THE
DAMNED

A CRUSADE
NOVEL

Also by Nancy Holder
and Debbie Viguié

The Cursed Ones: A Crusade Novel

Wicked
Witch & Curse

Wicked 2
Legacy & Spellbound

Resurrection

THE DAMNED

A CRUSADE NOVEL

NANCY HOLDER
& DEBBIE VIGUIÉ

SIMON AND SCHUSTER

First published in Great Britain in 2011 by Simon & Schuster UK Ltd,
1st Floor, 222 Gray's Inn Road, London WC1X 8HB
A CBS COMPANY

Published in the USA in 2011 by Simon Pulse,
an imprint of Simon & Schuster Children's Division, New York.

A CIP catalogue record for this book is available from the British Library

ISBN 978-0-85707-084-5

10 9 8 7 6 5 4 3 2 1

Printed and bound in Great Britain by Cox & Wyman Reading RG1 8EX

To Ann Liotta, one of the most
courageous people I know, who always stands up
for what she believes in
—D. V.

To Karen Hackett, a good and true friend
—N. H.

ACKNOWLEDGMENTS

In the writing of this book I have been reminded of all those men and women, both known and unknown, who have stood up and fought for the cause of freedom. To them I owe so much and would like to offer my gratitude for their courage and strength. To my wonderful coauthor, Nancy, I would like to give my profound thanks for all that she does and all that she brings to our books and our friendship. You are amazing. Thank you to her fantastic assistant, Erin Underwood, who has been a great help in spreading the word and getting people to join us on this Crusade. I'd also like to thank my own personal Crusaders, those who work tirelessly to help me, to promote me, and to keep me sane: Howard Morhaim, Katie Menick, Kate McKean, Annette Pollert, Scott Viguié, Barbara Reynolds, Rick Reynolds, Juliette Cutts, Calliope Collacott, and Marissa Smeyne.

—D. V.

I echo Debbie's gratitude to those who put themselves in harm's way, most especially, in the case of my family, the chaplains of the U.S. Navy. Deep, heartfelt thanks to Debbie, my wonderful coauthor and dearest friend. To my assistant and friend, Erin Underwood: You are brilliant and tireless, and I'm so grateful that you're in my life. *Muchas gracias* to our agent, Howard Morhaim, and to Katie Menick and Kate McKean of Morhaim Literary. Thank you to Laura Navarre for help with the Russian and to Lawrence Schimel for the Spanish. All errors are mine. And thank you so much to Team S&S: our miraculous editor, Annette Pollert; Mara Anastas; Bethany Buck; Paul Crichton; Bernadette Cruz; Lucille Rettino; Karen Sherman; and Jessica Handelman, our designer. To Georgia McBride, Scott Viguié, Belle Holder, Juliette Cutts, and my three amigas — Pam Escobedo, Beth Hogan, and Amy Schricker — and to my family, my gratitude — especially to Belle, who puts up with so much.

— N. H.

BOOK ONE
APIS

This light guided me
More surely than the light of noonday
To the place where he (well I knew who!)
was awaiting me —
A place where none appeared.

—St. John of the Cross,
sixteenth-century mystic of Salamanca

CHAPTER ONE

*For the last two weeks I've led the Salamancan
hunters. What a disaster. I can't believe that Father
Juan's prayers and magick spells told him I was the
one for the job. I'd laugh, if I wouldn't cry first.*

*Sometimes I dream that I have awakened from
this nightmare and there are no vampires, that
I'm home and loved and safe with my sister and
my parents and my grandparents. Then I wake up.
The Cursed Ones are real. My grandfather is dead.
My sister has been converted. She is one of them,
and my father is responsible. He betrayed her. He
betrayed me.*

*Even if the war ended tomorrow, nothing would
be okay.*

*But, of course, the war isn't ending tomorrow.
Unless we lose. I'm starting to think that's*

inevitable. Humanity is fighting an unwinnable battle, and sooner or later there won't be other bands of hunters to take our place as we fall.

I can't think that way, not if I'm the leader. But I do.

I enrolled at the Sacred Heart Academy Against the Cursed Ones a little more than two years ago to learn how to kill the vampires. I come from rebel stock—my grandparents were radical protesters in the 1960s, fighting for social justice and paying for their actions by remaining underground for the rest of their lives. Esther and Charles "Che" Leitner are legendary for their bravery and sacrifice.

In honor of them I dreamed of becoming the Hunter—the warrior who would be given the sacred elixir that would endow me with super strength and speed. That honor fell to another, Eriko Sakamoto. But then our master, Father Juan, broke with tradition and gave Eriko a backup team. There are five of us, known also as hunters. She was our leader, until New Orleans fell.

Eriko never wanted to lead; the Hunter has always fought alone, and that was what she had expected. She asked Father Juan to relieve her of command. He did, and gave me her role. But of all of us I have the fewest skills—I'm not supernatural, and I had no fighting experience before I came to

4

Salamanca. I think of myself as "just Jenn," and I feel like a fraud.

The Cursed Ones are coming down hard on us. None of our allies survived our attack on the vampires of New Orleans. During the battle courageous New Orleanians rose up and joined the fight, but they were massacred. On the news, on the Net, there was not a word about it. But people heard; they knew: It was useless to fight the Cursed Ones. The vampires would always win, and they would show no mercy to the losers. Better to obey them to survive.

As the hunters of Salamanca, we push and we fight and we make trouble. And so the terrified people are beginning to think of us, and not the vampires, as the problem. Spain, where we live, is one of the few nations that has not signed a treaty with the Cursed Ones. Spaniards have been proud of us, calling on us to save their cities and villages from the vampires that brutalize them. But people on the streets have begun to mock us. They call us pulgas—"fleas," a nuisance, an irritant.

If the resistance fighters like us lose the trust of humanity, we lose everything. The hunters of Salamanca need a victory. Something that can make everyone feel like there's hope. We need it for the people looking to us for salvation. We need it for *ourselves, to remind us that we can fight and win together as a team. And I need it for myself, so I can be the leader that we so desperately need.*

My fighting partner, Antonio de la Cruz, says that I need to have faith. I have no idea how he can say that after all that's happened—to us, and to him. I wish I could have faith. But in this world faith—like hope—is in very short supply.

—*from the diary of Jenn Leitner,*
discovered in the ashes

PAMPLONA, SPAIN
TEAM SALAMANCA: JENN AND ANTONIO, SKYE AND HOLGAR, AND JAMIE AND ERIKO

Where's our contact? Antonio wondered as he searched the shadows of the narrow brick alley, detecting shapes and movements only his crimson eyes could see. He spotted a few rats pillaging among the garbage cans, and a big black cat stalking them. The rats squeaked warnings to one another, but none of them ran away. They were used to cats, and humans, and vampires.

Then suddenly the rats squealed and screamed. At the same instant, the cat stiffened and yowled, then flashed past Antonio.

Antonio saw what had frightened the creatures of the night. At the other end of the alley Holgar Vibbard stood silhouetted in his bomber jacket and jeans beneath a watery streetlamp. The Danish werewolf chuffed low in his throat, a greeting tinged with wariness. Holgar must be thinking the same thing as his vampire counterpart: *The local resistance has failed to show for our meeting. Has something else gone wrong?*

Antonio crossed himself—black cat, bad luck. He'd grown up in a small village in the Spanish countryside in the 1930s, when faith and superstition had been more tightly bound.

The absence of Moncho was another very bad omen.

It was ten o'clock at night in Pamplona, and Antonio smelled vampires everywhere. Of all the Cursed Ones, the scent of death lingered most lightly on Antonio himself, or so Holgar said. Being a werewolf, Holgar had a highly developed sense of smell, better even than a Cursed One.

Ever since Antonio's escape from his sire in 1942, he had never been tempted to return to the vampire fold. His loyalties lay with humanity, hopeless though their cause might be. His love, though intended for God alone, lay with the girl walking beside him. She was Jenn Leitner, the leader of their vampire-hunting team, for whose sake he had kept vigil every night for more than two years, and whose sister he had sworn to save from the stake. Heather Leitner had been changed into a vampire by their enemy, Aurora Abregón, and for the last two weeks Antonio had been attempting to reawaken Heather's humanity, if indeed it was still there. He was beginning to have his doubts.

Ay, Jenn, you're so beautiful tonight, he thought, admiring the tangles of dark red hair escaping from the black knit cap that gently brushed Jenn's jawline. Petite, deceptively delicate in appearance, she could hold her own if a band of Cursed Ones came calling. Still, every protective instinct within him remained on high alert. During her two years of training at the Academia Sagrado Corazón Contra los Malditos—the Sacred Heart Academy Against the Cursed Ones—he had looked out for her. Now he served as her unofficial bodyguard, though none knew it. Antonio had been born in a time when men fought the battles and women preserved everything worth fighting for. Traditions, culture, children. There were so many things he couldn't give Jenn, and it made him feel powerless and ashamed. The least he could do was offer his own life in place of hers, should such a moment arise. Maybe tonight would be that night.

Jenn's skin was awash with the brilliant light of a storefront window. Her face was filled with longing as she watched a young couple a few meters ahead of them pointing into the store's second window. Antonio's acute hearing picked up the threads of their conversation—the girl's birthday was coming up, and her boyfriend was going to buy her a ring. They were two Spaniards, attempting to live a normal life under the fang.

Antonio followed Jenn's gaze and saw the couple ges-

8

turing at pearl rings. In the next case rows of dangling ruby hearts were clutched in the claws of gold and silver bats — since the war against the Cursed Ones, it was the most recognizable icon on the planet, the symbol of women saving themselves for a vampire's kiss. Antonio caught Jenn's reflection in the glass as her face hardened at their sight. He, of course, cast no reflection.

Wistfulness mingled with his tension. There was no chance for them to be like that couple; he would never throw his arm around her as she tried on rings and he pretended to be dismayed by the prices. She would never giggle and rise up on tiptoe to kiss his cheek to take the sting out of his financial sacrifice. They were hunters, and he was a vampire. And he had long ago promised himself to God alone, as a man intent on becoming a priest. Though he was a man no longer, his vow remained.

The couple wasn't as happy as they were pretending to be. Antonio could smell their fear, watch their eyes dart anxiously up and down the boulevard. But they were trying very hard to take joy where they could find it. Jenn was just eighteen; she didn't understand how people could continue to act as if the vampires hadn't won the war. How Spain could pretend it wasn't capitulating. But Antonio knew what it was like to fight against a truth so brutal that you had to find a way to forget, even if only for a few moments, the horror of what had happened to you.

Jenn glanced at Antonio, and he gave his head a quick

shake—*Nothing to concern you*. He forced down his blood-lust as she nodded back at him. She was unaware of the temptation she presented as she stood so close. He scented her, felt her heat. He wanted her. He always wanted her. But he would never have her. If he had still had the right to offer himself to her, he would have been faced with a terrible choice: break his vows of poverty, obedience, and chastity so that he could love her as men loved women, or deny the truth of his existence—that he had fallen in love with Jenn—and remain an obedient son of the Church?

Perhaps God Himself had blessed Antonio with vampirism, so that the choice would never have to be made. He balled his fists at the absurd notion. There was nothing blessed about what he had become. There was a reason vampires were called the Cursed Ones. A hundred reasons. And the God of his understanding didn't work that way. The Father of Heaven wasn't a capricious spirit, rigging tests and torturing His children to see if they deserved His love. God wanted to help. But He had to be asked.

Antonio stared at the crimson hearts reflecting a scarlet glow against Jenn's cheeks. There was no choice to be made. And yet he couldn't stop turning the question over in his head. He was obsessed with it. Vampires were known for their powers of mesmerism, able to charm their victims as men could charm cobras with the dip and lilt of a flute. Humans did it in their way—what else was flirting?—and for vampires it was just as natural and automatic. He fought constantly not to mesmerize Jenn. But had she succeeded in mesmerizing him instead?

"Antonio?" Jenn murmured softly, as if detecting his increased agitation. There was cautious distance in her voice, where before there would have been warmth.

Before Jenn's sister had been changed into a ravening monster.

Antonio had seen a similar thing happen back during the war — World War II, *his* war — when the atrocities of the Nazis had become so hideous that the people of Europe and the Americas lumped all Germans into the same category. To them every German was a Nazi, evil to a man, to be hated and feared. Now that Heather had been changed — "converted," in vampire parlance — it had become very hard for Jenn to distinguish him from the rest of *los Malditos* — the Cursed Ones — and to look upon him as the good vampire, the one she loved.

New Orleans had done this to them. Aurora Abregón, another Spanish vampire, had kidnapped Heather to lure Antonio to New Orleans, so that Aurora could present the traitorous vampire to her sire. Not only had Antonio avoided capture, but he had rescued Heather as well.

Who Aurora's sire was, Antonio did not know. All of vampiredom hated Antonio for abandoning his sire and siding with the pathetic human race. His sympathies made him a target, and he saw now how dangerous it was for him to be around the team.

11

Around Jenn.

"Antonio?" she said again.

"Estoy bien," he replied, assuring her that all was well with him. But it was not.

They walked past the happy pair. Antonio heard three heartbeats. The humans were going to have a baby.

To a casual observer he and Jenn looked like any other teen couple crowding the tapas bars and clubs and spilling onto the Spanish streets, though perhaps not as trendy. Jenn wore a dark gray hoodie over a black sweater and flared black jeans with clunky Doc Martens. Antonio had pulled on scuffed cowboy boots, low-slung jeans, and a simple black T-shirt. Jenn's heartbeat picked up whenever he wore the boots. So he had taken to wearing them whenever possible.

It's not good to tempt her. Or myself, he thought, but who on this earth was perfect?

Holgar's position at the far end of the alley was accounted for. Half a block up, Jamie O'Leary, another teammate, was pacing and smoking like a chimney, a seemingly endless supply of cigarettes stashed in the pockets of his black duster. He wore black jeans as well. Nearly bald and heavily tattooed, the Irish street fighter looked like the 'kicker he'd always been. He hated Antonio and Holgar both, and Antonio knew a day would come when Jamie would strike out against them. Not tonight, when Jamie had need of backup, but it would come.

12

Jamie's fighting partner, Eriko, had pinned a black bob wig over her two-inch spiky hair, and she wore black leather pants and a black silk T-shirt with the Chinese character for "death" embroidered in red sequins. The hunters of Salamanca had fans as well as enemies, and they could be recognized. They had opted for disguises over magickal glamours, so that the sixth member of their team, the English witch Skye York, could save her energy in the event of an emergency. Given their track record since New Orleans, there probably would be one.

Skye had gone into Gades, a club two blocks up, to look for their contact, José Ramón, also known as Moncho. Gades was Moncho's base of operations, and he was an hour late.

Father Juan, the team's teacher and master, had sent the Salamancans to Pamplona because the Cursed Ones were to hold a festival celebrating Apis, one of their gods of death. Apis had originally been worshipped in ancient Egypt as the Apis bull, symbol of the risen pharaoh, and god of the underworld. The festival was to be a mockery of Pamplona's Running of the Bulls. The real Running of the Bulls was held every July, and people—mostly men—would dress in white shirts and trousers, red sashes and kerchiefs, and run ahead of the bulls stampeding toward the bullring. Later, in the afternoon, those bulls would be killed by matadors in a highly stylized dance of death. It was said that the tradition had sprung from the practice of driving the cattle to market, but according to Father Juan, the real founders had been the bull leapers of Bronze Age Crete. Also according to Father Juan, the ancient Cretans had been plagued by vampires too.

Moncho had informed Father Juan that the vampires were rumored to be planning a running of the humans, perhaps on the feast day of St. Joseph, March 19. It was March 16, and the team had just arrived. Antonio wondered if Aurora was behind the plan, still hoping to capture Antonio himself.

Antonio touched the ruby cross that he wore in his left earlobe. Five tiny stones in a vertical line, two on either side of the fourth. To him, the seven rubies represented the very worst of the many mortal sins he had committed as a Cursed One. Sergio Almodóvar, his sire, had presented them to him with great ceremony during an orgy of death and debauchery, celebrating his fledgling's fine achievement—the murders of seven prominent Spanish Catholic clergymen.

Sergio had given Antonio the list of seven names. Five beloved parish priests; a bishop; and the most exalted and therefore the most difficult to attack, a cardinal. One by one, coldly and methodically, Antonio had tracked down these shepherds of God, ripped out their throats, and drunk them dry. Antonio did not transform them. There would be no conversion to vampirism for them, as there had been for Antonio. God had chosen them; let God take them.

"My evil priest," Sergio had murmured adoringly.

Antonio's sire had accompanied him to each vicious death, to observe, to savor, to gloat. He said that Antonio killed with the style and grace of a flamenco dancer or a matador.

At the time Antonio had not known that all seven men were descendants of Catholics who had been active during the Spanish Inquisition. Descendants of the religious who had tortured and condemned heretics to burn at the stake. Sergio nursed a personal grudge against the Inquisition, the details of which he had never shared with Antonio, his protégé.

No one held grudges like Sergio.

No one mourned those deaths like Antonio. He remembered their faces, and prayed for their souls. Antonio had taken the rubies when he'd escaped, thinking to sell them to pay for lodging. Instead he had found shelter at the University of Salamanca and had had the rubies made into an earring, to remind him that he had fallen — and could fall again.

As he crossed himself, he and Jenn ambled past the entrance to another alley. Holgar was keeping pace. Ahead, Jamie dropped a cigarette to the ground. Antonio could smell the burning tobacco; the onions, garlic, and *piquillo* peppers cooking in the kitchens of the clubs and bars; wine; a dozen fragrances on the women. And vampires.

Then Jamie looked over his shoulder, turned, and straightened. Skye was flying down the street in her scarlet petticoats, black lace-up boots, and black velvet jacket.

"They're coming!" Skye screamed, her white-blond

Rasta braids bouncing like coiled springs as she raced toward them, waving her arms. "We've got to get the people out of here!"

"Oh, God, it's happening *now*," Jenn said.

God, protect her, Antonio thought. *Let me die for her, if need be. But keep her safe.*

CHAPTER TWO

For it is written that in the Blood Times we shall walk in the light with our gods, and all shall be as has been foretold. We cast down the scourge of humanity, and inherit the earth. This is our holy calling, and our crusade.

*—from the diary of the Unnamed,
sire of the Vampire Kingdom*

PAMPLONA, SPAIN
TEAM SALAMANCA: JENN AND ANTONIO, SKYE AND HOLGAR, AND JAMIE AND ERIKO

"Prepare for battle! Spare all innocents!" Jenn shouted. The air was charged with terror as waves of humans ran toward Antonio and her, faces contorted in fear. Jenn grunted as the Spanish girl who had been window shopping slammed into her from behind. The boyfriend grabbed his girl's hand and dragged her toward the dark alley beside the jewelry store just as Holgar burst out of it. He looked human, but the girl began screaming, clinging to her boyfriend's arm. Then Jenn saw the army of rats scurrying before Holgar as if eager to join the fray. They bumped against Jenn's ankles.

"Go, go, go!" Jenn yelled to the young couple.

"Go into the alley!" Holgar shouted at them, forcibly herding them out of the chaos. Then he galloped ahead of Jenn and Antonio, waving his arms. "Stand in the doorways! Get away from the crowding! *For helvede, amigos!*" He was stressed, mixing his English, Danish, and Spanish.

At the back of the mob Cursed Ones were laughing, shouting, "*¡Toro! ¡Toro!*"

Jenn knew they must have moved in precision to start the hysteria, invading the clubs and restaurants, driving the patrons into the Pamplona streets.

From overhead something hit Jenn's head, hard, and she staggered, then caught up to Antonio. Blood dripped into her eyes, and she shook her head fiercely as she ran, trying to clear her vision. Droplets went flying; one of them hit Antonio on the cheek. He snarled, eyes suddenly awash with red bloodlust.

It's too much for him, she thought frantically. *All the vampires, and the blood, and the fear.*

Antonio turned and scanned the crowd. He and Jenn moved against the tide, looking for their team. "I see Eriko

18

and Jamie," he reported to her. "And Skye. They've taken on the vampires."

"Is Holgar ahead of us?" she shouted.

"I don't know."

The two were swept along in the stampede, in as much danger of being trampled by humans as they were of death dealt out by the vampires. It was a stupid place for the team leader to be. Blood dripped into her field of vision, and she was already starting to get woozy from the loss of blood.

"They're driving us to the Plaza de Toros," Antonio shouted to her.

The bullring. Once locked inside, the humans would be cows ripe for the slaughter rather than the fierce fighting bulls that gave Pamplona its bullfighting reputation.

Jenn glanced at the buildings on either side of the street, desperately looking for an open door. They were all shut. Through balcony windows she could see people watching, faces white with fear and shock. It was New Orleans all over again. The majority of the local populace was too afraid to do anything. Safer to watch the slaughter of friends and neighbors than to chance a brutal death themselves.

When the Cursed Ones had made their presence known six years earlier, the world had been lulled by the vampires' assurances that they wanted only peaceful coexistence. Solomon, their leader, was rock-star handsome, charismatic, and suave. But soon the world learned what some had always known—that vampires were monsters. Too late, nation after nation declared war on them. But the vampires were as savage as they were cunning. One by one, countries rapidly capitulated, adopting the fiction—the lie—that a truce had been negotiated. There was no truce; it was surrender, and it was wrong.

Spain was the final holdout. But the Spanish government was showing signs of capitulating. It was futile to resist an enemy so powerful, so difficult to kill.

So it fell to the hunters, the few who had been especially trained to fight vampires, to save the world. As Jenn raced beside Antonio, she realized she'd be lucky if she could save herself for another hour, let alone anyone else.

In front of her a man tripped, crashing to the ground and knocking over two others. Jenn leaped over the bodies on the cobblestones, hating herself for not stopping to help. But with a half-crazed mob around her and rampaging vampires behind her, to stop would be to die by trampling or bloodletting.

"We have to get clear!" she told Antonio.

"*¡Sí!*" he yelled back. "I'm looking."

Her heart thundered, and the hard rhythm of blood filled her ears, louder even than the pounding feet around her. Suddenly Antonio grabbed her around the waist, looked up at a low-hanging balcony just above their heads, and shouted, "On three! Jump!"

She placed her hands on his shoulders. "One, two, three," she yelled, bending her knees and pushing up through the soles of her feet. She sprang; he tossed her up onto the balcony, leaping up after her.

Jenn landed in a martial arts roll, then pushed up to a standing position. She forced herself to take several deep, slow breaths as she scanned the sea of humanity beneath her, searching for her teammates. At least three hundred people streamed past, nearly all of them screaming.

There was no sign of Holgar, but after a moment Antonio pointed toward the rear of the mob. There, barely ahead of the Cursed Ones, bobbed Jamie's and Eriko's heads. Eriko, very short, was nearly swallowed up.

"She's hurt," Antonio said.

Fear pricked Jenn's heart. Antonio leaned over the rail and whistled loudly. Miraculously, Jamie heard; his head swiveled toward them, and he tapped his partner on the shoulder. Jenn and Antonio angled their way toward them. Eriko's left arm was hanging at an odd angle, with bone jutting out of the skin. Though she had drunk the sacred elixir reserved for the Hunter of Salamanca, which gave her speed, strength, and the ability to heal quickly, she looked to be in terrible pain.

As they approached, Antonio leaned down low, extending both his hands. Jamie and Eriko jumped, each latching on to one of his hands. He hauled them up onto the balcony. Jenn thrilled at Antonio's show of strength, which never ceased to amaze her. Cursed Ones were by far faster and stronger than humans.

"What are the Cursers waiting for?" Jamie bit out as soon as his feet hit the balcony floor. "They could have killed a hundred people easy by now."

"They're holding back," Eriko said, unable to keep her pain out of her voice.

"They're herding them all toward the bullring," Jenn added. "I guess they're not planning on killing anyone until they get there."

"Wouldn't want to ruin their bloody appetites." Jamie balled his fists. He looked as if he wanted to leap back down off the balcony and tear the vampires apart with his bare hands.

Eyes glowing with hellfire, fangs glistening, the vampires whooped and laughed as they ran beneath the balcony. The streets were clear behind the last phalanx of Cursed Ones. A few curious humans began sticking their heads out of doorways. Some were foolish enough to start following slowly behind, and Jenn grimaced in disgust.

"You're hurt too," Antonio said to Jamie.

"Give the feckin' vampire a prize," Jamie wheezed, gripping the balcony with white knuckles. "Curser broke a couple of my ribs. I see *you're* not the worse for wear," he added, eyeing Antonio suspiciously.

Jenn scrutinized the silhouette of the Plaza de Toros rising in the distance. "We have to reconnect with Skye and Holgar. Whatever the Cursed Ones are planning, we can't let them get away with it."

"After you, Fearless Leader." Jamie gestured to the street.

Jenn hated it when he called her that, but she refused to let him bait her.

"Maybe you should sit this one out," she said snidely, "since you managed to get yourself hurt." Then she added more gently, "You too, Eri."

"On a cold day in hell," Jamie shot back, glancing at Eriko, clearly disliking what he was seeing—that she was in terrible pain. He ticked his attention back to Jenn. "Maybe we *are* in hell, but I'd storm the gates of heaven to stake meself a sucker."

Eriko gestured to Jenn's forehead. "Jenn-*chan*, you're losing a lot of blood. You look very pale. Are you all right?"

"Blood must be driving you wild, bat," Jamie sniped. Vampires didn't change into bats, or wolves, or mists. But Jamie liked to taunt Antonio. And blood did drive him wild.

"Let's go," Jenn said.

"I'll back you up," Antonio said to her.

"Same here."

For a second things were back to normal between Antonio and her. But his surprised smile reminded her that her heart had frozen up.

Flushing, she vaulted over the railing, landing in a crouch as she had been taught to do in her training at the University of Salamanca, where they had all learned to hunt and kill vampires. No matter how many times she engaged the enemy in a battle to the death, it still jolted her and sent her heart skittering in fear. But fear was a luxury she couldn't afford. It diminished her focus. It could get her killed.

She heard the others hit the ground behind her, but she didn't turn to look. She just took off. Before her the bullring rose like a circular stone skyscraper toward the starlit sky. A dull roar of *"¡Olé! ¡Toro!"* emanating from inside it set her teeth on edge.

A dark blue car sat at a haphazard angle in the middle of the road that led to the entrance of the ring. People were swerving around it, and about half of them were racing to the left, disappearing down a small side street. Behind the car the huge bullring gate was swinging shut.

Two figures jogged toward her, and Jenn increased her pace as she recognized Holgar and Skye.

Skye's black bustier was shiny with wetness, and there was blood in her Rasta braids. Holgar's bomber jacket was torn at the sleeve.

"What happened?" Jenn asked as she came to a halt in front of them.

"With Holgar's strength and a little bit of magick we were able to shove that car into the road just before the mob got here," Skye explained, catching her breath.

"Just like stampeding animals, they split around it," Holgar said. "That was our plan, *ja*? We shunted about a fourth of them down that street. They're still running, but they're safe."

Jenn nodded. "Good work."

"How many humans went into the bullring?" Antonio asked from behind her.

"A couple hundred, as near as we can tell," Skye replied with a frustrated sigh.

The fighting partners paired up and formed a line. Although Jenn was the leader, Eriko was the Hunter, so she and Jamie took point. Then Jenn and Antonio, and then Holgar and Skye. Crouching, they darted forward into the shadow thrown by the arena.

As they neared the curved brick wall, Jenn's stomach plummeted. She could see through the gated entrance to the illuminated ring and, beyond that, twenty vampires and half a dozen humans lounging in seats. Lights blazed everywhere, casting garish bluish-white stripes across the faces of the eager spectators.

"No Aurora," Antonio said, "at least that I can see. Nor my sire."

"Yeah, about him," Jamie said. "He going to be coming around too, now that word's out you're fighting with us?"

As Jenn watched, a half dozen Cursed Ones dressed in heavily embroidered and spangled bullfighters' suits, with black caps on their heads and red capes draped over their forearms, emerged from a passageway beneath the stand where the spectators sat. As soon as the audience of vampires and complicit humans spotted them, they began cheering. At the same time the humans who had been driven inside the bullring milled about in panic and confusion, shoving at one another and crying. The humans were the bulls. But no bulls had ever stood this helpless before those who would slaughter them.

25

"We can't let this happen. We have to go in," Jenn said.

Jamie and Antonio both crossed themselves.

"We'll be slaughtered too," Eriko replied. There was no fear in her voice; she was simply stating the obvious.

"So, what do we do?" Skye asked.

Jenn took a deep breath. "We go in swinging. But first we need an exit plan."

"You honestly think any of us are making it out of there alive?" Jamie asked, pressing his hands against his rib cage and grimacing.

"Even if we kill the matadors, the vampires in the seats would love to take us down," Holgar said.

"And their human minions," Jamie added with a grunt.

"I don't know if any of us will survive," Jenn replied. "But if we don't have a plan, then we definitely won't."

Antonio inclined his head in agreement.

"Tell us what you want to do," Eriko said.

They all looked at Jenn. The failure of New Orleans hung heavy on her shoulders. Her stomach clenched. And then she began giving orders.

"Skye, can you weave a spell so that if we punch a hole through this wall, no one will see it?"

The witch sucked in her cheeks as she thought about it. After a moment she nodded. "We won't be able to see it either. But if we all mark exactly where it is, we can find our way back to get out."

"That's good enough, *bruja*," Antonio said gently. He

was kind to Skye; he liked her and believed in her. Jenn believed in her too.

"Let's go for it," Jenn said.

Skye hoped that her protective spells were good enough as they entered the bullring. She bit her lip. Magick had strict rules, and technically she hadn't broken any. *An it harm none, do what thou wilt.* There was nothing about creating the hole that could be considered anything but defensive. Still, she had been really pushing the boundaries about using offensive magick—which could be why she was the only White Witch who had trained to become a hunter.

Of course, other witches were involved in the war.

I see you, Skye, a voice whispered inside her mind. *Te veo, mi amor.*

She shook her head, fear filling her as she heard the words. She couldn't deal with her ex, the Dark Witch Estefan Montevideo, when she was about to go into battle. Maybe not ever.

She glanced over at Eriko. She had set the other girl's arm quickly. It was a sloppy fix, but she hadn't had time to do a proper healing spell. The same for Jamie. One of his broken ribs had nearly punctured a lung.

He could have died. A swell of emotion overtook her. *He still could. We all could. Focus!*

Skye turned and stared at the six vampiric matadors,

who were unfurling their capes and walking toward the humans as someone, somewhere, played the traditional trumpet fanfare announcing the beginning of the bullfight. At Jenn's signal Skye and her teammates spread out slightly so they wouldn't be one big target. So far it appeared that the Cursed Ones didn't know that the Salamanca hunters had entered the ring. The other humans were completely panicked, knocking one another down in their efforts to escape. In the stands the onlookers laughed.

She moved her hand and whispered a dispersing spell; the people eased away from her and Holgar, leaving the field around them clear. It was safer for everyone that way. *Protective magick; it's okay.*

Holgar gave her a lopsided smile as he tugged on the wooden cross Father Juan had given him at graduation. Hanging from a leather cord around his neck, the cross had a lamb carved into its center, and the arms of the cross ended in intricately carved wolf heads.

"Christians, witches, beasts — I guess sooner or later we had to end up in a coliseum," Holgar said.

Skye couldn't help but grin back. No matter how bad things got, Holgar always managed to find the lighter side of a situation, or at least pretend to. Not that there was a light side to getting slaughtered, but somehow his attitude made it easier to cope.

The bullfighters were performing a sort of ballet of stylized grace. Their red capes were draped over small swords with sharp-looking tips, which flashed with the vampires' movements.

"We'll have to dodge those swords," Skye said.

"I will if you will," Holgar told her.

Discreetly they placed themselves between the vampires and the hysterical captives. The plan was to thin the ranks of matadors as much as possible before the hunters started herding the humans toward the invisible hole. Skye was fairly sure the presence of the hunters had not yet been detected. For the moment they held the element of surprise.

She cast one more glance in Holgar's direction as the bullfighters took off their black caps and bowed to the stands. It appeared to be the signal that the fighting was to begin. One of the matadors headed her way, a cocky grin on his face. Gold tassels swayed against scarlet satin and ebony silk as he advanced. Skye held her ground. Eyes glowing red, fangs extended, he brandished his cape and shook it at her, engaging in the ancient ritualistic death dance.

"¡Olé!" the vampires cheered. The few humans among them cheered too. Collaborators, fraternizers. Skye had other, harsher words for them. Maybe they were simply people, so afraid of dying that they would do *anything* to survive. Perhaps they were to be pitied more than hated, but Skye was not yet that evolved.

The matador had closed up the space between them and thrust forward his cape, shouting, "¡Toro, toro!" at her. Rather than cower, as he seemed to expect, she spun to the side, grabbing for the cross she had tucked in her waist-band. As he charged her, she pulled it out and thrust it into his face. The crowd began to jeer and hoot, as if she'd been caught cheating.

The Cursed One jumped backward with a snarl, raising his cape to shield his face as he stumbled, falling right onto the stake Holgar extended as he rushed to help Skye. With a whoosh the vampire disintegrated, turning to ash.

"Nice!" she cried to Holgar. He grinned at her, then scanned the ring for the next attack.

The crowd roared, but whether in approval or disap-proval Skye couldn't tell. A couple of the humans in the ring turned to see what had happened, sensing a shift in the balance of power.

If only they were all that easy, Skye thought.

A second matador approached, taller and more muscu-lar, and from his cocky demeanor Skye knew that this one would be much, much harder to kill.

"I'll take this one. Get some of these people out of here," Holgar said, moving close in. Vampire dust coated his cheeks.

Skye hesitated, not wanting to leave her fighting part-ner unprotected.

"I'm serious." He kept his eyes on the bullfighter, head dipped to avoid his mesmerizing gaze. "Save as many people as you can before the other C.O.'s get wise."

"Are you sure?"

"Yes, go!"

Skye ran toward a man and a woman who had stopped to see what had happened. They both looked dazed. She grabbed their arms and tugged.

"I'm going to get you out of here. Come with me! You, and you, let's go!"

Skye quickly gathered more and more people. Bewildered, nearly paralyzed with fear, they did as they were told, stumbling as they followed her toward the wall. Like the Pied Piper she gathered them with magicks, trying to reach them while attempting to remain unnoticed.

She had collected maybe twenty. When they were steps from the hidden hole in the wall, she turned and scanned the arena. No one else in the ring was looking at them, and those in the stands seemed to be fixated on the fighting. Eriko and Jamie were ducking capes with Krav Maga movements, but she couldn't locate Antonio and Jenn.

"It's a wall," one of the women protested.

"It's magick," Skye said, shoving them both through the hole.

She turned and headed for the next closest group of people, prepared to do the same, just as Holgar decapitated the second matador with one of the short swords. The head burst into dust, and the crowd in the stands booed.

Miss me? the voice asked in her mind, returning. She halted in her tracks, her own fear now vying with her need to get people to safety.

31

Then, shouting and booing, the Cursed Ones in the stands leaped down into the ring, grabbing at anyone they could, sinking their fangs into their necks, draining their blood in an instant, and dropping the bodies to the ground. The jig was up. It was time to go.

Antonio and Jenn ran toward her, herding as many people in front of them as they could. Eriko appeared behind Jenn and Antonio, carrying Jamie's body over her shoulder. The sight of him limp and bloody galvanized Skye into action, and she sprang forward.

"This way!" she screamed. "You can't see it, but it's there!"

Holgar loped across the blood-drenched dirt, shouting in Danish and pointing toward the location of the hole. Several dozen Spaniards poured through. Eriko darted in with Jamie. Antonio and Jenn were next, and then Holgar was dragging Skye along with him. As the hole began to close, Skye looked back. Dozens of bodies lay sprawled, their limbs at impossible angles, and at least fifty of the living raced around, shrieking—people the team could no longer help.

The hole closed.

Tears streamed down Skye's face as the team retreated, veering off from the locals, who were scattering to their homes or other places of safety. Enraged vampires denied their sport erupted from the bullring in pursuit.

With only seconds to their advantage the hunters wound

through twisting streets lined with gold-colored stone buildings with arched windows, racing away in full retreat. They
needed a safe house. Moncho was to have provided one, but
he had still not appeared.

They ran down passageways and alleys like fleeing
rats. Vampires shouted to one another, searching for them.
Human screams pierced the night as Pamplonans were
dragged from their homes and interrogated: *Have you seen
six humans traveling together? Are you hiding them?*

Spaniards screamed.

Died.

The hunters kept running. Draped over Eriko's back,
Jamie was pale as death. Skye gave them all a magickal
boost of energy, but she was exhausted. She couldn't go on
much longer.

"Goddess, help us," Skye murmured. "I am your faithful
daughter. Grant me this boon."

And then, as they passed a large house of weathered
brick with concrete medallions and a sloping tiled roof,
Skye felt . . . nothing.

"Jenn, here," Skye whispered sotto voce. She stopped
in her tracks and pointed at the ancient structure. Jenn
raised a hand, and the others stopped too.

Very slowly, a broad wooden door edged with wrought
iron creaked open. Leading the way, Jenn crossed the
threshold, the others following. The door slammed shut
behind them, and they stood inside a dark foyer.

Then the foyer melted away, and they were in a parlor, where half a dozen men and women had risen from dark wooden chairs set around a table covered with tarot cards and a crystal ball. The scent of burning sage—a cleansing herb—wafted in the air. Between oil portraits and landscapes on the walls, and on the bare stone floor, dozens of signs and sigils, markings of protection, had been painted or carved. Skye read them, understanding them at once, as she had been classically educated in the Art. These were medieval symbols designed to ensure the safety of the house and its inhabitants by making the house seem uninteresting. It was that void created by the markings that she had felt. Most places gave off their own vibe, much like people did, but this house was neutral, missing its echo of time and emotion. Only magick could do that to a house as old as this one.

"I'm a White Witch." Skye addressed the coven as a whole. She held up her ring, a crescent moon, and the Spaniards reacted, murmuring to one another.

A woman in a black dress decorated with silver crescents identical to Skye's ring opened wide her arms. "Welcome, *hermana*," she said in heavily accented English. "The blessings of the Goddess upon you."

"Jenn, we're among friends," Skye told her leader.

"We're hunters," Jenn said, panting. "I'm the leader. Please help us."

"The vampires seek you, eh?" the woman said.

"*Sí,*" Jenn replied. "We were in the bullring. We helped a lot of people escape, and now the Cursed Ones know we're in town. If you can keep us safe until they're gone, we would be grateful."

"Of course," the woman said. "My brothers and sisters, we must help these people. Carlos, Amalia, *por favor.*"

Her words galvanized the group. A man and a woman rushed to Eriko's side. They led her to an upholstered sofa, where she carefully laid Jamie down.

"Are you resis—," Jenn began, but Skye cut her off. If these witches were involved in the fight against the Cursed Ones, they would not join a resistance cell. They would be members of the Circuit, and she, as a Circuit member, had pledged never to reveal the existence of the group of witches dedicated to the freedom of humanity.

Of course, she'd broken that vow, blurting out the truth to Jenn. And after New Orleans, Skye had confessed as much to the Circuit, and they had cut her off, refusing to help her anymore.

"I am the High Priestess of this coven," the woman in the dress informed Jenn. "We will shelter you until the search is called off and you may safely leave Pamplona."

"Blessed be," Skye whispered.

"Merrily met," the woman replied.

"Not so much," Jamie muttered, his lids fluttering, and Skye's heart leaped. Jamie was as snarky as ever, which meant that he'd live. He sat up on the couch and yawned,

35

as if their near escape from death had been a trifling bore.

"Don't suppose you could spare a bit o' sumpin? Pint of ale, a bit of whiskey?" he asked the High Priestess.

The High Priestess's mouth twitched. "I suppose," she said. "But please, everyone, sit down before you fall down. All of you. Eva, Estrella, see to their injuries. I will get a 'bit o' sumpin.'"

"Thank you," Jenn said, taking a chair. She sank down wearily.

"No, we thank you. We are in your debt," the High Priestess said. "Unlike you, we cannot fight. But we can heal the fighters." Her eyes glinted like flint. "And we will."

CHAPTER THREE

Salamanca Hunter's Manual: Allies

As the Hunter, you must walk alone. Beware of entanglements. You cannot love as others do. You must love duty. You cannot have friends. Others will curry your favor, only to betray you in your darkest hour. Your sacred duty is not to save, but to hunt. Stake twenty vampires, and thirty souls will curse your name because a child was taken. Stake a hundred, and you will be hunted because the village burned. The Savior is aptly named, and so are you.

(translated from the Spanish)

PAMPLONA, SPAIN
TEAM SALAMANCA: JENN AND ANTONIO, SKYE AND HOLGAR, AND JAMIE AND ERIKO

The witches of Pamplona kept the hunters of Salamanca safe while the Cursed Ones went from house to house, searching for the humans who had dared to vanquish their matadors in the ring. The High Priestess, who was called Maja, created a spell to muffle the screams and shouts erupting from the night as the vampires terrorized the neighborhood. But Skye could hear them in her aching heart. How many were they killing in retaliation? Were any of them escapees from the bullring? Would it have been better for Pamplona if the hunters had not come?

"This is why we do not fight," Maja said to Jenn. "We only heal."

Skye stared down at the floor, and Jenn moved to her side. Protectively, Jenn laid a hand on Skye's arm.

"*Someone* has to fight," Jenn shot back.

"I don't mean to judge you," Maja said. "I agree. Someone has to fight. If, perhaps, more had fought earlier, we wouldn't be in such a desperate situation now."

Two of the witches and Holgar went on recon in an effort to assess when it would be safe for the group to head back to their well-concealed van. Everyone cleaned up, and the witches gave the hunters fresh clothes. About three hours later Maja herself joined an escort of four witches to magickally protect the hunters as they snuck back to the van.

Antonio drove. It was a distance of two hundred fifty miles, and they were cutting it close to sunrise. It was true that vampires could not walk in the sun. If Antonio stayed out of direct sunlight, he would be safe, but the rays of the sun fatigued vampires and made it difficult for them to function. They felt a pull to go down to the earth—into coffins, catacombs, basements, sewers—which was one of the reasons the gods of their faiths ruled the underworlds: Hades, Baron Samedi, or in the case of Antonio's sire, Orcus.

During their drive home Jenn called Father Juan and told him about their failure via cell phone. So many had died, and they still had no idea what had happened to the resistance members they had gone to meet.

"I'm sorry," Jenn concluded.

"Time for tears later," Father Juan replied.

Skye performed round after round of healing spells on the team, concentrating on Jamie, who began criticizing "the mission" as soon as the van doors were shut. He didn't have any specific criticism; he was just angry, and Jenn's "ineptitude" was fair game, at least in Jamie's mind. Skye made a few attempts to defend her, reminding Jamie that Jenn was in charge, not him, which made him even angrier.

"Yeah, about that," he began.

Finally Holgar growled pointedly, and Jamie fell to

swearing under his breath about things being all arseways.

It was still safely dark when they reached the gates of the University of Salamanca, but Jenn could hear the trilling of birds singing to the dawn. Father Juan shepherded them straight into the chapel, where he put on a white chasuble — a priestly overgarment, the color choice to honor the dead — and conducted a brief Mass for the repose of the murdered innocents, and to give thanks that the Salamancan hunters were spared. Jenn was not a Catholic, but she was respectful, and she knelt beside Antonio on the prayer bench. Cold emanated from him — he had no body heat — and he moved slightly away, as if he thought that was bothering her. Things were very different between them now, strained, since . . . Heather.

Grief flooded through Jenn, and she rested her face on the backs of her hands. She was exhausted. She'd been wounded in the chest in New Orleans, and while she'd been put back together and returned to the battlefield, there were times when her injury pained her. Or maybe her heart was simply broken.

Beside her, Antonio murmured in Latin and crossed himself. His rosary beads were wound around his hand like a bandage. No other vampire they had ever come across could touch a cross or any of a myriad of religious symbols without being severely burned. That meant he wasn't like the others. He was different. But it was hard for her to believe that anymore, now that her little sister had been converted. Heather

40

had been the sweetest person Jenn had ever met, and that sweetness was gone. If someone like Heather became so completely different, why hadn't Antonio? Maybe he was just a great faker, pretending to be good so that he could one day turn on them. Magicks might be protecting him from crosses and holy water.

No. I don't believe that. I can't believe that.

But doubt poked at her like the tip of a blade.

"Go in peace. The Mass is ended," Father Juan said in English. Jenn jerked slightly; she'd drifted during the service, as she often did. Maybe some of the others found comfort in the ritual. She tended to tune it out in favor of worrying about the dozens of things on her long, long list.

She gazed at Antonio, whose head was still lowered in prayer. Flickering candlelight caught the blue-black highlights in his hair. She wanted to run her fingers through it. Before she had known that he was a vampire, she had spent hours staring at Antonio, wishing he would look back. Practically every girl in their class had swooned over him like he was some rock star, chatting and flirting with him every chance they got. Everyone had been told that he was a seminary student — studying to become a priest — which made him even sweeter forbidden fruit.

And then, on the night of their final exam, Antonio had been paired with Jenn in this very chapel. And he had confessed his feelings for her. And why he could never act on them.

"It was you, Jenn. You who captured my heart." His voice echoed in her mind even now.

But I didn't know then what I know now, she thought. *I didn't know what it really means to become a vampire.*

An image of her sister rose in her mind.

"Jenn?" Antonio murmured, looking at her.

Everyone else was leaving the chapel. Jerking, she got to her feet and sidestepped out of the pew. Antonio bent his knee like a noble courtier, lowered his head in the direction of the large cross hanging over the altar, and crossed himself.

"Come to my sitting room. We'll talk," Father Juan invited them, leading the way. The private sitting room was very spare, dominated by a large olive-wood crucifix that hung behind a brown leather sofa. The priest went through another door to fetch a bottle and some glasses, and everyone sat down wearily.

So now we lick our wounds, Jenn thought. Literally, in the case of Holgar. Jenn turned away, unable to watch the werewolf as he surreptitiously cleaned a small wound on his wrist the way his wild brethren did. She focused instead on a calendar above a small table holding an electric teakettle, a sugar bowl, and some cups and saucers. The calendar featured the gardens and statuary of El Retiro Park.

Antonio hesitated, then sat in a leather chair facing the TV, away from Jenn. Skye plopped down beside her.

Then Jenn asked the question that had been plaguing her.

"How come Moncho never showed? He asked for help. We went. On the very night the vampires attacked, and we were caught off guard."

"Yeah, funny thing," Jamie said, grunting from his place slumped in a recliner.

"We keep going on missions like we did before New Orleans," Jenn persisted. "Someone asks for help, and we go. But it's not working."

"Yeah, funny thing," Jamie said again.

"But what about the worldwide resistance?" she asked. "How many groups are there like those in New Orleans, who are trying to fight back with the only skills and tools they have?"

"Why, you want to get them killed too?" Jamie drawled as he pulled a cigarette out of a pack in the breast pocket of the shirt one of the male witches had given him.

"Shut up," Skye said, an uncharacteristic outburst from the group's peacemaker. "We'd only just started going out as a team for two months before Jenn had to go to California. People around here found out about us and started asking for help."

"Your point?" Jamie said.

Skye's cheeks were pink. Jenn knew Skye had a crush on Jamie. Skye's lousy taste in men amazed her.

"So it makes sense the Cursed Ones heard about us too, yeah? So more of them are showing up at each mission. They're gunning for us. We're outnumbered," Skye said.

"Well said," Holgar told her, flashing her a smile. He was lounging on some decorative pillows on the floor.

Eriko didn't join the conversation. She was rubbing her shoulder and looking tired and wan.

Father Juan reappeared with a lacquer tray containing a water bottle, a dark green bottle of wine, and seven glasses. Jamie tapped his unlit cigarette against the cardboard container. Skye glared at the Irishman, who sighed and put the cigarette away.

"What are you all arguing about?" Father Juan asked.

"Jenn's wondering about other groups like ours," Antonio told him. "During the war there were resistance cells everywhere, struggling to survive, to fight."

When Antonio talked about the war, he meant World War II. Adolf Hitler had begun his campaign of terror, and Antonio had brazenly walked away from the seminary in 1941 to join the Free French Forces. He had been called a Maquis, after the thready brush by the same name, where they hid in the French forests. On one of his first missions he had stayed behind to offer a dying compatriot the last rites of the Church, and he had been attacked and "converted" on the battlefield. More than that Jenn didn't really know. He didn't like to talk about it.

"So it stands to reason that there may be lots of resistance cells today," Jenn put in.

Father Juan nodded as he set down the tray. "Perhaps it's time to reach out to these groups. Help them, and maybe get their help in return. At the very least we can try to coordinate our efforts. This is not a local problem. And if one day we could all rise up as one body and take on the enemy, perhaps we could win."

"Amen," Antonio murmured, crossing himself.

Father Juan's eyes gleamed with the hope that Jenn had lost. He decanted the bottle and arranged the glasses in a semicircle, but he didn't fill them. He was waiting for the wine to breathe. Jenn's chest was so tight that she couldn't breathe.

"Rise up?" Jamie scoffed. "We can't even trust the allies we do have."

"Maybe we need better allies," Eriko ventured.

"And more of them," Holgar added, in his singsong Danish accent. He quirked a half smile. "Preferably less cranky ones."

"Zip it, wolf," Jamie said, glaring. "There is nothing funny here." He gave Antonio a pointed look. "*Someone* told the Pamplona vampires to push up the date."

Antonio's answering stare was icy. "It's common in wartime to spread misinformation. They may have been planning all along to 'run the humans' last night. But I agree. Too often the vampires seem to know about our plans."

"Fancy that," Jamie bit off. "And now we've got *two* vampires livin' under our roof."

"Enough," Father Juan chastised them as he began to fill the glasses. He added a healthy measure of water into one of them, and handed it to Jenn. She still wasn't a wine drinker.

"Let's seek out these resistance cells," Jenn said.

"We're not diplomats," Jamie argued. "I came here to kill vampires, not start a club."

Father Juan ignored him. "Jenn is your leader, and this is a wise move. Skye and I will work magicks and try to discern who is safe to approach."

"We can't even trust each other, Father." Jamie's voice rose. "And meanin' no disrespect, but you and Skye ain't found the traitor who keeps telling the suckers our plans."

"Jamie-*kun*," Eriko murmured. "Please, don't argue with Father Juan."

Jamie clamped his jaw shut, the vein in his forehead bulging. He was barely keeping his fury under control.

Father Juan stood. "I'll ask Brother Manuel to make you all something to eat. You must be hungry."

"I'm sure *Antonio* is," Jamie said. "All that blood splatterin' about. Like starters for a big dinner."

"Jamie," Father Juan reproved.

The priest left, and the team sat for a moment, staring at one another, sipping their wine. After a minute Jamie picked up the remote control for the small television in the corner and clicked it on. A little television would help them unwind. And if they were watching something, they wouldn't have to talk about what had happened.

A news program came on. *"Bienvenidos, España,"* said the beautiful blond anchorwoman. Her coanchor, a man with salt-and-pepper hair, sat beside her and smiled at the camera.

"Today the Ministry of Economy and Finance unveiled a new benefits program for our senior citizens. All pensions will be increased by ten percent, effective November fourteenth. This will be accomplished without an increase in taxes, due to reductions in spending on national defense."

"Yeah, us," Jamie said. But the Spanish government had never footed the bill for the academy or the hunters it graduated. The Catholic Church had, and as far as Jenn knew, it was still paying.

"In other news," the male broadcaster said, *"there is a new art exposition at the Alhambra called Brothers. It features oils and watercolors by some of the world's leading vampiric artists. The queen will attend the grand opening, and political heads of state and celebrities from stage and screen are flying in to admire the beautiful canvases celebrating the special relationship between humanity and those who walk the night."*

The group groaned in unison.

A segment followed about a drop in violent crime in Madrid. So much of the news was propaganda, lies about the Cursed Ones or banalities in context of all of the fighting and dying.

"This is shite," Jamie grumbled, and Jenn had to agree. She looked over at Antonio, who was watching, stone-faced. He'd seen it all before—in other times, during other wars. After all this time was he still the idealistic man he had been more than seventy years before, giving his soul to God and his life to the people?

47

That's why I fell in love with him, she thought wonderingly. *He's like my grandparents, putting it all on the line to fight for justice. Like Papa Che. God, I miss Papa Che so much.*

She had left home and joined the academy because of Papa Che. She realized with a start that Antonio had been born about the same time as her beloved grandfather.

"Antonio, I need to see you," Father Juan called.

"Ya vengo," Antonio said in Spanish. I'm coming.

He got up and started to leave the room.

The anchorwoman looked mournfully into the camera, and a logo of a bat carrying a heart appeared behind her. *"In news from the United States, you may remember the tragic tale of Brooke Thompson and Simon Morton, the young lovers who were brutally murdered in Brooke's home in Berkeley, California."*

"Oh, God," Jenn said, feeling ill.

"Moved by their plight, Solomon erected a beautiful monument in their honor, which, sadly, was defaced last night."

A photograph flashed on the screen behind the anchorwoman. It showed a round Grecian temple with two white marble statues standing within.

"Fingerprints and other forensic evidence have pointed to the perpetrator of their murders, as well as last night's desecration, as a young human woman named Jennifer Leitner, a former schoolmate of Señorita Thompson."

An image of Jenn flashed behind the anchorwoman. It was her freshman-year high school picture.

Jenn felt her stomach plummet. After her father had

betrayed her to the vampires, Jenn had sought refuge in the home of her childhood friend Brooke, not realizing that Brooke's fiancé was a vampire. It hadn't taken long for the Cursed One to turn on them both, tearing out Brooke's throat before Jenn was able to stake him.

Hot tears welled at the memory of seeing Brooke lying lifeless on the floor. *I got her killed by going to her for help. He killed her. That's not love. Simon never loved her. If he had, he couldn't have done that.*

Her gaze ticked to Antonio, who stood by the door, watching intently, a muscle working in his jaw. For a moment doubt stirred her. There were many times that Antonio had had to restrain himself from hurting her even though he loved her. His vampiric nature was so powerful it was nearly impossible to fight, even for him.

She watched as he turned and left the room to join Father Juan.

"This is a pretty dead horse they're beatin'," Jamie remarked. "This happened, what, a month ago? Nearly?"

"They're using it as a symbol," Holgar said. "Symbols are very powerful."

"Solomon has stated that the vandalism serves as a grim reminder that despite the peaceful coexistence of vampire and human, ignorance and hate still exist. And it is in the interest of that peace and an attitude of genuine forgiveness that Solomon has invited Ms. Leitner to meet with him."

"What?" Jenn cried.

Then there he was on the screen: Solomon, the vampire who had orchestrated the war against humanity. Redheaded, with a turned-up nose and startling blue eyes, he was dressed in a black suit and a white, high-necked shirt. His face was somber.

Then the camera pulled back, revealing a second figure on the screen. Jenn blinked in astonishment as she recognized her father. Solomon's hand was on his shoulder.

"This is Paul Leitner, Jennifer's father. He has asked if he might say a few words to his dear daughter."

The hunters all stared at Jenn, then at the screen.

"What's he doing with Solomon?" Skye said. "Wasn't Aurora the one who attacked you?"

Jenn leaned forward, dizzy and sick at the sight of the man who had tried to trade her life for his, and Mom's, and Heather's.

"Is he a fanger?" Jamie asked. "Skye, you getting vibes?"

"I'd only be able to tell if he were physically present," the witch answered.

"Me too," Holgar said. "By the smell."

"If he was physically present, he'd be dead," Jamie said, holding up two fingers in the Irish version of the one-finger salute.

"Shh, please," Eriko murmured.

Jenn's father's face was drawn. Jenn could barely stand to look at him. His eyes were twitching, and he licked his lips once before beginning to speak.

"My daughter is a very sick young woman. I don't know what caused her irrational fear and hatred of the Cursed Ones, but I know that she needs help. Please, Jenn, if you're listening, come home. Everything will be okay. The authorities have promised me that we will get you the help you need, and if you come in, no charges will be pressed. Please, baby, come home. It will be better for everyone."

"What the *hell*?" Jamie cried.

"Oh, Goddess, why does Solomon want you?" Skye blurted in dismay.

"Maybe Aurora and Solomon are working together," Holgar ventured. "We know Aurora was trying to get to Antonio. So maybe Solomon wants Antonio too."

"Hate to say it, but he's just not that important," Jamie said, reaching for the wine bottle at the exact same time as Holgar. Jamie made a show of letting him take it.

Holgar handed it to Jenn. "Drink," he ordered her.

Staring at the screen, which now featured a commercial for a department store, Jenn got to her feet and left the room.

The familiar heaviness of the sun pulled on Antonio as he followed Father Juan down into one of the underground sections of the university. He wasn't sure what the space had originally been for, but they had been able to modify it to create a cell that even an insane vampire couldn't break out of. And newly converted, torn away from everything she knew, and denied the ability to hunt, Heather was one insane vampire.

After passing through a series of locked doors, each one more impressive than the last, they arrived at the room that contained the prisoner. Heather had wadded herself into the farthest corner of her cage. They had hosed her off, but her blond hair was matted, and dried blood was crusted under her ripped fingernails.

As soon as he felt she could endure being touched, Antonio was going to make sure she got a bath and clean clothes. He had no idea how he was going to accomplish it, but it would be an important step toward making her look, and hopefully feel, human.

Antonio sighed in frustration at her living conditions. When she had been captured by Aurora, Heather had also been kept in a cage. Two cages, two prisons—that made it hard for them to distinguish themselves as the good guys now that her circumstances had changed.

Heather stared at them, eyes filled with bloodlust, fangs clacking together. The scent of blood hung thick in the air even as he watched the evidence of a wound on Heather's arm slowly fade.

Antonio shared a quick glance with Father Juan. Heather was drinking from herself. That was not good. Father Juan looked worried too, as he produced a goblet from beneath his robes, along with a packet of blood that looked like it had come from a hospital.

"*Gracias, Padre,*" Antonio murmured as he took the items. Father Juan and one of the other priests at the *universidad* took turns supplying Antonio with the blood he needed to survive. Cursed Ones could only drink human blood. That was one more lie they had told the human race. Those who claimed to be able to drink from animals said so only to deceive mankind.

Antonio had been a vampire for decades, and he had trained himself to survive on very little. For Heather, newly converted, the need for a continuous supply of blood was too great for two or even four priests to provide. So Father Juan had needed to go elsewhere to secure a supply. Antonio suspected it had cost him greatly to do so, especially since the *universidad* didn't enjoy the same privileges it once had.

Antonio opened the pouch and poured the blood into the goblet. It wouldn't really quench her thirst. Living blood would nourish her far more satisfactorily. But drinking from a cup was just one more way they were trying to get Heather to reconnect with the humanity that had been ripped away from her. By forcing her to take her blood in a glass, he was trying to get her to remember all the other times, all the other liquids, she had drunk that way, and associate *that* with the proper way of getting her nutrition, not drinking from someone's throat.

Heather whimpered and moved to the front of the cage, stretching out a hand toward him as the smell of the blood hit the air. He walked toward her carefully, trying not to frighten her.

"How are you today, Heather?" he asked. The daylight

would sap her strength as well, make her a little quieter.

She blinked at him. The conversion process was so violent that it often left the victim in shock, unable to speak or even reason, sometimes for as long as two or three months. Antonio prayed fervently that she'd adjust soon. It would be easier to reach her when she had passed through this phase. At the moment it was like trying to converse with a rabid lion and hoping it understood you.

"Jenn is eager to see you. She misses you," he said.

Squinting her crimson eyes and showing her fangs, Heather whined as she stretched her hand toward the goblet. He consented, handing it to her. She snatched it with a victorious scream, then splashed the contents over her face.

"Ay," Father Juan said, as he moved his hands and began to chant in Latin. It was not a prayer to God but a magick spell to calm and soothe her. Antonio prayed that this time it worked. He always prayed, every time.

As Father Juan performed his incantation, Antonio crouched in front of the cell. Heather retreated back into her corner, busily trying to lap up the blood on her face and hands as she plopped down on the blanket and pillow they had given her. Her gray teddy bear was oozing stuffing from two puncture marks in its neck. Beside the bear lay the inhaler that she had needed in life for her asthma. She would never need it again, but Antonio was hopeful that, like the bear, it would serve to remind her of the girl she had been.

"Heather, we can give you more blood, if you'll only speak to us," Antonio said. "Please, *bonita*. We all miss you so much."

He heard steps behind him. There were few who came down here. Antonio turned and saw Jenn approaching in near panic.

"Father Juan," she managed. "My father was on TV with Solomon."

"What?" Father Juan and Antonio said in unison. They stared in horror at each other. Jenn tried to push past him to Heather, but Antonio blocked her. He didn't want Jenn to see her sister with the blood smeared all over her face. His mind raced. Could Solomon have killed their nemesis? Had Jenn's father escaped Aurora and sought sanctuary with Solomon? They needed to find out more immediately.

"What did they say?" Father Juan asked Jenn.

"They said there's evidence linking me to Brooke and Simon's murder. And that I vandalized their monument last night." She held back tears and tried to move around Antonio, but he stood firm.

"First one sister, then the other," Father Juan said. "It must be a ploy to get to you, my son. This settles it. I'll contact those other resistance groups and see if anyone knows anything."

Oh, Jenn, Jenn, Antonio thought, feeling the net tightening around them but caring nothing for his own safety. Only for hers.

"Antonio, please, stand aside," Jenn said, face white. "I need my family."

Antonio looked into her eyes and saw only pain there. She had had a terrible shock, and he feared seeing Heather would only make it all worse. He started to shake his head, but she put her hand on his arm. He could feel her warmth, and he closed his eyes briefly, savoring the sensation.

From behind them there was a sudden high-pitched shriek from Heather. She was throwing herself at the bars.

"Heather, it's me," Jenn called.

Jenn and Antonio turned around, facing Heather. Heather's eyes were glowing, her arms were flailing wildly, and she slammed herself against the bars in her attempt to get out.

"She knows me!" Jenn cried.

"Stay away, Jenn," Father Juan ordered her.

As Jenn darted toward Heather, Antonio wrapped his arms around her waist to stop her. Heather shrieked, thrusting her arms toward Jenn. Blood flowed from Heather's scalp where she had split it against the bars. She clawed at the air.

In her attempt to get to Jenn.

Not because she loves her.

Because she knows she's prey.

"Heather!" Jenn yelled again.

Far from calming the creature in the cage, Jenn's voice infuriated her further, and she began pounding on the bars and floor, screaming louder and louder, foam beginning to fleck on the corners of her mouth.

"Jenn, let me take you out of here," Antonio said.

"Let go of me," she shouted at him, raising her hand as if to strike him. "You . . . *monster.*"

"Jenn," Father Juan said. "You must leave."

The priest took Jenn's arm and firmly pulled her toward the door. As she screamed and wept, Antonio understood her pain, but her words cut deeply. She was right. He *was* a monster. He had learned to control the urges to subdue her and drink her blood, mostly, but they were still there. Only prayer and God's mercy had allowed him to push temptation down deep in his psyche.

Staring at Heather, he stared at himself. He had not seen his reflection in seventy years.

Until now.

"Father, it's not going to work," Jenn said, as she balled her fists and pressed them against her mouth to dam up the screams that were about to burst out of her. "Antonio won't be able to change her back."

"We don't know that," he told her, as he put her hand on the banister of the staircase that led to the main floor of the building. "You're in distress, I know, but you must have faith." He made the sign of the cross over her. "I'm going back to her now. To pray and work magicks."

She nodded, and he left.

Nausea ground her stomach. She lurched like a blind woman up the dim stairway, then along the corridors of the university building, sucking in the dusty mix of brick and old wood as she fought for control. She didn't know what was worse, seeing her father on TV, seeing her sister sneering like a demon, or realizing that Antonio had once been like that.

That he can be like that again.

Stumbling to a stop, she lowered her head against her knuckles. None of the vampires she had ever staked had seemed like people to her. They were so evil they were almost targets in some surreal video game. Stake a vamp, get a thousand points. Her mind had never really connected Antonio with those monsters. Or maybe it was her heart that had refused to admit that Antonio was a full-fledged vampire, a Cursed One, and not a "special" kind of human.

Maybe he wasn't even a special kind of vampire. He had savagely killed people. When he had first been changed, he hadn't been able to stop himself. Looking at Heather, how out of control she was, made Jenn doubt everything Antonio had told her about his past. She knew there was a lot he had kept from her, that he was weighed down by burdens he refused to share. She'd interpreted his reserve as a misplaced attempt to protect her. But now he couldn't. Heather was his mirror, and his secret was out.

"Oh, God," Jenn whispered. It wasn't a prayer. She

couldn't imagine anyone on the receiving end, listening, fixing it.

Her knees buckled, and she sank to the floor. If she hadn't gone with her father on the day Aurora attacked; if she had never gone to Spain to become a hunter; if only, if only, if only.

But then there would have been another day, a different betrayal. Her father had planned his meeting with Aurora. The vampires had won the war.

"Heather," she whispered, "come back."

She felt as if she were disintegrating, like foam on the waves. Below, the sharks swam deep. She was really losing it, and she didn't know if she could put herself back together again.

Then she pictured Gramma Esther at Papa Che's funeral—sad but composed, stoic, the family matriarch holding her dysfunctional family to account. And then, after Jenn had outrun Aurora, coming for Jenn and keeping her calm, giving her strength and support. It must have been so hard for Gramma to learn what a cowardly bastard her son was, knowing Heather was in mortal danger because of him, then letting Jenn handle it on her own.

We need her, Jenn thought. *I need her.* Gramma had texted her once since they had parted at the Oakland Airport. *Montana.* Gramma had promised to get her mom and take her someplace safe.

Montana was very big. And very far away.

Jenn kept hoping she'd text again, or, even better, call. Her grandmother was protecting both of them by maintaining her silence. But Jenn longed to hear from her. Her family was falling apart, and Jenn needed a shoulder, and strong arms around her. Someone who knew her, who loved her.

An image of Antonio blossomed in her mind. She shook her head. That one could not be him.

My father is with Solomon. He's a traitor to the human race. Did Gramma see him on TV? What's happening to us? To my family?

Shaking, she went to her room and crawled into bed, ignoring the soft knock on her door. Tensing, she thought — hoped, dreaded — that it might be Antonio, but it was Brother Manuel, the cook.

"Hunter?" he murmured in English. "I have make the breakfast."

He was sweet to speak English to her whenever he could. She turned her face to the wall and stared into the shadows.

CHAPTER FOUR

Cursed Ones, so we are named
But you're the ones whose hearts are maimed
Let us now come to your side
As our love burns deep inside
All that we are we bring to task
All that we have is yours, just ask
We love mankind for all you are
And take you each as a guiding star

THE IMPERIAL HUNTING PALACE OUTSIDE MOSCOW THE HUNTERS OF THE STARS OF DAVID AND THE SONS OF THE CRESCENT

The mission's failing, Noah Geller thought, as he fell to his knees in the moonlit snow. His back hunched, he leaned on his hands and panted like a dying animal.

Hideous creatures whooped as they dogged him through the forest—human eyes, vampire fangs, and wolf jaws.

Mustering all his strength, he staggered back up to his feet. He was sweating inside his winter jacket. He lurched left, stumbling into a slender, icy tree trunk; he grabbed on to it and then slid down, grimacing as splinters peppered his wound.

He'd run as long and hard as he could, but the injury had won. Dizzy, he crumpled onto his side. More blood bloomed from his white uniform, spreading beneath him like a red parachute deflating against the earth. His chest burned as if someone were dumping hot coals inside his rib cage, and just when he thought he couldn't bear the pain, he went strangely numb. Despite the five years he had spent in the Mossad, the Israeli special forces, he'd never been shot before, and he didn't know if this was how it was supposed to feel.

But as he examined the darkened snow in the moonlight, he knew it was bad. And the teams were running out of time. Dantalion, a centuries-old vampire, had commandeered the palace for his experiments, to create a vampire, human, and werewolf hybrid, a supersoldier to unleash on the human race. And those supersoldiers were chasing after Noah and the Stars of David, and Taamir's Arab team, the Sons of the Crescent. Some of the creatures had been hunters at one time, and their training plus their enhanced prowess gave them a terrible advantage over Noah and his teammates. Dantalion's minions had dragged off most of them; those they couldn't catch, they killed.

Before Dantalion, Russian government scientists had used the palace as a laboratory and created dozens of strains of viruses and plagues. People stayed well away from the palace grounds. All the plants in the once-lush gardens had withered and died. No birds flew. No frogs croaked. Babies born within a ten-mile radius came out wrong, and rarely lived. The palace's evil history served as a deterrent for some freedom fighters, but not all:

It was on this filthy, snowy ground that Noah Geller was about to die.

"Shit," he murmured. He pulled out his radio.

It no longer worked.

So he thought about Chayna, whose large Star of David pendant he wore around his neck. Chayna, his young wife, his true love, with her red hair and huge green eyes, and the gap between her two front teeth.

Seeing her as she was before he'd killed her.

Listening as heavy footfalls approached.

TOULOUSE, FRANCE
SKYE AND HOLGAR

It was ten in the morning, and the sun was poking through a murky layer of cloud cover. The old bridge was beautiful. The river was clear. Holgar had some old Gackt jammin' through the speakers, and he was singing along in Danish. Skye was staring at her scrying stone as if it were a GPS.

After Jenn's father had appeared with Solomon on TV, Father Juan had gone into high gear on the Internet, sending messages, seeking information, trying to form alliances.

The master had sent Eriko and Jamie to Venice to meet up with a resistance cell there in hopes of finding out more. Holgar and Skye had come to Toulouse for the same reason. Holgar was all for adding more numbers to their side of the equation. He was a pack man, after all.

Feeling hopeful, he pulled their white van into a car park near the center of the funky university town. Emblazoned on a pole, the city's ancient coat of arms featured the Lamb of God standing in front of what looked like a giant lollipop emblazoned with a stylized Crusaders' cross. Toulouse was located in the Midi-Pyrenees region of France, and the logo for the Midi-Pyrenees was a red banner featuring a gold Crusaders' cross decorated with twelve dots—for the Twelve Apostles. He liked all the Crusaders'-cross synchronicity. It made him feel lucky.

Ja, lucky to be away from Madrid, where everybody was losing their minds.

Jenn was a mess. Antonio spent most of his time trying to help her sister, and Skye went down there a lot too. But the little witch didn't hold out much hope for Heather. Skye was tired and irritable, and Holgar knew something else was going on with her. He just didn't know what it was.

Eriko wanted people to stop arguing. Jamie wanted Heather staked. He said she was a distraction they couldn't afford. Father Juan countered that if one vampire could be pulled back into the light—meaning Antonio—then perhaps more could be saved. What Jamie had said next was unrepeatable, and Father Juan had made him do penance by working in the kitchen with Brother Manuel. Peeling onions until he wept like a baby. Holgar couldn't help but enjoy that a bit.

And as for Heather, she just didn't bother Holgar as much as she upset everyone else. Ravening vampire, full-moon werewolf; wasn't it all the same?

Beside him Skye was murmuring in Latin. She smelled great; they'd had some French pastries on the road, and she reeked of butter and sugar. Her Rasta braids were coiled in a bun with a few dreads hanging loose over her shoulders. Big shiny tribal earrings with feathers brushed her chin, complementing thick black and turquoise eye makeup drawn to points half across her temples, as if she were an ancient Egyptian princess. Kohl was smeared beneath her eyes, and he thought she looked a bit demented, but far be it from him to ever tell her that. She might turn him into a toad.

Ah, Skye, such an adorable little terrifying person. Holgar couldn't help but smile as he slid the van into a very tight parking spot.

"Hey, that'd be something," he said aloud. "If you could turn the vamps into frogs."

"What are you going on about?" she demanded, glancing from the stone to him to the windshield. She startled. "Blimey, Holgar, you're going to hit that Mercedes."

"Never happen."

"Because I cast a spell of safety," she informed him.

"You just want to take the credit."

She huffed, and he chuckled. They got out. It was nippy; the students were bundled in their jackets and boots, listening to music with their earbuds, texting like mad. Kiosks advertised yoga classes, rooms to rent, and protest meetings—even ones to protest the incursion of the Cursed Ones. It was hard to believe that Toulouse was a town under siege, one about to capitulate to vampire rule. The Cursed Ones must be pretty cocky if they permitted so many freedoms. He couldn't smell any vampires around. Just because it was daylight, though, didn't mean they might not be lurking inside nearby buildings. He glanced at Skye.

"Do you sense the presence of any Cursers?"

She shook her head and studied her scrying stone with all the rapt attention of a texter or a gamer as they strolled. Holgar gently took hold of her forearm to guide her around a street sign.

"Something wrong?" he asked her. He smelled fear roiling off her in waves. He grabbed the stone from her. It was blank. He knew anyone could see into a scrying stone—

if there was anything to see. "Did you just erase this?" he demanded suspiciously.

She shook her head. Her braids flipped against her clavicles. "There was nothing there." She grabbed it back from him. "It's very rude to touch a witch's arcana," she informed him. "It's tuned to my vibrations."

"Forgive me," he said, but he had the sense that she had blotted something out rather than let him see it.

"It was just family stuff." Her voice was tight, nervous. "Father Juan said to go past the falafel stand next to the rug shop. Do you see a rug shop?"

Holgar spotted a small pull cart decorated with a dark blue awning. A deep fryer popped with grease as a dusky-skinned girl in vintage embroidered jeans dropped falafel nuggets in to cook. She had purple streaks in her raven-black hair, and she looked supremely bored.

"Is she the one?" Holgar asked.

"Let me check," Skye said, murmuring an incantation as she held the stone closer to her eyes. She paused, then shrugged. "I don't know."

"I didn't do anything to your stone," he said, feeling testy.

The falafel girl looked over at them and then inclined her head. She pulled up the mesh section of the fryer, allowing the falafel patties to begin draining.

"I think she *is* the one," he told Skye. "Let's introduce ourselves."

Holgar and Skye approached. "The cherry blossoms are

67

beautiful this time of year," Holgar said in Spanish, waggling his eyebrows up and down. "The eagle has landed. The spy has come in from the cold."

The girl frowned. "I beg your pardon?" she asked in French.

"Bonjour," Skye said, elbowing Holgar. "He's trying to be funny. We're from Salamanca."

The girl smiled. "Welcome to Toulouse," she said in English. "We've been waiting for you." She looked questioningly at Holgar. "I didn't know there was a code."

He sighed. "I've been to too many spy movies. I thought this was my big chance to say something like that. I'm very new to the spy business."

The girl scratched her nose. "That's *our* code," she informed him. "Someone else will watch the cart. I'll take you to the meeting."

Holgar mimicked the way she had scratched her nose. "Don't you want to check our passports, see some ID? What if we're imposters?"

She slid her glance to the left. Across the street, on the second floor of an old stone building, a window opened and a stern fellow about Holgar's age stared down at them.

"We've already checked you out," she said. "Let's go."

The girl walked across the street. Holgar and Skye trailed after her. Skye murmured in Latin, and Holgar raised an inquisitive brow. She had cast another safety spell, he guessed.

They entered the building and went straight through a

dingy foyer crammed with bicycles and with flyers papering the walls, then out the back door. A little greenhouse stood within twenty feet of the rear of the building. The supports were wooden and painted green, and the large plates of glass were cracked. Holgar saw six or seven people milling inside. The piquant smell of French roast coffee filled his nostrils. It was laden with a heavy layer of garlic and someone's rose-scented perfume. A tinge of fear wafted off someone. He'd have to figure out who that was, and see if they were simply afraid of being caught conspiring against the fangy overlords, or if they were spying for the enemy.

Heads turned as they entered the greenhouse. It was clear that they all knew one another well.

"People of Earth, we send greetings," Holgar continued.

Skye elbowed him. "Holgar, give it up. You are not funny."

A couple who had been unfolding chairs flapped two more open and set them down in the circle. The man—tall, smooth shaven, maybe twenty—smiled lopsidedly at Holgar and extended his hand to Skye. He had long, curly blond hair, white eyebrows, and blue eyes. He looked more Danish than Holgar.

"Bienvenue," he said. "I'm the leader of this cell."

"Hello," Skye replied, shaking his hand. "I'm—"

"No names," he replied. "We're glad to see you. Coffee? Tea?"

"Tea would be lovely," Skye said. "We'd both love it."

The others began to take their seats too. Holgar counted

three women besides Skye and the girl who had led them in. Three guys: Mr. Danish Pastry, Holgar himself, and the guy who'd been unfolding the chairs. The stern fellow at the window had not joined them.

"So," Holgar said, "you know who we are, even if we aren't saying our names. And why we're here."

"*Oui,*" said Mr. Pastry as he poured two cups of tea and brought them to the Salamancans. "We have some information for you. Here in Toulouse there is a local Cursed One named Philippe Gaudet. His brother controls the Vieux Carré in New Orleans. The French Quarter."

Skye nearly choked. "Blimey, I saw a little fanger get staked for saying that. By Aurora herself."

"Oh?" Pastry's eyes widened.

"We're pretty sure Aurora killed Christian Gaudet," Holgar confirmed.

"Hmm." Pastry processed that. "Well, Aurora and Philippe Gaudet met three nights ago. Here, in Toulouse. And she told him that Solomon 'doesn't matter anymore.' Those were the words she used."

Holgar was shocked. Solomon was the worldwide leader of all the Cursed Ones. When he had announced their existence to the world, he had described his role as "like your president." But he was more like a dictator—like Hitler, all smiles for the TV screen while ruthlessly taking over the human world.

"Blimey," Skye said again, her kohl-ringed eyes raccoon

enormous. "If that were true, if they've killed Solomon, oh, that'd be brilliant."

"Solomon's not dead," Pastry said. "But we think Aurora and Gaudet are hatching their own scheme. Maybe they plan to assassinate him. We don't know."

"How *do* you know any of this?" Holgar asked the pastry.

"We have eyes and ears," he replied neutrally.

"Maybe Paul Leitner is acting as a spy for her. Maybe that's why he's in Solomon's camp," Skye ventured.

"Who's Paul Leitner?" the pastry asked. Holgar and Skye fell silent, and Pastry scowled. "Trust goes both ways, my friends."

"He's a team member's father. Only he's on *their* team," Skye said.

"A collaborator." Pastry clenched his jaw. "When the war is over, they'll all be dead."

Holgar smiled at him. It was good to hear those words from another resistance fighter.

"But not by our hand," Skye said, looking anxious. "We're not about killing our own people."

"If they're with the Cursed Ones, they're not 'our own people,'" Pastry replied.

Holgar held out his cup. "May I have some more tea, please?"

"Of course," Pastry replied. "Anything for one of our people."

Beside him, Skye fretted.

71

VENICE, ITALY
JAMIE AND ERIKO

They were supposed to have parked their car at the entrance to Venice, but that lot was closed. So Eriko and Jamie had left the car two miles distant from their rendezvous spot with their Venetian contact, and hoofed it so that she wouldn't assume they weren't coming. But little Sofia, just ten years old, had faithfully waited.

Jamie was shocked to see such a biteen as herself wandering about on such a dangerous errand. Even though Sofia looked nothing like Maeve, she set him in mind of his dead sister. Maeve was his darlin' girl, ripped to pieces by a pack of Irish werewolves while the local Cursers looked on, doubled over in laughter. The anger burned deep and hot; it never went away. That was what he wanted; his rage kept him alive.

He hated this war, hated worse the spineless people in authority who failed to take action. They left it to children, Japanese samurai girls, and crazy Irishmen to do the work that must be done.

Ironically, many humans had fled to Venice when war broke out with the Cursed Ones. They had hoped, prayed, that the old stories about vampires being unable to cross water were true, and had sought refuge there because of all the canals.

They'd been wrong.

Cursed Ones had floated up and down the canals in their gondolas on *La Notte del Terrore*, the Night of Terror. The Venetian lagoon had sloshed with human blood. Sofia, who was only ten, told Jamie and Eriko all about it in a singsong, rehearsed voice, though she herself was too young to actually remember it.

They walked for nearly two miles more, past churches and palazzi grand in their elegant decay. Jamie spared no time to gawk. When Sofia crossed a street without looking, he went into a bit of a panic, even though there were no cars.

"Now we here," Sofia said, slowing in front of an opulent private palazzo. Three stories of elaborate stonework and mosaics glittered in the blessed sun. But it had gotten very late, and that sun was sinking fast.

Without hesitating, she crossed the threshold.

"Hold on," Jamie said, peering around her. Through the mosaic archway, everything was pitch-black. Though resistance cells took great care to disguise their rendezvous points, this place screamed ambush.

"Come," Sofia said, as she trundled on ahead.

"I don't like this," he whispered to Eriko, who put a finger to her lips to silence him. She followed after Sofia, but he could tell she wasn't happy either. But Father Juan had ordered them to meet up with Sofia and let her escort them to the meeting. Far be it from Eri to disobey the good father—even if it seemed that the man had not taken into account that a ten-year-old could not walk two miles as fast as two fighters could.

They moved through the corridor without incident. Jamie did not heave a sigh of relief. There was something off about the crumbling mansion with its arched balcony windows. The glass panes had long ago been punched out, and a breeze carried the odor of fetid canal water to Jamie's nose through the lacy frames. He couldn't smell Cursers the way Antonio and Holgar could. Neither could Eriko.

Sofia kept going. Shadows shifted over cracked white and black marble squares. A pile of rotting wood and velvet looked to have once been a settee. Beyond it, a harpsichord had long ago collapsed in on itself. Why meet here?

"They behind, they wait, you," Sofia said in broken English as she pointed toward another Moorish archway and the blackened expanse beyond.

"Aren't you coming with us?" Eriko asked. Sofia just stared at her. "You come?"

Sofia shook her head, glancing behind her at the setting sun. "Night, she come." Her smile was angelic, like Maeve's.

"Grazie, bella," Jamie said, struggling to keep the sudden emotion out of his voice. "Go home. Be safe." He swallowed hard, and cleared his throat. *"Ciao."*

She dimpled, giggling at his wretched accent, he supposed. He watched as she skipped out the front door, fading like a wraith into the twilight.

He and Eriko glanced at each other. In unison they

pulled stakes from quivers at their waists. With a nod he let her lead the way. Eriko had drunk Father Juan's magick mojo juice, which endowed her with strength and speed he could not match. But Jamie often caught her rubbing her elbows and knees, and rolling her shoulders, like an old lady. Every time he asked her about it, she insisted she was fine. She was their Hunter, once their leader, and his loyalty lay with her rather than Jenn, who'd taken over the role of commandant. Bad choice, that, even if he, Jamie, had gone along with it at the time. That had been a mistake. And on top of it something was wrong with Eri.

As if she could read his mind, Eriko waved her hand in front of her face, refusing to answer any questions he might ask, and they crept into the darkness. What was left of the light gleamed through more arched windows.

They approached a flared stairway. It too was marble, but still quite opulent. From the looks of it no one had gone up or down for a long time, as dust and cobwebs coated the stairs like a carpet. Jamie made out the banisters of a second-story balcony, and then more darkness.

Candlelight flickered through an arch facing the staircase. The resistance cell must be inside. He nodded at Eriko, and she nodded back.

Gliding like shadows, they reached the doorway. He followed her lead across the transom. Half a dozen people sat in a semicircle on ornate chairs with faded brocade upholstery. A guttering candle stuck in a mound of melted wax on a similar chair flickered weak light cast over their faces. Two were middle-aged; three looked to be about Jamie's age; one was a withered old gal wearing a black sweater and a kerchief. The old gal had something white pinned to her sweater. Jamie squinted at it. What was it, a piece of paper?

Eriko slowly approached the old bird and said, *"Buon giorno?"* She tapped the woman's shoulder. "Hello?"

Old gal was not talking.

Not moving.

Not living.

"Bloody hell, Eri," Jamie swore. "Trap!"

He and Eriko flew out of the room of dead people. With perfect timing, a Cursed One plummeted from the balcony above the stairway just as Jamie and Eriko reached it. Jamie dove at the sucker as he landed, sending the vampire onto his back. Shouting, he shoved the stake into the C.O.'s heart.

Something landed on top of Jamie as the vampire turned to dust beneath him. He heard Eriko's battle cry as he twisted to try to stake the feckin' vampire who'd jumped him. Eriko yanked the creature from Jamie's back and ripped off its head in one smooth motion.

Springing to his feet, Jamie raced beside her to the door, to sunlight and safety for as long as it lasted. Another bleeder leaped into their path, and Jamie dove at his feet, while Eriko got out a vial of holy water and threw it into his eyes. While the vampire screamed and clawed at his face, Jamie yanked another stake from his belt and killed him.

Eriko grabbed Jamie's hand, and together they made it to the front door and out into the waning sunlight. They began to sprint for all they were worth across the bridge back to the mainland, racing the sun.

As Jamie charged along, he glanced at Eriko. If she kept pace with him, they weren't going to make it to the car before nightfall.

"Go!" he shouted.

She frowned. "I won't leave you behind."

"I'm not asking you to. Go get the car and pick me up!"

She nodded and poured on the speed, bounding ahead. He made it to the other side. A few minutes later the car screeched around a corner as Eriko fought to keep control of it at the crazy speed she was driving. She slowed down; Jamie pulled open the door and barreled inside.

"Hit it!" he bellowed.

Eriko slammed the pedal to the floor, and they careened back toward the main road.

"So much for the Venetian resistance cell," Jamie muttered.

"Jamie, it was a note," she said, holding something out to him. The piece of paper that had been pinned to the old gal. "It's from Aurora."

Jamie held it to the window. The blur of the streetlights strobed against elegant black lettering.

Antonio, or all of you will end up like Heather.

A.

"Feckin' hell," he said.

"Yes, I agree," Eriko replied. Then, as Jamie moved to tear up the note, she held out her hand. "Master Juan will want to see it."

"Christ. That bloody Curser is nothing but trouble. Well, *I* know what we should do." He stared out the window. "About this," he added, in case she wasn't catching his drift.

Eriko was silent. Then her phone rang, and she dug it out of her pocket with one hand while taking a curve.

"Master, something terrible," she began, then interrupted herself. "What is it?" she asked. She listened.

Jamie caught his breath and took stock of his weapons, just to be ready. Wished he had a bazooka. Thought about the lovely gun he was building, a sleek darlin' that would shoot silver bullets. He'd been working on it for a while. He came from a long line of gunsmiths. A fella couldn't let knowledge like that go to waste. Next up, one that shot wooden bullets.

"We're on our way back now," Eriko said into the phone. "The resistance cell was dead when we got there. Aurora. She left a note. She wants Antonio, or she will convert us all."

Jamie counted the plastic vials of holy water in the pocket of his parachute pants. Six. Tested the sharpness of a stake on his thumb tip.

She listened. *"Hai. Hai."*

"What's going on?" Jamie asked after she had hung up.

"Father Juan wants to see the note. And he is planning to send us to Moscow."

"Fine with me," he said, "as long as we can get something *done*." He tested another stake. "Kill something, I mean."

In the window he pictured Sofia's sweet little face and then Maeve's. What the hell, what did it matter where they went? No place was safe.

As long as there were vampires and werewolves.

BELFAST, SIX YEARS EARLIER
JAMIE AND HIS GRANDFATHER

The three coffins were plain and rough, like the man and the boy who respectfully tossed earth onto the lids, caps in hand. Standing beside his grandfather, Jamie, who was ten, knew that men didn't cry.

They got revenge.

Through his unshed tears Jamie kept Father Patrick in his sights. He clenched his jaw so tightly that one of his molars cracked. The pain made him shudder from head to foot, but he was glad of it. He spat blood out on the turned earth, earning a smack on top of his head from his grandfather. Spitting on hallowed ground was not permitted. As if allowing werewolves and vampires to murder your family was.

Maeve. His ma. His da. His family were dead, and he was just standing there. Jamie was so ashamed. And so angry.

During the wake, while his grandfather got good and drunk, Jamie went down to the cellar where they kept the guns they ran for the Irish Republican Army. Various wooden boxes labeled POTATOES and O'LEARY GUNSMITHS were pushed up against the walls. Maybe it was too obvious that the O'Learys, makers of fine firearms for three generations, were the ones who stowed the illegal weapons of their local IRA cell. But they'd served the cause of freedom from English rule since Jamie's grandfather had been a tot, and never a one been caught at it.

Sure and the English had sworn to the peace in 1998, but never in their long and bloody history had the English given the Irish any reason to trust them. It was violence that had freed Northern Ireland—brawls, bombings, and shootings—and them that said any different were English sympathizers and cowards. Now there were vampires and werewolves to fight, and no decent weapons against them.

Jamie took a crowbar to one of the large wooden boxes and opened it. The potatoes were still coated with earth; he gathered up an armful and dropped them onto the basement floor, wincing at the thudding sounds they made, so reminiscent of the dirt clods falling against the coffin lids of his ma and his little sister as the undertakers began their work.

Jamie scowled at the first piece of the cache, a submachine gun. Too impersonal, and therefore not right for the job; he needed the proper handgun to deliver three shots, execution-style—two in the eyes, one in the forehead—and he needed a silencer. A bit more digging and he had his weapon— unlicensed military issue, could be used with a silencer.

"That won't serve, Jamie," said a voice from behind him. It was his grandfather, eyes rimmed with red. His wispy gray hair was matted with sweat.

"I'm killing him, Poppy," Jamie insisted. "Father Patrick stood by and watched while they, they—"

His grandfather approached, hand out for Jamie's gun. "We're Catholics, Jamie. We can't kill priests. Much as we might want to," he added sourly.

"But . . ."

"No buts, me boyo. There are certain things we don't do. Especially at your age."

Jamie's grandfather turned and gestured for Jamie to follow him to his workbench. He reached up and yanked on a thin chain, lighting a bare lightbulb that hung above their heads. A vise held a gun barrel; there were drills and presses and bits of steel all around. No one made guns by hand anymore except as a hobby or for show, but all guns needed repair now and then.

"We're the O'Learys," his grandfather said. "We've

been making firearms for over a century. That's what we *do*." He caught his lip. "We'll make a gun that shoots silver bullets, you and I."

Jamie nodded, hatred overflowing his soul and streaming down his face like tears. Ashamed, he tried to turn away, but not before his grandfather saw. He smacked him on the side of the head. Jamie's ears rang.

"I need you strong," his grandfather ordered him. "Now close up the potato box."

Steeling himself not to cry again, Jamie did as he was told. He would be strong.

As soon as it was light, he stumbled through the gray, miserable dawn to the churchyard. The sight of the fresh mounds of earth tore him open. Balling his hands against his mouth, he pushed all the grief back into his soul. He was a man now, and he had a man's business to tend to.

"Maeve. Ma. Da," he said to the graves. "We're going to pay 'em back. I was going to kill Father Pat for letting it happen. Poppy said no. I suppose I wouldn't make it to heaven to see you if I did such a thing. But we'll get the Cursers and the wolves. I swear it."

When he left, he felt better. He had a plan, a purpose. His hand was on the door to their flat when his aunt jerked it open. Her face was ashen, and she had on her nice coat, the one she wore to Sunday Mass.

"Jamie, Jamie," she said, grabbing his shoulders. "Father Patrick's been gunned down. He was in the rectory garden, watering the plants. It's said he might not live." She crossed herself. "I'm going to the church to pray for him. Come with me, darlin'."

He was thunderstruck. For a moment he just stared at her.

"I need me jacket," he said, as upset as he sounded, and hurried inside.

He raced down to the cellar to the crate of potatoes. He threw off the lid.

The gun was missing.

Father Patrick died that evening. Two days later Jamie's grandfather insisted they attend the funeral, and they knelt together, heads bowed. The casket was closed, because whoever had killed Father Patrick had shot out his eyes. Jamie was glad the priest was dead, but he felt no relief. Nothing inside him had changed. He still hated the priest. And the vampires and werewolves, even more than the English, and that was saying something.

That night he dreamed of Maeve. She was a vampire, white as porcelain, wearing her first-communion dress with its little crown and veil. She was knocking on his window, weeping.

"Let me in, Jamie, *please*," she whispered. "It's so cold out here. Me bones have frozen to ice."

In the morning Jamie woke with a start, to find his window open. For one instant, hope flared inside his heart that she had really come to him. But he had seen them tear her apart. There was nothing left of Maeve to be converted — and he would surely wish her dead and in heaven than eternally weeping at his window. Would he not?

It wasn't a question for the asking. No matter; he would warm her poor dead bones with the heat of his fury. And in that way, and only that, would his little sister live on.

Venice was miles away now, and with it all the dead folk.

"Jamie," Eriko said as they sped toward Marco Polo Airport, "are you crying?"

"Don't be daft, Eri," he said. "You've never seen me cry and never will."

Stonily he gazed out the window. Streetlights, bushes, other cars. That was all there was to see.

SALAMANCA, SPAIN
FATHER JUAN, JENN, AND ANTONIO

Let this be the right course, Juan prayed once more, as Jenn and Antonio walked into his office. He had cast the runes and entreated heaven to make his decision crystal clear. But as often happened when matters of life and death were involved, he was called upon to exercise his free will, and to ask those in his care to do the same.

Beyond his door the academy students bustled en route to their activities — training, studies, chores — and their lively young voices reminded him of the duties that lay across his shoulders. He had a sure hand in the future of humanity. He might not know everything, but he was certain of that.

Jenn and Antonio kept their distance from each other as they stood before his desk. He gestured for them to sit. They complied. He could remember a time when Jenn would take Antonio's hand, or Antonio would smile reassuringly at her. Those days had become a memory. The conversion of Heather had harmed their relationship. That was bad. They were fighting partners.

Perhaps what I am going to do signals a more permanent change, he thought.

"We have been asked to help two teams in Russia," he told them.

"Two?" Antonio said.

"It's a combined effort by an Israeli and an Arab team," Father Juan explained. "Numerous special-forces veterans were ranked among them, and they were expected to gain a significant victory for our side. Unfortunately, it's gone badly. Out of twenty members two hunters have survived, possibly three. Jenn, you will take the team to Russia and meet up with them, and together you will stop the vampire named Dantalion."

"Okay," she said.

Father Juan leaned forward on his elbows.

"We've had some intelligence since the teams went in.

Dantalion has been overseeing genetic manipulation experiments. He's been splicing werewolf, human, and vampire genes to make supersoldiers. Others combine human and Cursed One DNA in hopes of creating the perfect vampire."

"Perfect vampire?" Jenn repeated.

"One who is not affected by sunlight," he replied.

Jenn paled. "Cursed Ones who could walk around by day?" She glanced at Antonio, and Father Juan saw the longing there. He guessed she was imagining what kind of life they could have together if he were not forced to hide from the sunlight.

But then she looked away again, as if to remind herself that she and Antonio would never have a life together. The vampire bore the strangest expression.

"Has he succeeded yet?" Antonio asked.

"Not as far as we can tell. Although what he has created is far more frightening." He fell silent.

"Father?" Jenn pressed.

"*Bueno*. A few of Dantalion's experiments have either escaped or been set loose. They have been slaughtering everything they come across. It's only a matter of time before he creates enough of these creatures to take out the entire city of Moscow."

Both Jenn and Antonio seemed stunned by the concept. "That's millions of people," Antonio said, finding his voice first. "How can he do that? He's only one vampire."

"Antonio, you were in the war when the Germans

unleashed the panzers, the armored tanks. And the U-boats. You saw the blitzkrieg for yourself—thousands of bombs fell from the sky. The Allies thought the world was ending."

Antonio looked thoughtful. "That's true. And in this war there is also new technology."

"Vale," Father Juan said. "And just as the Nazis sought to conquer the world with their master race, so do the Cursed Ones."

"When do we leave?" Antonio asked.

Father Juan took a deep breath. "I've told the others to return. Eriko and Jamie have booked a flight. Holgar and Skye are already on the road. Barring any problems, the team will leave tomorrow morning." He hesitated. "With one exception. Antonio, I need you to stay here."

Jenn sucked in her breath.

"But why, Father?" Antonio protested. "My team needs me."

"Aurora made contact in Venice," Father Juan said. "She left a note with the bodies of the resistance cell Eriko and Jamie planned to meet with."

"The bodies." Antonio crossed himself. "So . . . she killed them all?"

"Yes." Father Juan also crossed himself. "She wants you, Antonio."

Jenn paled, but Antonio betrayed no emotion except for his sorrow at the deaths. "Are you keeping me here to protect me, Father?"

"No. I'm keeping you here to protect the team." Father Juan turned to Jenn, who looked stricken. "You don't need to bring that battle to Russia."

"But . . ." She swallowed hard. "If he's with us, then we can protect him."

"No." Father Juan placed both his palms on his desk, a signal of dismissal. "I am the master here, and this is my decision."

Antonio lowered his head, and Father Juan made the sign of the cross above it. Without another word Antonio rose and left the room. Jenn watched him go, then turned back to Father Juan.

"Thank you," she said. "It's the right thing to do."

"Powerful vampires like Aurora have enemies," he replied. "I'll continue to investigate."

"And pray that someone stakes her before she reaches Antonio?" Jenn asked.

He shrugged. "We would be very lucky if that were the case."

"I'll get ready."

After she left, Father Juan pushed back his chair and knelt on the stone floor, humbling himself before the One who knew all things.

"Let this be the right course," he prayed. "Your children cry out to You, Merciful Father." He made a fist and pressed it against his heart. "Protect us from evil, I beg of You. And I beg of You, stake her."

Then Juan rose and walked out of his study, and into the small walled garden. Rain wanted to fall; he felt it in his bones and smelled it in the air. The moon was wrapped in gossamer clouds, her face veiled in mystery and pity.

"I pray to you also, Lady," he said aloud. "I am still your son. Grant me this boon. Grant us relief from her.

"Blessed be."

Jenn walked to her room, wondering where Antonio had gone. Her face was numb, and her hands were cold with fear. Aurora's shadow loomed long and dark. The vampire had taken Heather. If she took Antonio, too, Jenn didn't know how she would stand it.

She shut the door and leaned against the smooth wood for a moment, wrestling with her emotions. Since her entry into the academy, Antonio had never been far from her, except when she had gone to Berkeley for her grandfather's funeral. That was when her entire world had been torn apart. When *they* had been torn apart.

What was going to happen in Moscow without him? If these two teams of veteran soldiers had been taken out, what chance did the Salamancans have?

Just breathe, she told herself.

She pushed away from the door and walked over to the small, simple table that served as her desk. Stakes were stacked neatly underneath the table. A rough-hewn cedar chest held vials of holy water and crosses, which the

Church provided. The hunters were allowed to carry any religious symbol they wished, since it was their faith and not the object itself that provided the power. Which confused her—she didn't have any religious faith, so why did crosses work? Because she knew that others believed they would?

All she wanted was to personally hunt Aurora down and kill her. She didn't want to go to Moscow.

If I get through this mission, I'll ask Father Juan to send us after Aurora. She will never hurt anyone I love again.

Did she love Antonio? Despite what Father Juan had told them—that the runes insisted they had a part to play in the future of the world, and that they must play it together— she still felt so guarded, so unsure of him. He kept secrets, mourned private matters he wouldn't share with her. Even before Heather's conversion he had held himself in check, constantly monitoring himself lest he hurt her.

Kill her.

She grabbed her duffel bag and her journal. After a moment's hesitation she put her journal down. Father Juan had given it to her when he'd made her the leader, charged her with writing a new Hunter's Manual, which would replace the centuries-old manual that was required reading for academy students. So far all she'd managed to do was prattle on about daily battles and her own inse-curities. Hardly the stuff to inspire new generations. But even that would have to wait. She had to travel as lightly as possible.

She arranged her battle gear, all black with some strategic pieces of body armor. The crest of the Salamanca Hunter was sewn on the shoulder: a red cross consisting of four curved arms of equal length—the cross of the original Crusaders. A blue knight's helmet crowned with three white feathers—the color for the Virgin, the feathers to honor the Trinity—perched on the top arm of the cross. Below, the word "Salamanca" was stitched in a font reminiscent of Spain's Moorish roots. Once a sole Hunter had carried the crest; now all six members of the Salamancans wore it. A black covering could be Velcroed over it when the team needed to hide their identity. She remembered her pride when she'd received it on the night of her final exam, just five months ago. That was the same night she'd found out that Antonio was a vampire. Not such a fine moment, that.

It felt strange not to be packing stakes or holy water, but Father Juan didn't want to raise any alarms. The Cursed Ones were tightening the noose around Spain. Security had increased at the Spanish airports, and the team had to avoid detection.

The world is going to hell, and it seems like we're nearly there. Of course, Jenn wasn't sure she believed in hell, or in heaven. She wanted to, but belief didn't come as easy for her as it did for Antonio, or even Jamie, for that matter.

She walked to the window and looked out at the moon, surprised to find Antonio standing a distance away, facing her window. He had told her that he had stood guard over her every night for the two years of their training; apparently he had continued to maintain his vigil. Misty moonbeams danced in his hair, and he didn't look cursed. He looked like an angel.

Don't die, she silently begged him.

He spotted her. A red glow crept into his eyes, and he turned away, disappearing into the darkness.

Don't be a vampire, she added, and moved back into the light.

CHAPTER FIVE

Cursed Ones, that is what we are
Distanced from you by so far
Yet we hope and often pray
That this is not always the way
For we wish to walk with you
Hand in hand in morning dew
Together we will watch the sun
And all your fears will be undone

SALAMANCA
JENN AND ANTONIO

About an hour later Antonio watched as Jenn walked into the academy kitchen, where Brother Manuel was preparing two large pans full of savory mixed paella, a saffron rice dish loaded with seafood and chicken. In deference to Jenn, who was a squeamish American, the chubby cook had omitted the snails that often accompanied the dish.

Antonio stood quietly in the doorway, uncertain if he should approach her. She had to prepare herself for the mission, and he didn't want to throw her off her game. They both knew this might be the last time they saw each other.

Deep red wine caught the light as the cook picked up one of the decanters and poured two glasses, adding some water to Jenn's. She had never become accustomed to all the wine everyone drank in Spain.

"*Salud,*" Jenn said to Brother Manuel as he handed her the watered-down beverage. To your health.

"*Y dinero y amor,*" Brother Manuel added. "*Y tiempo para disfrutarlos.*" And money and love, and time to enjoy them.

"What time is your flight?" Brother Manuel asked her. Then, as if he had to justify the question, "Should I pack something for the plane?" He arranged some cooked prawns over the mounded rice, stepping back to appraise his handiwork. "The food in Russia is terrible."

"Oh, have you been?" Jenn asked him.

Brother Manuel shook his head. "No, and I never care to. They are godless."

A fleeting smile crossed Jenn's face, and Antonio savored it. She hadn't smiled in weeks. Her face was gaunt, and there were shadows under her eyes. She was in no shape to go up against a vampire like Dantalion. The stories of Dantalion made Aurora and Sergio seem like kittens. Team

Salamanca had failed against Aurora, and Antonio shuddered to think what would ever happen if Sergio attacked them. Dantalion would crush them with the force of a bomb dropping on their heads.

"We're going to the airport around five in the morning," she said. "So this could be our last supper."

"Ay, Jenn, please don't say that," Antonio murmured, stepping into the kitchen.

"Hey," she said. She swallowed hard. "I didn't hear you come in."

"I didn't mean to startle you," he said. "I was just . . ." He gazed at her. He was so afraid for her.

"Jenn, if you wouldn't mind. If you would come with me, please," Antonio said.

He hesitated, then held out his hand. He didn't know if she would be able to bring herself to touch him. But she drank down half her wine, as if to give herself false courage, then slid her hand into his grasp. She was warm as embers against his cold skin. Grateful, he closed his fingers around hers.

Antonio walked her through the *sala* where the team took their meals together, bobbing his head at Holgar, who was finishing off a plate of uncooked venison. Holgar preferred raw meat, but he never ate it in front of the others. But Antonio, blessed—or was it cursed?—with a superstrong sense of smell, like Holgar's, always knew when Holgar had dined. Antonio had never made mention of it.

Holgar didn't run around announcing when Antonio drank human blood, either.

It was past time for Antonio to feed, and Father Juan had spoken to him about it before Antonio had come in search of Jenn. The priest had told Antonio that two students had come forward, offering to be donors for the esteemed vampire who hunted vampires. Antonio was both grateful and mortified. He hated taking blood from anyone; he had tried to hide the fact that it was more nourishing to drink directly from the living than, say, out of refrigerated blood bags or even fancy wine glasses. He didn't understand why that should be so. *Vale, vale;* if one tried to apply logic to vampirism, one would be sorely disappointed. How was it that he'd been alive for nearly ninety years, yet still looked nineteen, the age he had been when he'd been changed?

He wasn't sure that even God had the answers.

That did not mean that Antonio would stop asking them of Him.

Antonio took Jenn to the chapel. They walked through the side door of the sanctuary into the smells of the incense and flowers, the scent of paraffin from the votive candles burning in front of the statues of the Blessed Mother and St. John of the Cross, patron saint of Salamanca. The resemblance between the figure and Father Juan was pronounced, and many remarked on it. Antonio had vowed that before he died the True Death, he would learn just who and what the priest really was.

Fonts on either side of the entrance were filled with holy water; Antonio dipped his fingertips and blessed himself. A non-Catholic, Jenn did not partake.

Bending his knee as they faced the altar and the crucifix, he crossed himself again before sliding into a pew. Antonio didn't put down the prayer bench. He sat on the cushioned seat and took Jenn's left hand in both of his as she sat down beside him. Once more he was worried that he was taking liberties he was no longer permitted, but he had to touch her as much as he could, before she left—unless, in her heart, she was already gone.

"Ay," he murmured.

Jenn was silent. He didn't know how to speak to her anymore, to tell her the things he wanted her to know before she left on the new mission.

"I believe," he began, searching for words. "Jenn, I believe in a God who wants the best for us."

"Like my sister?" she asked bitterly. The anger in her voice made him want to weep for her and for the world. And even, in the recesses of his soul, to weep a few tears for his own betrayal those many years ago. Not because he thought he was pitiful, but because he still mourned what he could have become for God, whom he loved; what he could have been for the young girl whom he adored. And yet he never would have met Jenn had he not been turned.

His spirits lowered. This wasn't the conversation he had

wanted to have. But if it was the one she needed, he would do his best to keep his side of it.

"God did not turn your sister into a vampire," he said. "But God brought her here, where she has a chance." His voice cracked on the last word.

"A chance to what?" Jenn asked, pulling her hand away.

He was sorry that she had pulled away, deeply, as he searched for what to say. "God gives us grace."

"Oh, *that's* what it's called when you get turned into a monst—a Curser," she corrected herself.

Monster. That was how she saw him now, if she had ever really seen him differently. So his love for her *was* hopeless. *Bueno,* then he could love her as he should have in the first place: as a man who had taken holy orders and was dedicated to God. The way he wanted her to love him ran contrary to those vows and could only bring them pain anyway. At least this made his choice easier.

"Jenn," he whispered, her name the strongest prayer he knew. "Jenn Leitner."

She was quiet for a long time. He gazed at the altar, at the flames. Then, at the scent of her teardrops, he realized she was silently crying.

"Antonio," she whispered, and he shut his eyes tightly against the tide of his emotion. His name on her lips was the answer to his prayer. "Antonio."

She leaned her head on his shoulder. He felt her slump. He was just about to put his arm around her, to kiss her hair, her temple, her cheek. To humble himself as a man. Yes, he was one of God's men, but he *was* a man, not an angel.

No, I'm not, he thought. *I'm not a man.*

"If," she began, choking down a sob and clearing her throat. "If she doesn't get better, please, if you and Father Juan can't . . ." Jenn lowered her head. "I want it to be Father Juan who decides, not you. And—and I want him to be the one." She pressed a shaking hand over her eyes. "So I won't hate you."

"Heather will come to no harm while you're gone. I swear it," Antonio said, making the sign of the cross, then kissing his thumb, in the old Spanish way.

"Then I'll never come back."

"Don't say that. Never say that." He turned to her, cupping her chin and easing her to face him as he half turned in the pew. "I will pray without ceasing—I *am* praying. I've been making a novena for Heather, do you know what that is? I have been saying the Novena of Divine Mercy."

Jenn swallowed and moved her shoulders in a gentle shrug. She didn't believe in prayer. If only he could make her see.

"The miracles are already made," he said. "They're all around us. We have to adjust our vision, so that we can see them and accept them. Like when you fight vampires, Jenn. You can't see them move, so you focus on where they'll be next. It's as we say in the Church: 'Do not fear tomorrow. God is already there.'"

"Where was He when Aurora kidnapped her?" Jenn demanded. "And when she—when Aurora destroyed her?"

"God wants good to happen. He fights for it, through us. And through His priests. And through His crusaders."

"What, do you have a special line in to Him? His private number?" Jenn was making fun, but he heard the fury in her voice. He understood it.

"When I was called to become a priest, it was so that I could serve Him better. I spend hours trying to learn how to *listen* to Him, not to speak to Him. He already knows my heart. I am trying to learn His."

"Then I have really bad news for you, Antonio. He's heartless." Jenn slid out of the pew and headed for the door. "Tell Brother Manuel I'm sorry, but I'm not hungry. I'm going to bed."

"I can't let you go this way," he insisted, following after her.

She whirled around. "That's not up to you." She pointed to the chapel. "Go. Do what you do best."

"What I do best, *mi amor*, is love you," he said.

A dozen expressions crossed her face, a panorama of all human emotion. But in the end a numbness that hurt worst of all. "You're a vampire. You can't love anybody."

Then she turned and fled.

Defeated, he let her go. Antonio went back to the chapel, pulled down the prayer bench, and knelt, reaching for his rosary in the pocket of his jeans. He began to tell the beads in Latin, reaching up to loop his hair around his ear as it fell forward and obscured his view of the statue of the Blessed Virgin. His thumbnail grazed the ruby cross earring he wore in his left earlobe. His seven sins. The seven murders on his conscience. But there were many other deaths he had to account for. He had left his mother, brother, and sisters behind in their village. And Rosalita, who wanted to marry him. He had told her that he was already taken by God's bride, the Church, and would be faithful to Her.

Lita had died in the bombing. Quickly, he was told. She had not suffered.

But he had. He'd *left* her there. He was inside a seminary, studying about the miracle of the wedding at Cana—when Christ had changed water into wine—when she had been killed. His father confessor had told him that hatred and despair were sins. That night, sobbing before the cross, Antonio had sworn before Christ that he would never, ever again fail to protect a woman he loved. For yes, he had loved Rosalita, and now he loved Jenn.

And now Jenn was leaving to face Dantalion without him.

"God, give me strength," he begged. "Show me my path."

He returned to his rosary, and his fears.

Moscow
Team Salamanca Minus Antonio

"Well, that was fun," Jamie said, as they cleared customs in the grim and dingy Sheremetyevo-2 airport. Beneath strange brown decorative tubes that might have been some bureaucrat's image of interior decoration, the team waited in one of two serpentine lines. As everybody shuffled along like zombies, the guards would scare the regular people but let rich Russians jump ahead when and as they pleased.

Look at her nibs, and the other girls too, wearing their disguises. Jenn had on a black wig; Skye was wearing an olive-green beret; and Eriko sported a knitted cap, like Antonio's, that did nothing for her beautiful Japanese complexion. All three of them wore winter wear—turtleneck sweaters and heavy jackets, jeans, boots, gloves. Skye had cast glamours that were designed to deflect interest from them. He wasn't sure Skye had got the proper hang of it. Seemed like everyone had been staring at them as if they were pop stars.

Or hunters.

His girl didn't look well these days. Her cheekbones could cut cement blocks. If she caught him looking, she'd tell him she was cold. Pile o' shite, that was. All her aches and pains were getting worse. He'd planned to say something to Father Juan about it before they'd left, but the good father had said Mass for them, then gone back to rehabilitating Jenn's demonic little sis. Couldn't spare half a moment for the team he was sending away on another damned fool's errand, which was being led by their little American squirrel. Death trap, meet a complete and utter failure as a leader.

What did the American kidlets say? Epic fail. That was

for certain. Only reason Jenn was wearing that crown was Antonio wanted it on her.

"I'd begun to think we were going to start dating, that guard and me," Jamie went on, mostly to fill the silence as they headed for the exit. Not a fan of it.

"He wasn't," Holgar drawled. "I read his body language. You're not good-looking enough."

"And the sad thing is, you think saying that will bother me," Jamie shot back, hating Holgar more than usual today. Or maybe just on principle. Or maybe because he'd had to leave his nearly finished gun with silver bullets back in Salamanca. He'd been thinking a few more hours' work, a nice, dense Russian forest, a good firefight, and Holgar might not live to turn into a rampaging beast on the next full moon.

By Father Juan's edict they had been forced to leave all their gear home, even their holy water. Marc Dupree, the (dead) leader of the (crushed) Resistance back in (vampire paradise) New Orleans, had told them they were only kidding themselves if they thought magick spells would protect their luggage from being searched by airport security. It had worked well enough flying out of Madrid the last time. But no.

No worries; Jamie figured that in Russia, with only two hunters of the original twenty left to use the provisions *they'd* smuggled in, there would be a lot of extras lying around for the Salamancans. Things to kill Cursers with too.

"By the way, that woman guard *did* want to date you," Holgar said. "The one with the mustache."

Jamie grunted. "Then that wad of euros Skye slipped her must have been a down payment, not a bribe." He glanced over at Skye, who had in reality bribed the guard to stamp their passports, as everyone expected foreigners to do, while casting a spell so she'd stop being interested in them—a little trick Skye had picked up from her mates in Pamplona.

"Guys, please," Jenn hissed, and they emerged from the building into a crazy honking mess of snarled traffic. "Start looking for our contact."

The night was black and raining. One of the Fellowship of the Mid-East Stake, an eighteen-year-old Muslim named Taamir, was coming to pick them up in an old military truck. How the intel for the rendezvous had been relayed to Taamir's sultan back in Gaza, and from there to Father Juan, was a mystery to Jamie. If they could manage all that, why not send some more of *their* own guys to clean up *their* problem?

"There," Jenn said, pointing as a camouflaged box truck rumbled down the street. "That's got be him."

"Hai, hai," Eriko said.

"We're supposed to meet him around the corner," Jenn reminded them.

Jamie frowned at her. That was an idiotic idea, and she should never have agreed to do it. They'd look bloody conspicuous sauntering down the street toward a military vehicle. Any second now some Russian *polizei* was going to demand papers or a bribe, whichever struck his fancy. Maybe both.

But before Jamie could complain, they were down at the corner, scrambling into the cargo area of the truck. Jenn climbed up front with the Arab, and they bounced into the traffic. Eriko was squashed next to Jamie. Skye settled in next across from them, making room for Holgar, who pulled out an iPod and put in his earbuds. Holgar blinked, pulled out one of the buds, and put it in Skye's ear. They shared a smile. How darlin'.

Jamie closed his eyes and tried to sleep. He was in the mind of thinking about his dead sister and his ma. He wasn't sure why, just that the rage simmered inside him. *Another damn trip to save someone else's arse.* They'd gone to New Orleans for that, and look what a pile o' shite *that* had turned into. Venice, *another* mess. He swore in silence as colorfully as possible and set his jaw. He should just hop a plane to Belfast and to hell with the lot.

Except . . . Eriko.

He opened one eye to see her sneaking a rub of her ankles. He closed it quickly before she could glance his way. He had a thought: If this whole Hunter thing was taking too great a toll on her, maybe she'd give it up and come to Ireland with him. She could still do the fightin' and brawlin' if she had a mind to. But they could get away from all these misfits and, y'know, also lead a semi-normal life. Maybe eventually even have a little superbaby kid. If she was a girl, they could name her Maeve, in honor of his sister. Maeve Sofia.

SALAMANCA
ANTONIO, HEATHER, AND FATHER JUAN

The plane had taken off.

Jenn was gone.

Now Antonio sat in front of Heather's cell, empty of prayers, filled with worry. From the school's lost and found he had picked up a paperback copy of a novel about a girl who had fallen in love with a vampire. There were a lot of such novels, more than ever now that the Cursed Ones had revealed their presence to mankind, and he felt a strange sort of enraged tenderness as he turned the pages. This was not their reality, but Solomon and the others had exploited this romantic yearning to their advantage. So many young girls wore those bat-and-heart necklaces now. Would their vampire "boyfriends" drop the act at some prearranged signal, ripping out their throats?

Because that's what we do, Antonio thought. *We rip. We don't sweetly pierce and gently drink. We attack. We drain.*

We kill.

"Hasn't the Church banned that one?" Father Juan asked, chuckling, sitting beside him.

"Do you think Jenn's read it?" Antonio mused. He

106

looked through Heather's bars. She had pulled a blanket over herself and lay inert, as if she were sleeping. But vampires didn't sleep.

"If you're asking me if Jenn thinks it adds to your allure, trust me, she doesn't," Father Juan said bluntly. "She wishes you weren't a vampire."

"So do I." Antonio closed the book. "I think the people in this book are very sweet. He struggles every day to be worthy of her. And she expects it of him."

"Vale, vale." Father Juan cupped Antonio's cheek. "Antonio, you're old and yet filled with youthful idealism."

Antonio cocked his head. "And what of you, Padre? How old are you?"

A silence fell between them. Antonio looked hard at Father Juan. He saw the same face as on the images of St. John of the Cross—the saint whose name in Spanish was the same as his own, *de la Cruz.* A priest who gazed into crystal balls and swung pendulums over tarot cards. A child of God who left flowers in the woods for the Goddess. Antonio had followed him, watched him honor her and call himself her devoted son.

"Are you the saint?" Antonio asked sharply. "Are you here because these are the end times? Are the angels coming to help us?"

"Better, perhaps, to ask yourself what *you* are," Father Juan replied.

Then Heather started screaming. She threw off her

blanket and leaped to her feet, spinning in a circle with her head thrown back. Her shrieks pierced Antonio's ears; then she raced forward, flinging herself against the bars, wailing.

"There! Blood! She's there!" Heather screeched. Her voice was inhuman. She sounded possessed. But they were her first words since her conversion.

"She's *there*!"

"Heather," Antonio said, as he and Father Juan rushed forward. Antonio reached for Heather's hands, but she thrust herself backward, landing hard on the floor. She kept screaming.

"A bad dream?" Father Juan said.

"We don't dream," Antonio reminded him. "We don't sleep."

"No, no, no, no!" Heather cried, arms outstretched again, backing away as she stared at the ceiling. *"Dantalion!"*

Father Juan and Antonio traded looks.

"What about Dantalion, Heather?" Father Juan said calmly. "Can you tell us?"

She screamed.

Antonio opened the cell and stepped in, shutting the door behind himself. Cautiously he approached her. She didn't seem to notice him, only continued to scrabble away from him.

"Listen to me, to my voice," he said. He crouched over her, holding her chin in a viselike grip. Her eyes jittered from left to right. He exerted his influence, pushing.

"Listen." Antonio pushed again, and her voice dropped to a horrible, mewling whimper. He put his forehead against hers, forcing her to look into his eyes.

"Antonio, *cuidado*," Father Juan said. "Be careful."

He saw nothing in her eyes but fear. He sought to overcome it, whispering softly, "It's all right. You're safe with me. You're safe."

"She's . . . there," Heather said. "Dantalion!" She burst into tears and batted at him, flailing, kicking. As he tried to hold her, he pushed one more time.

"You're safe. With me," he said gently. "Tell me about Dantalion."

She stared at him, and sighed heavily. Then her eyes rolled back in her head, and she collapsed into his arms.

"*Dios,*" Father Juan said. "What was that?"

"I mesmerized her, to calm her," Antonio replied, easing her onto her back. He opened one eye. Heather appeared to be unconscious. "But she fainted, perhaps to avoid talking to me."

"Did someone else mesmerize her, perhaps from a distance?"

"We can't do that," Antonio said. "At least I can't. I must be able to look into the eyes of the person." He opened her other eye; then he lifted his arm and pushed back his shirt sleeve, preparing to place his wrist against her mouth. "Perhaps if she fed, we could wake her. Human blood would be better, but she can get sustenance from mine."

"No, don't," Father Juan said quickly. "Don't you feed her."

Antonio frowned. "Why not, Father?"

"I'll get some blood from the refrigerator for her. Just . . . don't." Father Juan gestured for him to come out of the cell. "Drinking from you is still drinking from flesh, and it could undo all the effort we've put in."

Antonio parted his lips as Father Juan unlocked the cell. Surely in the midst of a crisis they could forgo the niceties. Nevertheless Antonio came out and shut the door, making sure it was locked. Heather stirred. Then she lifted her head, sniffing the air. She rolled over onto all fours and charged the iron bars. Babbling and yelling, she reached for Father Juan.

"Tell us about Dantalion," Father Juan said.

She kept raving and gibbering, making no sense.

"It was a vision that she had," Antonio said. "From magick, maybe. Or from God." He looked at Father Juan. "I'm going to Russia, Father."

"Antonio, no." Father Juan looked at him. "We don't know what this means. I forbid you."

"Then forgive me, Father."

Moscow, Russia
Team Salamanca Minus Antonio;
Taamir and Noah

"We're here," Jenn announced, standing at the back of the truck. The door was still shut. Skye was leaning over Jamie

110

and moving her fingers in quite a suspicious manner; Jamie wondered if she'd put him—all of them—to sleep with a spell. He yawned and cricked his neck, then rolled his eyes as Holgar yipped in his sleep. The wolf did it again.

Jamie swore in colorful Irish, then said to Skye, "Can't you shut him up? If the foreigner hears him, we'll be in trouble."

"I *did* shut him up," Skye said. "I turned Holgar down nearly to zero."

"And why didn't you go *all* the way to zero, hmm?" he queried.

She pursed her lips. "Because I'm tired, Jamie. Magick costs, just like everything else."

"Jamie-*kun*, please," Eriko said.

The door opened into gloomy, snowy sky, and an olive-skinned lad with big ears nodded a greeting to Jamie and the others.

"Hello. I'm Taamir," he said. Since everyone except Jenn had hopped into the back without being properly introduced, no one else had actually met him. "Noah is at the camp with the noon meal."

"Neat," Jamie said. "Especially since it's teatime." Four p.m. He was starving. Brother Manuel had packed them some sandwiches, but he'd devoured his before he'd even sat down in the Madrid airport waiting area.

"The camp's about ten kilometers away," Taamir added. "We'll march in."

111

Jamie swore again. Not so much because he was tired, but because he didn't want Eriko to have to exert herself. But he knew if he said that, she'd probably kick him.

"Then let's go," Jamie said.

Jamie knows, Eriko thought. She fought not to limp as they threaded their way through dense, overgrown forests. Time and again she caught her boot on thick roots, wrenching her bones.

He couldn't know exactly what was wrong with her — she'd done her best to hide it — but he still knew that something was bothering her. On the night of their graduation from the academy, after Father Juan had selected her, Eriko, to become the Hunter, the priest had given her a cup of sacred elixir distilled from herbs so rare and precious that he could only make one dose a year. That year he had chosen to give it to her.

Eriko had loved her enhanced abilities, even though she wasn't positive she deserved them. She was as strong as Antonio and as fleet-footed as Holgar on his wolf nights. But both their bodies could accommodate their physiological differences. Hers could not. It was literally being torn apart, and she didn't know how much longer she could stand it.

I should have told Father Juan, she thought, as Jamie glanced over his shoulder at her. She was bringing up the rear in case the vamps were shadowing them, preparing to launch a surprise attack. But she'd been afraid that if she had told their master, he would have made her stay behind in Salamanca. It was bad enough that Antonio and Father Juan had remained in Spain. From what she had heard about this Dantalion, they needed all their fighting power.

Taamir had handed out stakes, holy water, and Uzis from a cache near the truck, and taught them how to scan their surroundings by sighting down the barrel. They all knew how to do that already, but Jenn told them to use the opportunity to brush up. Eriko hated firearms. They'd lost Lucky, one of Marc Dupree's freedom fighters, to friendly fire in New Orleans.

Catching her lower lip between her teeth, she moved through a particularly bad rush of pain in her upper thighs. Holgar glanced over at her, frowning slightly. He had a phenomenal sense of smell, and he could detect changes in body chemistry. He probably knew she was hurting, but he didn't say a word. Holgar was discreet. During their training at the academy he'd concealed Antonio's identity from them, as well as his own. Maybe she should talk to him. He would understand why she was hiding it. And he would honor her wish to keep it a secret.

But *oh*, if only the pain would go away.

In a haze of hurt she followed Jamie, glancing repeatedly over her shoulders, then up into the snow-sprinkled trees. Taamir whistled low like an owl. It was answered.

Then an entire section of foliage was pushed out of their way, revealing a guy dressed in white camouflage, his left arm in a sling, arranging what looked to be field rations on some metal plates. Short, curly brown hair framed an angular face with a freckled nose and large brown eyes. His lips were full, and his cheeks and chin were bushy with brown beard. There was something about him that Eriko liked very much, but she couldn't say what it was. Confidence, poise.

"Hello," Jenn greeted him.

We come in peace for all mankind, Eriko finished, feeling a tiny bubble of humor escape the pressure cooker of her anxiety. Skye had told her all about Holgar's spy code in Toulouse. Eriko, only sixteen, had been a little bit goofy like that before her world had ended.

"I am Noah Geller, Hunter," he said to Jenn. He looked older than the rest of them, maybe mid to late twenties. He bowed his head. "Thank you so much for coming."

"I'm our leader, but Eriko is our Hunter," Jenn replied, and she leaned slightly toward him, as if she, too, was affected by his charisma.

"Hello," he said to Eriko. She bowed, but stiffly, because of the pain.

Noah and Taamir passed out the rations. It was some sort of Spam-like product, which Noah was careful to mention was not pork, on pita bread, accompanied by raisins and other dried fruit and a vitamin drink. Eriko guzzled down the drink and accepted another.

The two soldiers cleaned up afterward. Noah moved with some awkwardness because of his injury, but Taamir filled in for him with ease. Father Juan said the Stars of David and the Sons of the Crescent had trained together for just three weeks before arriving in Moscow. The Salamancans had spent nearly four months fighting as a team and two years training before that, and they didn't come near the level of easy familiarity that Taamir and Noah demonstrated as they put the newcomers at ease.

After the meal, as everyone lounged on piles of leaves, Jamie said, "Don't suppose it would be wise to smoke."

Noah grinned and pulled out a pack of cigarettes from inside his sling. "I'm a smoker too. I've got a spot."

Jamie smiled faintly. "Thank God."

"Let's debrief first," Jenn said. "Father Juan said you weren't sure about a third survivor."

Taamir was loading their empty ration kits into a plastic bag. He looked up. "Svika. Leader of Noah's part of the group. Dantalion's henchmen dragged him into the building. We believe he's still alive, and we want you to help us rescue him."

"Wait. Hold on. Time out," Jamie said. "We are here for two reasons and two reasons only: to kill Dantalion and either destroy, incapacitate, or take possession of his experiments and all that shite."

Noah and Taamir traded wary looks.

"But we were told that was explained to you," Noah said.

Jamie thrust out his jaw and furrowed his brow. "Our big kahuna said nothing about rescuing anyone. Which is all to the good, because frankly, we suck at it."

"Jamie-*kun*," Eriko said quietly. "Please, don't say such things."

Taamir zipped the bag shut. "We would never leave a man behind. A brother."

"Your brother's got a Jewish name, mate," Jamie said.

"Yes, and I'm proud to call him brother," Taamir said.

"Things were very different before the war," Noah admitted. "The vampire war, I mean. A suicide bomber took out my entire family."

"And the Jews bulldozed our house," Taamir added. "In Gaza."

"And yet you've back-burnered all that," Skye said pointedly, looking hard at Jamie.

"Not back-burnered. Forgotten," Taamir replied. "This world doesn't have room for battles between humans. If we don't fight together, we'll die. All of us."

"Yeah, well, that's pretty talk, but that's a hella lot easier said than done," Jamie insisted. "Your governments aren't talking like that."

"That's why they're home, and we're here." Noah gave

Taamir a nod. "The older ones can't stop hating each other. But we can. *We have.*"

There was silence. Then Jenn said, "We have a lot to learn from you guys."

"*Hai, hai,*" Eriko said, sounding stressed. She looked over hopefully at Jamie.

Not me, Jamie thought. *Not me, ever.*

CHAPTER SIX

*It's hard to be a hunter. It's a lonely life. Family,
friends—you leave so many people behind. Loved
ones all. They can never prepare you for that when
you train. But even with your teammates, with
someone you care deeply about, you can still feel that
way. Because your thoughts, your fears, are yours
alone. And you die alone. That terrifies me. When I
was a kid, I used to think that death was something
that happened to very, very old people. It was like
I thought I was invincible. Now I know the truth.
Death happens to all of us, most of the time when
we're not even looking.*

*—from the diary of Jenn Leitner,
discovered in the ashes*

"And cut," Solomon said to himself, as he watched the film crew shoot his pet project, an epic film about the secret history of the Cursed Ones. Romance, drama, tragedy, and triumph—it was certain to enthrall both human and vampire alike. Most vampires had no idea of their own lineage. It was his joke to create one for them—and what a story it was. Lies from start to finish, but something that would give them pride, and the conviction that it was their destiny to put humanity in chains. It redefined the truth of their reality, and it would be his crowning achievement—other than ruling the world, of course.

Sure enough, the director yelled cut. Solomon had picked a good one.

Solomon had been converted in 1980, when he was just thirty-two and a rising star of the entertainment industry. He'd been Solomon Shapiro back then. The Shapiro had been dropped well before his conversion—he was a one-name wonder. Everyone in Hollywood had spoken of him as if he'd been their best friend, but in reality he was their worst nightmare—he smiled at them head on, then stabbed them in the back. His road to success was littered with stars, directors, and producers whose lives he had destroyed by making them promises he never intended to fulfill. He would do or say anything to get what he wanted, and in the end no one could hold him to account. He was too intelligent to leave evidence. More impressive, many of those who he had wronged the most had no idea he had done so.

In just a few short years many vampires had fallen under his spell—enough to consolidate his standing as leader. Hundreds of his opponents had been staked prior to the Valentine's Day that he brought the vampires into the light. The purges continued, and vampires trembled in his presence.

He had never met the old guard, though—ancient vampires like Aurora, Sergio, and whomever they served. He'd get them sooner or later. Preferably sooner.

Aurora was probably more dangerous than Sergio. She was wise to take over Vegas. It was a vampire's paradise. There was one way into Las Vegas, and one way out, and she had that heavily patrolled. So it was a perfect hunting ground. Aurora had left some lesser light in charge back in New Orleans. Solomon knew she was up to something, conspiring against him with Sergio. Those old-world vampires were hard to figure out, with their ancient, twisted allegiances, dusty histories, and worship of archaic hell gods. Liege lord *this* and king *that*, the code of the Transylvanian hills. She and Sergio, the love-hate of her life, had been duking it out for centuries like they were in a remake of *Dracula*. And as for this supersire of theirs, whoever, "the Big Bad," as they used to say on *Buffy*—

He'd be dust.

Let Aurora and company make their pathetic plans, scheme their little schemes. He had spies planted all over the place. He knew everything they were planning practically before *they* knew. And he knew something they didn't: Solomon had gotten the best news ever from his partner in Russia. The power in Vampireland had just shifted.

Solomon's future looked so bright, he was going to have to wear shades.

Because he was going to have a *bright* future.

He was going to walk in daylight. And whoever owned the sun wouldn't need Vegas, or New Orleans, or anywhere. Because he would own the world.

"Looking good," Solomon said to his cute little assistant, a tawny Barbie-airhead human who was wearing a plunging white tank top and jeans. Sparkling at her throat was the necklace he had designed *and* copyrighted—a bat holding a heart. Maybe he'd rip her throat out tonight. He liked doing that.

Because he could.

He winked at her—what was her name again?—and sauntered off the soundstage into the sweet Los Angeles night. Solomon Productions rented space from Paramount. He loved the old movie lot. It was where he'd begun his climb to fame, working in the mailroom.

This was his Solomon-in-L.A. persona. Of course, when

he was in Washington, he was a different Solomon—more grave, businesslike, *older*.

He strode into Makeup and Hair and swung into the first room on the right. A man sat in the chair, and Solomon watched in the mirror as pancake makeup appeared on the man's face. The sponge daubed his forehead, moving as if by magick, something out of an old ghost movie, but the makeup girl was simply a vampire.

Solomon made a show of tiptoeing up behind the man, then grabbed his shoulders and cried, "Boo!"

"God!" the man screamed.

Solomon chuckled and patted him on the back, whirling the makeup seat to the left and stepping in front of it. "Sorry, Paul, it was just too good a chance to pass up." He appraised the makeup job. "Perfect."

He smiled at the girl, then back at Paul Leitner, the father of Jenn, the hunter Aurora was after. That was one thing Solomon did not know—why Aurora cared so much about this one hunter. That bothered him. A lot.

Then Paul Leitner actually came staggering into one of Solomon's Talk Together offices in Berkeley and asked for his help getting his daughter back. Told him the whole intriguing story about Aurora and Jenn. Would anyone really go to all that trouble just to bag a little warrior girl? Heck, he'd taken out the American Hunter ages ago . . . and anybody else who tried to be a hero.

"Did you know Annie here used to work for a mortu-

122

ary? She made up corpses," Solomon declared.

"Never had any customer complaints," Annie said, grinning at Solomon.

"Except one of them was not a corpse. He was a sneaky vampire lookin' for love." Solomon let his fangs out a bit, flirting.

"Best thing that ever happened to me." Annie put down her container of foundation and picked up a brush.

"So, are you ready for scene two?" Solomon asked Leitner as he swung the chair back around to face the mirror. "Got your new lines memorized?"

Leitner hesitated for just a fraction of a second, and Solomon saw his anxiety, fear, resentment, hatred. Solomon felt for him, he really did. Aurora had treated him abominably. Betrayed his trust, reneged on their bargain, left him for dead in all that San Francisco fog. No wonder Leitner no longer thought he'd made a good decision offering up his delinquent, rebellious hunter daughter in return for the safety of his family.

"Let's run through it," Solomon said smoothly. "I'll feed you your first line. I've memorized all mine. Ready?" He cleared his throat and assumed his Washington, D.C., look.

He put his hand on the man's shoulder. "'We're still looking for her,'" Solomon said sadly. "'We understand the confusion she must be feeling. There's so much misinformation out there, so many false rumors. Jennifer Leitner, please, listen to your father.'"

123

He smiled at Leitner. "Your turn."

Fear rolled off Leitner. Both Solomon and the makeup girl caught the scent; it stirred them. Solomon kept his gaze fixed on his actor. Leitner clearly had second thoughts about his decision to ask Solomon for help. No matter. He'd be dead soon enough.

Maybe I should just mesmerize Leitner and be done with it. But this guy has it in him to deliver a convincing performance on his own. I'm sure of it.

"'Jenn,'" Leitner ground out. His hands began to shake, his finger to tap his knee.

"Cut." Solomon smiled at him. "Don't tap your knee."

"Sorry."

"It's okay, Paul. Let's move on. Your next line?"

Leitner took a big, deep breath. "'Solomon is right. We only want to help you, sweetheart.'"

"Perfect." Solomon beamed at him. "We'll shoot you in about an hour." He paused dramatically. "Not literally, of course. Shoot you. We would never *shoot* you."

The makeup girl giggled. Solomon started to leave, then paused again. "Maybe you *should* tap your knee a couple of times. Let her see that you're very worried about her. It's a thought."

He strode out, then down a flight of stairs to his office. Only he had a key. He let himself in, humming, and slammed the door. The human he'd had for breakfast was still chained to the wall. *And* still alive. Nice.

"Take two," Solomon said.

The human jerked his head. "No," he whispered.

In an instant Solomon's eyes glowed; his fangs extended. He glared at him.

"What did you say?" he shouted. He twisted the man's head so that his mouth was pressed over the guy's ear and yelled as loudly as he could, "What did you *dare* to say to me? *No?*"

The man gasped, and his eyes rolled back in his head. He was near death. If Solomon was going to have any more of him, he had to act fast. He had never in his thirty-odd years as a vampire drunk dead blood, and he sure as hell wasn't going to start now.

"No one says no to me."

Then he slowly pierced the man's ravaged neck with his fangs, knowing it would be torturous, as the man groaned and tried, very feebly, to protest.

Solomon chuckled and further drew out the pain. For a long, long, time.

Finally the man's heart stopped; his head lolled to the side, and his eyes stared at nothing.

"And that's a wrap," Solomon said gleefully. His cell phone buzzed, and he took it out of his pocket. It was his partner again.

"Danny," he said. *"Dobraye utro."* "Good morning," in Russian. He listened to a stream of Russian in response. His smile grew so wide he was afraid his face would crack.

"*Kruta*," he replied, which was Russian for "cool." "Of course I'll wire you more money." He frowned. "So there are just the two left, right? Two hunters?"

He huffed as the guy on the other end of the line continued to whine. "Oh, please, you can find two people hiding in the forest. Set your monsters after them. You can make *more*. They're like extras, Dantalion. Disposable. Yes? Okay, *kruta, kruta*. Later."

Solomon hung up. Dantalion was losing his mind, poor guy. Maybe it was time to dump him.

He unchained the human and dragged him into the hall. Called maintenance.

"Hybrids," he said to himself. "That's what we'll call them. Cool. *Kruta*."

He went back to the soundstage, daydreaming about sunscreen, and solar energy, and going surfing again.

Life was good, baby. Unless you were alive. And then it *sucked*.

RUSSIA
TEAM SALAMANCA MINUS ANTONIO;
TAAMIR AND NOAH

The food was stowed, the dishes packed away. Jamie and Noah had gone off to smoke. Jenn dozed a bit, then woke up as the two men returned, chatting and laughing about something. Jenn was certain that Noah was at least twenty-five. At least sixty-five years younger than Antonio. Noah had been checking her out too. It flustered her a little, but she liked it. It was nice to be around a guy who didn't have major baggage like Antonio.

Is that why you keep thinking about Antonio? she asked herself. *Wondering what he's doing every five minutes?*

Noah and Jamie sat down. They were a significant distance from their target, far enough to hazard a campfire. Jenn was grateful; it was very cold. The ground was snowy, and everyone's breath mingled and rose like ghosts above the flames.

"Before we get started discussing our mission, I want to tell you about Dantalion," Noah said, in his deep voice with his interesting accent. "He's very dangerous, and very old."

Taamir grinned at the Salamancans. "This will be good. Before he joined the Mossad, Noah was a writer. Pretty famous in Israel."

Jenn was impressed. She'd never met a writer before.

"Oh, that's fascinating." Skye glanced at Jamie, who was examining his Uzi. "Isn't it, *Jamie*?"

Jamie stirred. "Sorry, darlin', what?"

Skye gave the Uzi the same pained look she often flashed at Jamie's cigarettes. "Noah is a famous writer."

"We're sorry. We are listening," Eriko assured Noah.

"Yes," Jenn repeated, and when Noah smiled at her, her cheeks went hot. What was *wrong* with her? They were about to risk their lives, and she was flirting with a teammate.

127

Then again, why not? She and Antonio were a mess. She should move on.

And be alone, she told herself. Now was not the time to get involved with anyone. Not that Noah was just anyone. *I don't even know if he's available.*

Stop, Jenn!

Noah began.

The Russian people say that Dantalion is a demon who escaped from hell. They say that for centuries he lurked in the ice caves of the Ural Mountains, where special herbs grew that could cure many ailments—gout, and headaches, and digestive problems. Knowing this, Dantalion hid in the darkness, luring the villagers to come in with his whispers in the echoes of dripping water and the scurrying of rodents.

Come. I have what you want. What you need. Just be brave and come to me.

Come.

He would lull them with his singsong voice, and then attack them.

When the snow was so bitter that the villagers stayed inside, it is said that Dantalion crept along the sides of their huts at night, murmuring to the young girls to come out and dance with him.

Come. I have what you want. What you need. Just be brave and come to me.

Come.

Mothers told their children, "Go to bed, and say your prayers, or Dantalion will get you!"

Of a midnight, children would leave their beds and crawl out their windows.

Come. I have what you want. What you need. Just be brave and come to me.

Come.

Their priest hired a Hunter named Baradin from St. Petersburg. He strode off toward the mountains, to challenge Dantalion in the caves. He did not return. They found Baradin in the early spring, beneath the melting surface of a frozen pond, his contorted face ice blue, with two great holes in his throat.

If a Hunter could not destroy Dantalion, all hope for the people was lost. The villagers packed up everything and raced down the mountainsides while the sun brightly shone. The aged and infirm were left behind. Dantalion made short work of them. Then, starving, Dantalion howled like a rabid wolf from the mountaintops and raged through the deserted village. He set fire to the huts, the orange flames blazing for seven days and seven nights.

Meanwhile, it was said, the holy brother named Rasputin, known as the Mad Monk, was at an inn in Siberia. Rasputin had been engaged in a drinking contest in the tavern when he learned that the innkeeper's daughter had fallen very ill.

The girl's beautiful mother was hysterical. The pretty girl herself was panting and moaning, and on the verge of death. Not being one to turn his back on a loving lady or her lovely daughter, Rasputin offered his help. The mother gazed at him with forlorn and dewy eyes, and gave her consent.

Rasputin took the maiden's hands in his, forcing her to lie still, and ordered her to look into his eyes: Relax. Calm down. *And then, as if by some miracle, she could breathe. She felt no pain.*

Breathe, no pain.

Live.

Live.

Live.

Her terrified mother crossed herself as the girl sank into a swoon. Kneeling at the bedside, the woman told Rasputin she would give him everything she had if only he could make her child live.

"She will rise," Rasputin promised.

The next morning the girl woke refreshed and relaxed. But while the mother fell to her knees and kissed Rasputin's hands, some of the other townspeople were frightened.

"We had a demon in our village who could whisper to the soul like that," one of Rasputin's drinking partners murmured, holding up a cross. "He could lure a man into his cave, and rip out his throat. He would glide into our village and lure our children outside to meet him. And then he would drink their blood. It made him immortal."

That intrigued Rasputin. He began searching for this immortal blood-drinking creature. He came from superstitious stock, and he had heard of vampires.

To finance his search, he continued his practice of psychic healing. His gift, he learned from a lovely lady whose headaches he cured, was referred to in the scientific journals of the day as mesmerism, and it was a form of mental energy that could be manipulated, and used. But could it make him immortal, like a vampire?

Or was immortality only brought on by the drinking of blood?

In hopes of achieving eternal life, Rasputin began to drink blood. The stories say he drank in secret, from the veins of the willing wives of the Russian aristocrats in St. Petersburg. A peasant in his soul, he hated them all for their wealth and power while the peasants starved, and as he sucked their blood, he swore that he would suck their riches from them as well. They had no idea, of course. So he created a secret society and gave them all very important positions with fantastic titles like Daughter of the Dawn—in return, of course, for "love donations" of gold and jewels.

Still, he did not think that drinking blood had given him immortality. He felt no difference before and after, and as he looked in the mirror, he spotted wrinkles and liver spots—the telltale signs of aging.

He gained a reputation as a psychic, a mystic, a holy man who could heal the sick—even those near death. Alexandra, the czarina of all the Russias, heard of Rasputin, and begged him to heal her son, the heir to the throne, the Grand Duke Alexei. The child had hemophilia, which meant that his blood didn't clot. One scratch and he could bleed to death. The doctors could not help him and spoke only of an early death.

Thinking of the riches and status that he would gain, Rasputin met with the czarina in St. Petersburg. He made her promise to keep the medical doctors away and began his mesmerism program. Sending the boy into swoons gave the little body a chance to recover from each episode. And so the czar and the czarina believed that Rasputin was curing little Alexei, bit by bit, none of them realizing that stress relief can stop the bleeding in hemophiliacs, but not cure it.

Meanwhile Dantalion had wandered the steppes in search of blood, and the stories of the magickal city of St. Petersburg had reached his ears. Electricity! Motorcars! He blew in like an ill wind, himself mesmerized by the beauty of the modern, technologically advanced city.

Surrounded by such glorious wonders, Dantalion was overcome with self-loathing. He had lived like a savage in his ice caves. Wrapped in furs, he had attacked filthy peasants, and mud and cow dung had mingled with their blood when he drank. For how many centuries? He didn't know, couldn't even remember his own beginnings. And while he relished his immortality, he had no idea how he could remain in the glittering city without being detected. He couldn't go out by day. The sun would destroy him. But he was so hungry to live—to join the swirl of humanity.

He must have the sun!

Then he heard about Rasputin, the mesmerist who was curing the Russian grand duke of his fatal blood disease. Such a man must know a lot about blood chemistry. What if Dantalion's blood could be altered, such that he could endure the sunlight?

"I present myself," he said to Rasputin, appearing one night at the door of the monk's sparse flat. Dantalion was splendidly attired in a huge fur coat and hat, and a cane. He wished he could see his reflection, but he knew he was very grand.

"Vampire," Rasputin said delightedly. "Come in, come in."

Be brave and come to me.

Come.

So it began. Each wanted something from the other, and both needed money to achieve their ends. Russian coins — rubles — were the bullets of their day, and the two men were relentless in their pursuit. Money made Rasputin powerful; money gave Dantalion access to scientists and laboratories.

But Russia was in a shambles from fighting disastrous wars for more territory. Thousands of Russian sons were dead, and the survivors were penniless and hungry. The czar and czarina held their balls, wore their furs. The common people hated them and their associates — among them Rasputin.

Rasputin had nearly as many enemies as the czar, especially the husbands of his noble female fans — and they murdered him in 1916. First he was poisoned, then beaten, then shot, then beaten again, and then finally bound and thrown in the half-frozen Neva River.

It is now known that Rasputin was so hard to kill because Dantalion had been experimenting on him. Rasputin was his first attempt at making a new kind of vampire.

The czar, czarina, and all their children were executed by the rebels in 1918. St. Petersburg was no longer safe for unconventional persons such as Dantalion, who returned to the shadows again. He was not seen again until after Solomon made his appearance on Valentine's Day and brought the vampires back into the light.

"And now he's back. And what he does to the people he experiments on . . ."

Noah Geller trailed off, and Jenn roused. She had lost herself in his hypnotic voice as he'd woven his story about their target. "We have to get Svika out of there," Noah concluded.

Jamie pulled out a cigarette and tapped it against his submachine gun. "Well, why the bloody hell not take Dantalion out by force? Just nuke the hell out of him? The government's protecting another big scientist Curser, lad. It's clear as day."

"I have to agree," Holgar said.

Jenn cleared her throat. "That doesn't matter."

Noah looked at her and smiled faintly. Then he inclined his head. Her chest tightened, and her cheeks grew warm. Nice things started happening to her insides.

"There's a lot of dirty dealing in this war," Noah said. "Politicians trying to gain favor from those in power, as Rasputin did. Hoping that if they do what the Cursed Ones want, they'll be spared. Or converted."

He pointed at Jenn and Jamie. "I think both of you are right. Dantalion *is* being protected, but that doesn't matter. We're here on a mission to destroy him."

"Bloody hell." Jamie's voice was thick with disgust.

"Jamie," Jenn reproved, turning in Jamie's direction. Then she followed his line of sight and saw what—or rather, who—had caused his reaction.

"Buenas noches," Antonio said, standing at the perimeter of the camp. The moon tipped his blue-black hair with silver, aging him slightly. Making him seem different, not like the Antonio she knew. If she had ever known him. His dark,

deep-set eyes focused on her, only her, and bone-chilling fear consumed her.

Heather. Something's happened. They killed her.

She leaped to her feet, then stumbled backward. Skye raised a hand toward him in greeting; everyone else stayed where they were. Jenn's heart stopped. Everything stopped. If she didn't ask, if he didn't say anything . . .

She swayed.

"Jenn?" Skye said.

Jenn was mute. Everything in her world depended on Antonio.

"*Ay*, no." Comprehension dawning, Antonio gave his head a quick shake. "She's all right, Jenn." But there was a catch in his voice.

"Then w-what are you doing here?" She was embarrassed by how timid her voice was. She was the leader of this team—*his* leader—but she sounded like a twelve-year-old.

"Who is *he*?" Taamir asked from behind her, his voice dangerous, on alert.

"Antonio's one of us," Eriko said quickly. "Our other teammate. He wasn't able to leave with us . . . so he caught up."

"How did he find us?" Noah demanded, every muscle tensed. He and Taamir were on their feet. Antonio stood quietly and calmly, deflecting any confrontation.

"GPS. I put a tracker on my cell so he could find us." Holgar sounded completely convincing.

"And you came into our camp without telling us that?"

135

Taamir half shouted. A look from Noah, and he lowered his voice. "This is *our* camp. *Our* mission."

Was, Jenn thought. They'd failed. That was why Team Salamanca was there. It was their mission now, and she was in charge of it.

"Excuse me, but I believe our masters have discussed it," Eriko replied, lying through her beautiful white teeth. "Antonio tracking us."

"*Ja*. Father Juan said it was arranged." Holgar's voice was smooth as glass.

Jenn silently blessed both of them for their quick thinking. If their new friends knew that Antonio wasn't supposed to be there and that he was a Cursed One, it surely would be a deadly test to the boundaries of their fragile alliance.

Jamie, for a miracle, was staying silent. Jenn glanced over her shoulder and realized it probably wasn't a miracle. Skye had her hand on Jamie's shoulder. She'd have to thank the witch later for that.

But she could tell by Antonio's posture that something was still wrong.

"We're going to walk the perimeter," she called, voice deeper, firmer. She was their leader.

Antonio fell into step beside her as they pushed their way out of the small clearing and into the forest. Their feet crunched in the snow. Her breath blew out like smoke. His didn't.

As soon as they were out of earshot, Jenn whirled on him. "What are you doing here?"

He looked at her, eyes so dark it was as if they were made of the night sky. "Your sister . . . she had some kind of vision. She said something about 'her' and 'blood' and 'there.' And then she cried out Dantalion's name."

A chill seized Jenn's spine. "'Her'? Me?" She thought a moment. "Aurora?"

Antonio shook his head. "I don't know. But I was worried about you. I couldn't let you do this alone. I tried, but I couldn't." He kept gazing at her, a telling distance between them.

So many emotions jumbled inside her that she had trouble keeping track of them. With him here watching over her, that put Heather, and the others at the university, in more danger. And him, too, maybe.

But she couldn't deny her relief. He was here, with her.

"I know we parted badly," he began. "It was my fault, Jenn, and I'm sorry."

The dam inside her broke, and she realized that despite everything that had happened, she needed to be near him and feel this reassurance. She threw her arms around his neck and buried her head against his chest, breathing in the scent of him.

He lowered his chin against the crown of her head, resting his cheek there. His arms encircled her, strong and gentle. *"Ay, Jenn, te quiero, mi corazón."*

"I love you, too," she whispered. She might still suck at Spanish, but that she knew. "I do love you, Antonio."

He held her for what seemed like forever, stroking her hair.

"Tell me how she is," Jenn said.

Antonio related what had happened, and she paled. "But she was speaking in words?"

"Only during the vision," he admitted. "But that gives us hope."

Wordlessly, she nodded. Then she tucked a lock of his hair behind his ear. Leaned her head against his chest. No warmth, no heartbeat.

"Noah told us about Dantalion," she said. "Creepy guy."

"Noah? Or Dantalion?" he asked, sounding amused.

"Noah's a writer. Or was, before he joined the Mossad."

Antonio chuckled as if at some private joke. She looked up sharply and saw that he was grinning. She couldn't help but grin back.

"What?"

"I was just wondering if you've read any good books lately."

"I don't have time to read."

His grin broadened, and she frowned, puzzled. He bent forward and brushed her lips with his.

"I never thought I would be able to kiss you again," he said. His voice was filled with such longing that it made her tingle. She had thought she would never want him to kiss her again. She hadn't actually had a lot of experience with guys. The war had gotten in the way.

"*Bueno*, we should get back," he said, tracing her mouth with his finger. His fingertip was very cold.

"One more minute won't matter," she said.

"As you say." He kissed her again.

Then it was time to go back. They laced hands and walked back to the others, who were looking at the two of them expectantly. Correction: At *her*.

Jenn took over.

"Okay, we're going to take turns patrolling for two hours each with teams of two. Noah, Taamir, I'm going to pair you up with members of my team so we can start learning to work together." She turned her eyes to her own teammates.

"I'll go with Noah," Skye volunteered.

"I'll patrol with Taamir," Holgar added.

The two Middle Eastern hunters indicated their agreement, and Jenn had to hide a little grin of her own. Maybe she was getting the hang of this leader stuff.

"Thanks," she said. "Okay. Skye, you and Noah take the first patrol."

Skye stood up and brushed herself off. She smiled at Noah. "Shall we?"

He crossed over to her, and the two of them melted into the forest.

Skye was uneasy. She slowly walked the perimeter of their base camp and tried to calm herself. She had agreed to take watch with Noah. Holgar would patrol with Taamir.

She understood the need to get to know their two other comrades better. And she and Holgar had been the obvious choices. Taamir and Noah didn't yet know Antonio was a vampire, and she was pretty sure Jamie would say something obnoxious and start a fight. Still, she missed her partner.

She sighed.

"Okay?" Noah asked, his voice barely a whisper.

She nodded.

"You're very young," he noted.

Skye hunched her shoulders. She and Eriko were both sixteen, but Skye was the youngest. She had run away to the university when she was fourteen. Everyone had thought it was because she wanted to fight Cursed Ones. She did, but she had far darker reasons. *Estefan, where are you?* she wondered.

In her mind she compared Estefan to Jamie. Why was it she was attracted to bad boys? Of course, Estefan and Jamie only shared a dark edge and love of violence in common. Estefan was a witch who had sided with the Cursed Ones. Jamie was a human hunter who'd sworn to destroy the vampires.

"Nobody's young anymore," she muttered.

Noah nodded, seeming to take that as truth.

She was grateful that Antonio had shown up, though she didn't know why he was here. Clearly, there had been a change of plan, and it had taken Jenn by surprise as well.

As she walked, she wove four tiny spells. There was the one to give them both enhanced vision. There was another to keep their path free from roots and snares. A third enhanced hearing. A fourth made their footsteps silent. There were others she would have liked to perform, to mask their smell or to help them locate danger, but she was already tired from all the spell casting she'd done to get them through the airports earlier, and performing the four was taking everything she had.

"What are you doing?" Noah asked at last.

Skye hesitated for a moment. In Witchery it wasn't common to expose yourself to outsiders, but nothing about her journey since leaving home had been common. "I'm doing magicks to help us."

He was silent for a moment. "Magicks."

"I'm a witch. A White Witch," she added quickly. "A good witch."

"Your master told mine about you," Noah said.

So Father Juan had outed her. That worried her a little, but she also realized it was a good strategy. Back in New Orleans, Marc Dupree and his freedom fighters had been very angry that they hadn't been told. She doubted Father Juan had informed them about Antonio, though. Witches were not the enemy. Cursed Ones were.

"Is that why I can see and hear better than I should?" Noah asked.

"Yes."

"Would you please stop?"

Her heart sank. "You don't approve of witchcraft."

Noah half smiled. "I . . . approve of anything that will help defeat the Cursed Ones. But I'm attuned to my own senses, and this is, hmm, difficult to adjust to. I think it will hurt and not help."

She winced. "Sorry," she muttered as she released them both from the two spells. Unfortunately, she couldn't just release him, she had to release herself as well, and she stumbled into a tree with a grunt.

He reached out a hand. "You okay?"

She shook her head to clear it and then tried to recast the spell, but just for herself. She was too tired, though. She needed to rest.

"I'm—"

She stopped. Something was wrong. She turned her head, straining to listen. There was nothing.

Nothing.

And yet . . .

"Something's here," she whispered.

Noah half turned as a figure lunged at him from the darkness, grabbing him and tossing him into the air.

Terror galvanized Skye, and the adrenaline flowed through her body, giving her the energy to weave a spell to lessen the impact as Noah hurtled to the ground.

The creature turned toward her, and she shrank back. It was hideous. Its eyes were overly large in its face, its nose tiny and pinched, and its mouth bristled with longer fangs and more teeth than she had seen on a Cursed One. It looked more like the mouth of a wolf.

A werewolf! she thought. But the body was not wolflike; it was more humanoid, and dressed in black pants and a padded black jacket. It wore boots. It was nothing like anything she had ever seen.

The creature lumbered toward her, eyes glowing red. Skye sidestepped out of its path, surprised that her speed was on par with the beast's. It turned, slow as a human, and swung at her with hands tipped with curved claws.

Noah sprang up behind the creature and tried to drive a stake into it. She heard the sound of cracking wood, and with a shout Noah stepped back.

"The stake won't penetrate!" he yelled to her.

Her hands flew to her belt, and Skye whipped out a bottle of holy water and a stake. She uncapped the bottle, darted forward, and splashed the holy water in the creature's eyes. It stopped with a bellow and began clawing at its own eyes with its razor-sharp claws. It carved chunks of its flesh from its face until blood was flowing freely.

Skye took a precious extra second as she angled the stake upward, lunged, and then shoved. The wood stopped less than a quarter of an inch into the creature. The muscles were too strong, too powerful, to punch through.

She grabbed a cross next and slammed it against the creature's skin. It began to smoke and burn. And before

143

she could stop herself, she whispered, *"Incendio."*

The searing turned into full-fledged flames. The creature dropped to the snow, rolled, and extinguished them with a hiss and sizzle. Skye took a step back, blinking, horrified at what she had just done. Magick was only to be used for defense, never to hurt or attack.

Using only his free hand, Noah unsheathed a short sword from under the back of his coat and swung the blade downward. It cut halfway through the creature's neck and then lodged between the upper vertebrae of its spine. Grunting, he leaned, putting his full weight on it as the creature beneath him howled and writhed. One of the creature's claws slashed across Noah's knee, felling him instantly.

Noah sprawled on the ground near the creature's head, but he held desperately on to the sword, still trying to sever the neck.

"Help me!" he yelled.

Galvanized, Skye sprang forward, grabbing the hilt of the sword, taking care to avoid the clacking teeth and swinging claws, and she rammed downward for all she was worth, sobbing with the effort.

At first the blade didn't move. And then it did. Slowly, slowly, and then suddenly it sliced all the way through, cutting off the creature's head. Skye fell into the snow, panting, next to Noah.

While the adrenaline was still running through her

body, she reached out and touched Noah's leg, sending healing energy through it. Next she worked magicks on his arm. Now that he knew she was a White Witch, she could heal him without fear of discovery.

He groaned appreciatively. "Now, that I don't mind so much."

"What is this thing?" she asked, wincing as she stared at the decapitated head. The red eyes were smoking in the horrible, ruined face.

"It must be one of Dantalion's experiments," Noah said slowly as he wadded up his sling and crammed it into a pocket in his jacket. His voice caught. "If it's Svika . . ."

Laboring from exertion and fear, Skye fixated on the body as parts of it slowly turned to ash. It happened so slowly that it began to unnerve her. After two or three minutes all that was left was the head, which was decaying at a much slower rate. The lifeless eyes stared up at her. Then, as monstrous bits on the face began to crumble, the fact that this head looked very human could not be denied.

Cold chills turned to nausea, and she forced herself to turn away. She had hurt something that had been a person.

"Is it?" she asked him hoarsely. She cleared her throat. "Was it?"

"I — I don't know," Noah murmured. "But I wouldn't be surprised if Dantalion set him free to mock us."

Down among the dead men, as the poem went. His mind racing, Dantalion surveyed his domain of operating rooms, caches of surgical equipment, cages, cells. The smell was hideous. The screaming, annoying.

Hunters he had not yet used were chained to the walls, and heads dipped forward, unconscious. Vampires in cages raged at him as he swept through the basement of his headquarters, the Imperial Hunting Palace of the last czar of Russia. He was seething with anger and forcing the ragged edges of fear at bay. His chief scientist, Vladimir Khrushchev, walked beside him, unaware of the storm inside his superior.

"Can we go out yet?" Khrushchev asked. His fangs were extended, and his eyes glowed scarlet. He looked a bit thinner than usual. He gestured to the six vampires in white coats—his team of scientists. "We need to hunt."

"The last two hunters from the Middle East are still out there," Dantalion said, trying to sound calm and in control.

"Only two?" Khrushchev asked pointedly.

Dantalion didn't reply. He wasn't sure there were only two. It was impossible that two men could inflict this much damage on their hybrids. But he wasn't about to admit that.

"Perhaps it's time to send out more *matroyshkas*?" Khrushchev ventured.

Matroyshkas was their word for the hybrids they had created together, using captured hunters who'd dared to attack him; werewolves they had trapped from various packs they had identified; and vampires, some of whom had volunteered.

Dantalion and Khrushchev had dubbed the hybrids *matroyshkas* after the famous Russian folk-art nesting dolls that tourists liked to buy. Upon seizing control of the palace-cum-lab that he and Khrushchev now stood in, Dantalion had set out his souvenirs from his glory days with Rasputin in czarist Russia. One of these had been a set of *matroyshkas* of the czar, czarina, Alexei, and Rasputin. An in-joke of a sort, it had captured the attention of Khrushchev. Playing with the nesting dolls, Khrushchev had envisioned how to make the hybrids: putting the genes of one creature into the genes of another, then into the genes of a third—vampire, werewolf, and human, sometimes two vampires and a werewolf, or some other combination.

It was fascinating work. There were a lot of failures, some quite repulsive, but they were making splendid progress. Then, unfortunately, Solomon had heard about it and offered to pay for it in return for some hybrids of his own, and the information on how to make more. Dantalion had not wanted a partner, especially not the most powerful vampire known to the world. *Dantalion* wanted to be the most powerful vampire known to the world, and while he had some tricks up his sleeve to accomplish that, he didn't want to share the secret to making hybrids with a rival. He didn't even know how Solomon had found out about his plans. But Solomon had, and now Dantalion was stuck with him. On the plus side, Solomon had an unending supply of money, and Dantalion held back some of the crucial details of *matroyshka* creation, thereby retaining control.

But something was up. Something was wrong. He had sent out a dozen hybrids, and then a dozen more, and none of them had returned with their quarry—just two hunters. It didn't add up. He suspected reinforcements had arrived, but how many? Was it time to move to plan B?

"Send out more," he said to Khrushchev.

RUSSIA
TEAM SALAMANCA, TAAMIR, AND NOAH

Antonio realized he should have talked over his next order of business with Jenn first, while they'd been alone, but his mind had been on other things. That was bad. She was his leader, and he shouldn't surprise her like this. And he should have brought it up before Skye and Noah went on watch together. He was out of sorts. He didn't want Jenn to be here.

"There's something we need to discuss," he said.

"*Now* what?" Jamie said, groaning.

Antonio sat beside Jenn on a log, his boot heels crunching in the snow. "Do you remember those men with the black Jerusalem crosses? The ones who sent us home in the jet from New Orleans?"

"The ones who grabbed the scientist, the one who was working on the virus?" Eriko asked.

"Sherman," Jamie put in. "Yeah, those guys blasted in after we did all the heavy lifting."

"What scientist? What virus?" Taamir asked.

"It was a kind of anemia," Jamie said. "Sherman wanted to infect the Cursers with it, but they turned him first."

"Excuse me, Jamie-*kun*. It was leukemia," Eriko corrected.

"Well, it was germ warfare, at any rate," Jamie said. "Like these Russian lads were doin' before Dantalion took over."

"*Vale*, the same," Antonio said. "Well, I saw three more of them today."

The team stirred. Taamir watched them, baffled.

"Where?" Holgar asked.

"One of them was in the airport. I saw two more in a car, so I followed them. They're camping about a dozen miles from here."

Jamie swore.

Taamir leaned in. "Sorry, but who? *What?* A dozen miles?"

"That's about nineteen kilometers," Jamie informed him.

"You're not amusing," Taamir snapped.

Jenn took a deep breath. "Men wearing Jerusalem crosses were at my grandfather's funeral, too. At least one of them worked for the government."

"The Spanish government?" Taamir asked, clearly not following.

Jenn shook her head. "American."

"She's a Yank," Jamie said, stuffing his hands in the pockets of his cold-weather jacket.

"I think they might be part of a covert organization," Antonio declared. "Beyond the official American government."

"*You* show up, and now they're here?" Taamir said angrily. "And they were after *you*?" He glared at Jenn.

"I think they're *good* covert," Jenn said quickly. "One of them—I think it was one of them—said something to me at the funeral about filling my grandfather's shoes. His name was Greg. He wasn't hostile."

I should have asked Gramma about him, she thought. She wished she knew how to contact her. Jenn hadn't been able to reply to her grandmother's one text message: *Montana.* The phone her grandmother had used must have been a throwaway; Jenn's *Thank you* had bounced. The message had come in after they had parted, when her grandmother had put Jenn on a plane so she could go rescue Heather. Then Gramma had picked up Jenn's mom, and the two had escaped from San Francisco.

"Dantalion," Eriko said. "They must be here for him too."

"Yeah, but to kill him or kidnap him? Or maybe they want him to work on the virus. They've obviously got a thing for Curser scientists," Jamie said.

Jenn shook her head. "Dantalion's on the wrong side to help people wearing crosses."

"What should we do about them?" Eriko asked.

Antonio looked at Jenn. She was the leader, and it needed to be her decision, but something told him that these men were very, very dangerous. Each time the two groups had crossed paths, the men had carried themselves like predators.

And that just might be a good thing.

"We should try to make contact," Jenn said. "Reach out."

"Lovely, we'll invite them for tea," Jamie snorted.

"No way," Taamir said angrily. "We're on a mission, and we don't know these guys. They could even be working for Dantalion."

"I don't think so," Holgar said.

"I agree with Jenn," Eriko added, bobbing her head, looking uncomfortable as confrontation reared its head.

"Jenn's the leader; it's Jenn's call," Holgar said briskly.

"Dantalion wiped out your team," Jenn reminded Taamir. "If these guys can help us, we should get together with them." She flushed. "So to speak."

"No. It's a risk we shouldn't take." Taamir folded his arms across his chest. His cheeks were red. Antonio wasn't sure if it was from the cold or because he didn't like being reminded of his team's failure.

"So, how do you want us to go about it, *Jenn*?" Holgar asked pointedly, turning away from Taamir. "Antonio could take you back there. We've got a van, and Antonio, you must have a car."

"I do," Antonio confirmed. "Listen, Father Juan's been contacted by a number of masters. They want to put together more teams like ours. You'd be surprised at some of the places where Hunters have been fighting Cursed Ones."

"So surprise us," Jamie said.

Antonio wasn't about to discuss it any further in front of a stranger. Besides, they were getting off the subject. "Back to the black-cross agents," Antonio said.

"We go," Jenn said. "Now."

"Hey," Taamir protested. "Noah and I have a say in this too. And I don't think—"

There was a sudden rustling in the underbrush.

Antonio glanced up as Skye and Noah entered camp. Noah tossed something onto the ground, which rolled slightly before coming to a stop in front of them all. It was a human head, only slightly decayed, and bristling with teeth.

Eriko clicked on a flashlight, aimed the beam at the head. "What is that?" she asked.

"Something we killed ten minutes ago," Skye said.

"Bloody hell," Jamie spat, as Holgar picked it up to examine it.

"How come there's a head?" Jenn asked, her voice filled with quiet horror.

"One of Dantalion's experiments?" Antonio guessed. Holgar tossed it to him, but he let it drop in the snow, not wanting to touch it. There was something so unnatural about it that it unnerved even him. He forced himself to look down at the twisted features. A huge jawbone, lots of teeth but with the canines missing. Possibly those missing teeth had been vampire fangs. Human skin, mostly, although ash was creeping across the cheeks and forehead.

"Yes," Skye said. "It attacked us. The body disintegrated, until only the head was left."

"It's decaying too," Eriko noted as she bent over to take a closer look.

"Yes, but very slowly," Skye repeated.

"What does this mean?" Taamir asked.

"It means we can't afford to give Dantalion any more time to run his experiments," Jenn said, face pale but voice resolute. "We have to move against him now. Tonight."

A surge of pride swept through Antonio. Jenn was taking command. And suddenly Antonio smelled something. The odor was a bit off, but there was no mistaking it: the death scent of Cursed Ones. He lurched to his feet at the same time Holgar did. Holgar growled, and Taamir and Noah jerked their heads in Holgar's direction.

"What?" Jamie asked sharply.

"We don't have to move against him," Antonio snarled. "He's moving against us."

CHAPTER SEVEN

Salamanca Hunter's Manual: Casualties

On occasion, a friend or a person who has offered you aid will be put in harm's way. Your impulse will be to save him, but you must always choose the destruction of a Cursed One over saving the life of even the kindest and most self-sacrificing person. When a good person dies, he will surely join his Father in Heaven. But a Cursed One left unchecked is a grievous sin, one that falls upon you. Thus, you must always kill a vampire as soon as you encounter him, even if it costs the lives of innocents.

(translated from the Spanish)

Holgar growled as everyone jumped up and fanned out in anticipation of an attack. Then, to his horror, the growl deepened in his throat, changing into a lusty, violence-loving werewolf howl.

"For helvede!" he muttered—which meant "damn it" in Danish—prickling with alarm as Taamir and Noah stared at him. They separated from the Salamancan hunters in a flash, grabbing and aiming their submachine guns at him. Holgar's heart raced. He hadn't meant to growl. It had just burst out of him.

"What the hell?" Noah whispered. "What was *that*?"

"What is he?" Taamir said under his breath.

"He's okay," Jenn whispered back as she scanned the darkness. "He just howls!"

"That was *not* human!" Noah retorted.

"I'm okay!" Holgar held up a hand and waved it, trying to show that he was very human. He glanced at Antonio, Skye, Eriko, and Jamie, who had positioned themselves on the defensive, their attention divided between whatever was approaching and their possibly former allies. He hastily added in Danish, "I'm a werewolf, but I'm a *good* werewolf." But of course two guys from the Middle East wouldn't understand Danish, and he was so freaked out he had forgotten how to say it in

English. And although his Russian was also excellent, it, too, had abandoned him.

He couldn't think. His brain was sloshing with adrenaline. Noah had an Uzi, and Taamir had a Kalashnikov, a Russian weapon. *Ja,* maybe they spoke Russian. All Holgar had to do was remember how to say "Please don't shoot me" in Russian in the next two seconds, and he would live. It was all so absurd that Holgar started laughing. The real bad guys were coming, and he needed to stop howling, he had to stop, or those guys were going to blow off his head, but that was why it was so *funny* in an intensely horrible way.

"Nej," he guffawed, helplessly waving his hands. His normal human hands—thank God it wasn't the full moon—but it was bad that Dantalion had managed to use werewolf bits that could change. That meant fully mature wolves. *For helvede,* he had to focus on his dilemma and keep it together. But he kept laughing.

And then, disastrously, he howled again. This one louder still.

It was answered by whatever was coming at them from the forest, a noise that grated like metal on metal or metal on bone, on its way.

"He's signaling them!" Taamir whispered.

"Nej, nej!" Holgar said, laughing, horrified and terribly amused all at the same time.

"Are you *high*?" Skye flung at Holgar. "Shut up!"

"You shut him up, witchy!" Jamie told her.

Skye flushed and moved her hands.

Taamir spread his legs wide to brace against the recoil of his gun while he got ready to let 'er rip. Holgar freaked. God, those Russian guns worked only half the time; Taamir was just as likely to blow himself up on the spot as hit Holgar. Holgar *had* to get hold of himself.

The inhuman cries from the forest were louder.

Closer.

And then Skye's spell took effect, and Holgar went blessedly silent.

"Don't shoot him!" Jenn bellowed.

"Incoming!" Jamie yelled.

All of Holgar's worries about Noah and Taamir evaporated as a row of raging, ugly *things* shot through the trees too fast for Holgar to track. He was thrown backward into the snow. His breath knocked out of him, his heart pounding, he grunted for air as blurred red eyes and enormous teeth flashed like images caught in strobe lights. *Is its face melting? Wait, is it a werewolf?*

In an instant he'd lost his giddy hysteria. A sharp pain from something attacking him needled his chest. Another. He roared, and his training kicked in. *Sight the foe's next move. If you can't see the foe, strike where his blow is most likely to land.*

Still on his back, Holgar made a fist and swung with his right. Then he swung with his left. He hit something, but just as quickly it wasn't there. Unseen fangs or claws slashed his cheek. He bent his knees and rocked back, jamming them against a blurring shape straddling his chest. Shouting erupted all around him; then the shape was gone.

Holgar rolled onto his side and pushed himself up. In the flickering moonlight he saw Eriko hoisting a misshapen hulk above her head.

With a grunt she tossed it into their campfire. It began to scream and thrash. Taamir shot it with his Kalashnikov, the *rat-tat-tat-tat* bloating the battlefield with noise.

On the other side of the fire something with abnormally long, hair-covered arms—no they were batlike wings, maybe?—had Jenn by the hair. Holgar threw himself at the monster, grabbing one of the winglike appendages and wincing as his hands began to burn.

Holgar hissed, unable to yell. Defensive poison. He held on, tugging at it to loosen its grip on Jenn, as Jenn panted in agony. He bent his knees, allowing his full weight to hang from the wing. It didn't budge.

Then Jenn tucked in her head and executed a forward roll, dragging the monster with her. Holgar let go so as not to impede the momentum, then grabbed the creature's legs—beefy things, covered in long, matted hair, with people toes—as Jenn scrambled from beneath it. It flailed on its back like a furious drowning shark as Holgar anchored it by the legs. Jenn grabbed its wrists and looked up at Skye, shouting, "Skye, stake it!"

Holgar held the creature just above the knees, fighting

to keep it supine as Jenn struggled with its wings. Holgar smelled burning flesh. Jenn's, and his. From the poison.

Skye leaned over the monster and froze.

"Skye!" Jenn yelled at her in desperation.

Holgar spared a glance at his fighting partner. With her stake in both hands Skye dropped to her knees, driving the wooden spike into the creature's chest.

It gasped. Vampires didn't gasp. They didn't need to breathe. Wheezing, it fought to free itself.

"Again, Skye!" Jenn ordered her.

C'mon, min lille heks, Holgar mentally urged as he clung to the creature, holding it fast.

"Mama," it said in a guttural slur.

"Oh, God," Skye said, jerking away. "I can't! It's a human!"

"Shit!" Jenn cried. She grabbed the stake out of the monster's chest. Her hands were actually smoking from the monster's poisonous touch. Awkwardly she tried to hold the stake high enough to use her momentum to ram it home. Holgar let go of one of the legs and gripped his hand around hers. Then he slammed the spike down with all his might into the creature's chest.

It sagged. Jenn scrambled off, spreading her fingers in pain. Skye, seeing that Jenn was hurt, began saying her spells. Holgar was hurt too, but he could manage. He pushed himself to his feet and ran to assist Antonio, who was brandishing a cross at one of the other invaders. It had a vampire face, only . . . wrong, with a flat forehead, batlike ears, and a wolf snout. It was snarling at him, scarlet eyes glowing, fangs extended—just like Antonio's. *For helvede*. Antonio hissed back at the creature like a Curser and not the team's holy man.

Kablamblamblamblamblamblam. Noah was laying out a thunderstorm of ammo as if he'd given up trying to decide who was friend and who was foe. Holgar dodged the barrage.

Antonio advanced on the monster, which was a hideous mishmash with werewolf haunches and legs and human arms. It was so focused on Antonio's cross that it didn't notice Holgar advancing on it.

Suddenly the incessant chatter of submachine gunfire went silent. Holgar hoped that was not bad news—as in Noah might be dead—but kept his focus. He didn't need to be a hero, just backup, as Antonio kept the creature at bay. Pulling a cross from a pocket in his trousers, Holgar held it out, preparing to spring into action if the thing decided to make a run for it. It held its arms out and shuffled back and forth slightly, like an animal nervously pacing inside a cage. Or a bull, facing down a matador.

Holgar looked beyond the two, wondering if they had the time to spar with this thing, or if they should just rush it from both sides. Eriko and Jamie were taking turns staking a huge monstrosity that they'd flung against a tree trunk, so they didn't seem to be in any imminent danger. Skye was kneeling over Jenn, her hands on Jenn's head, doing healing magicks, he supposed.

Their Middle Eastern friends were nowhere to be seen.

Antonio remained still, prepared to spring, and it occurred to Holgar that with Antonio's Spanish appearance beneath his vampiric features, and his taut bearing, he did look like a matador—a vampire matador, just like the Cursed Ones in Pamplona. Holgar fought down a chuckle of ironic appreciation. They had serious business here, life and death. He was useless if all he did was act like a court jester.

The creature jerked and half glanced over its shoulder, spotting Holgar.

"Got your back," Holgar said to Antonio in Spanish. He could talk again! "But Taamir and Noah have run off."

"*Cobardes,*" Antonio spat. Then in English, "Cowards."

"English?" the monster ground out. Holgar blinked and stood his ground.

"Yes," Antonio told it.

"Kill me," the thing said, its knees buckling. It flung wide its arms. "Is good, kill."

Antonio remained as he was. "How many of you? How many vampires with Dantalion?"

"Dantalion! *Nyet, nyet!*" it cried, shielding its face as it staggered backward.

"How many of you are there?" Holgar asked in Russian. Thank God he'd studied it in school.

The monster glanced at Holgar. It snarled and lunged. Holgar stuck out his cross, and it recoiled with a wail.

"You're going to die. Tell me what I want to know, and I'll kill you quickly," Holgar continued in Russian.

"But Dantalion will know that I betrayed him," the thing protested. Its face was filled with longing and despair. "I cannot go to heaven. I accept that. But Dantalion will drag me down to hell. He swore that to any traitors. Anyone who *tells*."

Holgar scoffed. "He can't drag you anywhere. He's a vampire, not the Devil."

The creature's red eyes grew huge. "But he *is*. He is the Great Duke of Hell, with thirty-six legions of demons under his command."

"Nej," Holgar retorted in Danish. "And anyway, hell is a myth."

"What is going on?" Antonio demanded. "What is it saying?"

"Dantalion is a duke of hell," Holgar snickered, then thought a moment. Antonio was a very devout Catholic. Could he possibly believe such a thing himself? "Dantalion told them that if they talk to us, he'll damn them."

"There is a duke of hell by that name, in an ancient grimoire," Antonio said. "I came across that name while researching spells for Skye."

"Then why didn't you say anything?" Holgar burst out, indignant.

"I spoke of my concerns to Father Juan," Antonio informed him, rather haughtily. As if he thought Holgar's question was out of line. "We felt he was simply a vampire trading on the name."

"Well, you could have *mentioned* it to the rest of us," Holgar snapped.

The Russian burst into tears, as if their arguing had sent him over the edge. Weirdly, Holgar found it less strange to hear the malformed nightmare crying than to listen to his own spontaneous howling.

"I don't want to go to hell," the creature wept. "I am boy, Russian boy. *Ya russkiy. Ya russkiy pravoslavniy.*"

"He's Russian Orthodox," Holgar said, "and he's scared shitless."

The extremely former Russian boy wailed. He stretched his hands toward Antonio's cross, then recoiled. "I want to kiss crucifix! Give me back soul, oh, please!"

The hellish glow left Antonio's eyes, and his fangs retracted. He looked much more like a man with a soul than that poor monster ever would again.

Antonio said, "Interrogate him. We need information. Fast."

"He won't tell me. Dantalion said that anyone who betrays him will go to hell."

The monster nodded eagerly. "Hell. I no be Judas."

Antonio said nothing. Holgar felt his mouth twitch. It really was too crazy, wasn't it?

"Shall I tell him that we can make a hell of living for him?" Holgar said. That didn't sound quite right. He started over in Spanish. *"Podemos hacer—"*

But no one was listening. The creature stared hard at Antonio. *"Vuy ponimayete. Vuy tozhe vampir,"* it—he—said.

"He says, 'You understand,'" Holgar translated. "'You're a vampire too.'"

"Tell him that I am a priest," Antonio said in Spanish, "and I will hear his confession. After he's finished, I will absolve him." He pointed to the cross that he held in his hand. "Tell him that I will say Mass for his soul, and I will ask the Blessed Mother to intercede for him."

"Pretty tricky, Antonio," Holgar said, meaning it as a compliment. But Antonio's face clouded over.

"I *will* ask the Blessed Mother to intercede for him," the Spaniard said frostily.

Oh, these Catholics. Nitpickers and madmen.

Nevertheless Holgar quickly relayed everything Antonio had said to the vampire thing. Holgar pointed to Antonio with his free hand. "Look, he's a vampire and he's holding a cross. He is on God's good side."

The vampire let out another sob. He was trembling, afraid.

"We have nothing to eat," he said, which was not what Holgar had been expecting. "Dantalion withholds our . . . rations. Starves us until he sets us loose."

Like hunting hounds, in the Viking days. "What are your rations?" Holgar asked him.

The creature shook his head. "Just kill me, *tovarich*. My friend, release me."

"What do you eat?" Holgar repeated more forcefully, trying to get any information out of him. The Cursed One didn't answer.

"Can you walk in daylight?" Holgar asked him.

"Dantalion says we can."

One way to find out. Holgar looked at Antonio. "I asked him if he can walk in the sunlight. We can keep him here until morning," he said in English. So much English and Russian. *Why* hadn't he remembered all this crap when he'd started howling?

Antonio's expression wavered. Holgar figured he was worried about the sunshine himself.

"Antonio, it won't be a problem," he assured him. "For you, I mean. We can—"

"Bloody hell, what are you two doing?" Jamie bellowed, as he and Eriko screeched to a halt beside Antonio. "Anyone happen to notice we had to stake that guy about three dozen times? Now we've got to catch up with our boys from the sand dunes, and I've no doubt Dandylion has more foot soldiers on their way."

Holgar frowned. "What do you mean, 'catch up'?"

"Noah and Taamir saw their friend," Eriko informed them. "Svika. He was changed, but he didn't attack them. He told them he escaped. They're going to try to follow him into the palace."

166

Holgar and Antonio traded looks of disbelief. The creature slid his gaze from one to the other, clearly not understanding, but aware of the change in the air.

"So we need to go," Jamie said. He blinked and took in the scene. It began to snow, and he hazarded a glance upward. Then he yanked a stake out of the quiver at his waist, walked forward, and slammed it into the chest of the monster. He drove it in hard, and the creature gasped, grabbing at Jamie's hand. Its legs gave way. Jamie swept its feet out from under it, and it went down onto its knees.

"Bloody hell. Someone finish him. We're asking for it, staying here." Jamie reached in his quiver for another stake and tossed it to Antonio. "Eri, ducks, c'mon."

Jamie trotted over to their stash of submachine guns and threw one to Eriko. Moving in tandem, they began to thread their way through the trees, into the darkness. Antonio studied the stake in his hand.

The creature was panting, his head bobbing toward his chest. His hands hung at his side. He was mumbling, whispering.

"He's saying his prayers," Holgar told Antonio.

"Go with them," Antonio said to Holgar. "I'll catch up."

Holgar huffed, scowling in disbelief. "Antonio, we don't have time for this. Jamie is right. We have to get out of here."

Ignoring him, Antonio dropped the stake to the ground. He walked forward, shifting the cross to his left hand

and placing his right hand on the Russian monster's bobbing head. Antonio began to mumble along, the monster in Russian, the vampire in Latin, and Holgar threw up his hands in frustration.

Holgar trotted away, spotting Skye and Jenn at the perimeter of the camp. Jenn's hands were outstretched, and Skye was moving her hands over them. Still in need of healing, then. Holgar grabbed three submachine guns and carried them over to Skye and Jenn.

"Time to leave?" Holgar asked, essentially requesting her permission.

"Yes," Jenn said, taking an Uzi from him and looping it over her head. "What's Antonio doing?"

"Sending the Russian boy to heaven," Holgar replied. "He'll catch up."

"Maybe I should stay with him," Skye offered, her voice strangled as she watched Antonio with the suffering monster.

"Fighting partner," Holgar reminded her gently.

"Holgar's right. We need you with us. I wish we had more people." Jenn lowered her hand to her side and checked her quiver of stakes. Then she broke into a trot. Holgar and Skye followed behind.

"You know this is probably a trap," Holgar called after her.

"Life's a trap," Jenn replied, and put on a burst of speed.

"Well, we're cheerful tonight," he said, smiling wryly.

*   *   *

Skye wove behind Holgar through the dark forest, sickened and horrified. That monster had been more human than anything else they'd fought. And she had inflicted terrible pain on it.

An it harm none, do what thou wilt.

She had harmed it grievously. And in doing so she had betrayed everything that she, as a White Witch, stood for. Every vow she had made she had broken. First she had confided in Jenn about the Circuit, never dreaming that Jenn would assume the leadership position of the team. Back in New Orleans, Jenn had told her to reveal the existence of the Circuit to Father Juan, and Skye hadn't.

These hybrids are people. She tried to tell herself that Antonio had stayed behind to minister to that wretched boy physically as well as spiritually, but she really didn't think that that was true. If it were, he would have asked for her help. All her traditional magick revolved around blessing and healing—it was what her parents had taught her, what she had grown up with in their coven. No other White Witch had so publicly joined in the struggle against the Cursed Ones by training to become a hunter.

And even there her motives were not pure. She had run away to Spain to join the academy in hopes of learning how to protect herself against Estefan and whatever he had become. She kept hearing him in her head, and still she had told no one.

I'm doing this wrong. It's all wrong!

To their right, a tall, craggy mountain overlooked the hill they were ascending. It was a perfect place for an ambush. Ahead of her, Holgar disappeared into the trees. Skye lagged behind, tired from healing Jenn's horrible burns. She had also attempted to give Jenn a magickal boost of energy— she'd been trying to duplicate the effects of Father Juan's elixir, or at least come close to it—and she herself was doubly exhausted from the effort. Her mind raced. Holgar had touched that creature as well. He must be in pain. They needed her to patch them up, not—not to hurt that poor *thing*.

If they infiltrated the lab, what kind of tortured monsters would they find?

A cold wind slapped her cheeks, forcing her to concentrate. They were in the middle of a mission.

"Skye?" Holgar called softly as he bounded through a copse of oaks. She nearly jumped out of her skin as she reflexively grabbed a stake from the quiver at her waist.

"You're so far behind," he said. He was a tall, powerful shadow in the dark wood. "We have a long way to go. Are you all right?"

Mute, she nodded. Before she realized what he was doing, he took her submachine gun from her and put it around his neck, then gathered her up and slung her piggyback, threading his arms around her legs. She wanted to protest and tell him to put her down, but he was right to do it. She couldn't keep up.

Holgar loped along, his gait more wolflike than human, dodging tree limbs and sailing over roots. The guns around his neck clanked. The snow fell more heavily, and she tucked in her chin against his shoulder. Her white balaclava was bunched around her neck, but she didn't want to let go to pull it up.

As they broke through a stand of trees, moonlight shone on a tiny, glittering object far below them in a valley. It was their target, Dantalion's lab, housed inside a symbol of imperial Russia. Grand and mighty, it had been favored by Nicholas Romanov, the last czar, who had used it for his hunting retreat before he and his family were executed in 1918. First shot, and then their bodies burned.

What is in there now?

Noah and Taamir had camped quite a distance away. Holgar grunted and hunkered down, and Skye slid off his back. He took her hand and stealthily crept to the right. Past bare branches iced with snow, they darted down into a small dip where the rest of the team had assembled. Jamie had a submachine gun aimed at Noah's head, and he and Taamir had their hands raised in the air. As Skye drew closer, she saw that the two men were huddled around a stranger. A man. Or maybe . . . not a man. His skin was bone white, and his dark eyes looked like black holes. He didn't appear to be a vampire, and he wasn't monstrous, like the other creatures they'd encountered. But he didn't look "right."

"This is Svika," Jenn told Skye.

"Goddess be praised," Skye said sincerely.

"Maybe. Maybe not," Jamie retorted. "Something's happened to him."

"It's horrible," Svika said, in a thick accent that Skye couldn't place. "Dantalion . . . he's experimenting on humans, vampires, werewolves." He looked at Taamir and Noah. "Yes, there's such a thing as werewolves."

Jamie snorted.

"There's a tunnel," Svika went on. "About five kilometers from here. It's how I got out. No one saw me."

"So he *says*," Jamie bit off.

"We can get to Dantalion. I swear it." Svika locked gazes with Jenn. "There are more of them searching for Noah and Taamir. But he doesn't know about you. About your team. He'll only send reinforcements when he realizes there are more hunters. Now is our chance to strike."

Jamie looked at Jenn. "I say we kill him."

"How far back is Antonio?" Jenn asked, looking back the way they came.

"Who gives a damn?" Jamie made a show of wagging the submachine gun at Svika. "This is a load. How convenient that the one tosser these two want 'escapes.' No one *missed* him back there in the madhouse?"

"I think we should leave," Eriko said. "We have Svika. We can drive to the men with the black crosses and join forces."

"In the middle of the night," Jamie said. "With vampires on the loose."

Eriko looked at Jenn and tipped her chin. "But of course it's *your* decision."

"Skye, can you scry anything?" Jenn asked. "Do you have any intuition you can share?"

"Intuition?" Jamie echoed, sputtering. "Oh, this is brilliant! Yes, Skye, why don't you turn around in a circle three times and consult with the feckin' Oracle of Delphi?"

"Leave off," Skye snapped at him, cut to the quick. Jamie knew she had real powers. "I *can*, Jenn."

"Whatever you are going to do, hurry," Svika urged her. "If I *am* missed—"

"Double hurry." Holgar looked at Taamir and Noah, who were both clearly very uncomfortable around him. "Okay, all right, but I'm a *good* werewolf," he said in English.

They stared at him. After a beat Noah said, *"What?"*

Her heart pounding, Skye closed her eyes and searched for calm. She was trembling. Danger swirled around them. It was palpable. She thought of refuge and prayed to her Lady Goddess: *Conservate me, conservate me, conservate me. Protect me.*

She hadn't done this sort of thing very many times. What she hoped to see were symbols, messages from that part of her being that was attuned to the larger magickal fabric of the world. Something such as a black well, to represent the tunnel Svika wanted to take them into, or a snowstorm, representing the need to abandon the mission, retrench, and try something different. Or the black Jerusalem crosses worn by the agents Antonio had mentioned, symbolizing . . . what?

Instead, the tattoo at the small of her back grew warm, and she fell into a memory, long buried . . . by Black magick.

OUTSIDE LONDON, THE HELL FIRE CAVES, THREE YEARS BEFORE
SKYE AND ESTEFAN

While Estefan got them wine and laughed with his coven brothers from Cadíz, Skye closed and locked the door to the loo. Like the other rooms in the caves, which served as a clandestine meeting place for witches and other sorts who danced close to the edge of danger, the bathroom was illuminated by candle- and torchlight. A mirror veined with gold sat behind a black crystal vase containing five blood-red roses.

With trembling fingers, Skye loosened the scarlet laces of her black corset and pulled up the black lace blouse beneath it. Turning around, she craned her neck and looked into the mirror, moving the vase for a better view. She squinted at her reflection.

She caught her breath. She didn't remember getting the tattoo at the base of her spine, which was why Estefan called her borachín. *Little drunk one. But there it was, ugly, a misshapen gargoyle holding a heart in its mouth. The tattooed heart was bleeding. As if it were meant to bleed.*

Biting her lip, she daubed the heart with tissues as best she could, careful to flush all traces of her blood down the toilet. A magick user who got hold of a witch's blood could work powerful spells. Same with her hair, her nails . . . and her own heart, the one that was thundering inside her chest.

He's bad, *she thought*. I shouldn't be here with him.

"What's the matter?" Estefan asked her, when she came out of the bathroom. He was wearing a black ritual robe lined in crimson, the hood flung back, revealing his thick, blue-black hair. His black brows were knit over his dark eyes. His mouth—lips so soft, so warm—curled into a curious smile.

Whomever he had been talking to moved into the shadows, and he was making an effort not to look in that someone's direction. Was it another girl?

Skye's heart seized in her chest as tingles played across her face. She heard inside her mind a strange, low vibration. Fear washed down her spine, so cold she half imagined the tattoo would begin to give off steam.

And then she knew.

She crossed to him and desperately gestured for him to come with her. Her feet were numb inside her black lace-up boots, and her terror made her awkward.

"Estefan, there's a vampire here," she whispered. She glanced fearfully into the shadows.

Twin eyes glowed ruby red back at her.

"Goddess," she ground out. She grabbed Estefan's wrist. "There! There it is!"

"Nonsense, mi amor," Estefan said, moving his fingers in front of her face. Murmuring a spell under his breath. She fought it, struggling. He persisted.

"Estefan," she whispered. "We're all in terrible danger! The Cursed Ones are hunting witches! We have to get out of here! We have to warn everyone!"

"Everything is fine," he assured her.

"Stop it. Stop!" she insisted.

"It's fine."

"No. There's a —"

"There is nothing there."

She blinked. The room, which had seemed to swirl, was once again rock steady beneath her heeled boots. The air, fragrant with wine and candle wax. Soft laughter. The murmuring of voices preparing for ritual.

There had been danger, no?

No?

Her lids fluttered. She put her hand to her forehead, then lowered it to her side.

"Now, what were you saying?" he asked her pleasantly.

"I — I don't know," Skye murmured, swaying as Estefan caught both her hands in his.

Kissing her forehead, he chuckled. "Sit down, borachín. You've had too much to drink."

Skye rubbed at the small of her back through the layers of satins and laces. "Something feels funny. Wait, Estefan. I remember! There's a Curse —"

He moved his hand, and whispered in her ear.

"There is nothing. Nothing but my eyes." He pulled a black half mask studded with rubies out of the pocket of his robe. "And my lips."

He pressed his mouth over hers, and she forgot everything. She felt like the Sleeping Beauty, being awakened by a kiss.

"Te amo, mi amor," he said as he finished the kiss. "I will always love you. Always."

"Estefan," she murmured, closing her eyes. "Kiss me again. Never stop kissing me."

"Never," he promised.

Near the Imperial Hunting Palace
Team Salamanca, Taamir, Noah, and Svika

"No," Skye murmured, aghast. *Now* she felt like the Sleeping Beauty, awakening from slumber.

Estefan Montevideo had cloaked memories from her. She hadn't remembered that night in the caves, the vampire in the shadows. Estefan had hidden the fanger from her. He'd conspired with it. Had the others done so too?

What else had happened? What more had he hidden from her?

In the nearly three years since she'd last seen him, she had grown as a witch. So why, while she was focusing on another matter, had this vision been revealed? There had been a Cursed One at their wild parties in Lord Dashwood's

Hell Fire Caves. Perhaps more then one. She *would* tell Jenn about that, and soon; but now she had more urgent business.

She refocused. And then, in her mind, she saw three deep tunnels, one left, one right, and one central. The one on the right glowed with warm light.

Her eyes flew open. She said urgently, "There are tunnels, like Svika said. We take the one on the right."

"Yes." Svika regarded her gratefully. "There's an outbuilding. It was a carriage house. It's to the west. And there's a tunnel inside it that leads directly into the lab."

"Oh, right," Jamie said. "And if she'd said to take the tunnel on the *left*, you'd conveniently have a different outbuilding to point out, to lead us to our deaths *that* direction—"

"Jamie-*kun*," Eriko said gently, "you know that Skye has abilities that we don't have."

"Eri," Jamie said, looking peeved, "I *do* have a brain." Then he blanched as Eriko pursed her lips and dipped her head. "Sorry."

Eriko nodded without looking at him.

"We're going in. Now," Jenn declared. "It's three miles to the carriage house, and then we'll enter the tunnel."

"I'm *not* going," Jamie said, jutting out his chin.

Jenn gave him a hard look. He was completely unfazed.

"After we got back from New Orleans, you agreed to follow me," Jenn said to him. "You nominated me to be your leader. *Now let me do my job.*"

She's grown too, Skye thought, impressed. And relieved.

"I am following Jenn to the tunnel," Eriko said, and Skye knew Eriko was speaking to Jamie, fighting partner to fighting partner. The Hunter didn't realize Jamie was in love with her. Just as Jamie didn't realize that she, Skye, was in love with him.

Eriko looked steadily at him. Jamie huffed, and Skye knew Eriko had won the battle of wills.

"Bloody hell." Jamie looked at Jenn. "As long as the monster goes in first, and you give me permission to shoot him when I decide it's best."

"Done." Jenn looked past him to the Middle Easterners. "Taamir, Noah, what do you have with you? Any grenades?"

"Jenn," Skye said, shocked. "The germ warfare. There are things inside we should not unleash. What about the people who live near here?"

Jenn paused, then shook her head. "We have a mission to destroy Dantalion."

Skye shook her head violently. "No."

"Yes," Jenn said. "We kill vampires by any means necessary. That includes blowing up their lairs." Still, Skye could read the uncertainty in her face. What would they unleash if they did this?

"We need to win this war," Noah affirmed, and she felt that same warmth toward him as before. He reached in his pockets and handed Jenn two grenades. "We're hunters, not peacekeepers."

"I should go first," Svika said. "Follow me across. There

179

are land mines all over the grounds."

"Then we'd better step lively," Jamie quipped.

"And form a line. Step where the guy in front of you steps," Jenn said.

"Unless he gets blown up. Then I'd try a different route." Jamie made a point of planting his Uzi in Svika's back.

They assembled into a line.

Noah said, "Do you think we still have the element of surprise on our side? Has Dantalion figured out that there are more hunters out here than just me and Taamir?"

"Let's assume he doesn't know," Jenn said. "So we don't want to inform him otherwise by making any noise. Agreed?"

Noah nodded. "That's how I would play it."

"Okay, we'll fall out on my mark," she began.

"Goddess, protect us all," Skye said, holding out her hands in benediction.

Just then Antonio burst from the trees and half ran, half rolled into the ditch.

"Go, go, go!" he shouted. "The woods are packed with them! They're everywhere!"

"Follow me!" Hunkering down, Svika raced down the slope. The hunters followed.

And the forest shattered behind them.

BOOK TWO
VELES

Oh, night that guided me,
Oh, night more lovely than the dawn,
Oh, night that joined Beloved with lover,
Lover transformed in the Beloved!

—St. John of the Cross,
sixteenth-century mystic of Salamanca

CHAPTER EIGHT

Humans, lend us now your aid
Fight for us with law and blade
There are those who hate us still
They're the ones that you must kill
Safety, peace, our common goal
War takes an unpleasant toll
Now we put your love to test
Lay our enemies all to rest

University of Salamanca
Father Juan

Father Juan ignored the pain in his knees as he knelt in the university chapel, praying. He had been that way for most of the day, as unmoving as the statues of saints that kept silent vigil with him. He prayed for his team out in the field, for the students training at the university, for the war, and for the Church. There in the chapel he wrestled with demons of his own, struggling to find the hope that he needed to believe in so that he could share it with the others. For the first time since the Cursed Ones had announced their presence to the world, Father Juan felt completely hollow.

Maybe it was the end. Maybe the Antichrist walked among them. Maybe he had fangs and red eyes. What if Solomon, or one of the others, was that abomination, and they were suffering the end times? Doomsday cults had risen up over the last few years; they believed it. The end was not near—it was here.

Juan had done his best to ignore such hysteria. To admit that the war might be the fulfillment of prophecy would do no one any good. People tended to become complacent in the face of prophecy. The vast majority of the world had already rolled over and given up. Those who still fought couldn't afford the luxury of believing that their fates were sealed, the future already upon them.

They needed to believe that there was a better world waiting on the other side of their struggle.

Even if there wasn't.

They needed to believe they had a chance.

Even if they had none.

They needed to believe that love and faith would win the day.

Even if the day was already lost.

184

Father Juan took a deep, shuddering breath. He prayed finally for himself, for renewal of spirit, of purpose. He needed to stay the course. The years weighed more heavily upon him than usual. He knew the students wondered who he was. It was better to let them wonder than to tell them the truth. He had once been told that proof negated faith. He had been a young man at the time and hadn't understood what that meant. Over the years, though, he had come to see that it was true. Doubting Thomas wasn't blessed for his faith, because in the end he hadn't had faith, but proof.

On December 2, 1577, St. John of the Cross was taken into custody by the superiors of his order, with whom he had taken issue. He and St. Teresa of Avila argued that the Order of the Carmelites had grown corrupt and required reform. St. John's captors tortured him, whipping him and imprisoning him in a tiny room barely big enough for him to stretch out in, with no window, no doors. He endured for nine months.

A dark shadow flitted across Juan's mind, and a sickness surged inside him. It was done. He could feel it. The unthinkable had happened. He had cast so many spells and said so many prayers to try and prevent it, but in the end he could only alert himself to the moment it happened. He squeezed his eyes shut and continued to pray, knowing that everyone in his charge needed prayer now more than ever.

It was another two hours before Diego joined him,

silently sinking to his knees beside Father Juan. Diego was the bishop in charge of the university, a longtime friend and the only one still living whom Juan had ever trusted to hear his confession.

An hour passed as the two of them prayed side by side. Finally Father Juan rose from his knees and settled himself into a pew. With a sigh Diego joined him.

"So they've done it," Juan said, not asking, because he already knew.

"We feared this day was coming," Diego said, sounding old and tired for his sixty years. "Rome is close to making a treaty with the Cursed Ones. As a gesture of good faith they are officially closing the training academies they oversee the world over."

Father Juan felt each syllable like a blow against his chest. "That's half a dozen schools with teens who are training to become hunters."

"I know."

"Unofficially?" Juan asked, with a flicker of hope.

Diego pressed his hand to his eyes. "I heard from Archbishop Malachi. He's been a friend of mine for years, but he said that if we don't close the school, they will."

Misery settled around Juan's shoulders like a stole. "The Church is declaring war on us."

Diego nodded. "It would seem so. What do you want to do?"

The hollowness lessened. He was not alone. He had

friends. Father Juan studied the cross suspended behind the altar. Friends, and a Protector. "We can't surrender."

"I agree. I just don't know how we can fight both Spain and the Church."

"We can't," Juan replied. "But we can fight the Cursed Ones and reach out to the other hunter teams and resistance cells. If we could strike a real blow, it might encourage those who are still sympathetic to our cause to come forth and join us."

Diego stared at him. "Your idea is intriguing, but I'm wondering what you think we can accomplish on a large enough scale to regain the support of the government and the Church."

While imprisoned, St. John of the Cross wrote his Spiritual Canticle *on paper snuck to him by a friar charged with guarding him.*

"If they can take out Dantalion, it will be a start."

Diego shook his head. "Even if they can manage that, it's too isolated a victory. We need something a bit more public, more theatrical."

Father Juan thought of Pamplona. "Like the Cursed Ones? They love to create spectacle."

"Exactly like the Cursed Ones," Diego said. "*We* need to create a spectacle."

"What exactly did you have in mind?" Juan asked the bishop.

Diego raised a brow. He almost smiled. "They have a

spokesman; we need a spokesman. We need a voice, crying in the wilderness. Loudly. With a broader reach."

"The Internet?"

"Too controlled," Diego replied. "Think . . . older."

Juan blinked at him. "You're crazy. No television station is going to give us airtime. And if we try to take one by force, they'll just spin the footage. *After* the hunters are thrown in prison."

Diego shrugged. "Surely you remember that before there was television, there were other methods of communication."

Juan's lips parted. "Radio."

"Exactly."

Juan considered. "In New Orleans we heard a radio broadcast, a man named Kent, who said he was the Voice of the Resistance."

"As was done during World War Two," Diego pointed out.

"Sí, vale," Juan said thoughtfully. "We need a way to get the truth out, to share information."

"We can also use it to help people find safety and avoid cities that are Cursed One strongholds."

Juan brightened. "And maybe we can both find resistance cells and help grow the resistance worldwide." He looked again at the cross.

On August 15, 1578, St. John escaped through a window in an adjoining cell. With St. Teresa he reformed the existing monasteries and founded many others.

"A larger calling. We have the expertise, the training . . ."

Juan closed his eyes in gratitude. "And the faith," he replied.

In 1726 he was made a saint.

Diego nodded and clapped a hand on his shoulder. "Now you've got the idea."

"With God's help," Father Juan said.

"With God's help," Diego replied.

Both men crossed themselves.

Russia
Team Salamanca; Taamir, Noah, and Svika

Monsters—hideous, deformed things that had once been men or vampires or maybe even werewolves, or all three— charged the hunters. Eriko froze for a moment as Jamie shouted at Svika to move; then Svika and Jamie started running, weaving through the minefield toward the carriage house.

The danger of that maneuver took Eriko's breath away. Also the wrongheadedness. They should fight first and continue to the lab second. *Fight the battle that's in front of you.* That's what her father had said, after she'd told him she was leaving Japan to train to fight vampires in Spain. She hadn't completely understood what he'd meant until now.

Only she, Holgar, and Antonio had the strength to outrun those creatures, but even if they could, it didn't mean they wouldn't be blown up by the land mines for their efforts. And the other hunters? Blown up as well, or torn apart.

Skye rushed past her, following Jamie and screaming a spell of some sort. As the adrenaline flooded Eriko's body, she wished, just once, that Skye would do some sort of spell to wipe out the enemy attacking them. Couldn't a witch do that? It was dishonorable not to fight your hardest, do everything you could to protect your own people.

As Holgar ran after his partner, Jenn and Eriko locked eyes.

"Follow me," Jenn said. It was more of an entreaty, not an order.

"We won't outrun them," Eriko said, even as Antonio staked the first creature to come within arm's length. "I will stay, fight. I will join you in the palace as soon as I can."

"You won't know the way," Jenn said.

"Yes, she will. I'll stay with her. I can see your footprints in the snow and will follow them to you," Antonio said.

The creatures were a dozen jumps away. Eriko whipped two stakes from her belt and braced herself for battle.

"Run, Jenn, hurry!"

And Jenn ran.

Eriko and Antonio squared off, and Eriko was grateful he was there. She hadn't trusted him when they'd first formed their team. But now there was no one she'd rather have next to her when she was making her final stand, even if she hated the fact that he, too, held back when he fought. She did it from pain, he from fear that he would revert to the monstrous evil that cursed him.

The beasts attacked them like a shock wave, and Eriko spun in a circle, planting stakes in two different chests and catching a glimpse of Antonio doing the same. It was like some insane sort of ballet. Spin, jump.

Kill.

Antonio grabbed her and whirled her around to face an enemy approaching on his right side while he stabbed another one standing in front of him. The creatures that filled Eriko's vision had muscle denser than any human's, and it took more strength to pierce the flesh near their hearts. That was the point; their own bodies served as a kind of armor, making them all but invincible to a human of normal strength.

But there was nothing normal about Eriko, or Antonio for that matter. Behind her she heard the *rat-a-tat-tat* of a machine gun, and her stomach lurched. *Don't think about what's happening to the others. Just focus.*

Noah was worried as the line raced along through the minefield. They zigzagged across it like some drunken snake. At every footfall he expected to be blown up, but no mines went off. He finally began to wonder if the field was actually riddled with the bombs at all.

And then a more chilling thought hit him. How did

Svika know the way through it? He stopped so abruptly that Jenn ran into him from behind, and for a moment they grappled together, trying to maintain their balance and stay on their feet.

"What?" she hissed.

"Something is wrong."

"What?" she asked again, glancing behind as the others slowed down, looking at her anxiously.

"How does Svika know the way through this field?" he asked her.

She blinked. "Maybe Dantalion showed it to him." But she frowned. "Or . . . he *is* a plant."

"But why not just blow us up? Why lure us in?" Noah pressed.

"Dantalion wants to perform more experiments? He wants to make sure he's killed you and Taamir?"

He took that in. "He's guided us almost across. But you saw him. He's not human anymore. How can we trust him?"

"Come on!" the werewolf shouted as he looked back at them, having slowed his pace.

So, he was running behind a werewolf. And there was a witch. And their Hunter wasn't their leader. It was a crazy team. What other secrets could they possibly be hiding? They acted like they had lots of secrets.

Especially Jenn Leitner.

Panting, Jenn heaved a sigh of relief as they reached the carriage house. Her lungs were burning. As she bent to catch her breath, she glanced over her shoulder, hoping to see Antonio and Eriko following, and fearing that she would see the monsters instead.

But she could see no one through the reflections of moonlight on falling snow, just the forests and the mountainside they'd run down, with a higher mountain towering over it, black silhouettes in the swirling whiteness. Her stomach clenched. Brushing her damp hair away from her face, she ran on, reaching a tumbledown wooden structure that reminded her of a barn.

"The tunnel entrance is in here," Svika said, touching a canted wooden door, as the group hustled toward him.

"Jamie?" Taamir said, barely winded.

"Yeah?" Jamie replied.

"Stab him in the shoulder."

And before anyone could move or think, Jamie whipped a stake out and did just that. Taamir clapped his hand over Svika's mouth as Svika dropped to the ground.

"What the hell?" Holgar whispered.

"Tell us what Dantalion's planning," Taamir said to the writhing man. He glanced at Noah. "He's not himself."

Noah nodded grimly.

"I can't—I didn't—," Svika protested

Taamir backhanded him across the face. "Tell us, or I'll let Noah ask you."

Jenn stared hard at Noah, wondering how he would

take this treatment of someone who was, in essence, family.

"You don't want him to interrogate you. You know what he can do," Taamir said quietly.

"Skye, is there anything you can do?" Jenn asked. "Maybe work a spell of some kind?"

Skye just looked dazed. Then her eyes ticked past Jenn's shoulder, as though she suddenly saw someone standing in the snowy woods. The look on her face raised the hair on the back of Jenn's neck, and Jenn turned quickly, legs spread in a fighting stance, stake in her hand.

There was no one there. She turned back to Skye. The English witch still wore the same horrified expression.

"Skye?" Jenn asked, looking from her to the empty space and back again.

Skye didn't move. Noah pressed his hand against Svika's injured shoulder, hurting him. Things were quickly spinning out of control, and Jenn began to sweat, wishing she knew if and when the trap was going to be sprung.

She strode forward and snapped her fingers in front of Skye's eyes. Nothing. Forcing herself not to panic, she grabbed Skye's shoulders and shook her hard.

"Skye! What is it?"

Skye turned to her, lips trembling. "He's here. I don't know how, but he's here." She reached for a cross from her belt.

"Who's here, Skye?"

Skye screamed in utter panic. "Oh, God, he's found me!"

"*Who?*"

"Estefan! Oh, my Goddess, he's *here*!"

Jenn blinked and stared at the falling snow. "Who?"

And then, in the sudden stillness, Jenn heard the sounds of battle.

RUSSIA
AURORA AND ESTEFAN

From the towering mountaintop, shielded by tree branches, Aurora ran her hands along her fabulous ermine coat and watched through the snowfall as Antonio and the Hunter fought off Dantalion's monsters. She'd been picking the disgusting creatures off for days now, thinning them—she hoped it was driving Dantalion mad—but now it was time to let *them* pick off the hunters.

Beside her, Estefan stood in black body armor and a heavy black wool coat—he could still feel cold; Aurora just liked fur coats. The haughty and very sexy warlock looked supremely smug and self-satisfied. It irritated her, but if *she* was going to have a witch on her side, she could do worse than Estefan Montevideo.

"I can feel her," he chortled.

"Which means she can feel you, too, yes?" Aurora reminded him.

He hesitated, and she raised her brows at him. The egos of men rendered them so stupid.

"Maybe. I don't know," he admitted.

She sighed. Estefan's obsession with his ex was inconvenient, but understandable. He was still in love with the little witch, even though he also hated her for setting him on fire.

It was like that with her and Sergio. She was tired of being a slave to how he made her feel. He wasn't worth it. She had resolved that she was going to kill him. Their master would either thank her for it or kill her himself. He had always loved Sergio more than her.

Just as Sergio had always loved Antonio de la Cruz.

Watching the hunky priest, she wondered why it was that Sergio was so obsessed with him. She guessed Sergio was embarrassed by what he saw as his failure. No other Cursed One had ever been able to maintain his humanity and thereby so utterly reject his sire. Sergio hated and feared Antonio because of that. And yet, on those many occasions when Sergio could have killed Antonio, Sergio hadn't been able to bring himself to do it.

Yes, Antonio was Sergio's failure, his weakness. But Antonio's misguided strength of will made him truly spectacular, a lone specimen of rebellion among the Cursed Ones. Dantalion would have done well to capture and study Antonio, not create monstrosities in his labs. For all they knew, Antonio would one day will himself to walk in the sun—and wouldn't *that* change things.

She assumed Dantalion was unaware of all the drama

taking place outside his fortress. From her vantage point Aurora watched the battle between Hunter and Cursed One, and the hybridized *things* Dantalion had made. She saw the glint of the rubies in the cross earring Antonio wore. *Her* rubies, from the crucifix she had carried when she was human. The one that her master had taken from her the night he converted her, in that filthy cell. Her family had been tortured and burned, and the Spanish Grand Inquisitor, Tomás de Torquemada, had threatened to do the same to her. Then *he* had come . . . and saved her.

By damning her for all eternity.

Her sire had broken that cross to bits and handed out the stones to favored members of their court when they had performed a particularly noteworthy task. Sergio had been favored with more than a dozen of them. She had not been around during the year that Antonio de la Cruz had been converted. She and Sergio had had one of their frequent rows, and she'd been off sulking in Rio. She hadn't really stopped sulking since.

Behind Aurora two dozen of her vampires waited, silent, watching her and anticipating her signal. They would do her bidding without question. They only represented a portion of those faithful to her. Some she had converted herself, others were older than her, but all had come to trust her, to follow her.

She was tired of sharing power and jockeying for position with Sergio. It was time to end it once and for all. She turned to Louis, her lieutenant, who appeared to be in his late fifties, with thin, graying hair. She liked Louis. He wasn't one of the preening ones who liked to look pretty. He was tough, loyal, and utterly bloodthirsty.

"When I give you the word, destroy those hideous things and bring me the vampire," she said.

"And the Hunter?" he asked.

Aurora shrugged. "Kill her if she gets in the way, but don't waste effort on her otherwise."

She had been watching the Hunter. The girl was good, and the special elixir—oh, yes, Aurora knew all about it— definitely enhanced her natural fighting abilities. But she reeked of pain quite a distance away. Her body was wearing out. Without a miracle the girl wouldn't survive the year without her organs failing her. There was no sense risking the lives of her warriors doing battle with that one. Not when Aurora had Sergio in her crosshairs.

Louis nodded, and the first dozen of her Cursed Ones snapped to attention. They looked magnificent in their padded vests, which, like the hybrids' leathery bodies, made them difficult to stake. And they were armed with human-made weapons that they knew how to use with killing skill.

She looked toward the palace, caressing her long black braid, which coiled over her shoulder. Dantalion probably couldn't hear them from this distance and had no idea she was there. His experiments with sunlight were intriguing and could be put to good use. His little Frankenstein's monsters, on the other hand, were an abomination. Ones she was sure, now that she had seen them, the master would not approve of.

"What are your orders?" Louis asked her.

"Let's see what the Salamancans are capable of," she replied. She raised her hand.

"Go," Louis told the vampires. "Bring him to Aurora."

Flipping off their safeties and priming their weapons, her fighters charged down the hill as the light snowfall turned into a raging storm. She raised one brow and looked at Estefan, who shook his head, pulling his coat more snugly around himself.

"I didn't do it," he said. "Do you want me to stop it?"

She shook her head. "Save your strength."

Below, on the slopes, her warriors reached the battle. Antonio and the Hunter had fought Dantalion's abominations well. But both were injured, and both were exhausted, and there were still a lot of the monstrosities left.

"Send in the second wave," she told Louis.

More vampires joined the first rank, and together they mowed down the creatures with submachine-gun fire. Purple blood, and red, burst from wounds. The monsters shrieked in Russian and howled like wolves. Some died from submachine-gun fire. But any creatures containing Cursed One body parts had to be staked or beheaded to be destroyed. Then they hissed as those parts disintegrated into dust.

Aurora's henchmen allowed a few wounded survivors to stumble back toward the palace. Let Dantalion find out who had been killing off his monsters.

The path cleared; Aurora's vampires turned their attention to the prize. She smiled as Antonio was too late to counter an attack by three of her fighters. They knocked him unconscious while the Hunter managed a few round-house punches and kicks. A vampire aimed a pistol at her, sighted it, then twirled the pistol like a gunslinger, bringing the heavy butt end down on the crown of her head. The girl sprawled in the snow.

The gunslinger kicked the Hunter in the head, while the others tied Antonio up. She lunged forward, grabbing his ankle and toppling him off balance. As he landed, he kicked her again, this time in the face. She grabbed his foot, leaped to her feet, and, moving as fast as a vampire, whipped out a stake to slam through his chest. It didn't go through the padding.

Aurora guffawed, enjoying the sport. She'd heard about Pamplona, and had been sorry she hadn't been there. But this more than made up for it.

Four others glommed on to the Hunter, holding her as the slumped Antonio was trussed like a wild boar fresh from the hunt. One of the victorious raised a proud fist in the air, then hefted Antonio's limp body onto his back like Quasimodo, the hunchback of Notre Dame.

The vampire zigzagged back up the incline, sinking up

to his thighs in the snow, while the others kept the flailing Hunter from intervening. Once Antonio was safely away, they danced out of the girl's reach, laughing and taunting her. The Hunter began to give chase, but wobbled, her knees caving beneath her, before toppling face-first to the ground.

"These Salamancans are not so special, are they, Estefan?" Aurora asked.

He blinked. "*Lo siento,* Aurora, what?" he said distractedly.

She narrowed her eyes at him. "What are you doing?"

"Nothing." He shook his head. When he felt her eyes on him, he jerked. "I'm not doing anything."

She was unconvinced. Maybe he was communicating with his little English witch. Maybe he was even warning her.

It was time to go. Not because she feared the rest of the Salamancan team. She simply didn't want to risk anything happening to Antonio. And if Estefan was being indiscreet, she needed to put time and distance between the two exes.

The Hunter lay inert in the snow. From that distance Aurora couldn't tell if the Hunter was dead. Either way, it didn't matter. She had what she'd come for.

As her troops rejoined her, Aurora led the way back into the woods, where she had a fleet of all-terrain vehicles waiting for them. One eye on Antonio, another on Estefan, she pulled her furs around herself and smiled brilliantly. It was such a fine night to be Aurora Abregón.

He's so beautiful, she thought, staring down at Antonio as he was loaded into one of the Humvees. *More beautiful even than Sergio.*

Blasphemous thought, but true.

"*Vámonos,*" she said happily.

"Where are we going?" Estefan asked her.

She cocked her head. "Where do you think?"

Eriko sobbed in fear and frustration as she tried to push herself out of the snow, but her tortured, twisted limbs gave way. One of the remaining monsters lumbered toward her through the falling snow, and she sucked in her breath and squeezed her eyes tightly shut, her fingers still curled around a stake.

Nothing happened. The world began to drift away. She floated in a haze of pain and cold.

No. Wake up! she told herself.

Gasping, she forced open her eyes. The creatures and the Cursed Ones were all gone. She sat up slowly, pain sending tears down her cheeks. They had kidnapped Antonio, and she had let them. What would they do with him?

"Jenn," she croaked in a gravelly voice. She had to catch up to the others, get help.

She tried to stand, but her legs collapsed again.

She wondered how any other Hunters managed to survive the twisting of bone and muscle. Maybe they never reached this point, having been killed within days or weeks of graduation. She was lucky, but lying there in the snow with blood running down her chin, she didn't feel lucky.

She felt weak, and vulnerable. Two things she had never wanted to be ever again.

I'm failing, she thought, and then, with sudden clarity: *I'm dying.*

CHAPTER NINE

*Being a hunter is as much about instinct as
anything else. Training, knowledge, can only
take you so far. You have to learn to trust
yourself, even when you don't want to. The
mind notices thousands of minute details that
we don't even consciously register. This is what
people call intuition. Sometimes your gut knows
more than you do; you have to pay attention.
Sometimes the details you've overlooked are
miniscule. Sometimes they are glaringly obvious
and you just didn't want to see them. Because
you were afraid to.*

—from the diary of Jenn Leitner,
discovered in the ashes

RUSSIA
DANTALION

"What the hell?" Dantalion thundered as he watched a dozen ragged hybrids stumble back onto the palace grounds. He stood on his balcony, gentling Rasputin, his Russian wolfhound, and stared down at the terrified *matroyshkas* as they smacked into each other like windup toys. Their vampiric handlers approached cautiously to corral them and drive them back to their cells. The hybrids that still had mouths were shrieking like teakettles, roaring like apes. And Dantalion didn't see the new one he had sent out with them, Svika, who was supposed to lure his two hunter friends into the palace. Dantalion thought he had thoroughly mesmerized Svika, but maybe he had run away. Maybe they'd killed him.

This can't be the work of two hunters, can it?

Then Dantalion heard the *rat-tat-tat* of submachinegun fire. The hunters? Dantalion's own, protecting his borders?

The high, arched windows, fortified with foot-thick unbreakable acrylic, were foggy with a cascade of white. The damned snow. He couldn't see anything.

Rasputin whined.

"Easy, boy," Dantalion told him.

He aimed a remote control at a locked, reinforced box. It opened, revealing an enormous bank of readouts. Land mines, check. Electrified perimeter, check. Maybe Svika had been killed. Dantalion had ordered him to find his old friends, then lure them back through a "secret" tunnel. Instead Svika was missing, and the *matroyshkas* he had sent out to back him up were, apparently, being slaughtered.

Time to declare an emergency. He pushed the alarm code. Klaxons whooped. The stupid dog panicked and bolted. His scientists, Cursed Ones and humans alike, poked their heads out of their offices, wondering if they were having a drill.

"*Now* what's going on?" asked Khrushchev, as he joined Dantalion beside the control box.

"Just go downstairs to the basement," Dantalion said irritably. "I have the situation under control."

But just in case, there was another switch on the panel — one that would deliver poison gas into the subterranean labs. All the humans and most of the *matroyshkas* would die. The Cursed Ones like himself could not be poisoned in such a way. So next a bomb would go off, taking care of the rest and eliminating any trace of his experiments.

While he, of course, would be long gone.

Dantalion picked up the red landline phone inside the box and pushed the first button. The connection was made before he even heard a ring.

"Apples are red," he reported, speaking in Russian.

"The orchards are yellow," came the correct code, also in Russian. "Situation?"

"Uncertain. I may need you."

"We're ready."

Dantalion hung up and headed for the basement.

Russia
Team Salamanca Minus Antonio and Eriko; Taamir, Noah, and Svika

At the perimeter of the snow-covered minefield, Jamie turned in slow circles, looking for some sort of target.

"Skye, there is no one here!" Jenn said, as she sliced the air with a stake, while Holgar slashed at nothing with a wicked Israeli special-forces knife Taamir had given him from their cache of weapons. Vampires moved fast enough to seem invisible, but the falling snow would have given them shape if there had been any present. Just in case, Jamie had wanted to shoot off a few rounds with the Uzi he'd grown quite attached to, but he stayed his hand. The fewer combatants Dantalion thought there were out here, the better.

There was silence all round them, save for Skye's hysteria and Svika's groaning.

Of the two, Skye was freaking Jamie out worse. And that was saying a lot, considering what Svika was.

"He's watching us!" Skye said, grabbing Jenn's arm. "He's up somewhere high!"

Jamie looked down at the enormous palace. It had once

been very grand, but pieces of the gingerbread decorations had fallen off, and slabs of what looked like concrete had been set in their place. "Is this 'he' in there?"

"Who *is* he?" Holgar stared into the darkness. For once Jamie was glad to have a werewolf around. Holgar could see things, smell things, that no one else except Antonio could.

Skye kept whimpering.

"Bloody hell, witchy! Spill it!" Jamie shouted at her.

"He's a witch, like me, only not like me," Skye said, her voice cracking. "He's with the Cursed Ones."

"With Dantalion?" Jamie asked, horrified. "And this is some friend of yours?"

Her eyes widened. "He's with someone. Jenn, I think it might be Antonio!"

Jenn's mouth dropped open, and she went green. Typical of her to go all drama queen instead of keeping it together to lead the team.

"Why didn't you tell us this before?" Jamie demanded. "That some *friend* of yours was here and —"

"He just popped into my head. He *does* that!"

"*What?*" Jenn and Jamie said in unison.

"But — but he's really here. I can feel it." Skye hugged herself. "And I think he's gotten hold of Antonio."

"Where?" Taamir asked, painting the black night with the barrel of his Uzi. Noah kept a boot heel on Svika as he writhed on the ground.

"What about Dantalion?" Jenn asked. "Is he working with him?"

"What about Eriko?" Jamie asked Skye.

"I don't know. I'm not sure." Skye was shaking. "He's dangerous, Jenn."

"So's Dantalion. Look at that bloke," Jamie said, gesturing to Svika, "acting the maggot."

No longer writhing, Svika stared straight ahead, and for a second Jamie thought he had died. That could be good or bad. Jamie pushed past Jenn, knocking her shoulder hard, and pressed the Uzi against the center of Svika's forehead as Noah kept him pinned. The bugger was losing a lot of blood.

"Dantalion," Svika whispered. *"Da, ya podchinyus va . . ."* As Svika gasped, he fell silent.

"He's speaking Russian," Holgar said. "Talking to someone about obeying."

"Her friend," Jamie said, glaring at Skye.

"No, he's not Russian," Skye said. Her face was white. "He's a Spaniard."

"Bloody hell!" Jamie yelled at her. "All this time we're living in *Spain*, and you didn't think to mention it?"

"Keep your voice down," Jenn said between clenched teeth. "The fighting's over for now, and—"

"It bloody well is *not* over," Jamie replied in a cold voice. *"She's* the one in league with the Cursed Ones, don't you see? The traitor."

209

"No, Jamie. Blimey, I'm not." Skye held out her hands. "He's a Dark Witch, and we were together before the academy. I haven't seen him since."

"You're lying," Jamie flung at her.

"Listen to me," Jenn said. "They're going to count heads, and Svika's still out here."

Jamie could barely contain himself. "Yeah, and thanks to Skye, it seems our *Hunter* is in there. And perhaps so is your *boyfriend*. Who would make a lovely experiment, now, wouldn't he?"

Noah frowned at Jamie. "What do you mean?"

"Jamie, shut up," Holgar said, growling.

"Your *heartthrob*, who knows so much about resistance fighters?" Jamie added. "And if this Dantalion wanker wants to know about *that*, well, then, maybe he'll stab Antonio in the shoulder. Or drive a nice sharp *stake* —"

Holgar growled and leaped at Jamie, punching him so hard that the Irishman fell backward into the snow. Holgar yanked the Uzi out of Jamie's arms. Jamie sprawled, sputtering. Holgar loomed over him, bending down, putting his face close to his, imitating the way Jamie had aimed the Uzi at Svika.

"Leave off," Jamie said between clenched teeth. "I'm only saying what should be said."

"Dantalion, ya privozhy ich k vam," Svika said in a dull flat voice. He was panting hard.

"What's that mean?" Taamir demanded.

"He says, 'Dantalion, I'll bring them to you,'" Holgar informed them, his Uzi still trained on Jamie.

"Ya vash rab."

"'I'm your slave,'" Holgar said.

"He's mesmerized," Jamie said. "Dandy's soddin' puppet. I *told* you, didn't I? Jesus, Mary, and Joseph. We should blow his feckin' head off!"

"But he wasn't acting like this earlier. And vampires can't mesmerize you from a distance," Jenn argued. "Skye, is this witchcraft?"

Jenn moved in front of Holgar and held out her hand to Jamie. Glaring at Jamie, she jabbed it at him.

"Get up," she said.

"Well, Jenn, what a pair." Ignoring her hand, he got up on his own.

She fixed him with a hard look. "We need to assess the situation."

"Assess, hell!" Jamie said.

"We'd better think of something fast," Holgar growled. The sound made the hairs on the back of Jamie's neck stand on end.

"The tunnel," Svika said in English.

"Right, straight across to the grounds of the palace it is," Jamie said.

"You can't," Noah protested. "They'll pick you off."

"Listen, Israel," Jamie said. "Berserker girl here says that some bloke has got them in the palace. We were heading to the palace anyway; it just puts me in mind to get there bloody faster."

"Don't be an idiot," Jenn said to him.

Jamie wasn't an idiot. He was terrified. Terrified of losing Eriko and terrified of dying there for nothing when he should be back home defending Ireland.

"You got a better idea, any of you?" he demanded, looking around at faces that were just as strained and tired as he felt. Holgar stared at Jenn, and Skye was still locked in her own little world of terror.

Jamie yanked his gun back out of Holgar's hands and aimed it at Svika. "You! You must have a better idea. Tell me how to get into the palace or I'll shoot you in your good shoulder. Better yet, I'll shoot your bleedin' head in."

Sweat rolled down Svika's forehead, and he was beginning to shake, though whether from fear or shock, Jamie couldn't tell.

Skye was too catatonic to even protest, and that freaked him out even more. Her ex could be doing heaven knew what to his Eri while they were wasting time.

"Noah," Svika said, then mumbled so low that Jamie couldn't hear him. Noah lowered his head and listened.

"He wants justice for what's been done to him." Noah said. "He says that Dantalion did mesmerize him. But he's fighting it. He's got something in his pocket that will help us."

Taamir dug in Svika's pockets. He pulled out three objects that looked like electronically activated car keys.

"Feckin' hell," Jamie said, whistling, as Taamir showed them to everyone. "Are these what I think they are?"

"These disarm the mines?" Taamir asked.

Svika nodded.

"Two are decoys?" Jamie probed.

"All . . . work," Svika whispered.

"How do you know about those?" Jenn asked Jamie.

"IRA. But I've never actually seen one, only heard about them."

"They're all the same," Svika replied.

"Brilliant." He looked at Jenn. "If I take one, that leaves the others for you lot."

He snatched one from Taamir's hand. He grabbed an Uzi and headed back toward the minefield.

"Jamie, wait!" Jenn shouted. "We don't know if they're in there!"

"You're just afraid for *him*. This is our mission," Jamie accused.

"Even if that thing gets you through the minefield, they'll have sentries. You won't get within a quarter of a mile of that place without getting cut down," Taamir insisted.

"We're going to lose the advantage. One of those monsters will tell Dantalion about us. Maybe that freak Antonio was giving last rites to didn't go to hell. Maybe he went back to Dantalion. Maybe Antonio sent him with his blessings," Jamie finished, angry at himself for standing there arguing with them.

"But what if Dantalion *doesn't* know about us?" Holgar

argued. "And he sees a stranger on his grounds?"

"Then let's all go *now*. Our job is to take him down!" Jamie shouted. He clenched his jaw. "Give us the order."

"Not. Yet," Jenn gritted. "Noah, ask Svika for the layout of the—"

"Now," Jamie insisted. He whirled in her direction, gripping the Uzi. He could see the fear flare in her eyes. Jenn was wondering if he would force her to do the right thing and send the team in.

Holgar growled; tears slid down Skye's face. Noah kept hold of Svika as Taamir cautiously observed the power play. For that was what it was, plain and simple.

"Skye, *are* they inside the palace?" Jenn said. "Give it everything you have. Please."

At the sound of her name the young witch shuddered.

"I don't know, I don't know," Skye cried. "Oh, God, I'm so scared, Jenn. I'm sorry. This is why we're not supposed to do this. Witches."

"Well, you're here, and you are doing it," Jenn shot back. "Come on, Skye. We need you."

Jenn looked at Noah. "Okay, then. Make Svika tell you exactly how to get in there. Do whatever you have to do."

"No, wait, please," Skye said, *finally* pulling herself together. "I can try to take the mesmerism away."

"Bloody hell," Jamie said, spitting on the ground. "Best you just stay out of it. Jenn. This is all arseways. Let me go in. I'm good at this. This is how I grew up."

214

He waited one beat and was just about to take off when she gave him a nod.

"You can go," Jenn said. "On your own, Jamie."

That was all he needed, permission. And then it struck him. Why did he need her bloody permission to do anything? Rebellion and rage burned inside him, but it was best spent on finding Eriko and killing as many Cursers as he could.

Jenn recognized the inner struggle that raged through Jamie—it was the same one raging through her. She knew that if they both lived through this mission, a showdown between them was inevitable. That was fine; she'd gladly embrace it, if only because it would mean that they had both survived.

"No, don't let him go," Skye cried. "Please, Jamie, don't do it. Wait a few more minutes."

Jamie said nothing. He took off running into the darkness. Jenn wondered if she'd just given him permission to go on a suicide mission.

Skye balled her fists against her chest. Then she straightened her fingers and held them out, murmuring in Latin. Probably a spell of protection. Then she lowered her arms and frowned at Jenn.

"You shouldn't have let him go."

"Dantalion," Svika murmured in English. "I hear you. I hear you."

"He's falling back under the spell," Taamir ventured. "Or whatever you call it."

"Noah, do what you need to do to get through to him," Jenn said. Noah licked his lips, nodded, and leaned harder on Svika's shoulder with his boot. Svika groaned.

"No! Let me try!" Skye pleaded.

Then Svika screamed, a high-pitched sound that didn't seem like it could come from something that had ever been human. Noah cupped Svika's mouth; behind his hand the sound ended on a keening note that jittered along Jenn's nerve endings and set her teeth on edge. His entire body shook.

Svika took a deep breath and looked up at them with eyes that were clouded by pain but more alive than they had been. Tentatively, Noah lifted his hand.

Svika whispered something.

"What?" Jenn asked, moving closer. Noah joined her, and together they leaned over his friend. Suddenly Noah grabbed her hand and squeezed hard. Startled, she saw tears in the hardened soldier's eyes. She realized that this was torture for him. Svika was his comrade and teammate.

"Go to the right. Not the tunnel. The palace. There is a blind spot, broken camera," Svika said.

"Are you sure?" Holgar asked.

Svika nodded. "No trick."

"Skye?" Jenn asked.

But the girl had grabbed one of the two disarming devices and was sprinting after Jamie. Holgar whined deep in his throat and stared after her, then turned back to Jenn.

"What else?" Noah asked.

"Don't look in his eyes." Svika shuddered. "His eyes."

Jenn looked at Noah. "We're moving out," she said quietly, giving his hand a squeeze. "If you want to stay here . . ."

Taamir reached down and took Svika's hand.

"My friend," Taamir said in English. "What else can you tell us?"

"Nerve gas. Torture," Svika said. "Better that they all die." He gritted his teeth. "Let me go."

"No. No, Svika," Taamir insisted, glancing up at Noah. "We can carry him."

As Noah looked down at Svika, he let go of Jenn's hand. A long, low shudder worked its way through the Israeli soldier. He picked up the wicked, sharp knife Taamir had been carrying and held it by his side.

"Go on ahead," Noah said to Jenn and Taamir. His gaze was fixed on Svika, who was staring up at him. "Go on ahead."

"Noah," Jenn said, her voice strained.

"I've done this before." His voice was gruff. He pulled out a pack of cigarettes and placed one in Svika's mouth. "Go now."

With the last remaining device clutched in her hand, Jenn led the race to catch up with Jamie and Skye. With every step she was terrified that the device would fail or that it was a decoy, and that a bomb was about to blow her to bits. She also kept running toward the palace, expecting a fresh wave of monsters to pour across the snow.

At one point she thought she heard the roar of half-dead creatures in the distance, but a moment later it was gone. A figure loomed suddenly in the dark, and Jenn slowed in time to avoid running into Skye.

The witch was standing with her back to Jenn, hands moving as though pressing against an invisible box. She flipped her head frantically from side to side, white-blond Rasta braids flying around her.

"Skye!" Jenn shouted.

Skye just pounded on the wall that she alone could see.

Skye stood in the middle of a house of mirrors. Terror gripped her. She had made it this far only to be trapped, her reflection reflected into infinity. Everywhere she turned she couldn't get away from herself or from *him*.

She couldn't find a way out, and she had to if she wanted to save her friends. She saw Estefan's face projected in front of her, and she pounded at it in frustration. Everywhere she turned, she only saw more mirrors, no exit, no salvation. And everywhere Estefan's laughing face. If only she could break the mirror, then she could fight her way through the impossible labyrinth.

Skye had been lost in a mirror maze when she was a child at a local fair. She'd begged her parents to let her go with a family who had no idea the Yorks were witches. Then she had been stuck for two hours until a kind stranger took pity on her and led her out. But there was no kindness here, only evil.

She had told that story to Estefan.

She turned and ran to her left, suddenly convinced there was an exit there. She had to follow Jamie, stop him, save him. She made another left, and another. Then she slammed into another mirrored wall. The disarming device she held in her hands went skidding away, and Estefan's face loomed larger and larger.

"You can't escape me, *borachín*. I'm everywhere."

"No!" she screamed in fear and rage.

"*Sí.* And my friends are far more powerful than yours, so there is no protection for you."

Her reflection blurred, disappeared, reappeared. She pulled back.

And there, in a mirror in the far corner, an image shivered briefly, and Skye realized she was seeing Estefan's thoughts, thoughts he didn't want her to see. She focused on the image, struggling to ignore his leering face, which appeared in every other one.

It was fuzzy, but she pushed, and slowly it became clearer, until finally she could see the vampire Aurora, bending over a man who seemed unconscious. Skye shifted slightly, and then his face too came into focus. Skye trembled. Antonio. Aurora really did have him. It was Antonio and not Eriko who had been captured.

And not by Dantalion.

And they weren't in the palace.

Jamie was about to sacrifice himself for nothing.

Suddenly the image vanished. Estefan's laughing rippled in surprise and quickly turned to rage.

"I'll teach you to reach inside my mind!" he roared, his voice rattling the mirrors.

"Skye!"

A different voice called to her from far away. *Who is it?* She had to get out of the maze. Why didn't Estefan just kill her instead of toying with her?

Because he can't, she realized at last.

Because he isn't really here. He's only inside my head.

Skye took another look around and realized that the mirror maze was the exact one she had been trapped in as a child. It wasn't real. It was just a memory.

"Skye!"

The voice was louder this time, and Skye recognized it as Holgar's. She twisted around, trying to see Holgar, and the minefield, and the dark, instead of Estefan, the mirrors, and the garish light. For just a moment the mirrors shimmered as if they would fall away, which provoked a laugh from Estefan before they solidified again.

"So, you finally figured out this place isn't real?" he asked. "A little slow, *borachín*."

Skye screamed in frustration, and ran, focusing on a mirror in the distance, willing it to disappear. It began to pulsate, as though fading in and out of reality. She called up all that was within her and threw herself forward faster, until her left boot landed on a bit of metal that made a loud click.

A mine!

Petrified, she tried to stop herself, her right foot sliding out from underneath her, and she began to fall.

I'm dead.

Then something hit her with tremendous force and speed. She heard an explosion and felt wind rush by her, driving bits of dirt into her eyes and mouth. When she hit the ground hard, something heavy fell half on top of her, knocking the wind from her lungs and cracking one of her ribs.

Skye's lids fluttered against the stinging of the dirt in her eyes, and they teared up. When her vision finally cleared, Holgar was lying on her, whining quietly.

"Holgar! Are you okay?" she asked, fear washing over her.

"Unfortunately, I'll live," he groaned, sliding off her but staying on his stomach.

She sat up and saw that his back was a bloody mess, embedded with bits of shrapnel.

"What did you do?" she asked, her distress so great that when she brought her hands over his back she couldn't think of a single healing incantation.

"He knocked you off the bomb you were standing on," Jenn said quietly from a few feet away. "You dropped this while you were out of it." Jenn lifted one of the two disarming devices she was holding.

"No human could have done that with enough speed and strength to save you both," Noah said softly. "Lucky for us that you're not."

"I've always thought so," Holgar wheezed. He pushed himself up and tried to stand, then collapsed back onto the ground with a high-pitched cry that sounded like an injured animal.

"You broke that ankle," Taamir said. "You won't be any good to travel."

"Never underestimate a werewolf," Holgar said through gritted teeth.

Skye moved her hands over his ankle. *Goddess, help him,* she silently prayed.

"Or a witch," Holgar added. "She'll fix me up."

"We don't have a prayer of catching up to Jamie," Jenn said. "But we have to go in after him."

"Three minutes," Skye asked, working as fast as she could.

This was Estefan's fault. He had done this to her and put Holgar in harm's way. It was bad enough that he wanted to hurt her, but now he had hurt Holgar, and she could feel the rage building within her. It wasn't good; it distracted her from helping Holgar heal.

She breathed in, trying to feel the earth beneath the layer of snow that was quickly turning crimson around him. Every second that she lost to her anger was a second more that Holgar was bleeding and in pain, a second more that Jamie was alone and in trouble.

Jamie, we're coming. Don't do anything stupid before we get there.

*　*　*

Jamie knew it was stupid, but he went in through the front door. Alarms were going off, and the place appeared to be on red alert. Stupid blighters didn't even bother to lock the door when they were under attack. Maybe that was their exit strategy.

He made his way toward the stairwell and stopped a moment to study an evacuation plan mounted on the wall. It was in Russian, and he couldn't read any of it, but a giant red arrow pointed out the door he had just come through. Since no one seemed to be coming his way, he figured they were either holed up somewhere else or using an entirely different exit.

Svika had mentioned underground tunnels leading in and out of the building. And the basement was where he'd go if he were expecting an attack.

Smart money said that they'd have Eriko down there and not aboveground where she might throw someone out a window. And then jump to freedom. That was his girl.

He kicked open the door to the stairwell and ran down, taking them two at a time. The door on the next landing was made of reinforced steel and locked. Jamie gave it a tentative kick before continuing downward, encountering one sealed door after another, much to his frustration.

At the bottom of the stairs there was an unlocked door. Jamie ran through it, crouching low, gun in one hand, stake in another. Red flashing lights illuminated the hallway, and he saw a few people, or maybe Cursers, in lab coats, scurrying around at the far end.

Why do I keep ending up in the labs of mad scientists? he wondered, heading down the hall away from the people. The first two rooms he passed were offices with papers scattered about. The third held rows and rows of freezers and benches with high-powered microscopes and beakers and test tubes. Along the wall, text scrolled across the screens on a bank of computers, and a nearby printer spat paper at an impossible rate.

No sign of Eriko.

Jamie moved on to the next room. The door was closed. Jamie braced himself, then flung it open and stepped inside.

The room resembled a hospital ward with rows and rows of cots. Bodies lay on the cots, sheets tucked up to their chins. Sleeping, dead, or comatose, Jamie couldn't tell. He walked slowly down the ranks, scanning each face for Eriko. Or even Antonio.

The first few appeared human, but as he walked, the creatures in the beds began to resemble those they had fought in the woods, all fangs and twisted features. They appeared to be in comas, tubes running in and out of them.

Janie heard a strange hissing and picked up speed, desperate to find Eriko so they could torch the place and get out of there.

He turned to the next cot and froze as a pair of eyes met his gaze.

It was a girl, no more than eight. Her pupils dilated in

fear as she stared at him. There were straps over the blanket that covered her, pinning her down to the bed. IVs were hooked up to both of her arms, and there were fang marks up and down her throat. Tears slid out of her eyes and down her cheeks. She opened her mouth, and he could see that her tongue had been cut out.

He swore and moved to her side, quickly unbuckling the straps that held her down. As he grabbed the last one, he heard a noise behind him, and spun to see a man in a doctor's coat, his hands raised above his head as if to show that he was unarmed.

The man spoke in Russian over the clanging of the alarms, and Jamie shook his head.

"English, lad," Jamie said.

"I wouldn't do that if I were you," the man said in English.

Jamie covered the man with his gun, trying to decide whether or not to shoot him. "And why is that?" he asked as he flipped the last buckle open.

In an instant the girl jumped on Jamie, clawing at his face.

"Hey!" Jamie shouted, trying to pry her off.

She grew fangs before his eyes. Her mouth clacking, she strained to bite him. Jamie screamed and jumped backward. Then he managed to throw her clear.

She landed on the ground on all fours and made a horribly breathy sound—a hiss without a tongue. Her knees bent the other way, like an animal's, and her hands and feet were tipped with six-inch talons.

The girl turned, saw the doctor, and threw herself at him, sinking her fangs into his throat. Jamie opened fire on them both, killing the doctor before she could. Then, while she was recovering from the gunfire, Jamie staked her. As she slowly turned to dust before his eyes, she gave him a ghostly smile.

Sick to the bottom of his soul, Jamie turned and ran the rest of the length of the room, scanning the beds for Eriko and Antonio until he reached a set of bassinets. He could hear strange cries coming from the infants, but he squeezed his eyes shut, unwilling to see what was inside. He turned and staggered out of the room.

He had to find Eriko, kill this Dantalion, and blow up this place. No one could see this. No one could repeat this. It had to end here and now.

She could have been my little sister, he thought, the girl's face coming back to him and merging with his memory of Maeve. Jamie tried to push the image away, but couldn't. He faltered as he turned a corner and came to another set of doors. He didn't want to know what was behind any of them.

Then someone grabbed him and slammed him into the wall, clamping a hand over his mouth.

CHAPTER TEN

Faces lifted to the sky
The silvery moon hears our cry
Laugh or cry it matters not
Dead now those whom we have fought
Servant, master, all a name
Power, politics, just a game
For we're entwined, every part
Spirit, mind, flesh, and heart

SALAMANCA
FATHER JUAN

Father Juan woke suddenly from a deep sleep. He had been dreaming of his childhood, after his father died, when he and his mother and siblings had been living on the streets, doing whatever work they could find, going hungry. Those times had taught him much, toughened him physically and mentally, and given him a spiritual strength that had served him well.

They also taught him the value of home. For years the university had been his home, the place that sheltered him when he fought his own fears and dreamed dreams that were still as prophetic and mystical as those of his youth. He turned on his side, savoring the feel of the pillow beneath his head. Home was where you were safe and comforted. His little room was all his; more than just a place to rest his body, it was a sanctuary for spirit and mind.

He took a deep breath, inhaling the scent of incense, and *knew* as surely as if an angel had whispered in his ear:

Someone had invaded his sanctuary.

Someone who meant to kill him.

Father Juan sat up just as a knife arced through the air toward him. With a shout he grabbed the wrist that wielded it and twisted it sideways. The skin was warm to the touch—a human. *Who? How?*

His attacker was off balance, and his body followed as Juan wrenched his arm. The assailant fell to the ground hard, grunting as he did so. Without letting go of his wrist, Juan stood up and pressed his foot down on his assailant's neck, ready to break it at a moment's notice. The knife fell and skidded under the bed.

"Help!" Father Juan shouted, loud enough that he

would be heard by Diego, who was staying overnight in the room next door, but hopefully no others.

Seconds later Diego shot into his room. The bishop flipped the light switch and stood there in his pajamas. Father Juan squinted against the light and looked down at his attacker.

He gasped in dismay as he recognized the normally jovial features of Brother Manuel. Although the cook was grunting beneath the weight of Juan's foot, he made no effort to get away. He simply lay there passively, barrel chest heaving.

"What is going on?" Diego burst out.

"He tried to kill me," Father Juan said through clenched teeth. He pushed on his foot slightly, glaring down at the man who had cooked a thousand meals that he had trustingly eaten. "Tell me why."

"I was ordered to," Brother Manuel whispered.

"By whom?" Diego asked sharply, stepping forward. "Did a Cursed One put you up to this? What did they promise you, immortality?"

Manuel shook his head, as much as he could with Father Juan's foot still on his throat.

"Then what did they promise you?" Diego demanded.

Again Manuel shook his head.

"It wasn't a Cursed One, was it," Father Juan said quietly.

Manuel squeezed his eyes shut.

Diego turned to Father Juan. "You don't think—"

"I do," Father Juan said, heart and voice heavy. "One of us, someone from Rome, most likely."

"But, they *can't* have told him to harm you," Diego said incredulously. "Shut us down, yes. Force us out, probably, but *kill* you?"

It was not the first time Father Juan had been attacked by others of his kind for standing up for what was right. "It's an old tactic." He looked down at Brother Manuel, and he was filled with sorrow. Brother Manuel was a good man, but he didn't know how to question, how to stand up for himself. He was at the Salamanca academy because he'd been told it was his duty, not because he believed it was his sacred calling, above and apart from even his calling as a priest.

Father Juan eased his foot up enough to let the man talk. "How many others were you supposed to kill?"

"Just you," Manuel said, his voice tinged with genuine regret. "They believed that without you the rest would obey."

Father Juan closed his eyes. *Obey*. It was a word that had enslaved countless generations. One that he had fought against time and time again. It was the antithesis of responsibility, individuality, conscience.

"What do we do with him?" Diego asked, deferring, as was his wont in times of crisis, to Father Juan.

"We send him back to Rome," Father Juan said with a

sigh. "A pity, too. He was a good cook, and he didn't mind feeding the werewolf."

It was a joke, a poor one, but a joke nonetheless. Holgar would have been delighted. The werewolf was clearly rubbing off on him.

He thought of his team out in the field and said a prayer for them. He wouldn't tell them of this. They needed to believe in the academy, believe it was a sanctuary, as he once had. He would make it safe for them, even if it would never again be safe for him.

RUSSIA
TEAM SALAMANCA MINUS ANTONIO AND ERIKO; TAAMIR AND NOAH

"What are you doing here?" hissed the man who had grabbed Jamie. Speaking English. *American* English, through the vocal distorter of a gas mask. He was dressed all in black, and he had on a silver helmet emblazoned with a black Jerusalem cross.

"Bloody well the same as you, I figure," Jamie shot back.

"I very much doubt it. Get out of here before you screw it up. Go!"

"Not until I find my girl."

"The Hunter? She's not here."

"How do you know?"

"Dantalion's monsters didn't bring anyone back with them."

If that was true, then maybe Eriko and Antonio had sent the fang gang running.

"But there's a male witch, yeah?" Jamie asked.

"No, no witches here except yours," the man replied. "Come with me. Poison gas is coming in through the ducts, and he's set the place to blow. Thinks his handlers are on their way."

"Dantalion might know where she is," Jamie said.

"He'll be dead in five minutes," the man replied. "You will too. Let's go."

Jamie was about to argue with the man when they heard steps running down the hall from the same direction Jamie had come. Helmet dragged Jamie through an open doorway a foot away. Three beasties—huge fangs, rubbery lips, bloodshot eyes, and horribly misshapen bodies—streaked past them. Before the other guy could say anything, Jamie twisted out of his grasp and charged after the trio.

His eyes began to water, his lungs to burn. The guy was right; there was something in the air.

Wherever the beasties were going, they were in such a hurry that they didn't notice they were being followed. Jamie trailed a few steps behind as they twisted through the corridors. He tried to keep the layout straight in his head so he'd be able to get back out again, but he was having trouble focusing. His lungs were on fire, and his eyes were tearing up so he could barely see. Poison gas could kiss his ass.

Jamie picked up speed as the trio skittered down a hallway into darkness. Jamie bounded after them, then came to a T-junction. Light spilled from a doorway on his right. Slowing, hugging the wall, he moved closer. Behind him he could hear quiet footfalls, and he risked a glance over his shoulder. Helmet guy was coming up behind him. Jamie turned back, fixating on the doorway. He couldn't hear over the alarms, and crept closer.

"—hell happened?" It was a male voice with a thick Russian accent. He was speaking in English. Lucky break for Jamie. "Where are all the *matroyshkas*?"

"Two hunters took them down." More English, very American.

"The two men from the Middle East?" said the thick Russian voice.

"No. A vampire and a little Asian girl."

Antonio and Eriko!

"Where'd they come from?" asked the Russian.

A creature jumped Helmet. The two grappled. Helmet gained the upper hand, so Jamie stayed planted, listening.

"Unknown. They're no longer a problem. The other vampires took the vampire."

"*Other* vampires? What are you saying?" asked the Russian.

"The vampire with long black hair?" the American replied.

233

Aurora, Jamie thought. *She's here? She got Antonio? But Eri, what about Eri?*

"*What?*" the Russian said. "Who?"

"Yeah, I thought they were with you. Well, anyway, after they took the vampire into custody, they killed the girl."

Jamie blinked. Eriko. His breath stopped. Eriko.

Eriko, *dead?*

Rage tore away his sight, his thoughts. "*No!*" he bellowed, seeing nothing, feeling nothing as his reflexes took over.

If Eri was dead, then so was everyone else.

Jamie leaped into the room, and suddenly saw everything in ultrasharp focus. A white-haired vampire in jeans and a black sweater sat at a computer terminal. A man in white cammies and a gas mask was standing in front of him.

Then, from another door in the back, the three monsters charged into the room. They headed straight for Jamie. Jamie sprayed all three with his machine gun, but they kept coming. He dropped the weapon and jumped forward, staking each of them in turn.

"Get me out of here!" the Russian—the vampire—shouted at the man in the white cammies.

"First send Solomon the data. *All* the data," said White Cammies, moving backward, putting both Jamie and the vampire in his line of fire.

"Don't be an idiot!" the vampire yelled.

"Now!" the man bellowed.

The white-haired vampire typed frantically. The white-cammie man fired and nearly took off Jamie's left foot. Jamie flung himself behind a metal shelf, listening to the ping of gunfire as the man strafed him.

"Get out!" hissed Helmet Guy as he darted behind the shelves, crouching down beside Jamie. He handed Jamie the machine gun he'd dropped. "We want the vampire. That's Dantalion!"

The guy in the white cammies sprayed bullets at Helmet and Jamie.

"It's sent!" the white-haired vampire shouted.

Then the poison hit Jamie. It seared his eyes, his face, his nose. Everything fell away. He couldn't feel, didn't know if he was moving. Inching forward, he patted his jacket pockets. *Grenades*, he thought. *In my pocket. Eri.*

Then someone screamed, "Detonator!"

Eri, Jamie thought.

Darkness. Pain. Cold.

A growl pierced the ringing in his ear. Holgar?

Jamie looked up. A Russian wolfhound was staring down at him as he lay sprawled in the snow.

Jamie dropped his head back. Damn it. Goddamn them all. The Cursers and the war and the werewolves and just feckin' everybody.

The dog grabbed his sleeve in its teeth and tried to pull

him through the snow. With a harsh sob Jamie staggered to his feet and stumbled after the dog into the night. Jamie was sopping wet and covered with ash. He prayed to the Blessed Virgin that it was all that was left of Dantalion. Had he pulled a grenade? He couldn't remember.

It didn't matter. Because Eri was dead.

The animal began to bark and veered sharply to the left. Maybe the dog had come with people looking for survivors. Jamie slammed into a tree, spinning around to see flames and oily black smoke shooting into the air. Screams and explosions from the palace formed a wall of sound.

He fell down, unable to move. It didn't matter, if she was dead. Of course she was dead. Everyone he cared about was dead.

A minute later the dog began to bark in a frenzy. He'd caught the scent of something.

Silhouetted against the red and black, Holgar ran toward Jamie.

The dog lunged forward at the sight of him, and for a moment Jamie thought it was going to try and tear out the wolfman's throat. Instead the dog began to lick Holgar's hands and face in welcome.

"Jamie!" Skye burst out, lurching forward from behind a tree. "Jamie, oh, my God, what's happened to you?"

"Did you get him?" Noah asked, as the rest of the team—minus Antonio, minus Eriko—raced toward him.

For a moment Jamie couldn't make sounds come out of

his throat. And the first sound that did was a wail of fury.

"Eriko's dead." He couldn't move as tears and blood ran down his face. *"God."*

Stunned silence followed.

"What?" Jenn asked finally.

"The vampires killed her." His throat was raw.

More silence.

"How do you know?" Noah asked.

"Some American told Dantalion. Before the place blew."

"American?" Jenn echoed

"So you saw Dantalion? Is he dead?" Noah pressed.

"Blimey, give 'im a moment, will you?" Skye spat. "Look at him. He's half dead himself." She began to murmur a healing spell in Latin. He wanted to tell her not to bother.

"You didn't see a body?" Holgar asked.

"The place *blew*!" Jamie yelled.

"Not Dantalion's. Eriko's," Jenn said gently.

Jamie shook his head, trying not to fall apart in front of them.

"Eriko's strong," Jenn said softly. "She might have fooled them. We have to find her. Maybe she's okay after all."

He hated himself for glomming on to that slender hope. He nodded slowly.

"How'd you get out?" Noah asked him. "Someone help you?"

Ignoring him, Jamie sat up. "Does anyone know the way back?" he asked, taking a ragged breath.

"I do," Holgar said. He bent down and seemed to whisper to the dog for a moment. The animal disappeared into the night.

"What did you tell him?" Skye asked Holgar.

"I told him he was free to go find someone who could actually love him," Holgar said. Then he began to head off at a lope. Noah and Jenn reached down and each took one of Jamie's arms. Slowly they eased him to his feet.

Jamie began staggering along. And he couldn't help but think bitterly that at least the dog was going to get a happy ending.

It was a simple thing to trace his way back to where they had left Antonio and Eriko. As it turned out, though, it was a lot easier than even he had anticipated.

Holgar smelled blood, and lots of it. He took a deeper breath and underneath it all could smell Eriko. Her scent was still fresh, but fading as though she was retreating or . . .

"Skye!" he called. His partner scrambled to keep up with him as he raced forward. Holgar was going the right direction, but the scent was fading, only to be overtaken by another, most unpleasant one.

"What is it?" she gasped.

"She's dying. We've got a minute or less."

He could run far faster, but Eriko needed Skye's healing skills. He didn't have to say a word as silent understanding passed between them. Holgar swung Skye onto his back.

He hissed in pain at the contact with his wounds, which were still healing, but put on a burst of speed as he headed for a thicket of snow-covered trees.

"Eriko!" Skye cried, pointing straight ahead.

Holgar saw the shape of a human lying in the snow. As soon as they reached her side, Skye dropped off his back into a crouch next to the dying Hunter. Her hands began to fly over every cut, staunching the flow of blood that was carrying Eriko's life with it.

Holgar touched Skye's back, knowing that witches sometimes had ways to draw energy from other beings — defensive magicks — but not knowing if she could, or would, do it.

He could *feel* Skye's momentary hesitation, but his entire body began to tingle, and fatigue crept over him. His own body protested as its attempts to heal itself were placed on hold, the energy being diverted instead to Skye.

Holgar could scent the fear on the others as they approached. With an anguished cry Jamie collapsed to his knees next to Eriko's head, but wisely did not reach for her like he so obviously wanted to. Instead he began praying, his voice cracking, entreating every saint and Buddha and Allah and every other deity Holgar had ever heard of and then some to intervene on behalf of the dying girl. After a moment's hesitation, Taamir and Noah knelt on either side of Jamie and began to pray as well, one to Allah, one to Adonai. The three men's voices began to blend together, their words different but their faith strong and intertwining.

Holgar glanced up at Jenn, who stood there looking helpless. He knew that she questioned religion, and he could tell at that moment she desperately wished she could join her prayers with the others. But something held her back. She glanced down at him and saw the way he was touching Skye, and understanding lit her eyes. She carefully knelt beside him and placed her hand next to his on Skye's back, helping to fuel the young witch as she practiced the healing arts of her religion. All this to keep Eriko from prematurely experiencing one of the key elements of *her* religion: death and the subsequent reincarnation of the soul.

Skye's back felt hot where Holgar's hand was touching it, and the energy practically crackled from her fingertips as she worked. Jenn began to droop, and he very gently pushed her back, breaking the connection. Skye hunched her shoulders a little, but he knew she understood. It did no one any good if the efforts to save Eriko put Jenn in danger. It was taking its toll on him, as well, but he had more strength to give. Holgar dropped his head to his chest and dug deep.

When at last he was teetering on the verge of losing consciousness, the other three men eased him out of the way and offered their energy without even a breath's pause in their prayers.

Ten minutes later Skye removed her hand from Eriko. Everyone stopped, waiting for a sign.

"I think she's going to make it," Skye said, her voice hoarse. "We're going to need to stay here for a while, though, before we can move her."

"How long?" Jenn asked, her voice strained.

"I don't know," Skye said. "I'll work around the clock, Jenn. I'll make her better."

"I can stay with her. Maybe you lot should go after Aurora," Jamie offered.

"No," Jenn said, her voice quiet but firm. "We get in trouble when we split up. We'll stay until Eriko can travel. Besides, she's not the only one who needs to heal." She looked at Jamie.

"Then this is our place. Our ground," Jamie said. He reached up and yanked his tattered Salamanca patch from his shoulder, jabbing it into the snow.

"We didn't put down our flag in New Orleans," Skye said.

"We failed New Orleans," Jenn murmured.

"I don't know what happened here," Jamie said. He looked at the smoky sky. "Wonder if there's survivors. Ain't gonna look."

Skye trailed a fingertip down Eriko's forehead. "We need to take care of our own."

Holgar nodded, then with a sigh lay down, cheek to the snow, wishing like anything he were a wolf and not a man, even as the dawn spread its rays in the east and the reign of the night came to an end.

Jamie, ever so gently, lay down next to Eriko and stroked her hair while Jenn, Taamir, and Noah made quiet plans. Skye turned and looked at Holgar, eyes full of pain, and he lifted up an arm. She hesitated for only a moment and then scooted over next to him before lying down, using his arm as a pillow. Her body was tense, as though she were unsure about the contact.

"I didn't bring them here; I didn't," she said. He heard the pleading for understanding—and perhaps for forgiveness—in her voice. "I should have spoken up about *him* before, but I didn't know he was working with Aurora."

"Get some rest," Holgar whispered and she nodded.

"I should have—"

"Shh. We all have secrets, *min lille heks*." He stroked her back as she slowly relaxed.

Including me, he thought.

Skye lay still, feeling the warmth of Holgar beside her, wishing she had the strength to heal him. He had saved both her and Eriko, and she knew he was in excruciating pain from his wounds. Even his ankle wasn't fully healed. She could tell from the way he'd run when he was carrying her.

How had everything gone so horribly, horribly wrong? The lab was destroyed; that was a good thing. Dantalion had been stopped for good. Mission accomplished. But at what cost?

Antonio knew everything about the resistance cells they had been gathering information on across the world. People who were already risking their lives by standing up to the Cursed Ones were in even greater danger now that Aurora had captured Antonio. The Salamancan hunters had to rescue him before something happened. By now, though, Aurora and Antonio were long gone. And so was Estefan. She hadn't felt him in her mind since Holgar had saved her. It was a relief, but it worried her because she was pretty sure they were now far away.

Where are they taking Antonio? She thought about her glimpse into Estefan's mind. She tried to focus it. The mind was a strange thing. It could show you perfect replicas of certain memories, like the house of mirrors. Other times it presented images that were tinted by emotions and context, almost like impressionist paintings. She stared closely at the vision of Aurora and Antonio held in her memory, trying to tell if there was anything else she had seen in Estefan's mind at that time.

Goddess, help me to remember, she prayed silently. She breathed deeply in and out, to cleanse herself of fear, anger, uncertainty, even the sensation of Holgar's warm arm beneath her cheek. She tried to focus on that image, tried to put herself in it.

What had Estefan been thinking of Aurora and Antonio at that moment? Aurora was standing, while Antonio lay unconscious at her feet. She was clearly the victor. She was the master, and Antonio was the servant. And there, behind Aurora, had been a shadow. It was Estefan, laughing at Antonio's plight, himself victorious because Aurora was victorious. Himself a master because she was a master.

Fascinating, but it told her nothing that she wanted to know. Skye sighed. When she woke she'd cast the runes, see if she could get a sense of the direction that they might have traveled. Though something told her they were heading back to America.

Why? Was it because that was where she'd seen Aurora before, so she associated her with America? Why not Spain, since Aurora was Spanish? She could be anywhere on the planet. China, Australia, Alaska to see the aurora borealis.

Alaska. America. Aurora borealis. Swirling, pretty lights. Natural lights. Not like the lights they would be seeing. Not like the lights reflected in Aurora's eyes.

Skye focused on the image again. There were lights reflected in Aurora's eyes. She concentrated as hard as she could, trying to empty herself completely, trying to decipher the picture.

There was a word. A word spelled out in the lights. It meant something to Estefan. It was what he thought of Antonio and Aurora together. Where they were, no, where they were going.

The word was . . .

"Mei," Solomon said to his assistant as she was shown in to his home office. He was writing an e-mail at his desk. Solomon had a lot of desks in a lot of offices. This one was made entirely of glass — glass desk, glass chair with black cushions, black leather sofa, glass block fireplace. Spare. Very New Hollywood.

He also had lots of assistants. He just seemed to run through them so *fast*. But he had taken an interest in Chinese hottie Mei. Fangs a bit extended, he smiled approvingly at her bat-with-heart necklace. Everyone was wearing them. Even vampires.

As he hit send, he gestured for her to sit on the couch. "Please."

She complied. "You said you needed to speak to me right away?"

Although she was smiling, he could see she was afraid. That didn't surprise him. Most humans were afraid of him. The smart ones, anyway. Which left him with an interesting dilemma: Should he and Danny start testing on the smart ones or the dumb ones first?

"Here's the deal. We're going to start shooting the Russian section of *History*."

"Russia?" she cut in, shifting nervously. "I didn't know we were planning a Russian section."

"It's been under . . . development." He sat next to her. Her heart was thundering. "So this is what I'm pondering—casting the parts. We'll have to make sure we use an international superstar for the lead. It's a vampire named Dantalion. Heard of him?"

She shook her head.

"You will. But as we go on down the food chain, so to speak, I'm wondering how many actors we ship over there versus looking around in Russia, maybe some of those other countries over there—Lithuania, Mongolia. Thoughts?"

Mei crossed her legs and played with her necklace. He figured she was dying for him to change her into a Cursed One.

"Can you tell me more about Dantalion? What's the Russian part about?" she asked.

"I'm waiting for confirmation on the script right now." He couldn't help a chuckle.

Ping. He glanced at his in-box. Well, well, well, speak of the devil. The new message was from Dantalion's lab. His Danny boy. *Kruta.*

"Hold that thought, Mei." He clicked on the attachment icon. A folder opened with dozens and dozens of attachments, and each was so massive they were probably going to eat up all his memory. He looked at the names of some of the files, labeled in Russian and English, like all Dantalion's reports on the hybrid project. The attachments kept downloading. It looked like it was all of Dantalion's files, as if he had sent the entire contents of his computer to Solomon.

Good. Solomon had told his people to promise to rescue Dantalion once he hit the panic button, if and *only* if he sent Solomon all the data.

Promise to rescue, but not deliver on the promise.

His phone should ring any second.

It did.

"Mei," he said, looking up.

She'd been politely staring at the fireplace. She jerked and flashed a cautious smile at him.

"Go find something to do."

"Okay, Solomon," she said. "Sure."

He connected to the caller.

"Dantalion has been neutralized, sir," an American voice said on the other end of the line.

"Killed," Solomon confirmed.

"Yes, sir."

"No complications?"

"Black crosses attempted to extricate him. They were repulsed."

"Excellent. I'll expect a full debriefing in an hour."

"Very good, sir."

The line went dead.

The files continued to download.

RUSSIA
TEAM SALAMANCA MINUS ANTONIO;
TAAMIR AND NOAH

Using Noah's "smoking room"—a cave—as temporary shelter, Jenn checked in with Father Juan via Noah's radiophone, and he confirmed that they had to put as much distance as possible between themselves and the smoking ruins of the palace as soon as they could. She glanced around at her sleeping teammates and decided that in late afternoon they would take the truck and head for the nearest village.

She confessed to Father Juan that they had no idea if Dantalion was dead.

Same with Antonio.

Late afternoon came, and Jenn was the first member of the team awake, for the simple reason that she hadn't slept. She had replayed the disaster over and over in her mind, trying to figure out how she might have done things differently, all so she could try to keep from thinking about the fact that Antonio had been captured. She couldn't think about it yet, wouldn't think about it yet. If she did, she wouldn't be any good to anyone. And first they had to get out of Russia.

Is Dantalion dead? Did the black-cross guys show up because they'd been following us? Who are they?

Late in the evening she walked about a quarter mile from their camp and checked back in with Father Juan.

She conferred about her team's injuries, asking if he had heard anything, scryed, or had a vision that would tell them what to do.

Nothing.

"So, do you have a plan yet?" he asked her.

She was caught off guard. She had expected him to tell her the plan. She hadn't expected him to leave the next move up to her.

She took a deep breath. "We have to get Antonio back or . . . stop him from telling Aurora what he knows." She was a coward; she couldn't bring herself to say *kill him*. Not yet.

"Bueno," he said. "Now the mission is defined. If you need anything, call my cell. Don't call my office number."

"Are you away from the university?" she asked.

"Not exactly," he said, after a pause.

His response piqued her curiosity, but she had learned when she first started at the academy that there was no getting information out of Father Juan until he was ready to share it. She would just have to wait. After she hung up, she returned to their camp, and found Noah quietly heating some rations over a fire. He was smoking a cigarette. Without thinking, she waved her hand to dissipate the smoke.

He smiled at her and dropped the cigarette into the fire. Flushing, she crouched next to him and smiled faintly back. It felt like a bit of a miracle, after the death of Svika and the loss of Antonio, that either of them could smile. She took it as a good omen for the future.

"We're going after Antonio," she said quietly, so as not to wake the others.

"I know."

"What will you and Taamir do now?" she asked.

"Well, Jenn," he said. "That's up to you."

She raised a brow. "Aren't you needed back home?"

"Everyone is needed everywhere," he said. "But we're here. With you." He gazed steadily at her.

A warm tingle played at the small of her back. She thought maybe she should discuss the possibility with the others. Noah and Taamir were great fighters, and though she felt a momentary pang at adding outsiders to their little group, she realized that there was no cohesion to the Salamanca team anyway and the addition of the two could only help them. Maybe it would even give them a little more discipline, though as her eyes drifted to Jamie, she sincerely doubted it.

"We could use you," she said.

"You already did. You should have told us that Antonio was a vampire," he said.

She felt herself go white. He gave her a little confirming nod.

"Yes, I know. When he and Eriko volunteered to stay behind, I saw a flash of red in his eyes, and his fangs came out, just a little," he said.

"But you didn't say anything."

Noah shrugged. "He was on your team. You're his leader."

"Yeah. And he's been captured."

He put his hand under her chin and raised it. There were tan lines around his eyes. This was a guy who spent a lot of time in the sun.

"We'll get him back." She was aware of his touch. She was lonely and scared, and she needed arms around her, someone's shoulder to cry on. She could tell he knew it, and would welcome it if she went to him. He was warm, and brave, and here. And he was human.

"Thanks," she said, pulling away. "I need to check on everyone."

"Anytime." He looked at her steadily. "Just say the word."

She moved away and went back into the cave. Everyone was swaddled in sleeping bags. Eriko was breathing more easily than she had the night before. Holgar's back, though hideous-looking in the sunlight, seemed to be healing well. Jamie's mottled skin was beginning to scab over.

Skye's eyelids flickered, and then she sat up suddenly, her eyes zeroing in on Jenn's. "I know where Aurora has taken Antonio," she said.

Jenn felt her heart skip a beat. "What?"

"I saw it."

"Where?"

"Her new stronghold. Las Vegas."

LAS VEGAS
ANTONIO AND AURORA

"You might as well kill me," Antonio panted. "I'll never tell you anything."

Aurora made a clucking sound. "Do you really think that's why you're here? Information? No, I have other ways, easier ways of getting that."

She sat back in her white satin chair. Everything in her suite was white—walls, furnishings, carpet.

"Then what do you want from me?" Antonio gasped. He was bound between two pillars in the foyer, dangling above a white marble floor.

"You're going to be a little present," she said, resting a hand beside his head. "Sergio's little lost lamb, the one he couldn't find and bring home."

Antonio felt sick at the mention of his sire, at the monster who had made him a Cursed One.

Aurora was wearing a tight white dress with gold accents that made her look like a Grecian goddess. Slowly, sensuously, she pulled a dagger out from a holster strapped to her thigh and held it up for Antonio to see.

"This blade is so sharp it can cut through anything," she purred. "I've been testing it out, trying to find a flaw, a weakness, but so far—"

She made several swift swipes, and his shirt hung in tatters. She pressed the tip of the blade against his chest just above his heart and drew a line downward, then crossed it with another one in a mockery of him and his beliefs.

"It cuts through everything," she said as she plunged it into the middle of the cross and pierced muscle and bone to stab his heart.

Antonio screamed with pain as he felt his putrid blood flowing out along the blade. The knife was silver, not wood, so the impact did not kill him, but he had never felt pain so intense before. It made his entire body tremble.

"Antonio, the priest; Antonio, the good vampire; Antonio, the hunter. All of these you are, and yet I think there is one title that cuts more deeply. I think you are Antonio, the man in love with Jenn."

He jerked at the mention of her name, and the blood flowed more quickly along the blade.

"You know, that's what people don't understand. Sure, you chose to stop killing years before she was even born, but I think she was always here, in your heart," Aurora said. "That's why you don't break; that's why you don't bend; that's why you don't succumb to the bloodlust that is your nature, even when a spell is cast on you."

His thoughts flew to New Orleans, where he had struggled to control himself and the desire to kill Jenn, to drink her blood. He had thought it was because she was eroding his self-control. Had it really been a spell instead? That was part of why he had been keeping his distance from her. He was terrified that he would hurt Jenn, the closer they became to each other.

Aurora pulled the knife from Antonio's chest, and it hurt just as much as getting stabbed. He bit his tongue in agony. The wound began to heal quickly, but Antonio felt a little sick and weak, more than for a wound anyplace else. Aurora watched as the skin sealed over until he was whole again.

When the pain stopped, Antonio sagged against his restraints, relief flooding him.

"So, you would endure anything for her, deny your nature for her, be anything for her," Aurora continued.

"I would die for Jenn," he said, lifting his head defiantly. That was something no one could take away from him. He loved her, and he would give everything for her, sacrifice himself without thought to save her.

"I know you would," Aurora said, as she traced the tip of the blade over his chest and down his stomach. "I can't decide if it's romantic or pathetic, to be honest."

"It's what separates me from the animals, my capacity for self-sacrifice."

She laughed. "Spoken like a good priest. Only, are you referencing us when you talk about animals?"

Her eyes began to glow red, her fangs to lengthen. She looked like an animal, a wild, rabid animal who would kill him in a moment if he said or did something, anything, to upset her, or even nothing at all.

"You are less than an animal," he said.

She smiled. "Sergio doesn't understand how you feel. He doesn't understand your compassion for humanity, your longing to be one of them. He doesn't understand that Jenn is in your heart. He thinks that killing her will change everything. I disagree. Do you know what I say?"

"What?" Antonio whispered, fear for Jenn racing through him until he couldn't think straight.

"I say, since she's in your heart, don't kill her."

Aurora plunged the knife back into his heart and began to twist it.

"Cut her out."

CHAPTER ELEVEN

Sometimes the hardest thing you have to do is fight
when you'd rather just give up. You can't give up.
No matter what. Not even if your heart is breaking.
Not even if everything and everyone you love has
been taken from you. You must keep going. Because
sometimes, the fight is all you have.

—*from the diary of Jenn Leitner,*
discovered in the ashes

LAS VEGAS
TEAM SALAMANCA MINUS ANTONIO;
TAAMIR AND NOAH

Holgar couldn't help but stare. He had never seen anything like Las Vegas in his life. As they exited the plane, he

gaped in amazement at the bright, clanging slot machines that filled the airport. There were neon lights and scantily dressed women, both human and Curser, everywhere. Taamir looked like he was going to faint. Noah was steadily taking it all in.

"And this is only the *airport*?" Jamie asked in amazement.

Holgar was right there with him. He had heard stories of Sin City, grown so much more sinful now that the Cursed Ones had turned it into a stronghold, but he had a feeling that nothing could have prepared him for the reality.

Mixed couples—Cursed Ones and humans—held hands, kissed, touched. Heads were thrown back, and vampires sucked. The Salamancans and their two allies traded wary glances.

"Everyone's got bat necklaces," Jenn murmured, and she was right. Everywhere he turned, there were all manner of glittering necklaces on throbbing bosoms. "It means you only hook up with Cursed Ones," she told Noah and Taamir.

"Yes, we have them too," Noah said.

"'Hook up,'" Holgar echoed. "That's so American."

"Hook up, die, whatever," Jenn muttered.

"What the—," he heard Jamie say, and he turned to look. There was a long granite bar dotted with tall lacquered bar stools. A vampiric bartender in full fangs held out what looked like a hookah to two giggling young women. Behind him, backlit by an illuminated mirror veined in crimson, large clear cisterns bubbled with red liquid. The bartender cast no reflection.

"Blimey, it's a blood bar," Skye said, wrinkling up her nose in disgust.

"A what?" Taamir asked, looking nauseated.

"Like any other kind of bar, but instead of selling sake or beer, they sell different types of blood," Eriko said. "They started in Japan, I think."

"Look at those two. They're human," Skye said, horror filling her voice as she pointed at the young women at the bar. "They're not actually going to drink blood, are they?"

"The rules have changed," Eriko murmured.

"Or maybe not," Taamir said quietly. Holgar realized that prewar Vegas would have been too much for the conservative man's sensibilities, never mind the city's current state of decadence.

"Let's keep moving," Holgar suggested.

"Yes. Remain unnoticed," Jenn said crisply.

She missed Antonio, and she was terrified about what might be happening to him. Holgar understood that and did his best to hurry the others along. Of all of them he understood best how to nonverbally manipulate people. Wolves had complex codes of gestures and body language, and werewolves used them to their advantage in their dealings with regular humans.

Complying with his unspoken demands, they picked

up their pace. Outside the airport they caught a limo that would carry all of them. Even Eriko, who was still recuperating, gawked at the hugeness of the enormous neon signs flashing and strobing to entice the crowds. And the casinos! A castle boasted turrets and pennants; another was a pirate lagoon; a third looked like the city of New York.

"So extreme," Taamir said.

"So America," Jamie added. Then he turned to Skye. "You're absolutely positive that your boyfriend's not tracking us through you?"

"Yes," she said quietly. She'd been very contrite about the Dark Witch named Estefan Montevideo. "And I've created magickal wards around myself and all of you to be doubly sure."

"Wards?" Noah asked.

"Walls," she explained. "Barriers."

"So you didn't have them up before because . . . ?" Noah persisted.

"I have, on and off," she said defensively. "Magick costs, Noah."

"So does nearly killing your own teammate," Jamie said.

"Enough," Jenn said.

The van left the heart of the flashing casino district for the more sedate Desert Blossom, the hotel where they would be staying. They'd have adjoining rooms, one for the girls and one for the guys. Jenn had picked it to keep them under the radar. Holgar wondered if anything in Vegas could be considered under the radar. How on earth were they going to find Antonio?

He glanced at Jenn and could tell from her wide eyes and ashen expression that she was wondering the same thing. He felt for her. It was hard to be in love sometimes, harder still when you were separated by distance. Worse when you were separated by philosophy.

Gribskov, Denmark, Three Years Earlier
Holgar

Holgar awoke on the soft forest floor in a slow, hazy way. He was naked except for a pile of leaves that had fallen on him while he slept. Around him other members of his pack were slowly stirring or whimpering in the last minutes of sleep. The moon had been full the night before, and the pack had run together. Holgar ran his tongue over his gums, savoring the coppery aftertaste that confirmed that he had hunted and killed prey.

"Good morning," a young female voice said from a few feet away.

Holgar rolled over. Kirstinne lounged on the forest floor nearby. Her long blond hair cascaded around her naked body, and he watched as she stretched and yawned. She was beautiful and perfect in every way. He felt the familiar desire stirring inside him, and he whined low in his throat.

"Good morning," he replied.

"It was a fantastic hunt last night," she said, as she slowly sat up.

"It was," he said lazily.

"Like a dream, a wonderful, awesome dream," she said wistfully.

She crawled over to him and sat scratching his back. He contracted slightly so her blood-encrusted fingernails raked along his shoulder blades. Holgar sighed with pleasure. She bent over and kissed him, her tongue sliding into his mouth to tease him. He licked her cheeks eagerly.

Werewolves, like their wild counterparts, mated for life. And Kirstinne was his betrothed. They had been raised together, and they would be joined within the year. They would have a wedding for the mundane world to see, attend, and record. Then they would have a private ritual under the full moon, attended by their pack. When they made love for the first time it would be as wolves, as was tradition.

She was his and he was hers, and they could wait.

Both the man and the wolf in him yearned for that connection, that partnership, that foreverness. The way Kirstinne smiled at him, Holgar knew she yearned for it too. At sixteen they were still too young to properly raise cubs, though not by much.

A dozen feet away Holgar's father stood slowly, threw back his head, and howled. The older members of the pack answered in turn, while the younger ones, like Holgar and Kirstinne, could only manage a small, barking response while in human form.

Holgar and Kirstinne walked hand in hand to the duffel bags where they had stashed their clothes prior to transformation. One of his younger cousins ran over and playfully stomped on Holgar's foot. Holgar yipped and swung at him lazily. The boy darted away, laughing, and some of the younger girls giggled at his prank.

Life was good in the pack. Everyone knew their place and what was expected of them. From that came freedom to play, to laugh, to hunt—to just be. Holgar closed his eyes, savoring the smells of the forest and the scents of the other denizens who marked their path through it.

"Are you coming to Elsa's party tonight?" Kirstinne asked suddenly.

Holgar wrinkled his nose. Elsa was one of Kirstinne's closest friends, but she wasn't a werewolf. Nor did she know about them. Elsa's parties were always too loud, too hot, too crowded, and too full of smells. They made him sneeze, and his ears would often ring for a day afterward. And the worse offense of all? They weren't fun.

"I don't know," he said.

"Come on, this one's going to be special," Kirstinne said, and there was breathless excitement in her voice.

"Really? Why?"

"Yes. She's invited a Cursed One."

Holgar stumbled and caught himself. "Cursed Ones, here?" he asked.

"Yes. Apparently they're new to the area. Isn't that exciting?"

He cocked his head. "But Kirsti, they'll know what we are. They'll be able to smell us."

"So?" she asked with a shrug.

"What if they out us?"

She pulled her hand free of his and then wagged a finger in his face. "You worry too much, Holgar."

"Just because they want to go public doesn't mean we do. I mean, people are stupid enough to find their danger alluring. What about us? Half the world still fears normal wolves without reason. Do you think they'll find us sexy? No, they'll think we're monsters. I, for one, don't want to die from a silver bullet in my heart."

"That wouldn't happen," she said, rolling her eyes.

"Then why do you think werewolves have never staged a coming-out party? I'm not the only one who feels that way."

"Maybe because we don't have an international leader, like Solomon. Each pack has its own leader, and we don't interact with one another."

"Which makes it all the more dangerous. If people start hunting our pack, there's no one to help." He hated arguing with Kirstinne, but her casual attitude alarmed him. They had a comfortable life without anyone in their village knowing who they were. For centuries it had been that way. Why change it now?

He blamed the vampires. If they had stuck to the shadows, no one would have thought to do otherwise.

Kirstinne angled her head in a way that was both pleading and scolding. Holgar sighed. "I'll go to the party," he said. "I have, after all, been curious to meet a vampire myself."

She squealed and threw her arms around his neck. "You won't regret it!"

But Holgar did regret it. Twelve hours later, dressed casually in a Flight of the Conchords T-shirt, jeans, and sandals, he was standing with his back pressed against a wall in Elsa's kitchen when a Cursed One wearing all black came striding in. Black silk shirt, black jeans, black boots, black hair, black eyes. He looked like some weird emo goth.

Holgar crinkled his nose at the smell of rotting blood and death the creature exuded, which worsened as the vampire sidled up to him.

"Wolf?" it asked.

Holgar flinched inwardly but refused to give sign of it. "Yes."

The vampire smiled. "Also seeking prey?"

Holgar narrowed his eyes, not sure he took the vampire's meaning. "What?"

The vampire waved, gesturing to the room at large. "Which one of these lovelies will you feast upon tonight?"

"None," Holgar said, taken aback.

The man made a *tsk*-ing sound. "You should. They are, after all, ours for the taking. You and me, what carnage we could make, eh? We could divide up the girls for ourselves and then later torture the boys for fun."

Holgar felt like he was going to be sick. Staring into the creature's eyes, he knew the Cursed One was serious. He knew that they drank the blood of humans, but senseless killing was a far cry from feeding off donors.

The leader of the Cursed Ones, Solomon, had said that vampires could drink animal blood. Werewolves ate animals too, and didn't have to live off of humans.

At least that was the way it was supposed to work.

He tensed, trying not to let the memory back in. He'd buried it—or tried to—for years.

He and his father were chasing down a deer. A hunter stepped from behind a tree, his gun aimed in Holgar's direction.

Maybe the two wolves could have dashed for safety in time. Maybe the hunter was only pretending to line up the shot. Maybe he would have spared the wolf and gone after the deer instead.

No one would ever know.

Holgar's father had torn out the hunter's throat. But he hadn't stopped there. In a frenzy he'd ripped open the

265

body, his massive jaws clamping down on the heart—

Maybe werewolves and vampires weren't so different. *Not me. I don't kill people. I like people.*

The vampire surveyed the room greedily, his eyes glowing red. A gaggle of girls waved and giggled, and he waved back.

"That one," he said, pointing toward Elsa, "was kind enough to throw this party and invite me into her home. I'll kill her last."

Rage flooded Holgar. He had never particularly liked Elsa—she was so shallow—but she was Kirstinne's best nonpack friend, and he wouldn't see any harm come to her. To any of them.

"It's hot in here. Let's walk for a moment under the moon and talk," Holgar said, forcing himself to throw his arm around the vampire's shoulders.

"Whatever you say, my furry friend."

The night was balmy, the moon gauzy behind clouds. As soon as they were out from view, Holgar dropped his arm. "I don't want you hurting anyone here tonight," he said. "If someone offers to donate blood, that's not an issue, but I don't want anyone dead."

The vampire laughed as though he had just heard the world's greatest joke. "You are a funny one, my friend," he said at last.

"I'm not joking," Holgar said, staring into the other's eyes to show his commitment.

The vampire stared back for a moment, then stopped laughing. "Why do you care about these pathetic humans?"

"Because they are my friends. Because there is no need for bloodshed here, not now, not ever."

"That's where you're wrong. There will be blood here, starting with yours if you don't stand aside." The vampire took a step closer and straightened to his full height, trying to intimidate Holgar.

But Holgar had played far too many wolf games, seen too many power struggles, to let the Curser win so easily. He too stood up straighter, and clenched his fists so the muscles on his arms rippled in a show of strength.

The vampire lashed out at Holgar, taking him by surprise. Long nails scratched his cheek just below his left eye. Holgar jerked out of the way with a roar and then launched himself at the vampire, who easily sidestepped him, as though he were dodging an errant tennis ball.

They're faster than people say, Holgar realized as he steadied himself, wrenching a knee in the process. *How is it you kill a vampire? Stake through the heart? Decapitation?*

He panned the area for a weapon he could use. The only thing he saw was a birdhouse. He grabbed it, ripping the box free and smashing it. He grabbed a jagged piece of the roof and turned back to the vampire. The creature had the audacity to look bored, which enraged Holgar more. He lunged, swinging the stake toward the thing's chest.

The vampire slid out of his way, tripping him in the

process. Holgar barely managed to let go of the stake before he would have impaled himself as he hit the ground. He rolled onto his back, and the Cursed One bent down, grabbed his shirt, and hoisted Holgar to his feet. It bit him on the neck. Terror shot adrenalin through Holgar's body. He picked up the creature, ripping its fangs free in the process, then hoisted it over his head and slammed it down on top of the post for the birdhouse.

A moment later the vampire disintegrated into ash. Spent from all of the exertion, Holgar lost his balance and toppled to the ground.

As he lay there, he knew he had been lucky, and he was grateful. He could have just as easily been dead.

He dragged himself back inside. Kirstinne, who had been taking pictures of herself with her phone, came over when she saw him. She moved him away from the crowd, into a corner, and touched his cheek.

"Are you okay?"

"I got in a fight. Can I walk you home?"

"No, I'm spending the night here. Elsa's parents will be back from the movies around midnight."

He hesitated, wanting to tell her what had happened, but it could wait. There had been only one vampire at the party. "Be safe," he said.

"You too," she said. She gave him a quick kiss and then melted back into the throng.

His wounds began to heal and itch as he made his way

home. When he finally got there, he saw a strange car in the driveway. He slipped quietly in through the back door, intent on getting to his room before his father's company saw him in his current state.

He hadn't gone ten steps, though, when he heard his name.

"Good, Holgar. I wanted you to meet someone," his father called from their parlor.

Holgar went into the room, which was decorated with his grandmother's cross-stitches of the Danish flag and woodland meadows. Holgar's father and a stranger were seated on their sofa, holding mugs of beer.

The man stood up. He was tall, but not as tall as Holgar, with black hair pulled back into a ponytail, and thick brows and lashes. His nose was long and thin, and his eyes were dark.

There was no humor in his expression, and less warmth. He felt dangerous. Menacing.

Holgar realized the stench of rotting blood was not the lingering smell of dead vampire on his jeans, but new and overpowering.

The stranger was no man. He was a vampire.

"What is this?" Holgar asked bluntly in Danish.

"Buenas noches," said the vampire. "You are Holgar, *sí*? The son of my new friend." His English was heavily accented.

Holgar frowned. "Friend?" he asked, also in English.

"I've been forging an alliance between your pack and myself. We're going to work together to do great things," the vampire said with a smile, flashing his fangs.

Holgar could feel the evil rolling off of him, and it made his hackles rise. He looked to his father for confirmation, and his father nodded. There was a light in his father's eyes that he didn't like. The look of him, the smell, reminded Holgar of the night his father had taken down the hunter in the forest.

"Father, they kill people," Holgar said softly.

"Yes," his father said, his grin growing broader. His dark blue eyes shone in his tanned face. "And this alliance will ensure that we no longer have to disguise what we are from the world."

Holgar whined in his throat and hunched his shoulders. "It's wrong," he whispered.

Quick as a flash his father backhanded him across the mouth, so hard that Holgar tasted blood. There were consequences for questioning your alpha. Holgar had never before given his father cause to strike him. He had always been the good wolf, the one who knew his place, the one who followed his leader. But in his heart he knew that this was the wrong path and that it could only lead to destruction.

His father glared at him, and Holgar dropped his eyes submissively, standing as though he'd tucked his currently absent tail between his legs.

"Better," his father said.

After the creature left, and they were alone, his father challenged him:

"What are you thinking?"

"It's wrong to kill for sport, and that's what they do," Holgar said. "I know. I've seen their hearts."

"And have you not seen mine?"

"We're better than this, Father. We have a good life here," Holgar said, wincing as he waited for a second blow to land. It never came, though, and when Holgar raised his eyes, he saw that his father was amused.

"You're naive, son, and that's probably my fault. This is not a good life. This is boring. Hunting deer for sport? *That* is beneath us. We have a chance for greatness, and we will take our rightful place in history. Humans are just another form of prey. Evolution decrees that the stronger, the more evolved, live off the lesser. For millennia we've allowed humans to think they were the top of that evolutionary scale. No more."

"So, you're going to be the Cursed Ones' lapdogs?"

His father bared his teeth and growled low in his throat. "Not lapdogs; partners. Where they have been cursed, we have been blessed. It's balance, harmony, that we should join together. Equals in the new order. Tomorrow I'll call a pack meeting, and everyone will meet our new partners."

There was no talking him out of it, Holgar could tell.

He dropped his head and went to his room, where he spent a restless night.

The next day the pack met in the Vibbards' barn, which served as their meetinghouse. Kirstinne remained with her parents, flirting with Holgar from across the room. But he stood aloof and watched as his father delivered the news, hoping to see signs of dissent. He wasn't strong enough to oppose his father, but some of the others were.

Yet none of them challenged his father. They all agreed with him. He looked around at the faces of some of the others closer to his age, and they too seemed eager—excited, even—to move ahead with the plan. He couldn't see Kirstinne's face, but he hoped she shared his resistance.

"Now, we'll get a chance to meet our partners in about an hour. Until then, enjoy the food," his father said, gesturing to the tables that had been set up around the perimeters of the room.

The smell of the bloody deer meat made Holgar's stomach growl, but he had more pressing needs than food. As he listened to the excited chatter, Kirstinne sidled up to him, nuzzled his cheek, and picked up a haunch of meat. She offered it to him first, and when he waved it away, she took a nibble. As she chewed, her expression was thoughtful, and that gave him hope.

He took her arm and led her outside, away from prying werewolf ears.

"What do you think?" he asked.

She tried to pop a little piece of deer meat into his mouth. He gently rebuffed her.

"I'm not sure. It sounds . . . interesting. It just seems so odd, especially given what we were talking about yesterday."

"It's wrong," he pushed.

She shook her head slowly. "Not wrong, just one possibility."

Frustration rose in him. "The Cursed Ones are evil, and it is wrong to join them."

Kirstinne put down the chunk of meat. "What are you saying?"

"I can't challenge him. I can't stop this partnership from forming. But I don't have to stay here to see it happen. And neither do you."

Her eyes widened. "What?"

Holgar took a deep breath and grabbed her hand. "I'm leaving. I don't know where I'm going to go just yet, but I'll figure it out. I want you to come with me."

She stared at him for a moment before pulling free and taking a step backward. She shook her head violently. "I can't. This is my life, my family. I can't leave my pack. And I can't believe you, of all people, would ask me to."

"We can start a new pack," he begged, heart aching at the look of rejection in her eyes.

"No! I can't. This is where I belong. I follow my alpha, no matter what," she said.

"But Kirstinne!"

She put her hand on his. "Stay, Holgar, please. I won't tell anyone about this."

Stunned, he stared at her. "I can't stay," he whispered.

"Then there's nothing left to talk about," she said, with a catch in her throat. Without another word she turned and ran back toward the house, passing his father on the way.

Holgar stood his ground as his father approached. "She looks upset."

Holgar shrugged. "We both are."

His father's blue eyes narrowed. "So are our new friends. I just got a call. Apparently, one of them went missing last night. They've asked for our help to find him."

"Don't you have better things to do than look for one of their prodigals?"

"It's a gesture of goodwill and faith. Come back inside so I can brief everyone together. We'll start a hunt, find out when and where he was last seen. Hopefully, he just passed out in a strange lair last night. With any luck he won't be missing for long."

Holgar knew this was a moment he would never forget, no matter the outcome. His father had chosen the pack's path. *And Kirstinne has chosen hers*, he thought with genuine sorrow. With his next words he would choose his.

After a beat Holgar said, "He's not missing."

"He's not?" his father asked, looking perplexed.

"No."

"Then where is he?"

"Wherever dead vampires go, I suppose."

His father blinked. "He's *dead*? How do you know this?" his father asked sharply.

"I was the one who killed him."

His father looked like Holgar had slapped him. "There must have been some mistake," he said at last.

"No mistake. He was a vampire, and I killed him. And I'm not going to stay and make nice with the Cursed Ones."

His father turned white with rage. "Are you challenging me?"

"No, Father," Holgar said, his heart breaking. "I'm leaving you. All of you."

And he turned on his heel and walked away.

Three months later, tired, hungry, and covered in fresh scars, Holgar stood at the gates of the University of Salamanca. He had won a dozen fights with vampires, mostly through sheer luck and stupidity. But he wanted to fight so that he could kill them through skill and practice. Now he intended to spend the next two years training, studying, trying to become a Hunter.

From what he understood, the Hunter was a lone wolf, like him. Holgar had crossed the paths of two other werewolf packs. In neither case had he asked permission to join. Though he had physically left his pack, he could not let go of them emotionally. He had never imagined a life without them. When he slept alone after a hunt, he dreamed that they surrounded him, telling him that they'd been wrong and he was right. His father and Kirstinne joyfully reunited with him.

But it was only a dream.

Now he looked up at the massive gates, all gingerbread and bric-a-brac, so unlike the simple lines and spareness of decoration preferred by Danes. He had never seen anything so ostentatious.

LAS VEGAS
TEAM SALAMANCA MINUS ANTONIO;
TAAMIR AND NOAH

Until now, Holgar thought as he stared at the sea of flashing lights that made him squint against the brightness. It was so intense that it hurt. And his ears picked up the sounds of traffic, and the clanging of whistles, sirens, coins, and bells as they passed each casino entrance. It was nearly deafening, and he wondered how the Cursed Ones could stand it.

"Where do you think we'll find her?" he heard Jenn ask.

He glanced to the other side of the street and then pointed. "Somehow I think that's where we need to go," Holgar said.

The sprawling building's ancient Roman architecture, with white gardenlike statues, was very distinctive. The sign for the hotel appeared to have been altered; the letters in the first word were brighter and in a slightly different font than those in the second.

"You've got to be kidding me," Jenn said flatly.

"Ballsy," Jamie said, his voice almost admiring.

"It's got to be a trap," Eriko said.

"There's a bit of cheek," Skye groaned, as she read the sign aloud: "*Aurora's Palace.*"

CHAPTER TWELVE

Salamanca Hunter's Manual:
The Soul of Your Enemy
Know this: The Cursed Ones have no souls. Neither pity nor prayer can restore their souls unto them. They are truly, hopelessly evil.

Therefore, when it is the time to strike, do not be moved by your own grace and goodness. Mercy is as useless as a teaspoon riddled with holes would be against an incoming sea.

(translated from the Spanish)

SALAMANCA
HEATHER AND FATHER JUAN

She remembered her name. She blinked slowly at the memory. *Heather.* She said it out loud, testing it on her tongue.

"Heather." The word barely came out as a tiny puff of air. Another memory stirred. Someone else had called her by this name. When was it?

She shook her head slowly. She couldn't remember. She looked down and saw her inhaler crushed in her hand, the plastic cracked and flattened as though it had been run over by a truck. She brought it slowly to her lips and tried to inhale.

And panicked.

There was no breath in her lungs.

In fact she wasn't breathing at all. She gasped, sucking in air. Her lungs seared. Terrified, she recoiled, and her head slammed against the metal bars of her cage. She tried to scream, but it came out as a breathless screech that she couldn't even recognize.

What happened to me?

She heard someone coming. When she tried to breathe in, she smelled them. The door on the far wall clanked open, and she covered her ears against the sound.

"Heather?" someone asked softly.

"Yes," she managed to whisper.

Silhouetted in the doorway, a figure wearing a robe hurried forward. He was an older man, and he looked familiar. He carried a goblet of some sort in his hand, and her stomach lurched hungrily at the rich and spicy smell.

He stopped in front of her cell, and she took another tentative sniff and smelled blood.

Blood.

She wanted it more than she had ever wanted anything else. Only she didn't want it from the goblet; she wanted it from the source, from him. She wanted to bite *his* throat where she saw the vein pulsing above his priestly collar.

I'm a Cursed One, she realized with sudden, dizzying horror. *Oh, God, no.* But that could only mean one thing.

Jenn didn't save me.

LAS VEGAS
TEAM SALAMANCA MINUS ANTONIO;
TAAMIR AND NOAH

Jenn kept her head down as they checked into the Desert Blossom. Even though she was heavily disguised in a black wig and sunglasses, she still felt completely exposed.

She tried to force herself to relax. After all, Skye had also put a glamour on her. When Jenn had looked at herself in the bathroom mirror at the airport in Moscow, though, she had still seen herself. She had wanted to ask Skye if that was normal or if there was something wrong.

But the witch had been so distraught that Jenn had decided to leave her alone for a bit. Now she deeply regretted that decision.

"Are you sure I look all right?" she whispered so softly that only Holgar could hear her.

He turned, looked her up and down, and frowned. Jenn grimaced.

"What?"

"That glamour makes your butt look big," he dead-panned.

She grinned faintly. "I knew I could count on you."

A few minutes later, after they'd all settled into adjoining rooms, they reconvened in Jenn's. Pleasant, with white-washed furniture, art prints of howling coyotes and cacti, and bedspreads in Southwestern colors of brick and turquoise, it was almost homelike.

"How did you know about this hotel?" Eriko asked. "It really is off the beaten path."

"I came here with my family for my grandfather's six-tieth birthday," Jenn said. "He had always wanted to see Vegas, but we needed to keep a low profile."

"Low profile?" Noah asked.

Jenn realized she hadn't really told any of the team about her grandparents. "They were radicals in the 1960s," she said, and everyone stopped to listen. "They've been . . . my grandmother has been . . . underground my whole life."

"'Underground' means hiding out from the government," Skye explained to Taamir and Noah. Then she blushed. Jenn figured it was because after the war started, witches had gone underground too, to hide from the vampires.

"Impressive," Noah said. "So they were the resistance of their day?"

"They believed they were fighting for a just cause," Jenn said. She heard the tentativeness in her own voice.

"This is the same grandfather you mentioned back in Russia," Noah ventured.

Jenn nodded. "There were three guys in suits and shades up at my grandfather's funeral. One of them, Greg, was wearing a black cross, and he spoke with my grandmother."

"Were the other two wearing crosses?" Taamir asked.

"I never got close enough to tell," Jenn confessed. "But that was when Greg told me I had big shoes to fill. And that there were people who were hoping I would fill them." Her voice was soft; she was feeling shy about her leadership position. It seemed like some strange dream that they had unanimously agreed that she should take over the team. Even Jamie had said so. Now she wondered why. Father Juan had told her she was special. But she didn't see it. Didn't understand any of it.

"So the black crosses *were* following you to Moscow," Taamir said tightly.

"I don't know."

"It doesn't make sense. If they're so keen on you, why don't they actually speak to you?" Jamie demanded. He was sitting on her bed with his boots on the spread. Jenn gave him a look that he either ignored or didn't catch. "See, no matter where we run into them, they just push us out of the way."

"But we know they know who we are. And they got us back to Madrid from New Orleans," Holgar argued.

"And boy, did that freak out Father Juan," Skye said. She gazed into her scrying stone, then rested it in her lap.

"Freaked me out too. All of us." Jamie moved his head, cracking his neck. The loud snaps of his bones startled Jenn.

"I don't like it. Any of it. You're all very reckless," Noah said. "In the Mossad—"

"The Mossad ain't here, mate," Jamie snapped, cracking his knuckles. "And we *are*."

"Except for Antonio," Skye pointed out.

"Yeah, well," Jamie said, then muttered something Jenn couldn't hear.

Silence filled the room. Jamie pulled out a pack of cigarettes and toyed with them. Skye picked up and examined one of the decorative pillows on Jenn's bed, and made a face at Jamie, gesturing toward his boots.

The boots did not move.

"So. You came to this very hotel with your grandfather," Skye pressed on.

"Yes," Jenn said.

It had been a happy trip. Her grandparents, her parents, Heather.

Heather.

She felt guilty at the thought of her sister. She had been so worried about Antonio that she had nearly forgotten about her. Jenn hoped that Heather was all right and that Father Juan was helping her adjust to her new life—while still being Heather. In her heart, though, she didn't believe there was much hope, especially without Antonio there to guide Heather through the bloodlust. She shivered.

Jenn closed the blinds, then dumped her bag on the bed, forcing herself to concentrate on the present situation. Because of the airline regulations they'd had to leave their weapons behind, and that had made all of them unhappy.

Eriko flopped down onto one of the beds with a bone-weary groan.

"You okay?" Jenn asked.

Ever since they had found Eriko half dead, the Hunter hadn't seemed right. She had super healing abilities, but instead of getting better it seemed almost like Eriko was getting worse.

Maybe she's just getting worse at hiding her condition. Maybe it's always been bad.

Skye studied her scrying stone again. She was still really shaken by the encounter with Estefan in Russia. Jenn had been waiting until she calmed down to ask her more about it, about him, but she was starting to worry that Skye wasn't going to calm down.

We're falling apart. We're spent. And now, now we have to rescue Antonio. Aurora's Palace. I can't believe her nerve! How are we going to get in there to find him, let alone rescue him?

She remembered walking through the original hotel as

a child. It was enormous, and the shopping area alone was a marvel, with a ceiling that mirrored the sky and changed to reflect the time of day. What was it like now? Perpetual darkness?

There was only one way to find out. They had to get inside.

But not until they all got some rest. "Let's get some sleep," Jenn said. "We're going to need it."

"Best plan you've had yet," Jamie said, dragging himself off her bed and toward the adjoining room.

Holgar, Taamir, and Noah followed him through the open door, and she saw Jamie fall onto a bed. Holgar curled up on the floor, like his wild cousins. Taamir took the other bed, and Noah sat down on the rollaway cot. Noah glanced her way, locked her gaze, and held it. She didn't look away.

Help me find him, she thought. *Please.*

Skye started to get up from the bed and move to their cot, but Jenn stopped her with a hand on her shoulder. "I'll be up for a while," she said. "You take the bed."

Skye nodded sleepily and lay down, eyes drooping.

And for just a moment there was absolute silence. It was beautiful. But then the noise from outside began to intrude. Jenn heard people walking by the room, and she tensed, relaxing only when they were out of earshot.

Eriko began to snore, and from the next room she could hear Holgar and Jamie doing the same. She wondered if Taamir was praying to Allah. She knew Muslims said prayers at special times. All the things that had divided humanity—religious beliefs, land disputes—seemed so abstract and ridiculous now. She would have thought that in the face of such a terrible enemy as vampires, everyone would unite. That the threat of annihilation by the Cursed Ones would do what other threats—like nuclear holocaust—hadn't done: make the human race *one*. But it hadn't happened.

Let it happen to us, she thought. *Make us a team. We need to work together.*

There was nothing they could do until everyone had gotten a few hours' rest. She looked at Skye. The witch was still awake.

"Do you sense something?" Jenn asked quietly.

"I—I—no." Skye turned and looked at Jenn, eyes vacant. "But I'll try harder." She took a deep breath. "I think everyone's trying a little harder, you know? Jamie's not picked one fight. He's barely even criticized you." She smiled sadly. "Can't keep his bloody boots off the furniture, though."

Jenn smiled back at Skye. "At least he hasn't set off the smoke alarm." She changed the subject. "What do you think of the new guys?"

"Taamir's sweet. Gives off a lovely vibe. Noah. Well." She cleared her throat. "You know he's quite keen on you, right?"

Jenn nodded.

"And he's not a Cursed One, so that's a plus." Then she leaned over and squeezed Jenn's hand. "I hope you don't think I'm cold-hearted, talking about it while Antonio's still missing."

"We're good," Jenn promised her. "You should get some rest. All the glamours you're creating, plus the scrying . . . you're going to burn yourself out."

Skye nodded and lay back down, shutting her eyes. A minute later the witch's breathing changed as she, too, slept.

Jenn stood up and crossed by the open connecting door. The guys were all asleep as well. Noah's back was to her. His hair was very dark against his white pillow.

She took a hot shower, savoring the alone time. They needed to do some reconnaissance. Aurora had seen both her and Skye before, but not the others. At least to the best of Jenn's knowledge. So, should she send in two of the others, or should she and Skye work on their disguises and they all go in as a team?

We're going to look like a mob, she thought. Seven people in a hotel casino not gambling were going to look a little suspicious.

Jenn dried off and changed into the clothes she'd bought before leaving Moscow. Then she curled up in a chair at the table by the front door. A stack of magazines extolling the virtues of the many entertainments in Vegas was scattered on the surface of the table, which made her smile. Cursed Ones were in control, but some things would never change.

She flipped through a magazine, staring at the ads for Las Vegas shops and restaurants, hoping to relax her brain enough so that she'd have a shot at getting some sleep too. It was daylight, so she didn't think they needed to worry about setting up a watch just yet. All they had to fear were vampires' human minions. Antonio was the only vampire she'd known who was willing to risk the daylight.

Her throat tightened at the thought of him. Anxiety filled her, and then she let the moment pass.

As she turned the glossy pages, she let her mind drift. She thought about Antonio, Heather, her life before the vampires. She smiled at the sound of the snoring from the other room and tried to decide which guy was louder. Even in their sleep it was like they were trying to outdo each other.

She closed the magazine, not much closer to sleep, and pulled out the one underneath it. She idly opened it, then stared at an ad, realizing she had just found the answer to their immediate problem.

She got her backpack and fished out the credit card Father Juan had given her for emergencies. Then she picked up the room phone and dialed the number on the ad. When a man answered on the other end, she said, "Hi, I'd like to reserve seven seats for tonight's nine p.m. show of *The Magick of Myth* at Aurora's Palace."

LAS VEGAS
ANTONIO, AURORA, AND ESTEFAN

Antonio couldn't remember ever feeling so weak before. He had lost track of how many times Aurora had cut and stabbed him during the last twenty-four hours. She had offered him blood in a goblet, only to yank it whenever he tried to drink. His thirst was unbearable. Antonio had been fasting while he was praying and working with Heather, so he hadn't fed in nearly two weeks. It had been stupid. Father Juan had warned him against that.

Without feeding, a vampire's ability to heal himself slowed more and more, until the need to feed was completely overwhelming, and the self-preservation instinct kicked in.

Antonio was starting to fantasize about biting Aurora and draining her blood, and that wasn't good.

LAS VEGAS
TEAM SALAMANCA MINUS ANTONIO

When the radio alarm went off, Jenn lay still for a moment, wishing for a little more sleep. A country song played, one that had been old when she'd been young. It was cut off suddenly in a hiss of static, and it gave way to a male voice.

"This is our country, and we must fight to take it back. Those who didn't believe must now realize that the human population of

New Orleans has been devastated and that those who remain are starving to death."

Jenn sat up and turned up the volume. The voice continued. *"The city is lost, but we will take a stand elsewhere. I call upon all of you, for now is the time. We will not win this war and our freedom if we do not. In the west, San Francisco, Las Vegas, and Seattle are already lost to us. In the east, Newark, Detroit, Boston, and Charleston have fallen. There is still time to stop the same from happening to San Diego, Portland, Chicago, and New York. Resist always. The Cursed Ones must be stopped. This is the Resistance, and we need your help."*

There was another burst of static, and the country song was back, winding to a close. Jenn sat with her heart pounding. So, "Kent" was still broadcasting. She had heard him when she was in New Orleans.

There has to be some way to reach out to him.

"What's going on?" Holgar asked, standing in the doorway, yawning and stretching.

She took a deep breath. "Wake the others. We're going to a magick show."

Eriko couldn't help but feel little ripples of excitement and nostalgia as they entered the spacious "Temple of Myth," which was decorated like a Grecian temple. She was going out, like in the old days. Like when she was young and carefree.

"Look at this," Skye murmured. "It's incredible."

White marble pillars disappeared into the "sky"—cloud-shaped objects made of gossamer material that periodically puffed out mist scented with exotic spices. A huge illuminated moon hung from invisible wires.

Long marble tables seating six on a side were decorated with white candles inside Grecian-style braziers. On the walls, the large silver masks that traditionally represented comedy and tragedy bore an additional detail—long fangs protruding from the laughing and weeping mouths.

The stage was a concave semicircle decorated with Greek statues standing in various poses on pedestals. In the center of the stage sat an alabaster bowl as big as the family *ofuro* at home—the traditional hot bath where one could melt one's cares away. She thought of how wonderful it would be to lie back in a super-hot bath and rest her sore joints and aching muscles.

She thought of Kyoto. Back when she was fourteen, her plan had been to train at home, in Kyoto, to become the Hunter there. In retrospect she was glad that her father had refused to let her go, insisting that the honor be reserved for his only son, not his daughter. Had she become the Hunter of Kyoto, she would have quickly realized her motivations were purely personal, and her parents, used to indulging and spoiling her, might have encouraged her to quit. In Salamanca she had found her true purpose—not to avenge her best friend, but to rid the world of vampires.

Anger and a desire for revenge had pushed her out her

front door, and she hadn't spoken to her parents—or to her brother, Kenji—in two and a half years. She didn't even know if Kenji, a fellow Hunter, was still alive.

Maybe it's time to find out, she thought. It was almost as if Japan had ceased to exist for her. That was deliberate, she knew. She had needed space from everyone who had known her then. After what had happened . . . She stared into the flames, and remembered.

Kyoto, Japan, Four Years Earlier
Eriko, Yuki, and Mara

"Vampire boys are cutest," the Vampire Three sang in Japanese. Eriko, Yuki, and Mara were singing their latest song for an admiring throng on Eigamura Sunday. Eigamura was a combination Japanese movie lot and theme park, like the American Universal Studios, only a little less grand—okay, a *lot* less grand—and on Sundays pop groups performed in front of its gates. Sometimes inside, too.

"Vampire boys are sweet!" they trilled in their high, girlish, voices, Eriko posing with her hands folded over her heart, Yuki pointing to her mouth, Mara tapping the fake vampire bites on her neck. All three thrust their hips to the left in time to their recorded music.

The Vampire Three were dressed in their anime vampire schoolgirl finery—starched short skirts with red ruffles, knee socks decorated with little red hearts, and two tiny hearts on each of their necks, fangs'-width apart. They danced in a little circle and showed off their white satin bloomers. Their audience—lots of girls, and guys, too—clapped along. There were at least five hundred people there—the Vampire Three was the big draw.

"They are sugar hearts!" their fans yelled, singing along.

"True love, true love, vampire boys!" the Vampire Three trilled.

Cell phones were raised high as people recorded them. The Vampire Three was all for it. Eriko blew kisses to the crowd. Red plastic vampire bats holding sparkly hearts dangled from her ponytails. Her lips were bright red, like her nails, and she had on lots of makeup, almost like a geisha. All three of them had learned how to style themselves to look super good for YouTube. They had dreams of landing a big recording contract, maybe even a TV series. Their social-network pages were getting more and more hits. Along with their own poetry—Eriko wrote a lot of vampire haiku—they were posting tons of fan art, both pictures of themselves and ones cute boy vampires e-mailed to them.

On Friday they were finally going to meet their biggest vampire fan, a "Cute One" who called himself Shell Ghost Shogun. And he *was* cute. He had long black hair pulled up and back like a samurai, almond-shaped eyes the color of cherries, and *dimples*. He was going to send a limo to their favorite club, Missing Dreams. Was that not the most amazing, coolest thing in all of Japan?

293

Dead.

But on Friday, Yuki didn't show for the date with Shell Ghost Shogun. She was missing. No one was looking very hard to find her.

Dead.

Eriko and Mara started failing all their classes because they ditched school all the time to look for Yuki. So Eriko's parents *grounded* her. Eriko wouldn't even speak to them. She snuck out anyway, searching in the rain, wailing at the gates of Eigamura.

Dead.

The fans of the Vampire Three held vigils and sent letters of hope and poems to the website. Eriko and Mara kept searching, looking, asking.

Dead.

Then Eriko found Yuki.

Eriko was Skyping with Mara, which they had to do since they were grounded, and both of them were freaking out because someone had killed Eriko's mom's cat, Nekko. The message was clear: *Stop asking questions about Yuki.* Eriko was sobbing; Mara was swearing revenge.

Then, on the webcam behind Mara, Yuki appeared. She was dressed in white, and she staggered forward, hunched over with her long black hair in her face like a Japanese ghost. She swayed as she walked—no, lurched. Then she gazed up over Mara's shoulder into the camera with her bright red eyes, and grinned, revealing her fangs.

"Mara! Mara!" Eriko screamed, but it was too late.

Eriko watched—

She still had nightmares about it. Eriko never looked at the Vampire Three website again. Naive, gullible. Eriko hated herself for a long time.

But in the beginning she, Yuki, and Mara had had such *dreams*. . . .

"Those statues are alive," Skye murmured to Eriko. "Well, sort of alive. They're vampires."

Eriko studied them. Dressed in Grecian robes, wearing their human faces, they were unmoving. Of course they didn't have to breathe, which could have been a giveaway for a human "living statue."

"We'll have to be careful, then," Eriko whispered to her. Vampires had acute senses, able to overhear conversations most humans couldn't. Because of the elixir Eriko's senses were more developed than most humans', and matched some vampires'. Holgar was similarly favored. But not Jamie and Jenn. Nor Skye, unless she used her scrying stone.

They both turned around casually in their seats, spotting Jenn, who was sitting with Holgar, and Jamie, who was off by himself, chatting up the sexy woman beside him. Jamie was wearing a black V-neck sweater and black jeans, stark against his nearly bald head and tattoos. He and the woman, who was wearing a slinky red tank top and black leather trousers, were laughing together, and Eriko was startled by how charming Jamie appeared. She knew he had a crush on her, but he was such a . . . a *barbarian*. Rough, sarcastic, quick to anger. She couldn't imagine being Jamie's girlfriend . . . even if it did bother her a tiny bit, perhaps, to watch him having fun with someone else.

Still, she had to admire his hatred of the Cursed Ones. It was simple. Pure. And this new world was anything but.

She started to say something to Skye, then blinked at Skye's expression of longing, aimed in Jamie's direction. *No way*, Eriko thought, and was glad for the distraction when a waitress appeared to take their order.

"Cokes for both of us," Eriko said quickly, not wanting the waitress to card either of them. She hoped Jamie and Holgar, both Europeans used to ordering alcohol, would remember that in America the legal drinking age was twenty-one. Although not one of them was old enough to drink, all of them had killed vampires.

Taamir and Noah had opted out of the magick show, doing recon on their own. Jenn had neither given them permission nor objected to their decision. Eriko understood; Jenn hadn't really assumed command of the extended group. It was an uncomfortable place to be in, and Eriko was so relieved to be free of it.

Noah seems to like Jenn a lot. It would be much better if he took Antonio's place in her heart. Maybe Jenn will turn to him for comfort if we can't get Antonio back.

The audience was exotic, upscale. Eriko had never been

to Las Vegas before, but she'd seen YouTube, and the night-life appeared to be much fancier since the vampires had taken over. Maybe you had to be rich to dare going out at night. Maybe the humans bought some kind of protection. Away from the glittering lights it might be a different story.

As she scanned the crowd, Eriko noted some beauti-fully dressed Japanese girls in tiny minis making room for a Japanese man who had his back to her. His black hair was long, and he was dressed in a fashionable black silk jacket and nicely cut trousers. The girls were giggling and toasting his arrival with what looked like champagne, and she felt a wash of longing for everything that had been taken from her. She'd been a girl like that, carefree, with lots of spend-ing money and pretty friends.

Dead.

The Cokes arrived, watered down and filled with ice. Eriko tried to hold her glass gently, lest she shatter it with her strong grip. She was verging on a migraine headache — a new affliction. So far, muscular aches and joint pain had served as her companions, but not headaches. She won-dered if it meant that the elixir was affecting her brain. Had Father Juan known that it would hurt her like this? And given it to her anyway?

Who is he? Who is he, really?

"Ladies and gentlemen, and everything in between," a voice boomed. *"Welcome to our Magickal Temple of Myth!"*

Pan pipes and strings played over the audience as the

large moon and the glowing clouds burst apart and new white statues swung from silver trapeze swings and silk ropes. As the onlookers applauded, each figure opened a hand, and a small pillar of fire appeared in his or her palm, then disappeared. Next came a bubble of red light that burst, shooting red liquid—blood?—toward the audience. Startled shrieks burst from the lips of the well-dressed; then the liquid disappeared.

"Gods or magicians? Magicians or . . . magickal beings?" the voice pondered.

The room plunged into darkness. Music swelled. Then, no more than five seconds later, the stage was lit up by huge, fire-blazing pillars that stood in blocks of steaming ice. The statues circled them in a stately dance. A figure appeared, poised high above the stage, wrapped in white swaths of silk, posed with its arms extended to each side, Christ-like. It wore a skullcap, and its eyes were closed. Its features were smooth, and there was no way to tell if it was male or female; it seemed to be wearing some kind of bodysuit.

"From the dawn of time we walked. Immortal, invincible. We witnessed the birth of the stars."

The room filled with blazing points of blue-tinted light, which danced without any apparent means of support. One landed on Skye's shoulder, another on the lip of Eriko's Coke glass. The two looked at each other, startled.

Magick, Skye mouthed, and Eriko knew what she was afraid of, or rather, who: Estefan. "I should go."

Eriko shook her head. "You've warded yourself. Stay. You'll be noticed."

"We witnessed the birth of the oceans."

The lights disappeared. Over the walls silhouettes of whales undulated with slow, stately grace. The keening of humpback whales mingled with the pan pipes. Eriko smelled the sea.

"And saw the birth of humanity."

Lightning flashed and thunder boomed. On the stage, rain began to fall. The white figures all fell to their knees, and a holographic Greek comedy mask appeared on the ceiling, gazing down on them. The audience applauded.

"But what of myth?" it demanded.

"It is a myth that magick is not real," the white "statues" chorused. "Magick lives among us."

Then smoke and lightning billowed around the guests' tables, and when it cleared, some of the audience rose, appearing in different clothes: vampire actors in formal Victorian evening attire, Chinese robes, and the flounces of Gypsies.

"Magickal humans! Harry Houdini!" the voice announced, and a man in a tuxedo rose, bowed, and headed for the stage.

"Doug Henning!"

A man with dark brown hair and a mustache also stood, inclined his head, and walked from his table to the "temple."

"Harry Blackstone! Fu Manchu! Cardini! Kuda Bux! Dedi! Katterfelto!"

The magicians mounted the stage, some in tuxedos, others in Grecian togas. Fu Manchu wore rainbow-colored silk robes and a cap over his long, streaming white hair, his mustache just as long. They aimed their hands at the white figures. Suddenly the figures were encased in blocks of ice; then fire blazed around them. Steam rose, obstructing Eriko's view.

As the steam dissipated, women dressed in outfits from a 1950s evening gown to a grass skirt to a bustle to 1980s glam to the more understated post-vampire-war fashions appeared. They bowed and curtseyed, and the magicians approached them. They formed pairs.

"Assistants," Skye murmured. "From our tradition, only very mixed up. These aren't actual magick users. These are stage performers."

The audience began clapping as each magician performed a magick trick, aided by his assistant—rabbits appeared out of top hats; scarves became parrots or black cats. Enormous trees grew from seeds placed in palms. The assistants acted like spokesmodels, showing off their magicians' magical skills.

But three of the magicians had no assistants.

"Magicians require the yin and yang," the hologram announced. *"Magick works with male and female, positive and negative. Humans and vampires. Vampires, the true magickal beings."*

And at that moment Houdini's face vamped out—fangs

extended, eyes glowing red. There were giggles and cheers from the audience. No fear whatsoever.

"What are they going to do?" Eriko asked Skye as she went on alert. "What does this mean?"

"I don't know. But I'm freaking out," Skye whispered back. "This is not leading to something good. I can feel it."

"Houdini requires an assistant. Who will volunteer? A human, please. A lovely lady, hmmm?"

Hands raised. The hologram gazed down with red light gleaming from its eyes, scanning the audience until a redhead was selected.

Then "Fu Manchu" went vampire, his long "Chinese" mustache framing fangs that had been covered in jewels.

"And Fu Manchu also requires a lovely human. Perhaps . . . that beauty there!"

The red eyes gleamed over the audience, then focused on Eriko. There were good-natured groans from those not chosen. Then applause. Eriko sat frozen. Was this some kind of setup? A trap?

She glanced at Skye, who had gone pale. Then carefully looked for Jenn. She couldn't see her.

"Come, don't be shy!" the head exhorted her.

Eriko shook her head. The audience began applauding in rhythm, and a spot blazed down on her.

Fu Manchu headed for the stage steps. Obviously he was going to fetch her out of the audience. He wove his way through the tables.

Eriko got to her feet just as he reached her. There was no escape. He took her hand firmly, kissed it, and began to lead her back to the stage.

High-pitched squeals, almost like wounded piglets, made Eriko jump. Startled, she turned at the sound.

The Japanese girls in the audience had leaped to their feet. They were screaming and pointing at her.

"Vampire Three!" one of them cried. *"Vampire Three!"*

The man sitting with them slowly took off his shades. Her blood ran cold.

His almond eyes were the color of cherries, and as he grinned at her, she saw his dimples.

He was the vampire the Vampire Three—she, Yuki, and Mara—had been planning to meet on the night Yuki went missing. Shell Ghost Shogun.

In Las Vegas? Now?

In Las Vegas.

Now.

CHAPTER THIRTEEN

We weave a spell for all to see
With whispers of eternity
We are the past, the future, too
All you are and all you do
That is why we're here today
We've come in peace, and we will stay
Those who do not take our hand
Will find they make their final stand

LAS VEGAS
ANTONIO AND AURORA

Antonio wanted with all his soul to die.

No, that was a lie.

He wanted to sink his fangs into Aurora's long, sculptured neck. Aurora, the vampire queen, whose once-beautiful gown was now spattered with blood. Some must be his, but he had lost consciousness so many times, awakening to screams—human screams, his own—that he had no idea what had been happening. He smelled human blood, both fresh and aging, and the death scent carried by all vampires.

His desire for blood was as overpowering as the desire to exhale would be to a human holding his breath. If he could get free from his chains, he would tear open her neck and drink until every drop of her blood pulsed out of her body.

Her blood was dead.

But it was still blood.

Then I will take human blood. I'll drain one, then two, then three of them. Oh, dear God, no, por Dios. *I will never do that again.*

"Wake up," Aurora said, slapping his cheek, then tickling him under the chin like a doting mother. Her eyes glowed with hellfire.

"Buenas noches, mi macho."

Antonio remained silent.

Aurora ran her fingernail along his jawline, slicing it open. He was already in so much pain that this new injury barely registered.

"You've been very strong, and stoic, and priestly, but it's time to let go of that, Antonio. With your behavior you're shaming your sire, and his sire. And me. The entire Vampire Kingdom."

"It's a kingdom now?" he managed to slur out. "I thought it was a vampire nation."

"Nation? That's Solomon's idea. Not ours." She showed him the knife, the one she had been using to cut open his chest.

Ours. Who was she working for? Who was she allied with? She seemed to be competing with Sergio.

Antonio fought to stay calm, though the reflexive urge for self-preservation screamed at him to buck and struggle.

"The humans are falling because they are so divided," she said. "Into nations. They've deluded themselves into believing that their little bits and pieces of territory are worth fighting for. If they were united, *one*, they might have beaten us back. Once the Vampire Kingdom has been formed, we vampires will never have that problem."

She pressed the knife against Antonio's chest. He forced himself to focus on what she was saying. This was vital information.

"You're so handsome," she said with a sigh. "It's really too bad that I hate you as much as I do. And do you know why?"

She shoved in the knife, hard. But Antonio would not scream.

"I *don't* hate you for leaving Sergio. Or for betraying our kind. I hate you because of your loyalty to your church."

She shoved again. He grunted in pain.

"The Catholic Church condemned me to die a hideous death," she told him.

The knife twisted. He wrapped his fingers around his chains and gripped them, struggling to ride through his agony. Aurora's face filled his field of vision, her eyes glowing, her fangs sharp and white.

"My entire family was tortured and burned at the stake, and for what? Because we were Jews. Because we owned lands that the Catholics wanted. And *he* came to me, and offered me eternal life. And here I am."

The knife twisted again. He moaned, and detested himself for it.

"Is that not what your Savior offers to you?" she hissed. "Eternal life? Is it not said that the Pope speaks for God on earth? My sire has no spokesman. He's the Devil himself."

Antonio didn't respond. She jabbed the knife.

"The Devil," he rasped, to appease her.

"Yes. The Devil." She made a sound deep in her throat like the purring of a cat. "We vampires worship many gods—Sergio worships Orcus, *sì*? God of the underworld, bringer of light, punisher of those who break their vows. Are *you* in for it." She purred again. "Or you would be, if Orcus were more than a myth.

"The vampires of New Orleans worship Baron Samedi. That idiot Dantalion? Perhaps he worships Veles, the Slavic god. But all that will wither away, all the false gods will be extinguished, when *his* kingdom is established."

Is Dantalion still alive? Antonio wondered.

Silence fell. He realized she was waiting for his response.

"God did not torture you for being a Jew," he managed to say. "God did not torture you at all."

Her red gaze seethed with hatred. "I was tortured in *His* name. My baby sister was killed in *His* name. I watched my father burn!"

"It was not Go—"

"My sire will free us all from persecution. No one will dare to raise a hand to us. To try to *stake* us." Her voice rose, and she threw back her shoulders, raising her chin. Her blue-black hair tumbled down her shoulders. "What you see before you is the natural state of the vampire. Unbridled and passionate."

She yanked on the chain around his right wrist, forcing him to let go of it. The metal clanked as he dangled above the floor, head dropping forward.

"You're a sad dream, Antonio. You hold yourself down. You were wearing chains long before I put these on you. Your belief restrained you."

"No," he managed. Her talk of God made him wonder if this was the night he would die. If somehow it was for the cause—if it was for Jenn—he would gladly accept the Final Death.

She yanked again, harder. "I see how hard you've struggled against your true nature, and I don't admire you for it. I pity you. And I despise you. But you're the prize." She grabbed a handful of his hair and pulled his head back. "My sire wants to study you, then make an example of you."

She let go of his hair and leaned over him. "Just as I'll

make an example of every single human being in Salamanca. Of *her*."

"No." His voice was deep, loud, in command.

But after another twist of the knife he screamed.

"There's a way to stop all this," she whispered. "Let me tell you what it is."

AD 1490, TOLEDO, SPAIN
AURORA DEL CARMEN MONTOYA DE LA MOLINA ABREGÓN AND HER SIRE

"There's a way to stop it," the vampire had said, as he reached for Aurora in the filthy cell. His hooded robe concealed his features; she had seen only the crimson light of his eyes. It was the light of hell and of the bonfire that waited for her in the town square. "You have but to consent, and I will save you."

She had consented.

Gates and doors remained unlocked as he carried her lifeless body from the prison. The black coach that transported her to his castle raced against the sunlight, reaching the rusting portcullis as the first streaks of dawn washed over the wood piled in the main square of Toledo, where she was to have been burned.

Not a word was uttered on the streets about Aurora Abregón's disappearance. No one ever looked for her. Perhaps money had changed hands when she was carried out.

Perhaps the guards knew what had happened, and had stepped aside out of fear. Maybe Aurora's rescuer had made a pact with Tomás de Torquemada, the Grand Inquisitor by the grace of Their Royal Majesties King Ferdinand and Queen Isabella of Spain. Torquemada, the sadistic fiend whose name would ring out through the ages as the destroyer of innocence, under the guise of defending the Church from sin.

"I am forgotten," she had told her sire, as the nights became months, and then years, and then decades. And then the decades became centuries.

AD 1793, Madrid, Spain
Aurora, Sergio, and Their Sire

"No one in my family knows about me," Aurora murmured as she sat at the master's feet. They were in his vast library. Many of the books he had collected had been destined for burning by the Catholic Church. He also had a round globe and a telescope — marvelous things.

She and he had been playing various card games with the *baraja española*, the traditional Spanish deck. Then the message from Paris had arrived, and Aurora had grown too melancholy to concentrate. The French were cutting off the heads of the nobility, and an Abregón had died. But who had mourned for Aurora?

"No one remembers me," she went on.

"Your name is cherished by those who matter," Aurora's master replied. "Like . . . *him*."

He beckoned to the figure paused at the threshold, and Sergio Almodóvar strolled into the room. Aurora brightened, glad to see him, and he bowed over his leg to her, a courtly gentleman.

The three of them were wearing the latest in fashions. Aurora was in a simple white gown adorned with a red collar and a wide red sash. Sergio wore tight breeches, leather boots that came up to his knees, and a long, slashed coat over a simple, high-necked shirt. Their master wore a monkish robe, as he always did, this one black velvet embellished with tiny bats of scarlet satin. His hood threw his features into shadow, but Aurora had memorized them. She imagined herself his adoring mirror; he had but to look at her to see how beautiful and perfect he was.

It was October 15, 1793, and just the day before, the French revolutionaries had beheaded their queen, Marie Antoinette. People were terrified—rightly so, as France had become gripped in what they called the Reign of Terror. Alas for the Abregón family: One of the French queen's maids had been an Abregón, and she had died along with her mistress. But she had not been beheaded with the guillotine. Her instrument of death had been a rusty ax.

"I'm *glad* everyone has forgotten me," Sergio declared, bowing deeply to their master and planting a kiss on Aurora's mouth. Sergio's lips felt warm, although of course that couldn't be so. Sergio was a vampire, as she was. Yet she could not deny the heat. The passion.

"Being forgotten is like being dead," Aurora said.

"No, *mi amor*, it's not," Sergio insisted. "I owed thousands in gambling debts. If anyone knew where to look for me, I'd be in debtors' prison." He pulled a face. "For *eternity*."

Aurora laughed. Tonight she loved Sergio. A week ago she could have driven a stake through Sergio's heart for the way he'd treated her at the master's annual masked ball. But Sergio had wooed her — again; serenaded her at her balcony — again; brought her handsome men to drain — again.

"So. Today my two favorite children are not quarreling?" the master asked. "Today they are happy with each other?"

"Ecstatic," Sergio declared, lifting Aurora up in his arms. "As happy now as we were furious with each other."

"Ah, you're such Spaniards," the master said.

"A Spaniard knows the ways of love," Sergio whispered into Aurora's ear, and Aurora smiled brilliantly at Sergio. "*¿Con permiso, Maestro?*"

Their master chuckled.

"One moment," the master said.

Sergio and Aurora both looked at him.

"There is a thing called a Hunter," the master informed them. "One who goes up against such as we, for the purpose of murdering us."

The two lovers stared at him. "One who *knows*?"

"*Sí*. There is one here in Madrid." He made a show

of gathering up the playing cards. "Whoever brought this Hunter to me would receive a great reward."

"Then put me down, Sergio," Aurora declared. "I have work to do."

They chased each other out of the library, laughing.

Las Vegas
Antonio, Aurora, and Estefan

It was time. Aurora could feel it. She looked at Estefan, who had been enjoying Antonio's suffering almost as much as she had. While she had been working on Antonio, Estefan had been weaving spells to break the vampire's spirit, to increase his bloodlust, to help him forget who he was and why he had chosen the path he had.

And they were on the cusp of victory. Antonio was starving, half mad with hunger, and he was exhausted and delirious. Estefan helped along the rage that she engendered in Antonio, with more spells. And now, now for the finishing touch.

"Is she ready?" Aurora asked, looking at the back of the girl Estefan had lured into the hotel suite. He had bewitched her, in every sense of the word.

"See for yourself," Estefan said smugly, spinning the girl around so Aurora could see her. The glamour was perfect.

"I think it's time," Aurora purred. "Antonio's going to get exactly what he wants."

*   *   *

Antonio existed in a haze of cutting and healing. And blood, always the blood. He wasn't certain of his name, or where he was. He'd lost track, and he wanted only to die. But somehow he knew that wasn't an option.

"Antonio," a voice whispered, and he jerked hard on his chains at the sound of it. It was *her* voice.

He blinked, looked.

It was Jenn. Her dark auburn hair curled around her face—dark eyes, small mouth, lips parted. Her breath wafted against his lips, and he smelled the vanilla-scented soap she used, the lemons in her hair. Fresh blood.

Her heart was beating as fast as a hummingbird's.

"Oh, Antonio," she whispered. "I'm so sorry. But we got you out. You're safe."

"Ay, amor," he said through cracked lips. Then the beating of her heart washed over him like a tsunami, and he was drowning in the scent of her blood. A tantalizing fragrance that raised such a need in him that it was like holding a drowning man six inches beneath the surface of the water. He was helpless against it.

"No," he muttered.

"It's all right." She placed her fingers over his mouth. "Father Juan is working magicks to heal you. So is Skye."

"No time," he said. "Kingdom."

"What?" She cocked her ear close to his mouth. Her aroma was a storm on the waves.

313

He couldn't fight it. He didn't want to.

"Jenn, get away from me," he whispered, the words spilling out in Spanish.

"Aren't you glad to see me?" she asked in a small voice.

He jerked, suddenly aware that he was sitting in a darkened room and that she crouched beside him, his vampiric eyesight tracing the gauzy white nightgown she wore. There was a red satin ribbon at her throat, and she wore a scarlet sash. She reminded him of the runners at Pamplona, the poor humans fleeing from the Cursed Ones. From his kind.

"You can't believe what I've gone through to get to you," she said. "But we're together now. You're safe." She reached out her arms to him, the sleeves of the nightgown pulling back from her wrists. Her delicate blue veins pulsed just beneath the skin.

"No. Run," he said. "Get away from me."

Her eyes glittered; her lower lip trembled. "Are you glad to see me?"

"*Por supuesto*. Do you need to ask?" he whispered. His fangs lengthened. He reached his hands toward her, wishing for his chains.

Smiling, she slid into his embrace. He turned his head away from her, trying to shut his jaw. His fangs pierced his lower lip, and he began to bleed. Shaking, he licked at the dead blood, but it was like saltwater to a man who was dying of thirst.

Unaware of his desperation, Jenn lay her head on his chest. He kept licking the blood off his lips, ordering himself to be satisfied with it. To let it be enough.

But it wasn't.

"Get away from me!" he shouted.

Still she clung to him. With a roar of anguish he pushed her away. She sprawled backward, onto the floor. Antonio cried out, realizing what he'd done, falling to his knees beside her.

"Did I hurt you?" he asked brokenly, but before he knew what he was doing, he had grabbed her shoulders, pinned her beneath his weight, and sunk his fangs into her neck.

Ecstasy blazed through him. More. He had to stop. More.

A joy he had never known before filled his veins; rapture squeezed his heart, released it; squeezed, released. He soared, alive, nineteen years old and dreaming of the future. He drank. It was sweet, wonderful. He clung to Jenn, feeling as if she were being poured into him like water even as he was pouring into her like communion wine. United, in the way of vampires.

Grateful, he drank deeply, lustily.

Then, as her heart slowed, he realized what he was doing. What he had done. And he pulled away.

Or that was what he would have told himself later, if the girl beneath his fangs had not died. But the truth was that he kept drinking. He drank her dry. And when her heart stopped, he sank his fangs into the throat of another girl, who appeared beside the dead one.

He couldn't stop himself from killing that one, either. By the arrival of the third girl he didn't care; by the fourth he was glad.

He had never felt so liberated in his life. So free, so new. He threw back his head and laughed. He couldn't remember his own name, how he'd gotten into the room of dead girls. What did it matter? All that mattered was blood. And there was a world of it for the taking.

"I'm going to hunt," he told the vampire with the black hair. "I'm going to *kill*."

"Good," the vampire told him, as she led him to the window of her palatial suite. With the click of a remote the glass slid away, and the fresh air of the desert night washed across his skin.

"My city is your city, Antonio," she urged him.

So that was his name? He liked it.

"Before you go," said a voice behind him, "can you tell me, how is Skye?"

Antonio turned. A tall Spaniard faced him. He had a beating heart, and yet he wasn't exactly human. Almost a vampire, but somehow not.

"Skye?" the man prompted.

"Don't know her," Antonio replied.

Then he left to hunt.

Jamie gaped at Eriko as she stood in the hotel room she shared with Jenn and Skye. She looked amazing and ridiculous all at the same time. Three days had passed since she'd run into Shell Ghost Shogun at the magick show and he had insisted on a private concert. He'd made it clear that no was not an option. He'd been cheated out of enjoying some time with the Vampire Three before. He would not be denied the company of the "Vampire One."

After conferring with Jenn, Eriko had set a date—that Friday—and she, Jenn, and Skye had shopped for the proper clothes. If proper they could be called. She looked like a cartoon character, coating her face with white makeup, her lips drawn into a tiny cupid bow and her eyes outlined in shiny black eyeliner, with glittery red hearts dotting the corners. Stiff black petticoats stuck out from under a red satin miniskirt. White thigh-highs and black patent-leather heels completed her outfit.

"Are you having us on?" Jamie blurted. "What, were they all out of French-maid costumes?"

"Crikey, Jamie, where've you been?" Skye asked him.

"Fightin' for a free Ireland, and then a free human race," he shot back. "You?"

"Let me see your safe passage again," Jenn said, crossing to Eriko.

Eriko reached in her bodice and pulled out a folded document stating that the human bearing this document was a VIP guest of Shell Ghost Shogun and must be shown every courtesy.

Skye joined them, moving her hands over her scrying stone, probably giving the juice a boost. Jamie glowered. Eriko had to go, but did she have to go looking like *that*?

"This is a good thing. He might know Aurora," Eriko reminded Jamie. "He's staying at Aurora's Palace."

"He might know you're the Hunter." He pressed his knuckles against his forehead and exhaled slowly. Then he lowered his hands to his sides and shook his head, his eyes closed. "It's too risky."

"Jamie, we're hunters. Everything is risky." Eriko slipped on short white gloves trimmed in red lace. "Everything."

Jenn watched as Eriko stepped into the limo Shell Ghost Shogun had sent for her. Eriko had met the car in the turn-around of a different hotel about a mile from the Desert Blossom. Jamie followed on a motorcycle. Jenn, Holgar, and Skye were in a taxi; Taamir and Noah had rented a black van. The split-up had been Noah's idea. If something happened to one group following Eriko, she'd still have multiple backups looking out for her.

They had stakes and crosses—easily made from items

at hand. They'd hoped to buy some weapons, but humans weren't allowed to carry firearms in Las Vegas, and no one was willing to sell anything illegally to a pack of strangers. Requests to Father Juan to locate a resistance cell had gone unfilled. People were too afraid to resist, or so it seemed.

All six of them kept Eriko's vehicle in their sights. Jenn stared into the scrying stone. Skye had done well; she could see Eriko inside the limo. Behind the white geishalike makeup Eriko looked tired.

Then the limo pulled up to Aurora's Palace, and a Cursed One in a black suit helped her out. He was joined by another. They flanked Eriko as she went inside and entered a special elevator.

"Where are we going?" Eriko asked one of the vampires.

"We have sound?" Jenn asked, surprised.

Skye nodded. "I combined two enhancement spells. It worked."

"Nice," Jenn said appreciatively.

"Penthouse," the vampire said to Eriko. "Miss Aurora's suite."

Jenn caught her breath. Holgar reached over and squeezed her hand.

"We knew that Shell Ghost Shogun might know Aurora," Holgar said.

"I put a strong glamour on Eriko to keep her from being recognized," Skye reminded her.

"This is good. She can try to make contact with Antonio," Holgar added.

Jenn's cell phone rang. It was Noah.

"Jenn, I'm here. *We're* here," he amended.

"Thank you."

"I've got your back." His voice was low, and steady.

In the scrying stone the elevator door opened. Now Eriko was facing an ornate white door embellished with reliefs of fanged Grecian figures.

That door opened. A tall, dark, and very hot guy stood in the doorway. It was Skye's turn to gasp.

"Estefan?" Jenn guessed. Skye nodded. She looked ashen.

"She's with Estefan," Jenn said into her cell phone.

"Jamie will love that," Noah drawled. "We should hang up. They might be able to listen in. We could, back in Israel."

"Okay." She didn't want him to go.

After she and Noah disconnected, Jenn kept her eyes locked on the scrying stone as they exited the cab, nodding once at the black van as it rolled into the parking structure. She, Holgar, and Skye sauntered along in front of the massive complex, Holgar studying the topmost floor of the tallest building. Taamir and Noah appeared.

"Hey, sssssssexy," a woman dressed in a silvery tank top and red mini hissed at Noah, strolling boldly up to him. She was a Cursed One, her fangs extended. "Want to party?"

Noah winked at her. "Maybe later, baby."

The vampire sauntered away.

Jenn stared into the stone.

"Please, come in," Estefan invited Eriko.

Eriko minced across the threshold, acting a little uncertain and excited. She gazed around the room. The lights were dim, and about a dozen figures sat in chairs. Only their eyes were visible, glowing in the shadows.

One of the figures spoke to her in Japanese. Jenn was fairly certain that it was Shell Ghost Shogun. Eriko bowed several times, speaking in Japanese. Shell Ghost Shogun laughed.

Music played, total tween-style Japanese pop, and Eriko started a routine. She stuck out her butt and pointed to her cheeks. She hopped around in little circles, sounding twelve.

"That is *not* Eriko." Jamie said, watching over Jenn's shoulder. She hadn't heard him walk up. That was bad. Hunters had to be on their guard 24/7.

"Good. The glamour's working," Skye said happily.

"I mean, dancing around like an idiot." His voice was tight. "This was another gem of an idea."

Jenn refrained from pointing out that Jamie hadn't protested when Skye had infiltrated Aurora's nest back in New Orleans. He loved Eriko, and that was getting in the way. And he hated Antonio, and that was getting in the way too.

Eriko finished, and the assembled group applauded.

She hopped around and bowed. Shell Ghost Shogun said a few more words in Japanese. Eriko laughed and waved her hands in front of her face. Then the music started up again.

"Can't you do a spell to understand Japanese?" Jamie asked Skye. "Or make her sing something else?"

Skye shook her head. The song ended, and Jenn heard the pop of a champagne cork.

A young woman with two punctures in her neck appeared in their field of vision. She was wearing a white evening gown, and her pallor nearly matched the creamy fabric. Her hands trembled as she held out a tray of champagne glasses to Eriko.

Help me, she mouthed.

Then Aurora glided into view, and Jenn and the others stiffened.

"We're gonna kill you, bitch," Jamie muttered darkly.

"I wish Antonio had been here to meet you," Aurora continued. As she said his name, the girl holding the tray swayed. Eriko reached out a steadying hand to help her.

Monster, the girl mouthed. *Help.*

"Staci, we're *all* thirsty, not just our guest."

Staci shuffled away from Eriko, holding out her tray as she moved among the seated figures. Each took a glass of champagne.

"*Bueno*, Staci. You may return to Antonio's room and wait for him there."

"Oh, please, no," Staci sobbed. "Please, just kill me now. While he's gone."

"No," Jenn whispered, stunned. *"No."*

"Oh, God, Jenn," Skye said, grabbing her hand.

He's gone back, Jenn thought, *to what he was. To what he's always been.*

She would have dropped the scrying stone if Skye hadn't taken it from her. She would have burst into tears if she could have remembered how to cry. Or how to breathe.

"Maybe it's a trick," Holgar said, putting out a hand to steady her, much as Eriko had steadied the girl. "Maybe they know we're watching. They're saying that to provoke us."

"Well, I'm bloody provoked. I say as soon as Eri walks back out that door, we attack. Take Aurora now," Jamie said.

"With what?" Skye asked.

"What about Antonio?" Taamir added. "We should wait until he comes back. Make a clean sweep."

Noah gently edged out Holgar, who yielded his place at Jenn's side. "I'm sorry," he said, wrapping his hand around her hand. "I know what it's like to lose a teammate like this."

"We—we haven't lost anyone yet," she managed.

"We should have been more aggressive about finding weapons and people," Jamie said, pacing. "If he's gone over to the dark side, he's told them everything."

"Maybe he's pretending," Skye said hopefully.

"Did you *see* the holes in that girl's neck? And how terrified she was of him?" Taamir asked.

"Maybe she's in on it," Skye argued.

Taamir frowned skeptically. "Aurora obviously trusts him enough to let him go out on his own."

"So we're assuming," Skye countered. "Maybe it's just a show for us. Maybe they know we're scrying." Jenn knew she was trying to soften the shock, and she was grateful for the attempt. But it didn't work.

"You said Estefan wouldn't be able to detect your presence," Jamie said.

"I said I *hoped* he wouldn't be able to," Skye replied.

"Well, you know, there are just too many maybes for my taste." He rolled his shoulders, loosening them. "I say it's time to attack."

No one else spoke. From somewhere in her swirling brain Jenn knew they were waiting for her to respond. But she couldn't.

Antonio, she thought desperately. *Antonio.*

"Come here a moment," Noah told her. They walked a bit apart. Noah put his hands on her shoulders and positioned her to face him. Running his hands down her arms, he caught her hands in his. "They had to blow off steam," he said under his breath. "Now they'll listen to you. What are you going to tell them?"

"I can't do this," she whispered. "Noah, you don't really know me."

324

"I *do* know you," he countered, squeezing her hands. "I am you. And you *can* do this."

"No—"

"I was the scared kid. I was uncertain if I could step up when the time came. But I found out that I have strength deep down, deeper than most people can go. You have it. I can see it. That's why you're here. And that's why you kind of like me." He didn't smile. He meant every word.

"And that's why you have to go over to them and give the word. Just like you did in Russia."

SALAMANCA, NEW YEAR'S EVE, A FEW MONTHS EARLIER
JENN AND ANTONIO

> *"We are the vampire hunters.*
> *Our cause is holy.*
> *From Spain we come to save the world.*
> *Race from us into the sunlight, demons of hell!*
> *Better that you die in flames than by our hands!"*

As she stood in the icy chapel on the grounds of the University of Salamanca, Jenn sang along with the survivors of her class—down to little more than a handful—and watched Antonio de la Cruz. While the others sang, he prayed. Beneath his black ceremonial robe, his black hair curled along his jawline. He had amazingly long lashes, and he was buffed out. Jenn had been crushing on him for two years. So had every other girl in class, except maybe Eriko Sakamoto—who was all business—and Skye York, who had a crush on an Irish student named Jamie O'Leary.

Tonight was their final exam. After two years of training, one of them would become the Hunter. What would become of the others? No one was sure.

Father Juan, the head of the Sacred Heart Academy Against the Cursed Ones, signaled for them to file out into the foggy night. The university bells tolled; the vampires were waiting to pick them off, one by one.

"This way," Antonio said in his heavily accented English, as Skye and Eriko waved at them. They were part of a *grupo*, with Skye, Eriko, Jamie the crazy Irish guy, and Holgar, from Denmark. Holgar was a *werewolf*. Jenn still couldn't believe it. An actual werewolf.

And Antonio? He was deeply religious, and he was Spanish, and that was about all she knew about him. Like all the other girls she had told herself that the reason Antonio hadn't succumbed to her flirtatious skills was because he was studying to be a priest. She was glad he had her back tonight. He was a great fighter and strategist. Her grandparents had met in the underground, fighting for justice. No wonder she thought he was so wonderful.

When she thought about what was to come, she was amazed she'd made it this far. She wasn't the best fighter, or the fastest runner. She hadn't gotten the best grades in

Lore and Strategy. She was just Jenn. But somehow she'd survived when more than a hundred others hadn't.

"This way," Antonio told the five, taking the lead. Jamie was about to argue with him when Holgar loped past. Jenn fell in behind.

They moved soundlessly, like ninjas.

"I smell them," Holgar murmured.

They slowed. The dark covered them. Fog rolled in. Wind blew. Jenn started to get really, really scared. This was it.

The moon poked through the layers of fog as Antonio appeared before her. His robe hood was thrown back, and the silver light caught the angles and planes of his face. His eyes were deep-set, his lashes amazingly long. His nose was very straight, above soft lips she had dreamed of kissing a million times. He might die tonight. She wouldn't be able to bear it.

He gazed down at her, and she couldn't look away. It was as if he were casting a magick spell on her. He took a step toward her. Her heart raced.

"Jenn, tonight," he began. He fell silent. Then he raised a hand and cupped her cheek. His skin was icy, and she jerked, startled. He began to take his hand away.

"No," she said quickly, and he smiled. But it was a sad smile, stormy, and he did move it—to weave his fingers through her hair. His gaze swept over her features, as if he were memorizing them.

"Jenn, if tonight something happens, I want you to

know why . . ." He trailed off, cocking his head, holding her in his gaze like a hypnotist. "Why I didn't . . . act. It was you, Jenn, these last two years. You who captured my heart. But I couldn't."

His hand slipped from her hair to her shoulder. His touch made her knees buckle. She couldn't believe this was happening. Here, now. *Antonio de la Cruz.*

He cleared his throat. "I couldn't."

"Because you're studying to be a priest," she said.

"But now, when we fight them, you'll probably see why. I won't be able to stop it. And I want you to know that it changes nothing about how I feel. What I wish I could be. For you."

Then Holgar growled.

"C'mon, mates!" Jamie yelled. "Wolf's on the move!"

"Before we go," Antonio whispered. Then he bent his head over hers, and kissed her. His mouth was cold, but she felt warm. Tingles raced up her spine. Her heart was going a million miles a minute.

"Mi luz," he said. Her Spanish was bad, but she knew he had just called her "my light." *"Mi alma."* My soul.

"Oh, Antonio," she murmured, her eyes closed as he nuzzled her face with his mouth, his nose. "Have you known all this time that I—how I felt?"

"Sí. And I have thanked God for it. But, Jenn, you need to *know."* A pause. "Open your eyes."

And she did.

Las Vegas
Team Salamanca Minus Antonio;
Taamir and Noah

"We'll work something out, Jenn," Skye said.

It was only then that Jenn realized she was sitting on the curb outside Aurora's Palace. She didn't remember sitting down.

"Oh, Skye," Jenn whispered, her heart breaking. *"Skye."*

Jamie planted his feet in front of her. "Don't you do it, Jenn. Don't you bleedin' cry. You're our *leader*. Get it together." He glared at her. "So, what's the plan?"

Her body shook as she looked up at them. Holgar, Skye, Jamie, Taamir, and Noah, too, were all waiting to hear her grand, glorious decision. Noah gave her a quick nod. And something in her . . . shifted.

He's right. I can do this.

"We need to do what will cause the most damage," she said hoarsely. "What will help us win this war. We need to go in, now."

"Likin' that," Jamie said. "Good girl."

CHAPTER FOURTEEN

It's hard to let go. It's the most difficult lesson to
learn, regardless of whether or not you're a hunter.
We spend our whole lives seeking and building
connections—families, friends, mentors, lovers—
and then, in a moment, they can be taken from us.
These relationships can end along with a human life,
or these relationships can fall apart, until they are
as dead to you as if that person were in their grave,
though they still walk.

These are the hardest deaths in so many ways,
the deaths of a thousand tiny insults or omissions.
You wake up one day and realize that the person you
counted on most just isn't there for you. Worse yet, you
might not even care. This is the true horror. Physical
death is easy to understand, and no one blames you

when you mourn. Intangible death is so inexplicable,
that when you realize the loss it seems like the time for
crying has passed and you must hide your pain from
everyone. Even yourself.

> *—from the diary of Jenn Leitner,*
> *discovered in the ashes*

AD 1942, MADRID, SPAIN
IN THE COURT OF SERGIO ALMODÓVAR

Sergio Almodóvar, king of the vampires of Spain, sat on his throne and beamed at Antonio de la Cruz as he strode into his chamber with a lifeless human in his arms. Vampires crowded the walls, most dressed in the style of the day—women in black ball gowns with padded shoulders, and men in tuxedoes. Some had clung to the times when they had been converted, wearing remade court dress— hoopskirts and powdered wigs, Renaissance doublets, and frock coats. Sergio had many offspring.

But none of them pleased him as much as Antonio de la Cruz. The raven-haired youth had rained down destruction on the descendants of the men who had murdered Aurora's family and planned to burn Aurora herself at the stake. Sergio had planned the deaths as a present for Aurora, but unfortunately, they were having one of their lovers' quarrels and he had no idea where she was. Sergio wished she could have seen Antonio in action. In Sergio's opinion, the boy was a born killer. Antonio a priest? What a tragedy that would have been.

As reward for the seven murders, Sergio had presented Antonio with seven of the twelve exquisite rubies Sergio's sire had given to Sergio as payment for his various acts of service. Sergio had been more than pleased to give these sparkling stones to the jewel of his crown—Antonio.

Tonight Sergio had planned a grand fiesta in Antonio's honor. And apparently his protégé had brought a party favor. Intrigued, Sergio leaned forward.

"*Buenos tardes*, Antonio," he said. "What have you brought me?"

"My lord," Antonio said, dropping the body to the floor. As it fell, a wooden stake fell from a halter at its waist and clattered onto the stone. "A Hunter."

Sergio was speechless, overcome with pride.

"*Bravo!*" someone in the glittering assembly cried. All began applauding Antonio, the priest whom Sergio had found in the woods, praying over a dying Frenchman.

Sergio stood, arms outstretched.

"Antonio, you are a prince among vampires," Sergio declared. "Henceforth you are Duke Antonio de la Cruz."

"*Bravo!*"

Sergio swept down from the dais and embraced Antonio. Clasping hands with Antonio, Sergio led the boy to the royal room's focal point, not Sergio's throne but the statue of Orcus, with his bearded goat's head. His fanged mouth was open, and a mammoth fire blazed inside. Vampiric servants stoked the flames.

"Orcus, I present to you my servant, Antonio, duke of the vampires of Spain. He is my best, my pride, my joy. As I am bound to you, so is he, and I give you my bond that he will serve you faithfully. Swear faithfulness and loyalty, Duke Antonio. For eternity."

"I swear faithfulness and loyalty," Antonio repeated. "For eternity."

Sergio turned to smile at him, but at that moment a shadow passed over the handsome vampire's face. He blinked, and Sergio frowned. "Antonio?"

Antonio blinked again, and looked around, then at Sergio, like a man who had awakened from a daze. His mouth worked, but he didn't speak.

"Is something wrong?" Sergio pressed.

"No, no," Antonio said. He touched his forehead. "Forgive me."

"Then let us continue," Sergio said.

But Sergio should have paid better attention. That night Antonio de la Cruz left his court and joined the enemy. Sergio's sire nearly killed him, beating him for the shame and the humiliation. Sergio's court abandoned him.

"I will get him back," Sergio promised.

In 1942.

AD 1591, Ubeda, Spain
St. John of the Cross

St. John of the Cross lay on a pallet in a plain and simple room in December 1591, and everyone had given him up for dead. He held his beads, and made a prayer:

The soul takes flight, to repair the world. Oh, my soul, make good out of this long journey, so that I will achieve my true purpose and end my days in bliss.

Prayers are like magick, moving through the ethers of time and space. Like finds like, need finds need.

Fate finds destiny.

A prayer found the vampire Antonio de la Cruz.

In 1942.

Las Vegas
Team Salamanca Minus Antonio;
Taamir and Noah

Eriko sang. She kept having to fight her urge to throw herself at Aurora and try to stake her now. But she would be killed before her team could back her up.

However, in some ways, dying would have been preferable to singing and making cutesy faces at Shell Ghost Shogun. She had always suspected that he was the vampire who converted Yuki. And now he was here.

The girl, Staci, was serving a second round of drinks,

her hands still shaking. What had Antonio done to her? And looking at the row of Cursed Ones watching so intently, Eriko wondered what they were going to do to *her*. She had stakes concealed as stays in her top and a tiny cross tucked into her bra. Not much in the way of defenses, and she realized she hadn't thought through what to do if there was no easy exit.

She giggled and smiled and wished that she'd posted that she was going to be doing a private show at Aurora's Palace. Somewhere online. That way if she ended up dead, the team could at least use it to spread awareness of the fact that the vampires weren't all peace-loving like they pretended.

So many ifs. And some regrets:

She was sorry she hadn't kissed Jamie. She'd never kissed a boy, and he was so into her that it seemed a shame she hadn't tried it. She was sorry she hadn't checked on Kenji, to see if he was okay, if he was still alive.

She finished singing and did an elaborate curtsey, forcing herself to smile and giggle.

The Cursed Ones applauded, and Aurora stood up, approaching her, fangs clearly visible.

"Wonderful! Thank you very much for entertaining us this evening." Aurora cupped her cheek in her hand. "Such a pretty child, and so talented."

Eriko couldn't decide if Aurora was about to eat her or turn her into a pet. She slid a hand to her waist, ready to reach for a stake if need be.

Kill her now! her inner voice urged. *You'll never have a better shot.*

An explosion rocked the building, and Aurora turned swiftly away.

"What was that?" the vampire demanded.

Eriko smiled. She knew exactly what it was. It was Jamie, coming to the rescue.

SALAMANCA
FATHER JUAN

They met in the university chapel: students, teachers, priests. Father Juan stood up at the front and surveyed their ranks. They had fought the good fight; they had kept the faith. But now it was time to make the hard decisions. Diego stood beside him, offering his support. He took a deep breath and began.

"I've called you all here today because it's time you knew what was going on, and each one of you must decide your future."

There was murmuring as people shifted in their seats and looked to each other.

"The Church has negotiated a peace with the vampires. They have ordered us to cease hunter-training activities and close our doors."

Gasps and choruses of "no" echoed around the room. He held up a hand to silence them.

"I don't feel that this is the right thing to do. I've decided, therefore, to keep the school open, defying the orders from Rome."

Spontaneous applause and cheers broke out. Then Father Juan once again held up a hand to bring order.

"Those teachers who stay may continue to train whoever wishes to learn. But please, all of you, be aware that any Catholic who remains here risks excommunication. And the government may send in troops to force us to leave. We are completely on our own; no help or aid will come from any quarter. This school will stand against the forces of darkness to the end—hopefully the end of this terrible war.

"You have all trained and taught to the best of your abilities. You now stand at a crossroads. Anyone who wishes to leave this place should do so within the next twenty-four hours. No ill will will be harbored. Those who go do so with my blessings. Those who remain do so with my gratitude.

"Now, everyone should retire to their room for the rest of the day to think, pray, meditate, and decide their path. Thank you."

Father Juan stepped down from the stage and left through a side door. He headed for his office, followed by Diego, who walked beside him.

After a few minutes of silence Father Juan finally turned to the bishop.

"How many do you think will stay?"

Diego shrugged. "I think most of the students will stay. They're committed to what we stand for."

"And what of the teachers, the priests?"

Diego's eyes clouded. "That is a far different matter. Many of the teachers have families to care for. Excommunication is a terrible threat for the priests. To be cut off spiritually by the Pope is a terrible punishment."

Juan sighed. "I know. Which is why I think you should leave."

Diego started, his eyes flashing angrily. "Do you think me a coward?"

Juan put his hand on the man's shoulder. "No one who has spent any time with you could ever think that. But you have served the cause, and I think you might continue to do so in Rome. I need to know what they are planning."

"I can do that," Diego said. "I *will* do that. But the students—"

"I'll watch over those who remain. I can't watch what is happening outside these walls, though."

"If I leave, it will give the other priests impetus to go as well."

"I know. And it pains me, but if I have to carry on alone, I will."

"You don't have to protect me," Diego said stubbornly.

Father Juan laughed at the idea. "I know, my friend, but by sending you to the lion's den I fear I'm putting you in far greater danger than if you stayed."

They faced each other, possibly for the last time. Father Juan watched as Diego struggled with emotions that nearly overpowered him. Finally the bishop held out his hand, and Juan clasped it.

"I'll leave at the end of the twenty-four hours," Diego said. "I won't make my decision known before I go, so as not to sway others who are making their own choices."

"Agreed," Juan said.

The two embraced. Then Diego hurried down the hallway, and Juan watched him go. Sending him away was the right thing to do, but it would be harder to face the daily struggles without his companionship and wisdom.

Father Juan stared at the closed door of his office and didn't want to go inside. After a moment's thought he turned away. It was time to pay Heather another visit, to remind himself what they were all struggling for—and against.

Standing before her cell, he found her huddled in the corner, sobbing quietly.

"Heather," he called gently.

"What do you want?" she screamed in return.

"To talk," he said, pulling up a chair, still keeping several feet from the cage.

"I don't want to talk. I want to kill you."

"Why?"

"Because."

"Because why?"

She laughed, a hollow, mocking sound that made his hair stand on end. "Because you're food, and I'm hungry."

"You don't have to kill to eat. Antonio doesn't."

Heather half laughed, half sobbed. "Jenn never told me her precious boyfriend was a Cursed One."

"I imagine she didn't."

"Why?" Heather screeched and threw herself at the bars. Father Juan didn't answer.

"I'll tell you why. Because she's a hypocrite! She was my hero, saving the world from vampires. She couldn't even save me! And you know what? I'm going to kill her for it," Heather hissed.

There was no reasoning with her; Father Juan could see that. She wasn't scheduled to eat for several more hours, so after sitting with her a few more minutes he got up and left. He walked, wandering through classrooms and down hallways. Jenn was going to be devastated when she returned and discovered that Heather had found her voice, but that all she could do with it was express her hate.

Antonio, how did you overcome what you are? he wondered. He thought of him in Aurora's clutches, and his stomach churned. He prayed that the team would find him and save him. They needed to, because in his heart he didn't think they could save Heather.

Outside the student dorms, walking, Father Juan lifted his face to the sun and felt the warmth suffuse him. When he had worshipped the Goddess, he had embraced the moon.

His current work also kept him up at night. Sometimes he forgot the healing powers of the sun. He breathed in deeply of the golden air, wishing he could drink the light in to himself and illuminate the dark, shadowed corners of his own mind and heart.

With his eyes closed, he became aware of voices talking together quietly. He followed the sound until he found a bench under a tree and saw that two students, Maria and Marta, fifteen-year-old twins from Argentina, were sitting together, hugging and crying.

They didn't see Father Juan, and he lingered for a moment.

"They could excommunicate us," Maria said.

"But Father Juan is a priest. He can absolve us," Marta answered.

"Not if they excommunicate him, too. Then he's not a real priest anymore."

"Some things are worth fighting for. And if we survive, if we win, surely we will be forgiven," Marta said.

"I'm leaving. Please come with me," Maria said.

"I can't leave," Marta replied.

The two girls embraced, and Juan's heart broke for them. That was the hell of this war, the way it rendered families asunder. And now the actions of the Church were doing the same. Anger burned in his breast, and he fought to maintain control of himself.

Finally he stepped forward, startling the girls. He dropped to his knees next to them and embraced them both. They clung to him and to each other and cried as he prayed for them both, for their souls, and for their lives.

He stayed with them for nearly half an hour. Then he retraced his steps back to his office, still not entirely prepared to deal with the aftermath of his announcement. When he neared the door, his heart sank slightly as he saw someone waiting for him.

Master Molina stood, bag in hand, and Father Juan wasn't surprised. Their martial arts expert was also a member of the Spanish military. If Master Molina didn't leave, he would be disobeying orders.

"I understand, but I am very sorry to lose you," Juan said, reaching out to clasp the other man on the shoulder.

The warrior shook his head. "You're not losing me. I think we need to consolidate our forces; we're too far-flung, too vulnerable to attack."

Father Juan cocked his head to the side. "What are you saying?"

"I think we need to move the teachers, hunters, and priests to the student dormitory so that we're all together."

Father Juan felt a wave of emotion nearly overcome him, and he blinked back tears of gratitude. "Thank you, my friend. And you are, as always, right."

Master Molina nodded. "I'm going to go find an empty room."

Father Juan nodded. "I'll have the others who are staying do the same."

Master Molina nodded and turned to go. It was nothing short of a miracle, that Molina had answered a call that put him at odds with everything he believed in. He prayed they had several more such miracles. They would need them to have any chance of survival.

Las Vegas
Team Salamanca Minus Antonio;
Taamir and Noah

Noah had to admit that Jamie's knowledge of alcoholic beverages and their flammability was impressive. They had managed to blow out the glass in all the windows on the floor immediately below the one where Eriko was with the Cursed Ones. At least two vampire guards had been caught in the blast and had burned to ash. The vampire prostitute Noah had convinced to lead them up there got a stake in the heart for her troubles. No charge. It was a good start, but there was a roomful of vampires overhead who still needed to be dealt with.

Jenn led the charge up the stairwell, and Noah followed on her heels, proud of her for pulling herself together. The seven hunters burst into the room they had seen in the scrying stone. Eriko's shirt hung off her in tatters, and she drove a stake into Shell Ghost Shogun, who disintegrated nicely upon impact. The drinks girl, Staci, was screaming her head off in a corner.

Noah turned to the vampire on his right. He had clearly believed himself above the rabble of humanity here in Aurora's Palace, and now he found himself the dirt beneath Noah's boots. The hunter smiled, savoring the irony.

Noah found himself facing off against a massive vampire, probably a bodyguard. Out of the corner of his eye he saw the vampire leader, Aurora, saunter right through all the chaos and out the front door.

Las Vegas
Antonio

Antonio heard fighting as he returned from his hunt. The elevator was out of order, and he'd climbed the stairs, practically flying up them, he went with such speed. At last he set foot into Aurora's audience chamber, only to find her vampires locked in combat with humans.

He frowned, not seeing Aurora. There was something he wanted, needed to tell her, but he couldn't remember what it was.

He thought about joining the fight, but there was no one there he cared to protect or kill. The vampires could take care of themselves, and if not, they deserved to die for being weak.

He turned and left, to look for Aurora. He heard someone call his name, but it wasn't she, so he didn't turn around.

His left earlobe was beginning to itch. Antonio reached up to touch it, and hissed as his finger brushed his cross earring. Lightning fast, he forced himself to yank out the ruby-studded earring and drop it in the stairwell. The itching stopped.

He charged back into the desert air. It smelled of human sweat, fear, lust. Perfumes and exhaust entwined with desert sand in the dry night heat.

Antonio looked up and down the Strip, squinting against all the lights. Where would she be? If she was out hunting, maybe she had gone somewhere quieter, with fewer distractions for feeding.

He made his way down several streets, putting distance between himself and the Strip, until finally the lights and noises took on a more reasonable character.

The scents, too, were different, subtler and yet somehow richer. He stopped and cocked his head. Antonio could smell a mixture of incense, candle smoke, and something intangible. He followed the scent for nearly a block until he found a small whitewashed building. In a city known for its ostentatious flamboyance, the building was austere in contrast, with only a single stained-glass window visible from the street. It had a sign that read SINNERS WELCOME.

An invitation if ever there was one.

Antonio smiled and went inside. He counted thirty beating hearts, people gathered, praying. He recognized the words of a Catholic novena. Apparently, their special concern was for the city itself. He smirked as he half listened to their pathetic mumbling.

An elderly couple held a baby at the front of the small sanctuary, facing a priest in a chasuble and stole. The trio exchanged a few whispered words, which Antonio could hear from where he stood. They were grandparents, presenting their grandchild for baptism, hoping that the little girl would help bring new hope to the city.

They couldn't have been more wrong.

In the back pew a young woman sat, arms wrapped around herself, rocking back and forth. She was dressed in a short pirate skirt and tunic, seemingly just off work at one of the casinos. Antonio killed her before she knew he was even there. He laid her limp body down on the pew and wiped her blood from his lips.

No one even turned around, so intent were they on their prayers. It was fantastic. He killed three more, silently. Then it got more complicated. People saw him, screamed, "Cursed One!" They scattered, running, screaming. He caught one teenage boy when he was halfway out the door to freedom.

The old couple died defending their grandchild.

Antonio slaughtered everyone, saving the priest for next to last. The man died with his god's name on his lips and Antonio's fangs in his neck. That left the very best for last. Antonio picked up the squalling infant and smiled at her, imagining how she would taste. He bared his teeth. Her tiny fists balled, and she let out a loud wail. He was charmed. She smelled clean and fresh. A delight, like dessert.

Then something crashed to the floor behind the altar. He jumped, startled. It was a crucifix. Why hadn't it troubled him? Simply because he hadn't noticed it?

First he averted his eyes, but then he gazed at it. He couldn't stop staring at the crown of thorns, the sad eyes of Jesus, the plain brown boards, fascinated and repulsed.

Shouts outside reached his ears. He put the baby on the floor and spun to face the back of the church. Humans burst through the door, stakes and crosses thrust before them, bearding the lion in his den. He must have missed a parishioner, who'd run out and gotten help. It hurt to look at these crosses, but he couldn't look away with humans racing at him. A tattooed man with a nearly shaven head led the rush.

Hunters, he thought, judging by the skilled, organized way they advanced. Trained assassins.

Antonio waited for the tattooed hunter to come to him. Then at the last moment Antonio stepped to the side and snaked out an arm, grabbing the man around the throat and yanking him backward until he was helpless in Antonio's arms.

He smelled rage on the man. No fear. Just deep, hot anger.

Antonio dropped his head and sank his fangs into the man's neck. There was a strangled scream followed by kicking and flailing, but Antonio knew every move, every tactic, and he easily subdued his prey.

His blood tasted like smoke, and metal. It made Antonio shiver with delight. He fed quickly.

But something stabbed him, and he released the man, blood flowing from the twin wounds on the tattooed throat. Antonio turned to see a Japanese girl standing in short, stiff skirts caked in blood, her face contorted in fury. He twisted his arm behind himself, yanked out the stake she had put in his back, narrowly missing his heart, and drove it through her shoulder. He snarled. It was not a death-dealing blow.

He put his hand around it to pull it back out, then spun just as a tall blond guy slammed into him, bearing them both to the ground. Antonio kicked up at him, hard, and bit the man on the arm. The man rolled away for a moment to retrieve a stake on the ground, and Antonio sprang to his feet.

He was getting bored.

There were too many of them to kill quickly, particularly in a church, which afforded them so many additional weapons—now that he looked at the fallen crucifix, he cringed.

He smiled at the auburn-haired girl who seemed to be in charge. She looked so very, very familiar to him. He blew her a kiss and laughed when her eyes bugged out of her head. Then he raced out the side door, running into the night.

The cool air kissed his cheeks, and he kept running, enjoying the speed and chuckling at the sounds of their footfalls in pursuit of him. If they were fools, they would send their fastest on ahead to be killed quickly, leaving the rest of them that much more vulnerable.

He was only mildly disappointed when the sounds of

pursuit faded, but he didn't consider turning back to fight them. The night was calling. The night, and the horizon. He wanted to kill more people at prayer. It had felt so nice, and they tasted better somehow, more flavorful, the little slaughtered sheep.

He frowned. Where was he going to find enough of them to meet his needs?

Utah. Utah was the next state over, and hadn't he heard that Utah was Mormon country? Delicious. More innocence.

Aurora would understand. He would be back soon, once he had drunk his fill.

Jenn dropped to her knees next to Jamie even as Holgar, Noah, and Taamir went after Antonio. Skye had already pulled the stake out of Eriko and was doing what she could for her shoulder.

"Are you okay?" she asked Jamie, trying to block out the image of evil Antonio blowing a kiss at her.

"No," he said, looking up at her, eyes wide and face pale.

She was taken aback. This wasn't Jamie. Where was the snark, the profanity, the accusations? He was seriously hurt. How much blood had Antonio taken? How much blood loss could a human being survive?

"Skye! We need to get Jamie to a hospital, somewhere where we can get him a transfusion," Jenn said, trying to keep the panic out of her voice.

Skye turned, still working on Eriko. "There's no way

we'll be able to pull that off without getting caught."

"There has to be a way," Jenn said, struggling to keep her voice even despite the fact that Jamie was slumping back onto the ground. She twisted so she could put Jamie's head in her lap, and something scratched her thigh through her pocket. Antonio's ruby earring. She had found it back in the hotel stairwell and retrieved it.

Jamie, Eriko, and now she had bled for Antonio.

No more.

She had seen his glowing red eyes. The solemn, cautious guy she knew was gone, and a monster capered in his place.

Gone. Her heart shattered.

"Jamie, hang on," she ordered him.

Jamie tried to nod his head, but even that effort seemed too much for him.

"We have to figure out how we're getting out of here," Eriko said, grimacing. "Aurora's seen us. The airport is not an option."

"There's only one road in and out of this place; that's what you told us," Skye reminded Jenn.

"Then we'll find a way through the desert," Jenn said, setting her jaw. "First we have to get help for Jamie. And then we have to . . . we have to kill Antonio." She took a deep, long breath. "We can't leave Vegas until that's done."

Oh, God, please, no. Her stomach lurched, and the room began to spin. She tried to ignore the fact that Jamie's pulse seemed to be slowing.

"Actually, I think we have to leave Vegas to get that done," Skye said.

"What do you mean?" Jenn asked.

She hesitated. "I think, right before he left, he was thinking about Utah."

Jenn stared at her. "How do you know?"

"I'm not sure. I just heard him in my head." Skye started crying. "He couldn't have done this. I *know* him. He's not a killer. This is not him, Jenn."

Jenn's throat tightened, but she didn't respond.

As Skye wept, she pressed a hand to Eriko's forehead and murmured an incantation. Then she got up and sat beside Jamie. She cried harder as she began to work magicks.

"He needs blood," Skye whispered, herself growing pale.

"I'm a universal donor," Jenn said. "If we can just find someplace, someone who has the equipment, I could donate my blood."

"We can help with that," said a rangy voice at the door.

There at the entrance stood Greg, the man from her grandfather's funeral, flanked by two other men sporting the same suits and identical black Jerusalem crosses. Greg stepped over half a dozen bodies as he walked toward her, but he didn't glance down at a single one. He bent over and took a good look at Jamie, then motioned at the other two men. Wordlessly, they gently picked up Jamie.

"Hey, wait a minute," Jenn said, going after them.

Greg regarded her steadily. "We can save his life. We will."

"Where will you take him?" she demanded.

His black sunglasses reflected her careworn, blood-streaked face. She couldn't see his eyes, couldn't read his neutral expression. She ticked a glance past him to the door.

"Not just him—you, too," Greg replied. "He still needs a donor."

Jenn stood and turned to look at Skye, who was holding her hands in front of herself, fingers spread, concentrating hard. She gave Skye a quick, sharp nod.

"Go," Skye said. "I'm feeling vibes. I think they're friends."

"Well, we're certainly not enemies," Greg replied.

And Jamie didn't have time for them to discuss it.

"Skye, coming?" Jenn asked, making up her mind.

Skye shook her head. "I'll wait for the others. They might return here."

"We'll meet up tomorrow. Nine a.m., one mile from the northern border checkpoint, understood?" Greg asked Skye. "You know where it is?"

Skye nodded, biting her lip as more tears streamed down her cheeks. She looked so young. Just sixteen. What a world she had grown up in. Jenn knew she desperately wanted to go with Jamie; maybe that would be better, so she could continue to work her magicks on him.

"Do you want to switch places?" Jenn offered.

Skye shook her head. "I'm *not* a universal donor."

"Besides," Greg said, "it's you, Miss Leitner, whom we need to speak with."

Jenn nodded and, turning, walked out of the church with Greg. And as she stepped over them, she didn't look at the bodies either.

SALAMANCA
FATHER JUAN

It was time to say good-bye. Father Juan embraced Diego tightly, praying silently for his safety. The bishop pulled away at last, wiping at his eyes. His bags were next to him. He held out a piece of paper to Juan with a list of names on it.

"Ninety students have elected to stay. Those who chose to leave have gone already."

"And the instructors?"

"Master Molina alone of the Spanish military officers is remaining."

Juan nodded. "It's too much to expect them to go against both their government and their church."

Diego nodded. "The three civilian instructors are staying."

"All of them?" Juan asked, amazed.

"Yes."

"That is an unlooked-for blessing."

"One you're in dire need of, I'm afraid," Diego said grimly.

Juan didn't want to ask the final question. "The priests?"

"Leaving."

"All of them?"

Diego nodded grimly. "I can stay," he ventured.

"No, I still need you out there looking out for us."

"I'll do everything in my power."

"Do everything in God's power, and then we're fine," Juan said, trying to smile.

"I know some people don't see it, but you are doing God's work. He will take care of you. He always has. He won't let you die until you are finished with your work here."

Juan laughed bitterly. Diego spoke words truer than he knew.

Diego continued. "I don't believe the Pope knows what is happening here. I can't believe he is condoning all of this. I think the alliance, the shutting down of the academy, all are being orchestrated by others. As has happened before, in other wars."

"If that's true, then it's even more important that you go. Maybe you can get to His Holiness and tell him what's happening," Juan said. "Make him see that we need his support."

"I will try. Until then, good-bye, my old friend."

Juan watched Diego's car drive out of sight and then turned and went into the chapel, needing to pray and be by himself.

But a lone figure knelt in front of the altar, apparently having the same need. Juan approached slowly, not wanting to interrupt, but drawn to see who it was and whether they needed him to pray with them.

He was surprised when he saw that it was one of the younger priests, a young Italian with dark hair not unlike Antonio's. His shoulders were hunched, and he held his clerical collar in his hands.

"Father Giovanni," Father Juan said, "I thought you would have been gone by now."

Father Giovanni looked up at him. "I was gone."

"And?"

The priest tried to smile. "I came back."

"I'm glad," Juan said, kneeling next to him. "I'm just not sure why you did."

Father Giovanni gazed at Father Juan with an odd, far-away look on his face. "I—I had a vision. God told me I was needed here. That I had a purpose." He took a breath. "I think I'm going to die here."

Juan stared at the priest in alarm. "Are you sure?"

"As sure as one can be when one is having a vision," Father Giovanni replied, "for the first time in his life."

"Then why did you come back?"

Father Giovanni looked next at the crucifix on the wall. "God told me He needed me, but that it was my choice."

"To die in the service of God is the finest death anyone can have," Juan assured him, not sure what else he could say. "And we all die."

Father Giovanni nodded and then offered his collar to Juan. "I'm excommunicated, then, Father."

Juan shook his head. "Rome has made an error. You

wear that with pride. You are serving God. You are His priest. The students who believe need to see you wearing your collar, to know that you still have faith. It will give them courage."

Father Giovanni nodded. Anger again rose in Juan. God's people were dying for what was right, and they were being threatened for it by the very people who should be supporting and canonizing them. Why did it always have to be this way?

He heard a footstep at the back of the chapel, and soon Master Molina was kneeling beside them, bending his head in prayer. Then the other three instructors came in and joined them. So few of them left to care for ninety students.

He heard the shuffling of many feet as those students came and joined them, gathering around the teachers instead of sitting in the pews as they ordinarily would.

Juan closed his eyes. *I am not alone.*

We are not alone.

BOOK THREE
SEKER

Upon my flowery breast,
Kept wholly for himself alone,
There he stayed sleeping, and I caressed him,
And the fanning of the cedars made a breeze.

—St. John of the Cross,
sixteenth-century mystic of Salamanca

CHAPTER FIFTEEN

Did you think that we weren't there?
Did you think we didn't care?
We've seen every tear you've cried
Hung on every breath you've sighed
We want to dwell in your heart
Together always, ne'er to part
And when you taste our undying thirst
You will feel how we are cursed

LAS VEGAS
TEAM SALAMANCA MINUS ANTONIO;
TAAMIR AND NOAH

Jenn sat in the back of a black, windowless van with her arms folded across her chest, dividing her attention between

Greg, who sat across from her, and Jamie, who lay unconscious on the vehicle's floor. "Who are you?" she asked at last.

Greg gave her the ghost of a smile. "We're the good guys."

A minute later the van pulled to a stop, and Greg swung open the door. They were in a parking garage. Where, she wasn't sure, but it couldn't have been too far from the church. The two black-cross men who had been with Greg carried Jamie out of the van and into a waiting elevator. Jenn followed with Greg.

They exited into a penthouse suite, and Jenn marveled at the views of the city with all its blinking lights. A man in a black turtleneck, who was also wearing a Jerusalem cross on a chain around his neck, waved the men carrying Jamie over to a dining table, and they placed him on it.

"Don't worry, he's a doctor," Greg said.

As the man began to set up IVs for the transfusion, Jenn realized that she had been so tired and so stressed for so long that she had passed beyond worried. Sinking down into the chair, she gave serious consideration to what it would be like if Jamie's and her positions were reversed.

Death would be a blessing, a release from the fear and the fighting. There were moments when Jenn struggled just to remember why she was fighting instead of giving up, accepting the world the way that it was, and trying to get by in it until someone recognized her as a former hunter and killed her.

She shook her head. It was the exhaustion and the horror over Antonio that was doing her thinking for her. She needed to put those thoughts from her mind.

She didn't want to watch the doctor work, so she turned back to Greg and cleared her throat. "Now, tell me exactly who you are and what's been going on," she said.

He pulled up a chair and sat down. "We're part of a shadow organization working inside the United States government. We've never given up on winning this war. We've been working to create a weapon that will change the balance of power."

"Like the disease that scientist was working on in Madrid?" Jenn had been in America when her team had been sent to help safeguard Dr. Sherman and had failed. She had been told, though, that after the scientist was turned into a vampire, commandos wearing the black Jerusalem cross had snatched him from under the noses of both the Cursed Ones and Team Salamanca.

"Exactly like that," Greg said.

"And . . . you were in Russia?"

He grimaced. "Afraid we didn't quite pull that one off. We didn't get Dantalion or his data. Everything went up."

"We were going in," she said. "We could have done it. You got in our way."

He shook his head. "Then it would have been your people getting blown to smithereens instead of ours."

She closed her eyes. "Jamie heard someone talking to

Dantalion in English. An American, he said. From Solomon. Filling Dantalion in."

"What?"

"Telling him about Aurora. And us. He said that Eriko had been killed."

Greg leaned forward. "Did Jamie describe him?" He glanced at the fallen hunter as if he wanted to jostle him awake.

"The man was wearing a gas mask and white camouflage," she said.

"That doesn't narrow it down much. But it should come as no surprise to us that he and Solomon were working together. Solomon's got half the world working for him."

"You should have told us you were there. And what you were doing."

"Sorry. We can't move quite as freely as you can. This meet-up's not exactly sanctioned," he said, "and that's telling you more than I should."

She sighed. "Just our luck to have wimpy allies."

"We will win this war," Greg said. "We just need time."

"We're fresh out."

A cushy chair was brought in. Jenn sat down gingerly, never taking her eyes off Greg as the doctor wrapped a tourniquet around her upper arm and tapped a vein in her forearm. Greg's face was grave.

"I'm afraid that's true," Greg said.

"Here we go," the doctor said. Jenn winced as the needle went in.

"Why don't we team up? Why do you only help us in the ways that you do?" she asked him.

He shook his head. "We're not ready to be exposed like that. The best thing you're doing for this war is acting as an inspiration for those mustering the courage to rise. And keeping the Cursed Ones distracted, so they look your way instead of ours."

"We're bait?" she asked angrily. Their lives were worth more than that.

His expression never wavered. "Yes, and no. You're a mighty force to be reckoned with, and in time I think all of you will figure that out. But word about you is getting around. You could also become a public face to this conflict."

"You're doing great," the doctor told her.

Jenn had never thought of it that way before, but as her lids flickered, she could remember the excitement back at Salamanca when she would walk by the students. They looked up to her and the others, needed them, and aspired to be them. And soon those students would likely replace the Salamanca hunters.

She turned her head so she could look at Jamie. At the rate they had been sustaining injuries, it was only a matter of time before they all got killed.

"We should at least have a way of contacting you," she insisted.

"It's too dangerous. Tonight's events have done nothing

363

but underscore that. Don't worry, though. We're always keeping close tabs on Team Salamanca. And we're not the only ones."

"What do you mean?" she asked, beginning to feel a little woozy.

His face stretched and blurred in front of her. "You'll find the answer to that yourself, in time."

Greg wouldn't tell Jenn anything else, and she slept fitfully on a couch, worrying about Jamie and Antonio, fighting to reconcile the monster she had seen in that church with the guy who had kissed her so tenderly. Who had kept watch over her during their two years of training. She thought of something her grandfather used to say: *Fool me once, shame on you. Fool me twice, shame on me.* Had Antonio fooled her all this time? Father Juan had given Eriko the elixir, then "demoted" her from leader of the team. Had he given the elixir to the wrong person? And had he been equally mistaken about giving Antonio a position on the team?

If I had to go against what Father Juan told me to do, would I have the nerve?

Dawn came, and she hadn't really slept. She, Greg, and an unconscious Jamie were waiting at the rendezvous when the others showed. One look at their grim expressions told Jenn everything she needed to know. Antonio was still alive. Her heart sang for one moment before plummeting. If he was still running loose, there was a very real possibility that she herself would have to stake him. All the time that she had worried about Antonio, she had never seen herself in this position. Never the one to end his life. Would she have the deep-down strength Noah had spoken of? Or would she falter at the crucial moment?

Would he kill me, *then?*

The others greeted her and fretted over Jamie, who was still unconscious. Skye told Jenn that upon Eriko and Holgar's return, she had taken the baby to a nearby hospital, swaddling her in warm blankets and then leaving her at the entrance. Then she'd cast a summoning spell and had waited in the shadows until a hospital staff member had come outside and found the child.

They all piled in the van, which Greg had outfitted with some stakes, two crosses, and a vial of holy water. They huddled together on the floor, and Greg threw a tarp over them. He had explained that a well-placed hundred dollar bill and the proper guard would ensure that the inside of the van would not be looked at too carefully at the checkpoint, but they had to remain still nevertheless.

"And keep those weapons stowed," he added.

Jenn found herself holding her breath, wedged between Noah and Jamie as the van rolled to a stop. Noah took her hand, and she let him. Time passed; she wasn't sure how long, but she was sure they had been discovered. Then the van rolled forward, slowly, and picked up highway speed. Under the tarp it was hot and dark, and a few minutes later, when Greg pulled it off, she sat up in relief, her stomach queasy.

Half an hour farther on they pulled over to the side of the road. A beat-up pickup truck was sitting there.

"Here's your ride," Greg said. "I've heard Antonio's holed up for the day about three hundred miles north. Little town called Ridgeback. Population is practically nil. They've got a motel, a gas station, a couple of stores, and that's about it."

"Thank you," Jenn said as she exited the van.

"Don't thank me. Just keep doing what you're doing," Greg said seriously.

"We will," she assured him.

She held out her hand, remembering Gramma at Papa Che's funeral. She had shaken Greg's hand too. Maybe he thought of Gramma too, as he warmly shook Jenn's hand. Behind them the rest of her team piled out of the vehicle and descended on the pickup.

"Tell your grandmother hello," he said as he jumped back into the van.

Jenn waved and turned to her team, not having the heart to tell him that she had no way of contacting Esther Leitner.

Skye felt drained as she sat in the bed of the pickup with Holgar. She had volunteered, hoping that the feel of the wind and sun on her face would help refresh her, recharge her. She longed to take off her shoes and feel the dirt between her toes, and conduct a restorative ritual. She was going to need to take care of herself shortly if she hoped to take care of anyone else. Jamie had come around, but he was groggy and reserved—not at all himself. Skye could tell Jenn was worried about him too.

She leaned half against the cab and half against the werewolf. She could tell by the way he had his head lifted and was flaring his nostrils that he missed running through the forest. Missed being in nature. She did too. Although for Holgar it had to be a much more primal, intense experience. Sometimes Skye envied that, though not the reason why. She rested her head against Holgar's shoulder, and he didn't seem to mind.

When her hunting partner had come back with Taamir and Noah unharmed, she had been so intensely relieved it had momentarily eased her despair over Jamie and Antonio. As it turned out, each member of Team Salamanca was still alive. It was what Father Juan would call a miracle. And if they could kill Antonio, that would probably be a miracle too.

She had seen Antonio in that church, though, had felt his thoughts and then literally read his mind. Had that really happened? He had thought "Utah," and now they were headed that way after him. She must have, but how?

Maybe it was a sign. Maybe Skye was supposed to reach out to him, bring him back to his senses. Antonio had overcome his vampiric nature before. Could he do it again?

If he could, then maybe there was hope for Heather, or for all vampires.

Her thoughts turned to Estefan and whatever it was he had become. Less than vampire, more than witch. He had driven her mad on the palace grounds, if only for a few moments, and she had almost died because of it. Terrifying. She shivered.

Mistaking her action for physical discomfort, Holgar wrapped his arms around her to warm her. She closed her eyes, savoring his warmth, feeling the raw earthiness that was him. So much power, so much strength. And so much good. He was what Estefan should have been.

But Estefan loved his own worst nature and was trying hard to cultivate it. There had to be a special hell for those who chose to become like the Cursed Ones—if such a place existed.

Noah drove the entire distance—more than four hours—before stopping. They pulled up outside the dusty motel on the outskirts of Ridgeback. Skye hopped down from the bed of the truck and went into the lobby with Jenn to make sure that she wasn't recognized and that no identification was requested.

She murmured the spells as softly as she could while the transaction was carried out. Two rooms were obtained, and the team staggered inside, bone weary.

Skye sank down on the one bed and stared at Eriko. She looked like some insane anime character with her stiff, blood-coated skirts and her bra. Eriko's shredded blouse had been lost somewhere. Skye started to laugh.

"It's not funny," Eriko said, turning red.

Jenn turned to look, and then she, too, started to giggle. "It is, a little," she said.

All that they had brought to the States was still in their hotel room in Vegas, and lost to them now. Skye was glad she had left everything she'd cherished back in Salamanca. Moving slowly, Jenn shrugged out of her turtleneck. She was wearing a black tank under it, and she tossed the turtleneck to Eriko, who ran with it into the bathroom and closed the door.

A minute later Skye could hear water running, and Eriko emerged after a few minutes, hair wet. The turtleneck was mismatched with the mess of a skirt, and Skye wished she had some clothes to share with Eriko. Hopefully they could find a thrift store nearby.

After sleep, that was. Skye let herself collapse onto the bed. As she closed her eyes, her stomach growled. And after food. Sleep, food, clothes. That sounded right.

Jamie had slept for much of the ride in the pickup. Now he lay on his back, staring up at the ceiling and dreaming about how many different ways he could kill that Curser Antonio. The bite wounds in his neck hurt like the devil and were beginning to itch. He was still shaky from the blood loss and transfusion.

But he would find some way to kill that vampire if it was the last thing he ever did. To think he had trained with him, fought with him, *trusted* him. Okay, he had never trusted Antonio.

On the floor Holgar yipped in his sleep, and Jamie turned his head to stare at the werewolf.

And you're next, bloody animal.

They slept four hours and then rose. Holgar stretched his muscles. They needed to find and take down Antonio while it was still light outside and they had a chance of cornering him.

It was a shame. The old Antonio had been a good guy and deserved better. But this new Antonio was insane. Holgar had risen while the others slept, with the thought of going after him by himself. He wanted to protect the others, particularly Jenn and Skye. Jenn didn't need to have Antonio play mind games with her. And Skye needed a rest. Plus, his partner was so tender-hearted; he had a feeling she was going to try to reach out to Antonio, in an effort to bring him back to the good side. Even if it were possible, Holgar believed it would take time and resources they just didn't have to deal with a renegade vampire.

Ultimately, though, Holgar had waited. In a fair fight between himself and Antonio he wasn't sure who would win. And if he went off by himself and got killed, it would make it that much harder on everyone he was trying to protect.

Jamie teetered slightly on his feet. "You okay?" Holgar asked.

"Fine," Jamie said.

Holgar felt his hackles rise. It wasn't like the Irishman to go so long without being mouthy. It didn't bode well.

"All right, everyone, lock and load," Jenn said grimly.

It was kind of funny. None of them had guns. Holgar had taken count, and among them they had eight stakes, two crosses, and one vial of holy water. He'd gone into battle with less, but not willingly.

The map in the pickup truck's glove compartment had shown the town and an abandoned farm on its outskirts. They stopped at a combination hardware and feed store for some chain, an ax, and a large burlap sack, and Eriko rummaged through a rack of T-shirts and sweatpants.

As they drove to the farm, Holgar hoped that this would all be over soon. He felt as if he were going to an execution, and all his good humor deserted him. The situation was tragic.

He thought about his father, who had killed that human hunter so many years before. Holgar had always thought it had been his fault—that he'd darted into the man's line of fire because he was a pup who didn't know any better. That Holgar's father must have suffered equal guilt over taking a human life.

But he had allied their pack with Cursed Ones so easily. Insisted that werewolves needed to kill to express their true

371

nature. Holgar's father was wrong. Nothing in him wanted to be here or to do this.

As soon as they pulled up outside the farmhouse, he knew that Greg had provided good information. He could smell vampire. And not just any vampire.

Antonio de la Cruz was his friend.

And if he was in his right mind, he would want me to do this.

"He's here," Holgar said softly, though why he bothered when the truck's engine could wake the undead, he didn't know.

Skye nodded.

There were two structures, a house and a barn. They raided the house first, half of them going in the front at the same time the other half went through the back. In two minutes it was clear Antonio wasn't there.

That left the barn.

"We could burn it down," Taamir suggested, looking at the structure.

Jenn shook her head. "We need to know for sure he's in there, and if we do that, we won't."

It made strategic sense, but Holgar couldn't help but wonder if their leader was under the delusion that she could talk sense into her boyfriend.

"And we need to question him, find out what he told Aurora about the resistance cells," Skye said.

"I agree," Jamie said quietly.

Holgar looked at him askance, troubled by Jamie's

position on the matter. Would the Irishman take pleasure in torturing Antonio for information?

"Okay, so we're going in, but there's no need to be stupid about it," Jenn said, her voice steady, her face granite hard. She reminded him of a Viking Valkyrie, prepared to fight the last battle. "He can't be in the sunlight, so let's fill that barn with as much as we can."

Moving as fast as they could, they threw open doors and yanked back shutters. Holgar heard a hiss from inside. Antonio was in there, all right.

Holgar positioned himself just under one of the open windows, and next to him Taamir did the same. The others gathered in the sunlight, just inside the barn door, and waited.

Jenn's heart lodged in her throat as she stood where the sunlight met the darkness. She felt as if she'd been standing there for the last two and a half years. Everything had been a blurred dream, and this was the reality of her life.

"What do you want?" It was Antonio's voice, but deeper, harder.

"You," she said simply. Her hands trembled as she grabbed a stake and a cross, preparing for attack.

I don't want to kill you. Please, please be my Antonio again. She tried to make herself breathe. She couldn't. The shadows and sunlight wove a pattern of crosses, of bars. Then of nothing but lines. That was all a cross was, lines in the sand.

No. It's a weapon, she reminded herself.

After a long pause Antonio stepped forward so that she could see his face. His eyes were glowing, and his fangs were white and sharp. He was sizing her up, his gaze ticking past her to Eriko, Skye, Jamie, and Noah.

"Here I am." He hissed.

"What did you tell Aurora about the resistance?"

She could swear he looked almost confused. "What resistance?" he asked at last.

Jamie swore quietly, and Antonio turned to look at him. "Do I know you?" he asked.

"You know all of us," Jenn said, startled.

"I don't think he does," Skye whispered. "Maybe it's a spell. Or what happens when vampires . . . go back."

And somehow that made it worse. Jenn was about to kill her boyfriend, and he didn't even know what it was going to cost her. She began to shake with rage.

Aurora. Aurora had done this. Aurora had taken everything from her.

Antonio took a step forward, looking like he was trying to figure something out.

"Do I?" he murmured. "Do I know you?"

That was when Holgar and Taamir snuck up on him from behind. With the blunt side of his ax Holgar swung down hard on Antonio's head. Antonio crashed to the ground, and Holgar hit him again. Jenn winced with each blow as she and the others circled Holgar, Taamir, and Antonio, ready to offer assistance.

374

Taamir bound his arms and legs with the chains, and then the two shoved Antonio into the burlap sack from the feed store. They hauled him outside and dumped the sack in the sunlight. Even if Antonio woke up, there would be no way for him to escape with his life.

"What now?" Eriko asked. She didn't look good. In fact she looked worse than Jamie.

"Now we really question him," Noah said grimly.

Holgar cocked his head as though listening to something. A few seconds later Jenn heard it too.

Two VW buses careened up the road and slid to a stop next to them. Jenn and her team readied their weapons. The driver's door of one bus opened, and a woman stepped out and took in the scene.

It was Gramma Esther. A submachine gun was slung around her neck. With her gray hair tucked beneath an olive army cap, wearing a brown, beige, and white jacket over a pair of jeans, her grandmother was an aged echo of the radical idealist Jenn had seen in pictures from the 1960s.

With a cry Jenn ran and threw her arms around her grandmother, never so happy to see anyone in her life. Her grandmother hugged her fiercely, patting her back.

"Hey, baby," Esther said softly. "An old friend said you could use some help, so we've been driving all day to get to you. Now it looks like you don't need much help at all."

Squeezing her eyes shut, Jenn kept her arms wrapped around her grandmother. She wanted to stop time in this moment when she felt safe and rescued. And not have to face what must be done next.

"You okay?" Gramma Esther whispered.

Jenn forced herself to nod. "You?"

"Getting by. I promised your mother I'd bring you all back to our camp to say hello."

Mom, Jenn thought, dazed. *Oh, Mom.*

As they parted, Gramma Esther gestured to the sack. "What's in there?"

She hesitated. "Do you remember when I told you about Antonio?" But all she had told her grandmother was that she liked a boy back in Spain, named Antonio.

"Yes." She gazed levelly at Jenn. "Greg told me the truth about him. You didn't."

Jenn swallowed hard, but before she could say anything, her grandmother continued. "Is there a reason he's still alive?"

Jenn felt the world shifting and tilting again.

"There is," Skye spoke up. "We need him, and I think I can reach him. I—"

Esther raised a hand to stop her. "You had me at 'there is.'" She looked at Jenn. "You're the leader of your team, and I'm the leader of the Defender outpost. If you need him alive, we'll keep him alive. You can tell me all about it later. For now we'd better get going back home."

Home. With her grandmother and her mother together, it would almost seem like it. Almost.

Gramma Esther took in the rest of the team. "Seems you've been collecting some allies," she said.

"Where is this home?" Jamie said.

Gramma Esther cocked her head. "You must be Jamie."

"What of it?" he asked.

"I'm Eriko," Eriko said, bowing. "And this is Holgar, Taamir, and—"

"I hate to cut this short, but we need to get out of here," Gramma Esther said. "Home is well hidden, and better than a pickup truck in the middle of nowhere." She raised a brow at Jamie. "Okay with you?"

They ditched the pickup and split up between the two VW buses. It was a tight squeeze, but they got everyone in. Skye went with Antonio to keep watch and make sure he stayed unconscious. Holgar and Eriko stayed with them. Jamie, Taamir, and Noah rode in the bus with Jenn and her grandmother.

As Jenn climbed into the front seat next to Esther, she gave her grandmother a weary smile. "Next time you talk to Greg, please thank him for me."

Esther patted Jenn's check. "Already done, sweetheart."

LOS ANGELES
SOLOMON

Solomon rang for his new assistant, Marti. He tapped his fingers on his glass desk, impatient for his call to go through.

Sure, it was the president of the United States, a busy man indeed. But *he* was Solomon. And he was Solomon with all Dantalion's research at his disposal. Solomon, who was ready to push the war to the next level.

"Yes, Solomon?" The president sounded wary.

"Jack, how's it going?" he asked jovially. "Listen, I had this crazy idea. You want to hear it?"

There was a pause. "Of course I do."

SALAMANCA
FATHER JUAN

Juan sensed the live-wire tension of crisis, both at the academy and with his team in America. Three days had passed since Antonio's capture, and his condition showed no improvement. Jenn's team was not as welcome as they would have been had they shown up without Antonio. Half of Esther Leitner's band of freedom fighters wanted the Cursed One dead. The other half agreed that Antonio needed to be kept alive, but only until they found out exactly what he had told Aurora. The opposing viewpoints had split the group, and Jenn had implored Father Juan to come to Montana.

He had accepted that his hunters weren't going to be able to bring Antonio back to his senses without his help. Given his lack of success with Heather, he wondered if his presence would actually do any good. But he could try. He must try. He would pray over Antonio and cast magicks with Skye.

But how could he leave his small group of rebels alone in Salamanca after the mass exodus? He had no doubt that the students would listen to Giovanni and the four instructors. But would they be well protected? Father Juan was needed in two places at once. For the first time, he regretted asking Diego to leave.

"You wanted to see me," Giovanni said, entering Father Juan's office. Again his dark hair and eyes reminded Juan of Antonio, and he felt a terrible pang.

Composing himself, Juan told him what was going on. When he had concluded, Giovanni nodded. "You should go. We can survive a few days without you."

"And if you can't?" Juan asked bluntly, thinking about Giovanni's vision of dying at the university.

"Then your being here would only get you killed as well. Please, Father, go. I have a feeling you will be able to make a difference."

"Did you have another vision, my son?" Juan asked sharply.

Giovanni shook his head. "No, but it's a feeling."

"Okay, then I'm going. I'll bring the team back with me. We need to be united. Can you handle the . . . girl?" *The vampire? The ravening monster who would tear out the throats of everyone here, if she could?*

The priest lifted his chin. "I believe so."

"Good. Do whatever you have to." Juan hesitated. He didn't want to say what he had to say next. "If . . ."

"I will keep her alive. But I will not allow her to escape, no matter the cost."

Juan closed his eyes. He nodded. He was about to face a similar struggle with Antonio. He prayed both he and Giovanni would have the strength to make the hardest of choices, should it come to that—to destroy Heather and Antonio.

And perhaps, he thought fearfully, *to send them to hell.*

CHAPTER SIXTEEN

When I kept silence, my bones waxed old through my roaring all the day long.

For day and night thy hand was heavy upon me:

My moisture is turned into the drought of summer.

Selah.

I acknowledged my sin unto thee, and mine iniquity have I not hid.

I said, I will confess my transgressions unto the LORD;

and thou forgavest the iniquity of my sin.

Selah.

—Psalms 32:3–5

Montana
The Resistance: Father Juan, Esther Leitner, Team Salamanca, Taamir, and Noah

The sacrifices of God are a broken spirit: a broken and a contrite heart, O God, thou wilt not despise. It was Psalm 51, verse 17, and it had been going through Juan's head ever since the plane touched down in America.

Juan stood with his suitcase in the run-down bus station just outside Jordan, Montana. He was the only one who had gotten off in town, and he felt conspicuous.

The sky was clear and blue; beyond the station was a rise covered with fir trees. A car was due to come for him. He closed his coat around his black turtleneck sweater. To deflect unwelcome attention, he had opted not to wear his clerical collar.

Juan believed that both God and Goddess wanted him to reach the resistance enclave in Montana. He had prayed and conjured the strongest of magicks to ease his journey, and it was a miracle that he had gotten this far without incident. The number of armed humans and vampires in the airports and at checkpoints had doubled, maybe tripled, since he had last flown to the States. Everywhere there were images of Solomon posing with the governors and mayors of the towns Juan traveled through, and with the president of the United States. TV news shows featured stories about him, with carefully arranged photo opportunities in front of American flags, greeting workers at factories, and kissing babies. It was as if he were running for office. Which Juan supposed he was.

Juan's heart was so heavy. He believed in faith. Faith could move mountains, make miracles. That was why the prayers of believers—no matter what religion—were as powerful, in his eyes, as bullets. It was also why he could justify and condone the fact that the White Witches in the world, except for a very few, continued to use their magicks for healing, and not for fighting the Cursed Ones. Such magick use was prayer.

But these were hard times, and even he found himself growing angry that the devotions of millions seemed to have no effect. Were the words of comfort he had offered others for so long, so very long, as hollow and empty as he himself felt?

"Hey, John," a voice said casually.

He turned around to see an older woman standing just inside the bus station. Her strong features resembled Jenn's. She was Esther Leitner, then. Her gray hair was pulled back, and in jeans, boots, and a short navy blue coat she looked like a rancher on her way to buy feed.

He nodded and picked up his small black suitcase. He followed her into the station, then out the back. A rusty blue pickup truck was idling, and she went around to the driver's side while he placed his suitcase in the truck bed. Then he climbed in, and they took off.

"How are things?" he asked, as they drove away from the station.

"Bad, Father," Esther said, as she checked the rearview mirror. "He's bad. I think we may have to stake him." She studied him in the mirror as if to gauge his reaction.

Then she asked, "Why did you really elect my grand-daughter their leader?"

He was surprised. "Don't you have faith in her leadership?"

She waited. When he didn't answer, she said, "What told you to do it, your head or your heart?"

"My soul," he replied.

If his response surprised her, she didn't let on. They both fell silent, for a time, and then he asked questions, lots of them. The situation was as Jenn had told him—like a powder keg.

After two hours' drive they reached a thick stand of trees. The truck idled, and a dozen armed men and women of all ages fanned around. Holgar and Jenn were among them, and he smiled at the sight of them. They both smiled back, though Jenn looked as if she were about to break down in tears as she approached the truck. He rolled down the window and cupped her cheek.

"Father Juan," Jenn began. "You have to help him."

He turned to Esther. "May I walk from here?"

She nodded, and Jenn opened the door. Jenn hugged him, then moved back quickly, as if she had overstepped.

The Defender outpost was situated on the remains of a recently deserted ranch, dotted with several outbuildings of cinder block, a large barn, and a large, once-beautiful three-story brick home that had been partially burned down. There were three skinny cows in the barn, and a flock of chickens. The group had fed them, and now there were eggs and fresh milk. Spray-painted on an exterior barn wall was

U SUK CO'S! and a wealth of profanity. A handmade pennant tacked over some of the spray paint proclaimed the camp Defender Territory. The Salamanca Hunter's pennant was affixed below it.

Counting the Salamancans, there were thirty people in the camp. Juan made thirty-one. The majority of them were living in olive-drab tents. Esther and six of Che's and her old compatriots from the underground made up the core group and governing body of the Defenders. All of them had been at Charles Leitner's funeral. Jenn's mother, Leslie, had joined them, and they had gathered fourteen more Defenders. The Defenders ranged from a thirteen-year-old who had seen his entire family slaughtered by the Cursed Ones to a woman in her seventies whose husband of fifty years had denounced her to the vampiric overlord of their town in Wyoming. She had had to run for her life.

Father Juan noted the life-size photograph of Solomon riddled with bullet holes out in a fallow field. A vampire hung in effigy.

Many smiled at Juan. Others just looked. The thirteen-year-old stomped up to him and said, "Man, if you can't fix that sucker, I'm taking him out myself."

"If I can't fix him, *I'll* take him out," Juan replied, to the boy's surprise. The priest reached in his pocket and handed the kid a vial of holy water and a cross. Such things were permitted, if one was a priest.

The boy folded his arms over his chest. "That shit didn't

help my parents. You probably know we've got a wolf guy here, too."

"*Sí,* but he will not hurt you. I'll say Mass in an hour," Father Juan told him and Jenn. "Will you come?"

"No," the kid said. "Just get all these weirdos out of here."

He turned and stomped away, then picked up speed and traced a wide half circle as Holgar approached. Holgar purred low in his throat upon seeing Father Juan.

"Goddag," Holgar said, greeting him. "It's good to see you."

"How's it going, Holgar?" Juan asked him.

Holgar hesitated. "Good so far. I asked for a cage. I've been taking a lot of sleeping pills and tranquilizers. I don't want to howl and frighten the others." His face was tight, grim. "The full moon's coming. I won't be going out."

Juan nodded, but he was concerned. What would these people do to Holgar if he did get out?

"Vale," Juan said, tabling the discussion they should have about that. Antonio was his more immediate concern.

"Where are Eriko and Jamie?" he asked.

"Eriko's resting," Holgar said. "Jamie's sitting with her."

"She's all right, though?" Juan ventured.

"Right enough. She's having trouble sleeping. Taamir and Noah have fit right in." Holgar looked at Jenn. "That leaves . . . two."

Jenn took a deep breath. "Skye's with Antonio. She's been with him a lot and . . ." She trailed off and choked back

386

a sob. Holgar put his arm around her, and she lowered her head, pressing her forehead against his chest.

"Shh, shh," Holgar whispered.

There was a tenderness between them that intrigued Father Juan. He hadn't seen this side of Holgar before. He knew that wolves, though feared by many, were solicitous and loyal pack mates, while constantly aware that there was a pecking order that must be maintained. But what must the Danish werewolf think of his alpha, displaying such weakness?

"I was about to get something to eat. Rule one when you're living with livestock: Don't get hungry." Holgar smiled at them, recapturing his jauntiness. "That's a joke. Jenn's grandmother stole a whole truckload of field rations, and a team just brought back about a hundred apples. Are you hungry, Father?"

"No, thank you, Holgar." If he was going to say Mass, then he would fast.

Holgar moved away, leaving Jenn and Father Juan to walk alone. Father Juan took note of Esther as she drove the truck around a tent. She gave him a wave. The shadows were lengthening. Day was dying, and night would bring new challenges.

"Take me to him," he said quietly.

Jenn lowered her head, and he made the sign of the cross over it. Either she didn't notice it or pretended not to. She had no reason to have faith in God; he hoped He would give a better accounting of Himself in the days to come.

Not that God owes any of us an explanation, he thought.

Father Juan and Jenn walked into a copse of scrubby trees that appeared to be the remains of an orchard. His foot came down hard on a stone. Finally they reached a building made of concrete blocks, where a young man in paramilitary gear stood guarding the entrance. He had dark, curly hair like Antonio's and he wore a Star of David around his neck. He was holding an Uzi. The unpainted metal door behind him displayed the words CAUTION NO ADMITTANCE handwritten in black marker.

"Noah," Father Juan guessed. He held out his hand. "It's good to meet you, my friend."

"Father Juan. I wish it were under better circumstances," Noah replied. He looked at Jenn. "I have to warn you. He's worse." Then he ticked his gaze up at the sky.

"When it gets dark, it's harder for him to . . ." As before, Jenn couldn't finish her sentence.

Noah pulled keys from his pocket and unlocked the door. Jenn stepped in first, and Father Juan followed.

The light was dim. A canvas curtain had been pulled across the bare room. An electric light cast the silhouette of a cage on the fabric. It was similar to the one back in Salamanca that imprisoned Jenn's sister. Father Juan's heart went out to Jenn afresh. Her sister converted, her father a traitor, and now Antonio. Yet she stood there, reasonably composed. There was a miracle—the strength of the human spirit.

He hadn't answered Esther's question about Jenn's status as leader because he hadn't known the answer. As he guided the hunters, he prayed for them constantly. He also performed the same ancient magicks that, unknown to most, had surrounded the original Crusaders who rode for Jerusalem back in the Middle Ages. He invoked the wisdom of the Goddess and the power of God for the most useful parts each of the hunters could play. And the answer that kept coming was that Jenn Leitner, of the six, must lead.

Father Juan hadn't wanted to frighten his youthful warriors by admitting to them that his own wisdom hadn't governed his choice. They had no idea who and what he really was, and he knew he couldn't tell them. But he had faith that the runes he threw and the novenas he conducted on their behalf were good and right. That the answers he received were truthful. It always came back to faith.

Skye's profile was outlined behind the curtain, and she was murmuring an ancient healing prayer in Latin. Jenn and Father Juan both stopped and waited for Skye to finish. When Skye breathed a heartfelt "so mote it be," Father Juan crossed himself.

"No!" came a roar of fury from inside the cage. Metal rattled. Beside him Jenn caught her breath.

"Could it be that he's been possessed?" Jenn asked him quietly. "I know you've performed exorcisms in the past."

"You do?" He hadn't realized. That part of his life had been over long ago, before he'd come to the Academia.

"So do you think if you exorcised him, that would help?" she pressed.

"We'll have to see," he said honestly. He had no idea. He didn't know how to help Antonio. He didn't actually know what had happened to him.

"We'll have to see," he said again, "but we *will* do something."

Apparently satisfied with his answer, Jenn pulled the curtain away.

The cage, made of stainless steel, had been pushed into the corner of the room, and Skye was perched on a camp chair facing it. She turned at the sound, and her face lit up. Books, lit candles, and the sacred objects of the Craft— herbs, crystals, flowers—sat on a small wooden table beside her chair. Her Circuit had come through for her, sending supplies to her via a post office box in the little town.

All Father Juan could see of Antonio were his red eyes, glowing in the darkness like candle flames. But waves of fury radiated from the vampire, as powerful as ocean tides. They were the same waves that magicks rode, and prayers. Antonio's entire being expelled the passions of his personal demons—the forces that drove even ordinary men to evil, and sin. How much worse must it be for a man forcibly changed into a vampire?

Father Juan made the sign of the cross. "In the name of the Father, and the Son, and the Holy Spirit," he began, "peace be with you."

"Vete al diablo," Antonio replied in Spanish. Go to the Devil.

Skye rose and embraced Father Juan. She was trembling. Father Juan placed his hand on the crown of her head, blessing her. As she stepped back, he was shocked at the change in her. Her face was thin, and deep circles ringed her eyes.

He turned to Jenn. "Why haven't you told her to rest? She's exhausted."

Jenn's cheeks reddened, and he knew why. She was desperate to have Antonio back.

"Oh, she did try to make me take breaks," Skye said quickly. "I just wouldn't listen. Besides, I think I—I'm getting somewhere." She looked down. She was lying. Everything about her posture spelled futility. Was she sugarcoating her opinion to spare Jenn? Father Juan couldn't tell.

"Well, I'm here now. You should go rest."

"Really, I'm fine," Skye insisted.

"I won't hurt him. Go and rest. I'm saying Mass in an hour. Let the others know."

"Yes, Father Juan." Skye's lower lip quivered. "I'm so glad you're here."

"I'm not," Antonio said, as the little witch left the building. His voice was gravelly. He barely sounded like himself.

Father Juan looked at him. "And why is that, Antonio?"

"Don't say that name! That's not my name! I was converted, and I have a new name. The name of a demon!"

"And what name is that?" Father Juan asked calmly.

"Legion," Antonio said. "I am one of millions. We will swarm over the earth, and we will cleanse it of the vermin that infect it." His eyes blazed. His fangs seemed to have grown longer. There was nothing of the gentle priest who had begged God to lift the horrible curse of vampirism from him.

Juan pulled his missal from his pocket and opened it to the day's lectionary. "Do you remember when we would say our prayers together, my son? You often start your waking time with vespers."

"Get that away from me!" Antonio raged. He flung himself as far away from Father Juan as possible. "You!" he shouted at Jenn. "Let me out of here or I'll rip out your throat."

"Let me sit a while with him," Father Juan said. "Send Holgar in. Perhaps there's something you can do to help your mother or your grandmother."

"Mom's left with a team to rescue a spy in Solomon's movie company."

"Oh? That's very good." He managed a smile.

"Yes." She tried to smile back. "My mom's so brave."

"Like daughter, like mother." He tried to keep his tone light, although he was on the verge of despair. Antonio was so far gone. It hurt his heart to see the vampire this badly changed.

Or is he changed at all? Has this been lurking beneath his humanity all this time?

392

Jenn left. He turned to Antonio. Antonio's eyes burned. His fangs gleamed.

"We're coming," Antonio whispered. "You won't be able to stop us."

"Is that what Aurora told you?"

Antonio turned his back. "I don't speak to humans. I kill them."

"Even Jenn?"

"I don't know anyone by that name." His voice was icy. "That's a stupid name anyway."

Father Juan had arrived on a difficult night, and Eriko was glad he was there. Even though he had drugged himself, Holgar howled and yipped all night. With her strong hearing she detected Antonio flinging himself against the bars of his cage, trying to get out. Eriko was afraid the Defenders would turn on the hunters and drive them away. And she, for one, was in no condition to leave.

She was afraid that she was dying. The pain had become nearly unbearable, a throbbing deep inside her bones. Her entire body hurt, constantly, and like Holgar and Antonio she could find no rest.

On the third day that Father Juan had been at the camp, Eriko went to him and told him that she wasn't feeling well. She didn't want to tell him just how bad it was. She was ashamed, as if it were her fault, and she didn't want him to feel that it was somehow *his* fault, for giving her the elixir. In

Japanese culture it was very important to make sure your superiors saved face. So she minimized just how bad it was.

Father Juan and Skye conjured healing spells that worked for a little while, but then the pain came back with a vengeance. Eriko saw that the effort had taken a lot out of them, and she knew they were trying to help Antonio. So she lied, announcing that she felt much better and didn't need any more help.

I'm the Hunter. I'm needed, she reminded herself. But she could wait, until Antonio was helped.

At least that was what Eriko kept telling herself.

"Let's see how Antonio is doing tonight," Father Juan suggested to Jenn. "Perhaps there's been some improvement."

Jenn swallowed hard, and he felt so sorry for her. Had he been wrong to pair her with Antonio? The runes insisted that Jenn and Antonio shared a destiny. But what on earth could the nature of such a destiny be?

They entered his prison together. Skye was in her usual chair. There was a simple woven basket beside her on the floor. Antonio kept to the back of the cage. But Father Juan could still see his glowing red eyes. Could hear him hissing like a snake.

"*Mi hijo*, my son, how is it with you?"

Antonio's answer was another roar of outrage. Then he raced across the cage and threw himself against the bars. Father Juan jerked but stood his ground, and so did Jenn.

Skye dug her hands into the basket, then flung something white and crystalline at Antonio. Salt, Father Juan realized, for spell casting.

"By the Triple Mother and Her consort, the Horned God, I free thee from the chains of bondage!" she cried. "I release thee from thy torments! I return thy free will to thee!"

"I have my free will!" Antonio shouted, grabbing the bars of his cage and shaking them. "I finally have it back! I am a vampire! For half a century I denied what I was. I tried to act like one of you. But I'm not like you. You're my food, and I'm a god to you."

"He's begun to remember," Juan murmured to Jenn. "That's a good sign."

"Is it?" she whispered. "Antonio," she said loudly. "This is not you talking."

His glowing red eyes turned in Jenn's direction. Fury blazed there. And nothing else—no love, just a predator's lust for his prey.

"*Sí, idiota*, it is me. It's finally me."

"No. Because you wouldn't call me that." Jenn's voice quavered.

"Aurora freed me, *idiota*. All that misery, twisting myself into something I am *not*. To satisfy a myth."

"The god you believe in is not a myth," Father Juan said calmly.

"The god I *believed* in tortured Aurora and her family. Her sire freed her. I contain multitudes! I know the sins your god has perpetrated against us. And it's time we all fought back. We will crush you. All of you!"

Juan made the sign of the cross. Antonio recoiled.

"If my god is myth, why does the cross bother you?" Juan asked.

"Don't start with that! All symbols of human faith disturb us equally. But *our* symbols of faith are coming. You'll be helpless before them."

Juan kept his voice steady. "What symbols might those be?"

Antonio sneered at him. "We are not fools. *Or* traitors. You can stake this one out in the sun, and we won't tell you."

"Because you don't know. Aurora didn't tell you, did she? She didn't trust you with the information. Because she put you under a spell. It will wear off, and you'll come back to us." He didn't know that, but he wanted to shake the demons' hold on Antonio.

"Don't try your tricks on us." Antonio's eyes narrowed. "We don't care if you believe us or not. Aurora will come back for this one. With an *army*."

"And if she doesn't?" Juan asked. "If she leaves you here to rot?"

Antonio raised his chin. His fangs extended over his lower lip. His eyes burned. "I won't rot. I'm a vampire. I'm immortal."

Father Juan heard the change in Antonio's choice of words. Not "we," but "I." Was this progress?

"I know you're tormented by what you did," Father Juan said. "I know you want forgiveness. And deep in your heart you know that too."

Antonio's answering smile was cold. "There is no depth in my heart, you poor, deluded man. My heart is dead."

Juan put his hand on Jenn's shoulder. He could feel her shaking. "Your heart beats for this girl."

"My fangs extend for her, but that's all."

Father Juan felt a horrible chill. Perhaps Antonio could not be reclaimed. Jamie would gladly stake him, if it came to that. If only he could rekindle Antonio's depth of feeling for Jenn. Surely that would bring him back. Love was the most powerful force in the universe.

It was time to try a different way to express that force.

"Skye," Juan said, without taking his eyes from Antonio. "It's the full moon. After you've taken a nice, long nap and had something to eat, we'll draw down the Moon together."

"Oh, Father, really?" Skye cried. "I've never accepted the Goddess into my being."

"High time, then," Father Juan said. "I'll act as your high priest, with your permission."

Her tired, thin face took on light. "Thank you, Father."

"Go and rest." Juan made a show of sitting casually in Skye's vacated chair. "I'll stay with Antonio for a bit."

"Sí, sit closer," Antonio whispered, laughing, as if he had just made an excellent joke.

"Take Jenn with you," Juan added.

"Be careful," Skye said. "He's been trying to mesmerize me."

"He won't be able to mesmerize me," Juan replied.

"Closer, closer," Antonio murmured, gesturing with his fingers. "Come, little bull, to the matador."

"Antonio," Jenn said. *"Please."*

"You have but to ask, *señorita*," he replied. Turning, he focused his gaze on her. "Come to me, *Jenn*."

"Go, Jenn. *Now*," Juan ordered her.

Numb from head to toe, Jenn went with Skye out the door. Noah was standing as sentry. Jenn tried to dig down and find the strength he claimed she had, but she had nothing.

"Things will get better," Noah said to Jenn, and she tried to respond. But things were worse. She had seen Antonio through new eyes. He was a Cursed One, and nothing more. Whatever had made him special was gone.

"Jenn," Noah said, and she wanted to bury her head against his chest and sob. But if she did, she was afraid she would never stop.

"Father Juan and I are going to perform a very special ritual," Skye reminded her. "It might work." Her eyes glinted. "It *will* work."

"Thank you, Skye. Now go and rest," Jenn said, ashamed that she hadn't been more persistent about making Skye take care of herself. Antonio's need had seemed greater. But everyone on the team had needs.

Skye kissed Jenn's cheek and left. Jenn stood beside Noah. He smelled of soap and a bit of sweat. She felt his body heat. No matter how much she'd wanted to feel warm beside Antonio, she never had. He had no body heat, and his skin was cold to the touch. Maybe it had been a crazy thing to do, letting herself fall in love with him. But she hadn't "let" herself. She simply hadn't been able to stop herself.

"I don't like it that he's in there alone," she said, meaning Father Juan but thinking of Antonio.

"Me neither," Noah said. His voice was strained, and when she glanced up at him, there was a faraway look in his eyes, as if he were thinking of something else.

People were walking toward them in the lengthening shadows. Jenn squinted, making out the figures of her grandmother and Jamie, and she stiffened.

"Jamie's here to relieve me for sentry duty," Noah reminded her. "I'll go sit with Father Juan for a while."

"Thank you," she murmured, grateful to him.

"Jenn." Noah's voice caught, and she looked up at him. His features softened, and he reached forward, looping an errant strand of dark auburn hair around her ear. As he lowered his hand, her heartbeat stuttered, and she felt a flush rush up her neck.

"What?" she asked, her voice cracking.

He quirked a half smile at her, then turned as her grandmother and Jamie approached.

"Father Juan in there?" Jamie said, his voice ice cold. His neck was still bandaged.

"Yes."

"Eri needs to talk to him."

"I'll give him the message," Jenn said.

Jamie gave his head a sharp shake. "*I* will."

Fear shot through her, but she reminded herself that Noah would be in there too, and he would stop Jamie from doing anything crazy. She wasn't sure what she thought Jamie might do. It had been easier to deal with him when he'd been off his game.

"You're on guard duty, Jamie," Gramma Esther reminded him. "You can't desert your post. C'mon, Jenn. Let's walk."

"I will tell him," Noah said to Jamie, nodding to Jenn as he unlocked the door and slipped inside, leaving Jamie standing at the door, fuming.

Before Jenn could say anything, Esther turned and walked briskly away. Jenn followed.

"You're going to have to watch him," Gramma Esther said.

"We're not much of a team, are we," Jenn murmured.

Her grandmother grunted. "Oh, child, the fights we used to have back in the day." She shook her head. "It used to drive me crazy. I mean, we were fighting 'the Man.'" She made air quotes. "Did we have to fight each other, too?"

"That's what I keep thinking," Jenn said. "The Cursed Ones are threatening to annihilate us. Can't we all just do the right thing?"

"By whose definition?" Her grandmother took Jenn's hand and laced her fingers through it. "We need to talk about what to do next. Greg contacted both of us. What did he tell you? Did he talk about Project Crusade?"

Jenn's brows shot up. "Project *what*?"

"Crusade. Greg's people have been systematically contacting resistance cells. They're creating a database of information to help the cause."

"Like what?" Jenn asked. "What have they found out?"

"He hasn't told me. Maybe there's nothing to tell, yet."

"Well, like what kind of database? For making a weapon? Dantalion was trying to create supersoldiers, and vampires that can walk in daylight. Did they finally retrieve some of that data?"

"Like I said, I don't know, Jenn. But here's one thing I've learned: One person *can* make a difference. But no individual is more important than another."

Gramma Esther looked at her hard. "Our mission is not just to win the war. It's to wipe vampires off the face of this earth. You as a hunter must agree with that."

"Yes," Jenn said.

"And that's what Antonio was fighting for, when he was Antonio," Gramma Esther added.

"He still is Antonio," Jenn said, balling her fists. "I know it."

Her grandmother stopped. The setting sun cast a halo around her gray hair. "I thought I understood the human

401

heart. Before you and Heather were born, there were two people in this world I loved more than anything. Your grandfather and your father."

Her gaze grew steely. "But Papa Che is gone, and after what your father did, well, let's say that I'll never let my heart overrule my head again."

Jenn's throat tightened. "What are you trying to tell me?"

"We need to win this war by whatever means are necessary. Our leaders will be faced with hard choices."

She gazed at her granddaughter with determination. "And you, my dear, are one of the leaders."

Holgar's slurred, drugged howls hurt Skye's heart as she waited for Father Juan to join her for their ritual. The moon was full, and Holgar was so loaded up on tranquilizers he wouldn't be able to slip out of his cage—a pen, ironically, that had been used to contain livestock, same as Antonio's. Skye had thrown a tarp over it so that no one would be able to see him during his transformation.

Skye had spent an hour alone arranging branches and stones to make an altar for the ritual of Drawing Down the Moon. Then she had created a sacred pentagram with salt, and scattered rose petals that Father Juan had brought from Spain. She was touched to see that he'd also brought her an athame—a ritual knife—as well as a robe, herbs, oils, and crystals that could be used for a variety of rituals. When she'd asked him if he'd had any trouble getting any of it through security at the airport, he had simply smiled and shaken his head.

Now, in her dark blue hooded silken robe, Skye couldn't imagine a Catholic priest participating in this most sacred of witchly rites, in which the designated High Priestess of a coven's ritual would become filled with the Goddess Herself. Growing up as a White Witch, Skye had witnessed the miracle dozens of times, as each adult woman of the coven assumed the role. She had dreamed of the day that she would stand in the center of the coven's pentagram and greet each member by name, in the voice of their revered Sacred Mother. It was a rite of passage for female White Witches.

Such an honor had never befallen Skye before. It would happen only if everyone who participated in the rite pledged their loyalty to the Goddess. But Father Juan had dedicated his life to the Christian god.

In addition, Father Juan would be serving as Skye's Long Arm of the Law—the male who would ensure the safety of the High Priestess as she invoked the forces of magick. It implied a relationship built on deep trust. She had not been trustworthy back in Salamanca. When she had applied to the academy, Father Juan had asked her straight out if she had any enemies who could prove a threat. The whole reason she'd gone to Salamanca was to learn how to protect herself from Estefan, but Skye had lied to Father Juan, and had continued to lie every time she'd heard

Estefan's voice in her head and hadn't told anyone. Because of her untrustworthiness Eriko and Jamie had almost died, and Antonio had been captured by Aurora and made into what he was now.

"Blessed be," Father Juan said, stepping from the shadows and into the moonlight. He, too, was wearing a dark blue robe. He carried a long tree branch nearly as tall as he was in his left hand.

"Merrily met," she replied. "Please, come and join the circle." He lifted his hood over his head. She could no longer see his face.

She cleared her throat.

"Father Juan, I have to ask you—can you set your Christian god aside to do this?"

"Sí," he replied firmly.

"And focus only on the Trinity of the Goddess?"

"Maiden, mother, crone," he answered.

"And you will serve as my high priest and do all things that I ask of you, in service to the Lady."

"I will."

"Blessed be," she said.

"Blessed be," he intoned.

"And we will harm none."

"An it harm none, do what thou wilt," he assured her. "And I will make you safe."

"All right then. We are here to bring the Goddess into our midst, so that She can heal Antonio de la Cruz."

"So mote it be," Father Juan said.

"We are here to offer Her love and protection to Antonio de la Cruz, so that his spirit will no longer be troubled."

"So mote it be," Father Juan said again. Then he stood beside her and extended the branch, moving in a circle and touching each of the points of her pentagram with its tip. "I am the Long Arm of the Law. No evil shall enter our circle. No imp, no succubus, no incubus, no demon. I stand the protector of the Lady Goddess and all who love her."

A wind blew at the rose petals. Father Juan tapped them with the branch.

"All is calm," he proclaimed. "All is bright."

The wind died down.

Skye took deep breaths and felt the night all around her, the night that had grown so terrifying for humans. The moon had belonged to the Goddess, but the Cursed Ones had stolen it from Her. Witches were now afraid to worship under the stars, fearing Cursed Ones would slaughter them, and met in buildings instead.

Imagining moonbeams on her hair, she let go of her resentments, her fears, and her heartaches as best she could. The reigning principle of the Goddess was love, and, as was said, great love cast out great fear.

"I call out the name of three, three, three," she murmured, using the words of her family's tradition. She visualized the moonbeams traveling through her head and down

405

her body, filling her heart with light. Moving down through her lower body, through her legs and then her toes, and into the chilly earth beneath her bare feet. Then down into the soil and the roots, and the soul of the world. "Queen of all light, of all night, of all right."

"Blessed be," Father Juan said.

They moved through the steps, invoking the Goddess. Skye kept waiting for a sign that she was doing the ritual properly, but she mustn't hold any negative thought. She mustn't hold any thought. She must purify herself, cleanse her heart, and make herself a vessel for the Goddess to inhabit. She must freely give up her own will and ego so that the Goddess could live through her.

"Don't try, Skye," Father Juan said soothingly. "Just let it happen."

She could almost hear Holgar imitating Yoda: *Do or do not. There is no try.* Nervous laughter threatened to bubble out of her.

And then the moonbeams became brighter, and she sensed the descent of the Goddess from Luna, the Moon, down the silvery paths of light to the field, and to the star of rose petals and salt, and to *her.*

"Hecate, Selene, Diana," a voice rolled out of her. "I am known but little known. Know me now."

The Goddess was wrapped in incandescent light. Slowly She rose in the gauzy mists of the northern lights, colors rolling around Her like blankets of shimmering velvet. The heavens shone as She ascended back into Her sphere until, gazing downward at the sapphire planet—the poor, sweet Earth—tears of compassion streamed from Her eyes and became stars.

Love filled Her. Love was Her. And then the Goddess dissolved into Her vital essence, the one true particle that formed all creation: love. It billowed, and streamed, and filled, and danced. Love . . . *loved*.

> I have been with you in the beginning
> I shall be with you always
> in the endless spiral dance
> O soul,
> love in me

"Love Antonio, I beseech Thee," Father Juan murmured, as he fell on his knees before Skye. "Free him with Your love, my Lady."

"Antonio de la Cruz," the Goddess said through Skye. "You are my beloved son."

Inside Antonio's jail Esther and Jenn had finished their simple dinner of freeze-dried beef stew and were eating Oreos and drinking tea. It was their turn to sit with Antonio, who was guarded around the clock. Father Juan and Skye were performing a ritual, and Noah was walking the camp perimeter with Jamie and some of the Defenders.

No one knew how hard it was for Jenn to sit there. Or maybe they did, and it just didn't matter. Antonio had to be guarded. Jenn was one of the people who had to guard him. It was the mission.

She stole a glance at her grandmother. Tough as nails, yes, but she had always been warm and loving with Jenn and Heather. Yet she had spoken of sacrifices and hard choices. What had her life in the underground really been like?

Gramma Esther had commandeered a battery-powered TV, and they were channel surfing. There was nothing worth watching. At the moment they were both staring at an idiotic sitcom about a human family who lived in Las Vegas and worked in a vampire-run casino. It was called *Sun and Games*.

"Does anyone actually watch this?" Jenn grumbled.

"I hear the ratings are sky-high," Gramma Esther replied.

"Let me out," Antonio whispered.

"Stop it," Jenn said loudly, her stomach contracting. "We're not listening to you."

Gramma Esther changed the channel. "Commercials, infomercial, *another* sitcom," she said, groaning. She switched again.

"Gramma," Jenn said, stricken.

Her father's face filled the screen.

"Change it," Jenn pleaded, but Esther sat forward and turned up the sound.

"Let me out," Antonio insisted.

The camera pulled back to reveal Solomon standing beside Jenn's father, who was seated. Solomon's hair was red, like Jenn's. Even though she hated the sight of him, Jenn couldn't deny that he was rock-star hot. He was wearing a black suit and a white shirt with no tie, and a silver chain with a peace-sign pendant.

"We're still looking for her," Solomon was saying sadly. His hand was on Jenn's dad's shoulder. "We understand the confusion she must be feeling. There's so much misinformation out there, so many false rumors. Jennifer Leitner, please, listen to your father."

The camera zoomed in on her father. He seemed impatient, his arms folded across his chest, his right index finger tapping almost continuously against his left arm.

"Jenn," her father began. "Solomon is right. We only want to help you, sweetheart. Certain facts have come to light. We understand now that you weren't alone that terrible night. Someone forced you to do this awful thing." His voice was stiff, flat.

"He's been hypnotized," Jenn said.

"Wait," Esther said, moving toward the TV. "Oh, my God."

"It's Morse code," Antonio said. "He's tapping in Morse code."

Jenn leaped to her feet and looked at Antonio. But his attention was fixed on the TV.

"'Don't come,'" he said in unison with Gramma Esther. "'It's a trap. I love you. I love you. I love you.'"

Jenn's knees gave way. Gramma Esther put her arms around her and held her. Jenn was afraid she was going to pass out.

Antonio.

"Daddy," Jenn said, craning her neck over her grandmother's shoulder to look at the TV. Her father sat stoically, no longer tapping, then made as if to wipe his eyes. "Oh, Gramma."

"Thank you for listening," Solomon said on the screen. "If anyone has any information on this poor young woman, please come forward. We now know that what happened was not your fault, Jenn. Your father's waiting to be reunited with you. If you see this message, please, contact us. We're waiting for you with open arms."

Then the sitcom returned. The two women hugged each other tightly. Neither spoke.

My father, Jenn thought, suddenly so dizzy she thought she might faint. *Daddy.* He had betrayed her, literally throwing her to the vampires. To Aurora, who had destroyed Antonio. She had torn her father out of her heart. Her hatred of him was white hot. But this . . . he was warning her, telling her he loved her. She didn't know what to think, how to feel.

"He loves you. He needs your forgiveness," Antonio said from his cage.

Jenn swallowed hard and looked up at him. His eyes were dark brown, not red. And his fangs had retracted.

"Stay away from him," her grandmother ordered.

Kissing Gramma Esther's cheek, Jenn walked to the cage. Antonio turned sideways and looked at the floor.

"He needs your forgiveness," he said. Then he buried his face in his hands and sank to his knees.

Jenn couldn't breathe. She looked at the bowed head, the slumped shoulders. Was the monster in the cage gone too? Had two miracles occurred?

"First he needs his own forgiveness," Gramma Esther said, taking Jenn's hand and holding it tightly, as if Jenn might trust too much and get too close.

"Antonio, is it really you?" Jenn said.

He let his hands drop, and she saw the anguish on his face, the raw need for release, as he threw back his head and stared up, as if at God Himself.

In the distance Holgar howled, long, and low, and plaintively.

"I don't know, Jenn," he said, as tears slid down his cheek. "Who am I?"

CHAPTER SEVENTEEN

MARCH 3, 1941

TONIGHT I WILL LEAVE.

I HAVE PRAYED ON MY KNEES IN THE CHAPEL FOR HOURS, LISTENING FOR THE WORD OF GOD. FATHER FRANCISCO HAS ORDERED ME TO STAY HERE AT THE SEMINARY AT THE UNIVERSITY OF SALAMANCA. I WANT TO GO TO THE BATTLEFIELD. I WANT TO FIGHT AS A SOLDIER AND CUT HITLER'S ARMIES DOWN. BUT FATHER FRANCISCO HAS REMINDED ME THAT GOD IS FIGHTING BATTLES FOR SOULS, AND I'M CLOSE TO TAKING MY HOLY ORDERS—JUST WEEKS AWAY. HE SAYS THAT ONCE I AM ANOINTED, I WILL BECOME A LION OF GOD, LIKE ST. MICHAEL. I WILL FIGHT AGAINST SATAN AND HIS DEMONS.

BACK IN MY VILLAGE I WAS SO IN LOVE WITH LITA. SHE WAS BEAUTIFUL AND FUNNY; SHE WANTED ME TO MARRY HER, AND FOR US TO HAVE MANY CHILDREN. IT WAS WHAT SHE

WANTED, AND PART OF ME WANTED IT TOO. BUT I BELIEVED THAT GOD'S PLAN WAS FOR ME TO BECOME A PRIEST.

WHEN THE BOMBS FELL, SHE DIED ALONG WITH MY ENTIRE FAMILY. AND I WAS SAFE INSIDE SALAMANCA, SINGING CHANTS WITH MY BROTHERS. UNTOUCHED. UNHARMED.

I WAS SO ASHAMED.

REST IN PEACE, DEAR LITA.

ADOLF HITLER IS CONQUERING THE WORLD, SENDING THE HELPLESS TO HIS DEATH CAMPS. NOT JUST JEWS BUT GYPSIES, THE DISABLED, THE INFIRM. THIS CANNOT STAND. THIS <u>WILL</u> NOT STAND. GOOD MEN ARE JOINING THE CRUSADE AGAINST EVIL AND TYRANNY. AND I AM A GOOD MAN.

ONCE AGAIN THE WORLD BEYOND THE WALLS OF MY CHURCH CALLS ME TO THE BATTLE. THIS TIME I AM GOING. AND I SWEAR ON MY SOUL THAT I SHALL NEVER LET ANOTHER PERSON I LOVE COME TO HARM.

—FROM THE DIARY OF ANTONIO DE LA CRUZ,
FOUND ROTTING IN THE CATACOMBS

MONTANA
TEAM SALAMANCA, ESTHER, AND THE RESISTANCE

Flush with the apparent success of their ritual, Skye and Father Juan sat in chairs outside Antonio's cell. His own chair, safely behind the bars, formed the base of their triangle. In the center, in a circle of cumin, cloves, and juniper berries, a crystal ball caught the lights of candles Skye had placed at the north, south, east, and west. A white candle burned to invoke pure contact with spirit. A black candle burned, to repel evil and lay open Antonio's unconscious mind. There was turquoise, for humanity; gray, to neutralize evil. Father Juan had added a missal, his rosary beads, and a vial of holy water to the altar.

Antonio wore cuffs of silver, which Skye had exposed to the moonlight while praying for him. Around his head she had woven a diadem of silver ribbon. He was shirtless, and she had drawn a pentagram on his chest with the ashes of oak wood. He had pressed his body against the bars, eyes closed, while she touched the ash to his icy skin.

Skye's left and Father's Juan's right arms stretched between the bars of the cell. They held each other's hands, then took his hands in theirs, and Antonio caught Skye's slight jerk. Because she was still afraid of him, he knew, and because his hands were cold. Because his blood didn't circulate. Because he was a Cursed One.

Was it a curse that could be lifted?

Or is there a part of me that really doesn't want them to help me?

That part of him that had reveled in the curse of vampirism?

As a boy Antonio had observed the lonely existence of Father Pablo, the Catholic priest in his little village — denied a spouse and family, sharing the joys and sorrows of his flock without taking part in them. When Antonio had asked Father Pablo about it, the priest had told him that God approved of such a sacrifice and sent other, much more wonderful gifts in compensation.

Antonio had not quite understood, and as he was only a boy, and a sinful one at that, he didn't expect to. But he would become a priest like Father Pablo, and he would get those wonderful gifts. It would be like Christmas.

Years passed, and everyone in the village knew Antonio de la Cruz was destined for the priesthood. But when Rosalita Hernandez had arrived from Mexico to live a few houses down from his family's, Antonio had been tempted to deny his calling to the priesthood and marry her.

Then he remembered Father Pablo's words. He gazed around at all the proud faces of the villagers—one of their own would become a priest! He listened to his mother's prayers of thanksgiving to Mother Mary for the wonderful gift of her son, Antonio.

He couldn't betray their trust in him. So he'd stayed true to God and left for the seminary in Salamanca. Soon after, the bombs of the Spanish civil war had dropped on his village, killing Rosalita, Antonio's widowed mother, and his entire family.

From the safety of his monastery Antonio had grieved, and his religious community had gathered around him, prayed with him. The girls who came to Mass swooned over him—so handsome, tragic, and unavailable! He had grown closer to God, comforter of all, and even though Antonio had still been very lonely, he had not felt alone.

But in the dark Antonio wondered: *Did God make the bombs fall to make sure I would stay true to Him?*

"Yes, he did," Sergio had informed him, on the night they had met in a forest in France, in 1941, the war. "He did that to you, Antonio. Because he is a god of suffering. I offer you another path."

Then Sergio had converted Antonio, and he had lost God, or so he had believed. When the change had first come over him, he had lost his conscience and his humanity. He ran, free, overwhelmed by the passions he had denied his entire life. He found joy in lust, hatred, and cruelty. Sergio loved him for it, declaring him the finest, most heartless vampire he had ever run with.

"You're *magnífico*," Sergio would tell him, as they terrorized Madrid, and Antonio killed the priests on Sergio's hit list. "An inspiration!"

What had brought Antonio's humanity back to him, back in 1942? He remembered his pride at bringing a dead Hunter to Sergio's court on the night of the ball to be held in his honor. Antonio had just dropped the young man to the floor when something happened to him. Then and there he had become horrified by what he was doing. It was like waking from a nightmare.

But how? Why?

Antonio had known as he turned his back on his sire

that he had shamed and humiliated Sergio—and that he would be marked for Final Death.

After he had left Sergio's court and found sanctuary once more at the university, the kindly priest in charge of the chapel had allowed him to live in the basement—or what they had referred to in those days as the basement. There had been a misunderstanding; because he was a vampire and not a mortal man, he had pushed open a heavy door sealed a century before and had gone down more flights of stairs than the current inhabitants had known about.

Assuming he had reached the basement, Antonio dwelled in the deepest depths of the catacombs—the rooms of the dead, where the bones of the faithful had been stacked for centuries rather than buried in the churchyards. Perhaps Salamanca had suffered a plague or the churchyard had reached capacity. Such were the reasons for the catacombs of other cities. Skulls lined his walls; leg bones and arm bones marked the route he would walk to hear Mass, go to confession, and to drink blood from his friend. He was in an agony to be the best Catholic he could. Whatever he had done to save his soul he had to keep on doing, or he would be doomed.

But as he sat in the cage facing Skye and Father Juan, Antonio wondered if he had actually had nothing to do with his own reawakening. Had witches drawn down the Moon that time too? Had the prayers of men and women he didn't even know altered the energy of his life, and rescued him from hell?

Surveying Skye and Father Juan's careful preparations through the bars of his cell, shame rushed over him. *I didn't deserve rescuing, not this time. I would have killed that baby. They don't think I would have, but none of them is a vampire, like me.*

"There is no other vampire like you," Skye said, startling him.

Antonio's lips parted in astonishment, and he let go of both their hands. "Did you just read my mind?"

Skye looked just as surprised. "Blimey, luv, I guess I did."

"What?" Father Juan said.

"Um, well, he thought about how there are no other vampires like him," Skye said. She was lying to Father Juan, perhaps to protect Antonio.

"You *read* his thoughts," Father Juan said.

"*Heard* them. Clear as day," Skye replied.

"Try again," Father Juan told them.

The light from the candle flames reflected on Skye's forehead as she closed her eyes. Antonio and Father Juan both watched her in silence for a few seconds. Then Antonio closed his eyes, and concentrated.

I'm thinking about sunshine.

"Skye?" Father Juan pressed.

Skye opened her eyes and shook her head. "Nothing. Are you doing anything different, Antonio?"

"No," Antonio replied.

"What were you thinking about?" Father Juan asked him.

"The sun."

"Maybe it has to be something more emotional for you. Maybe a memory." She studied the layout of the candles and herbs, the crystal ball in the center. "I wonder if I added rosemary, for remembrance . . ." She returned her attention to him. "Try thinking about Jenn."

Try not thinking about her, he thought, and Skye cocked her head.

"Heh. Since I *told* you to think about her, maybe I'm just assuming that you are. But a picture of her face appeared in my mind."

"What precisely was he thinking when you first read his thoughts?" Father Juan asked, and Antonio shifted uncomfortably. "Tell me the truth this time," he added.

"He was afraid that he would have ki—hurt that baby, if he hadn't been startled." She cleared her throat and moved one of the candles a fraction of an inch, avoiding eye contact with both of them.

Antonio smiled grimly. "I was afraid I would have *killed* the baby. Skye, *brujita*, it's sweet of you to try to protect me, but in this case honesty is definitely the best policy."

She moved her shoulders. "It's not the way of my tradition to cause any sort of harm. And this is painful for you. Another sort of witch might be able to do it"—a cloud passed over her features—"but I'm your friend."

"Then *be* his friend," Father Juan said. "Aurora was

419

torturing and starving him, so we can assume she broke him down. But we need to know what built him back up into the Antonio we know. This is the second time Antonio has overcome the natural condition of the vampire."

"Did he have a girlfriend the first time?" Skye asked, and Antonio traded a look with Father Juan.

"Jenn isn't my girlfriend," Antonio said.

Skye raised a brow. "So much for honesty."

The two men fell silent. Then Father Juan said, "Our tradition is very different from yours, Skye. To you, denying your human appetites is an affront to the Goddess. To us, we offer those appetites as a sacrifice to God, so that we can channel our energy in service to Him and to His flock."

"Well, then, maybe he's gone off the deep end because of that," she said. "If he stopped trying so hard, you know . . . Maybe Antonio needs to eat, drink, and be merry. He's often rather dour, wouldn't you say?"

Antonio gave her a lopsided smile. "Is that how you see me?"

"We're at war, Skye," Father Juan said. "Antonio has been a soldier for decades. It hardens one. Toughens one."

"But he serves your god." She looked confused. "And your god does not like his holy men to kill people."

"He doesn't like it, but sometimes it's necessary. Sometimes, for the greater good, one has to make war," Father Juan said.

"But in your world 'good'—well, that's a moving target, isn't it? The Crusades of the Middle Ages—you killed people like Taamir by the hundreds of thousands."

"That's one way of looking at it," Father Juan said.

"In my world things are only good as long as no one is hurt." She sighed heavily. "Maybe that's why I'm the only White Witch I know fighting the Cursed Ones."

"Maybe if you told me how you came to that decision, it might help illuminate Antonio's decision as well." Father Juan picked up his rosary beads, kissed them, and put them back down on the altar.

At once the candle flames leaped and burned brighter, filling Antonio's cage with light. Skye gasped, and Antonio looked down at the pentagram on his chest. The ash was softly glowing in a silvery hue.

"Silver, the color of the Goddess. Is it possible she's claiming him?" Skye slid off her chair and got to her knees. She spread her arms wide. "Hecate, Queen of the Universe, is this a sign?"

Alarmed, Antonio crossed himself. "I'm a Catholic, nearly a priest."

"Let's join hands," Father Juan urged, "and see what Those of the Most High wish from us." He reached for Antonio's hand. Skye cried out softly as she laced her fingers through Antonio's.

"What?" Antonio said.

"For a moment your skin was warm," she said.

Father Juan's eyes widened. "I felt nothing."

Antonio let go of them and touched his face. Cold. "It must have been the heat from the candles." He made a moue of apology, as if he were somehow dashing Skye's hopes.

"Or it was magic," she retorted. "I *do* believe in it, you know. And we *are* here in a ritual setting, with, y'know, an *altar* and everything. So one might expect something to happen that's a little, I don't know, *special*."

Determined, she grabbed Antonio's hand again, then huffed and leaned sideways, taking Father Juan's. "And may I remind you gents that *I* am the High Priestess here, and I serve a Mother who *would* warm the hands of a child of Hers, if he were cold? Please, close your eyes."

Antonio did as she asked, feeling unaccountably light-hearted. There was a lot at work here that he didn't understand. Maybe if he could relax, then —

I didn't stop because I wanted to. I stopped because I was startled. How could I have let that happen? I am a prince among vampires. My sire is a king!

His eyes flew open, as did Skye's. Her chest heaved as she gazed at him in horror. Antonio looked down, seeking Father Juan's rosary to steady himself; instead he saw the crystal ball. Dark gray smoke swirled inside it.

"What is that?" Father Juan murmured.

"His aura. His thoughts. They're still very dark." Skye's voice shook. "He's not all the way back with us. Not even halfway."

Bite her wrist, a voice whispered in Antonio's mind. *Drink her blood.*

Skye cried out and jerked her hand away. She backed into her chair, knocking it over, and Father Juan instantly placed himself between Skye and Antonio.

"Fight it, Antonio." Father Juan reached down and grabbed up his rosary. He dangled it in front of Antonio, who recoiled from him.

"I only want a little," Antonio said calmly. "For the love of God, you're starving me."

"You fed just this evening," Father Juan countered. "Before Skye came." He pushed up his jacket sleeve, revealing his bandaged wrist.

"But your blood is thin, and old. Hers is young. Fresh." Antonio leered at her.

"Your eyes," Skye cried. "Father Juan, keep away from him!"

"Can you read his thoughts?" Father Juan asked, eyes fixed on Antonio.

"Yes. He wants to kill us both, and tell Aurora where he is."

"I *don't*!" he shouted. "You little liar!" Then Antonio trained his attention on her. "Skye, forgive me," he said sweetly. "I—I lost my temper, but I'm all right now. Come, let me prove it to you."

"He's trying to mesmerize you." Father Juan cupped Skye's shoulders.

Antonio flung himself at the cage bars. They clanged and rattled. Did they think they could keep him caged up like some *human*? "Don't you know who I am? Who *we* are? Legion! Legion! Legion! We are coming from the depths of hell!" he shouted. "Armies of us will fall on you! We'll rip out your throats! You *dare* to turn us to dust? You will be *less* than dust! You will be *nothing*! *Nothing!*"

He grabbed the bars and yanked. Enraged, he bellowed the names of the gods of hell:

"Orcus! Samedi! Hel! Baal!"

"Saint Michael! Saint Gabriel! Saint Raphael! All holy angels and archangels!" Father Juan shouted. "All holy orders of blessed spirits!"

"Do not try to exorcise *us*!" Antonio shouted. He spoke for all of them, the many inside him, the ones who were coming and would crush—

"Jenn!" Skye shouted at him. "Jenn! Jenn! Jenn!"

He gasped.

"Jenn!" she cried again. "You love her. You do!"

"No," he whispered. Suddenly he felt dizzy and empty. And hateful. And alone. "No."

"She loves you. She loves you," Skye said. "You are loved."

He slid to his knees. "Oh, Skye, oh, *Dios*. Help me, Father," he begged, lowering his head. "I'm sorry. *Lo siento. Mea culpa, mea maxima culpa.*"

Jenn had heard it all. Antonio speaking so earnestly, and then like someone in a horror movie.

The horror movie that all their lives had become.

Forcing down her tears, she gestured to Taamir. She had joined him on guard duty so she could eavesdrop, and now she wished she hadn't.

"Are you all right?" he asked her, munching an apple, as if he were accustomed to hearing Antonio's rages.

The door burst open, and Skye tumbled through it. She looked at Jenn, then put her arms around her tightly. Jenn held herself stiffly. She couldn't fall apart. She *wouldn't*.

"Taamir, please go in and stay with Father Juan," Skye said. "No one should be alone with Antonio. Are you on watch, Jenn? I'll take it from here." She took Jenn's Uzi from her and slung it over her shoulder. "Go on. You know it's best you find somewhere else to be."

Jenn took a deep, ragged breath and nodded. Wheeling away, she half ran past the other tents and buildings to the open field, where the life-size photograph of Solomon had been obliterated. Only scraps of the poster clung to the hay bales.

"I hate you. I hate you," she said, kicking it. "I'll kill you." She pounded at it with her fists, one at a time, and then both, doubled. She kept hitting and kicking, finally crying, punching it until the pieces of straw raised crisscross welts on her hands.

Then she slid down it, exhausted, still crying. She lay curled in the icy mud as the tears nearly froze to her face.

*　　*　　*

"Honey," said a voice, as someone gently shook Jenn.

She startled. She hadn't been asleep, exactly—now she was just so numb and cold she couldn't move. A blanket came around her shoulders. She opened her eyes slowly, and for a moment she was so stunned she couldn't focus.

Her mother was kneeling in the freezing mud, showering her face with kisses.

"Mom," Jenn said, throwing her arms around her mother. Jenn closed her eyes tightly and inhaled her mom's warmth, her scent, her. Her mother. Safe, alive, here.

"Oh, my baby," her mom said. "Oh, Jenn."

They held each other for a long time. Jenn's mom smoothed her hair and tried to help her get up. Jenn's leg was asleep.

"When did you get here?" Jenn asked. "How?"

"Just a few minutes ago. Gramma brought you here, yes? I've been looking for you everywhere." She raised a hand. "Here! I found her."

Noah approached. "Good," he said. Then he slid his arm under Jenn's shoulder and steadied her. He was solid and strong beside her. And warm. Tentatively, she pressed her weight on her tingling foot.

"Mom, I didn't kill Brooke."

"I know. We all know." Her mother kissed her cheeks, then sniffled and kissed her forehead once, twice, a dozen

426

times, and embraced her again, smiling shyly when her arm brushed against Noah.

"Mom, Daddy was on TV," she said. "He was trying to send me a message."

"Jenn," her mother said, pursing her lips. "I don't know about him. I . . . I'm not ready to believe anything he says.

"How's Heather?" her mother asked, changing the subject. "When did you see her last? Father Juan said she's in a safe house, but they can only call out, and since he's here, they're being extra careful. I've been *dying* to talk to her. She's all right, though, yes? Does she have someone to talk to about it? A therapist, maybe?"

"Oh." Jenn hazarded a glance at Noah, who stayed very neutral. He knew about Heather. It killed Jenn to lie to her, but she and Father Juan had both agreed that no one outside the team—and Noah and Taamir were part of the team—could know about Heather, not even Jenn's mom. The best way to protect her sister's life was to lie about her condition.

"I want to be with her. Father Juan is trying to arrange it," her mom added.

Jenn was surprised, and also very pleased. That was a great idea, if her mother could take the truth. It would help Heather reconnect, and it would reunite Jenn's family. As much of her family as was left, anyway. Would her father ever join them again? Jenn didn't know.

Beneath the moonlight her mom looked younger than

Jenn ever remembered seeing her. It was as if her new life agreed with her. Jenn thought of all the things her mother had done to try to be helpful in postwar San Francisco, like taking meals to shut-ins, many of whom had been injured battling the Cursed Ones. The local authorities had shut down her art gallery because some of the pieces she exhibited had been seen as "inflammatory" and "detrimental to the truce process." Even though she was Gramma Esther's daughter-in-law and not her blood relative, they were two of a kind.

"Your mother brought someone who's been spying on Solomon for the resistance," Noah told Jenn. "Your grandmother has called a meeting, and we've been out looking for you."

"Let's go," Jenn said. But as she tried to walk forward, she wobbled on her tingling leg. Noah eased her along, his side pressing against hers. His welcome body heat seeped into her. After what she'd seen and heard, it felt so good to lean on him.

"Can't we stop to get you a coat? You're frozen," her mother protested, trailing after them.

"Are you all right?" Noah asked Jenn quietly.

"It's so good to see her," Jenn replied. "I hate lying to her about my sister."

"Life is like that. The sweet with the bitter." He gave her a sad smile. "So one must remember to taste the sweet when it's available."

Jenn's joy was already beginning to sour. Maybe the meeting was also about Antonio. A thrill of deep fear made her stomach clench, and she slowed down, waiting for her mom. Jenn took her hand and squeezed hard.

"Thanks. I can walk now," Jenn told Noah.

"I'm not sure—," he began.

"I'm okay." She licked her lips and shifted her weight. Tingles raced up and down her leg.

She walked shoulder to shoulder with her mother into the barn. There were about twenty people, all familiar faces, many flashing smiles and gestures of greeting at her mom. Her grandmother and her two lieutenants, Sam and Bo, were seated at a rickety wooden table. A few others sat on wooden chairs, others on hay bales. Father Juan, Skye, Eriko, and Jamie were on the bales.

Skye mouthed, *Holgar is with Antonio.* Father Juan smiled gently, seeing her and her mother together.

A blond woman, very pretty, stood at the foot of the table, as if she had been asking Gramma Esther for a favor. She was wearing skinny jeans, boots, and an army jacket with a Jerusalem cross pinned on the lapel. But while the government agents wore black crosses, this one was white.

"Jenn Leitner," the woman said, extending her hand as Jenn and her mom walked to the table. "I'm Marti Swanson. I'm with the Resistance."

A bit mystified, Jenn shook the woman's hand. It seemed that there were a number of "resistances" in this war. Father

Juan and Antonio had explained that in World War II it had been the same way. But during that war most groups had worked within the borders of their own countries, fighting against invading armies. Jenn was the only person on her team from America, and she had gone to Spain for her training.

Jenn's mom pulled out two empty chairs from the table, gesturing for Jenn to sit with her. Jenn glanced over at her team, then took the seat beside her mom. Noah leaned against a post and crossed his arms.

"Some of you know that Solomon is planning a film about the history of the Cursed Ones titled, simply, *History*. Two weeks ago Solomon told an operative of ours, a woman named Mei Lao, that he was planning to film a section set in Russia about vampire supersoldiers. He was talking to someone named Danny about it. But we think that's a cover for something else."

All the Salamancans stared at her. Then they looked at one another.

"Dantalion?" Jenn said.

"Maybe? Who's that?" she asked.

"Dantalion was making hybrid human, werewolf, and vampire monsters. Really strong. Vampire supersoldiers, only for real. That could move in daylight," Jenn told her.

There was a stir around the room, and Jenn realized, belatedly, that this was news to all but a select few. So much had happened so fast.

"Was he successful? *Could* they walk in daylight?" Jenn's grandmother asked.

"We don't know," Jenn replied, trying to keep her voice steady.

Marti licked her lips. "I have more."

"Go on," Jenn said.

"We all wear these heart necklaces"—she lifted one up from around her neck—"with bugs in them. So far Solomon doesn't suspect that's what we're doing. I got this next bit myself, by standing outside his door. He does love his speakerphone," she added dryly.

"Camps are definitely the way to go." Solomon's voice echoed from portable speakers positioned around the room. *"We can round up all the undesirables and keep them in one place. Your thoughts, Jack?"*

Camps? Jenn thought, looking at the worry on people's faces.

"Undesirables would be . . . who, Solomon?" Shock registered on everyone's faces. "Jack" was Jack Kilburn, the president of the United States.

"I'm taking my cue from your World War Two. The people who stood in the way. The troublemakers. And the weaklings. Hell, your side locked up anyone who was of Japanese descent. You could make your own list, if you like. Do you have any enemies you want to lock up?"

Expressions of dawning horror gave rise to murmurs of alarm. Pleas for quiet accompanied a lot of shushing as people leaned forward to hear.

"You're talking about concentration camps. Like the Nazis," said the president.

"Bingo. And I have a feeling quite a few of you humans will be making a new home behind barbed wire."

There was a pause. *"But there are billions of us, Solomon. How many of these camps are you talking about?"*

"There's billions now," Solomon replied. *"But we can take care of that. In record time."*

The room went dead silent. People's faces drained of color. Jenn's mom reached for her hand.

There was a long pause. The speakers hissed with white noise.

"That's all we have," Marti said. "If Solomon told Kilburn what he was planning, I didn't pick it up."

"Oh, Goddess," Skye said, burying her face in her hands.

In the stillness Jamie stood. His neck was still bandaged from Antonio's bite.

"Why are any of you surprised? This is what governments do. Throw the people down in front of the tanks. This piece of shite is making a deal to save his own arse, just like Jenn's da here. It's you and me against the Cursers, no help from *them*. Always has been, always will be, till we wipe 'em out."

Gramma Esther and her old-folk Defenders nodded in agreement. "Jamie's right."

"We know that Solomon is planning a press conference on the mall in Washington, D.C., in a week. Someone in the

White House told us the president is going to be there too," Marti said.

"Good. We can take them both out at the same time," Jamie said.

"Jamie, there's no way," Jenn said. "We won't be able to get anywhere near them."

"She's right," Esther said.

"Oh, *God*! You're a pack of cowards!" Jamie looked around, then grabbed a metal watering can and flung it as hard as he could. It slammed into a post.

"Jenn's right," Noah said. "I've 'taken out' a few politicians in my time, and it takes months, years of planning. And a lot more manpower than we have."

Then Father Juan stood. His face was almost glowing. "But we can do something else. We could play that recording for the world."

"When Solomon and the president meet at the mall. The world will be listening," Gramma Esther said.

"God and the Devil, too," Jamie said. He shrugged. "It's better than nothing. And I guess it's all we're going to get from *you* lot."

"We'll try to do better," Gramma Esther said archly.

"See that you do," Jamie shot back, deadly serious.

The planning began at once. Jenn was in the thick of it, but she let Jamie do a lot of the strategizing because, as he put it, "my people used to do this sort of thing." The night wore on inside the barn, and even though she and the others were used to keeping the same hours as the enemy, her head began to bob.

Something caught her attention in her peripheral vision. Near the opened double doors of the barn, Father Juan was gesturing to her. Skye stood beside him, her face pale and wan.

Jenn pushed away from the table and went to see what was up. Father Juan put his arm around her shoulders as if bracing her for a blow.

"I'm going back to Spain, and I'm taking Antonio with me," he said.

CHAPTER EIGHTEEN

Sometimes, no matter what you do, no matter how hard you fight, you still lose. That's one of the most horrific secrets of life. Sometimes there is no victory, no beating the odds, no emerging triumphant. The deck might be stacked against you. Fate may have decreed your failure. I just know that sometimes, even when you think you've won, you've lost.

I hate it. I'm tired of losing. I'm tired of losing friends, family, the war. How do you change it, though? How do you swap out the deck or change your fate? Because I need to. If I can't, everyone I know will die. And it will be my fault.

I've heard it said that victory is won in inches. That may be true, but we don't have the time. If we win in inches, we'll still lose, because with every day that passes, hundreds more die.

How do I stop it?

How do I make my own fate?

How do I even begin?

—from the diary of Jenn Leitner,

discovered in the ashes

MONTANA
TEAM SALAMANCA MINUS ANTONIO;
ESTHER AND THE RESISTANCE

"Master?" Jenn's throat closed up around the word. Thoughts jumbled in her head—that Father Juan hadn't given up on Antonio, that Father Juan wouldn't be there on the mission to Washington. And that Skye also had something to say.

"My heart is telling me that I must stop fighting. But I can help Father Juan with Antonio and Heather." Skye spoke in a rush, nervous and anxious. "Antonio is better because of what Father Juan and I have done."

"Antonio is going to get in your way," Father Juan said to Jenn. "And I need to get back to the academy. And if Skye has been able to help Antonio, she may be able to help Heather."

Jenn bit her lower lip, and shook her head. "Skye, I can't let you go."

"Jenn," Father Juan began, but she shook her head again.

"Skye can reach the minds of our enemies. She might

be able to gather information that we need." Jenn looked at the gothy witch. "And if we get injured, you keep us going."

Skye frowned. Jenn sensed her confusion, and gave her a quick hug. "Please, Skye, don't abandon us. That would be causing harm." She looked at Father Juan. "Wouldn't you agree?"

Their master remained silent. Then he turned to Skye. "As you've pointed out, in my faith good people often do bad things. They take the sin upon themselves, for the greater good. But if you know what you must do, then so be it. "

"I don't know," Skye murmured.

"How soon are you leaving?" Jenn asked.

"Ten minutes," he replied. "Your mother is giving me her van so I can keep the sun off him. She's staying here. I told her I would send for her later."

Ten minutes. That wasn't enough time to prepare herself. But ten hours wouldn't have been enough time either.

"Why tonight? Why now?" she asked.

"While you were strategizing, I cast the runes," he said simply. "And I prayed."

"But . . ." Jenn's throat tightened.

He drew her into his arms and kissed the crown of her head. "You've had so many disappointments, Jenn."

She froze. *Are you taking him away so I won't be disappointed?*

"I want to say good-bye to him," she said.

Father Juan hesitated. "It would be better if you didn't see him now."

"No," Jenn blurted. "Oh, *no*."

"Jenn, be strong," Skye said, taking her hands. "Father Juan, let her see him. I believe it will help him like it did before."

The three fell silent as they reached the building. One of Gramma Esther's Defenders snapped to attention at the sight of Jenn, saluting her.

"I heard we're going to kill Solomon," the soldier said.

"Well, that's the eventual plan," Jenn hedged.

"Roger that, miss." He unlocked the door. Jenn looked at Father Juan and Skye.

"I want to go in by myself."

"Holgar's in there," Father Juan said. "I want him to stay with you."

"All right," Jenn said.

The room was dim. Holgar was already standing; he moved toward her and gazed down at her. He looked terribly sad.

"He's not doing well," Holgar murmured. "This shouldn't be your last memory of him."

"It's not my *last*," she said, flaring, not so much with anger but with a horrible fear that he could be right.

She walked forward, forcing Holgar to get out of her way. He did, standing back in the shadows.

Antonio was sitting cross-legged on the floor, gesturing

with his hands and whispering. She stood quietly.

"Antonio. I've come to say good-bye."

His hands stopped moving. His head snapped up. His eyes were red, but in the next second they were brown. He looked like a normal nineteen-year-old. Like the guy she'd crushed on for two years, before she'd discovered he was a vampire.

This was the guy she was still in love with.

"Jenn," Antonio said. *"Bueno."* He ran his hands through his hair, such a human gesture that it gave her hope that everything would be all right, somewhere, someday. "You should stay away from me." He paused. "And from Heather, too. Until we get better."

She wondered if Father Juan was really going to send for her mother to come and live at Salamanca. What would she say when she saw Heather?

Gazing up at her, Antonio threaded his fingers through the bars. Then he seemed to think better of it, and lowered his hands to his lap. The light cast a circle on his blue-black hair that looked like a halo.

"I've been thinking." Antonio's voice was hushed and quiet. "I'm rededicating myself to the priesthood. I can't become a priest, but I can put my focus where it should be. From where it . . . wandered."

Her breath caught as if he had punched her in the stomach. Her heart stuttered.

"What are you saying?"

"You know what I'm saying." His eyes glistened. "You need to have a life, with a man. That's your calling. I'm not a man, Jenn. And I never will be."

"No," she choked out. She fell to her knees in front of the cage and put her hands through the bars.

He hissed and pulled himself away from her. His eyes blazed with red, and his fangs extended.

"Get her out of here!" Antonio shouted. "Holgar, please!"

Strong arms gripped her and lifted her to her feet, putting distance between her and Antonio's prison. Holgar. She struggled against him, but he held her tightly.

"Antonio!" Jenn cried, reaching for him.

Antonio whirled around, his back to her, doubling over.

"Go," he ground out.

Holgar forcibly walked Jenn to the door, opened it, and pushed her through. She burst into tears. Then arms came around her — Father Juan and Skye. Weeping, she stumbled as Skye led her away. She tried to turn back, but Skye held her firmly.

"Don't look back, my angel," Skye said. "Just come with me. I won't leave you. Any of you. When we're done in Washington, I'll work night and day to figure out how to help bring Antonio back to us."

"He *is* back," Jenn said. But she knew that wasn't true. She cried harder, and when she thought she couldn't cry any more, fresh tears slid down her face.

Jenn began to feel rivulets of calm within the wild river

of her grief. The witch was casting spells to soothe her.

"Jenn," Skye whispered, "I'll bring the Circuit up to date on all this. The witchly communities will *have* to see that they must get involved."

"What about Estefan?" Jenn asked her. "Does he have a circuit, too?"

Skye hesitated. "I don't know. These are things we need to figure out. Things have been happening so fast."

A van lumbered past them. Skye gripped her hand; Jenn knew Father Juan and Antonio were inside. Jenn bowed her head as Skye murmured over her in Latin.

Good-bye, Antonio. Vaya con Dios.

She put thoughts of him away, as if in a box, to be opened later.

Then she wiped her face and headed back toward the barn, where the planning session was still in full swing. A figure was standing just outside the double-door entrance, an Uzi over his shoulder. Noah.

As she approached, he reached in his pocket and pulled out something. It was a pack of gum. With a trembling hand she took a stick, unwrapped it, and popped it in her mouth. It was cinnamon, her favorite.

"I'm quitting smoking," he told her. He quirked a lop-sided grin. "I noted that you aren't a big fan."

She tried to smile, to feel flattered. The best she could do was a nod.

"Jenn? Good," her grandmother said, as he and she

walked back inside. Esther held up a cell phone. "Marti just got a call. The press conference will be held next Friday. That's six days and eighteen hundred miles."

"Plenty of time, if we kick it," Jamie said.

"Not enough time," Noah murmured.

"It doesn't matter," Jenn told him under her breath, and went to join the others.

PARIS, FRANCE
AURORA

Aurora rested on the brocade settee, enjoying the view of Paris at night. She liked hotel rooms. No matter how bad the mess, one didn't have to clean it up. She rather liked the washes of red on this particular white carpet. It gave a touch of color to the gold and ivory design of the massive suite.

Louis, her lieutenant, entered her sitting room. The man bowed low, and unlike some, he meant the courtly gesture.

"Where do we stand?" she asked, crossing her legs as she leaned back her head.

"Our troops are assembling," Louis said. "And the resistance is back in America, chasing after Solomon."

"And Antonio de la Cruz is back at the university?"

"Our lookout at the airport confirmed it," Louis assured her.

She suppressed any telling reaction of relief. They had to believe that she was in full control. In truth, however, she was petrified that her sire would find out that she had had Antonio de la Cruz—and that she'd lost him. It had been stupid of her to take him back to Las Vegas. But she didn't have connections in Russia, and she'd been unnerved by what had happened to Dantalion.

She'd thought to frighten Dantalion a little by picking off some of his monsters before she grabbed Antonio. But after she'd left the palace grounds, his entire headquarters had blown up. She'd sent some vampires back to have a look. They'd sent pictures to her phone. The wreckage was incredible. There was no sign of Dantalion himself, but it was quite possible he'd been blown to such tiny bits that he was still "there."

"There's something else," Estefan said as he casually entered the room. Aurora was irritated with the Dark Witch for not knocking and asking permission to enter. Estefan was pushy and presumptuous. What *had* the little White Witch seen in him?

"Go on, Estefan," she said imperiously.

Estefan paused as if for dramatic effect. He looked so smug. Aurora had just about had enough. Louis looked irritated too. Maybe it was time to get rid of Estefan.

"Sergio Almodóvar is in Madrid," Estefan announced.

She and Louis both blinked at him in surprise. "Madrid?"

"*Sí.* And he's getting ready to go to Salamanca."

Alarmed, she leaped to her feet. Sergio would *not* take her prize. "Let's go," she said.

443

MADRID
SERGIO ALMODÓVAR AND PHILIPPE GAUDET

While Philippe Gaudet looked on, Sergio sat on his throne in the bloodstained chamber and remembered every detail of the last time he had set eyes on Antonio de la Cruz. In 1942. In the center of this very room, surrounded by Sergio's subjects. On a night designed to honor Antonio, the young vampire had presented Sergio with a Hunter. And then Antonio had fled. Why? What had happened to him that night?

Sergio wanted to know. Had to know. And so did Sergio's sire, who at this very moment stood on the brink of creating the Vampire Kingdom here on earth. His sire was very interested in Antonio. If one vampire could lose his way as completely as Antonio had, it could happen to another. To many. Such a catastrophe could not stand. Sergio's sire wanted to study Antonio—and Sergio would do anything to give Antonio to him.

"You're firm in your resolve," Sergio said to Philippe Gaudet. Philippe was a vampire like his brother, Christian Gaudet, who had ruled the French Quarter of New Orleans. After Aurora had murdered Christian, Philippe had come in secret to Sergio to exact his revenge. "You'll join with me to take Antonio before Aurora gets him."

Philippe nodded. "If you let me stake her. Aurora killed my brother. She's lower than the dust on my boots."

"Done," Sergio said. Sergio wanted to believe Philippe, but he'd been betrayed before. "And you're sure she's in Paris?"

Philippe nodded. "I have excellent spies. The resistance recaptured Antonio, and they took him to Salamanca University. He's there now. And Aurora's planning to go in after him."

Sergio smiled. "But she's not there yet."

"She's not there yet," Philippe replied.

Sergio tapped his fingers on the arms of his throne. "If only she'd come to me. She was always so competitive. I already told our sire what she did. She *had* Antonio, Philippe. But rather than bring him to me, or to our sire, she played with him." Sergio didn't add that apparently Aurora had managed to return Antonio to his natural vampiric state. He would force Aurora to tell him how she'd done it, before she died.

Philippe shrugged. "Then she deserves what's coming to her."

"Agreed," Sergio said, but his unbeating heart felt small and cold in his chest. The story of Aurora Abregón and Sergio Almodóvar was the stuff of legends.

Maybe I won't let him kill her. Love is so complicated.

And inconvenient.

"Then you have my support. The vampires of Gaudet will be there," Philippe said.

"*Vale,*" Sergio said, rising. He gazed at the exact spot

where Antonio had dropped the Hunter. Such pride. Such a vampire. He would have been a prince. Then he had become nothing but the lapdog of humans. Since Aurora had gotten through to Antonio, Sergio should reward her, not kill her.

After he captured Antonio himself.

"We should get ready," he told Philippe.

As Sergio's boots echoed on the stone floor, he heard: *I will kill her; I won't. I will; I won't.*

He just couldn't decide.

SALAMANCA
FATHER JUAN, ANTONIO, AND HEATHER

Heather had spent *forever* in the cage down in the dark, dank basement of the university. She'd heard rustling, movement—which turned out to be rats—and she couldn't get Father Giovanni to tell her anything about what was happening. He was afraid of her.

She liked that.

When the door opened, Heather was surprised to see that another priest and the vampire were both there. She remembered both of them vaguely, like a long-forgotten dream. This Cursed One seemed somehow different to her than her fragmented memories of him, though. More like . . . her.

"Heather, how are you?" the vampire asked very slowly.

She hissed at him.

446

The priest ventured closer than the vampire did, and he spoke low, soothingly. "We're sorry we've been gone so long."

"Jenn," Heather said.

"What?" the priest asked, looking at her. She remembered now: His name was Father Juan.

"I smell Jenn." She closed her eyes. Her sister's scent was coming, very faintly, from both of them. They had been with her. They had seen her.

"She's doing well," Father Juan assured her.

Heather hissed again. "I smell fear on you. I smell *terror*."

Father Juan bowed his head. "It's true. I am afraid."

"Not on you. On *you*," she said to the vampire. "And I smell other things." She backed away from him.

"What?" the vampire asked her. Antonio. That was his name. He loved her sister. Her sister, who was human. While she, Heather, was not.

"Death," she told him. "You reek of it."

En Route to Washington, D.C.
Team Salamanca Minus Antonio and Esther Leitner's Defenders

Our mission has changed so much, Jenn thought. *We were trained to kill vampires, not hijack the airwaves. This is more up Noah's alley. And Antonio's, when he fought the Germans back in World War II.*

447

Three dozen people in eight vans and cars were driving toward Washington, D.C. Jenn's mother had stayed behind in Montana. Jenn and Noah were sitting on the floor of a panel van with the passenger seats taken out for roominess. Noah had been trying to explain how "the operation" was going to work. He had diagrams and sketches of cell phones, cell towers, radio towers, and satellites, and her eyes were glazing over. Apparently, it was more complicated than holding up a boom box. She was having major doubts about the plan, and she had attempted to express them. But no one had paid attention. People were tired of sitting around in the wilds of Montana.

Noah, Jamie, Eriko, Skye, and Holgar were in sleeping bags on the floor. Taamir had gone in a different vehicle. Jenn and Noah were the only two still up. They were chewing cinnamon gum and staring at documents together. She had no idea how old he was. If he was in the Israeli special forces, he must be in his mid to late twenties.

Younger than Antonio by a long shot.

He sighed and looked at her.

"This is crazy, this whole thing," he said around his gum. "Washington will be crawling with vampires and loyal humans. Loyal to the established regime," he added. "We need more time."

Great minds think alike, she thought.

"We're out of time," she said, remembering her last conversation with Greg. "Maybe there will be a miracle."

"I'm very pragmatic," he told her.

"Hey, Israel, pipe down. Some of us are trying to sleep," Jamie groused.

"Jamie," Eriko reproved.

"The Voice of the Resistance said he'd help," Jenn reminded Noah. Through Father Juan's efforts to locate and unite resistance cells, "Kent" had e-mailed him and offered to help. He said he would put them on the air. Noah was double and triple-checking to see if Kent could deliver on that promise.

Jenn's cell phone rang. It was Father Juan. Her heart skipped beats as she connected. Noah very politely moved away as best he could, picking up a map of the National Mall, where Solomon and President Kilburn would hold their press conference.

"Jenn," Father Juan said. "How are things?"

She lowered her voice. "I'm kind of . . ."

"Having second thoughts?" he filled in. "Kent called me directly. He confirmed everything. He wants to meet in an Internet café off the I-70 in Maryland. He'll give me more details if you agree."

"Good," she said. "But I'll have to run it by the others."

Noah looked over at her, and she held up a finger to indicate that she'd fill him in later. He nodded and unwrapped another stick of gum.

"Very well," Father Juan said. "Your grandmother still has a lot of those prepaid cell phones, *sí*? We'll set up a call with one of those."

"Okay." She took a deep breath. "How is Antonio?"

"Hmm. It's hard to say, Jenn. He asked me to put him in a cell next to Heather. He says he has bad times and good times. I used Skye's arcana to cast a strong protection spell. Please thank her for allowing me to use them. And the Circuit has agreed to help. A witch is going to come to the university to work with me."

"Oh, that's great." She smiled hopefully. *"Gracias."*

"De nada, Jenn. Ah. Father Giovanni is signaling me. We have a new security system, very fancy. He's teaching me how to use it."

"Then I'll let you go," she said, not wanting to. She wanted to hear more about Antonio. "I'll tell everybody about the meeting, and I'll get you a number for the prepaid phone."

"Bueno. Go with God, Jenn."

"The same to you," she replied a bit awkwardly.

Then he stayed on the line a moment. She could hear him breathing.

"Father?" she asked.

"It's nothing," he replied. "Just . . . be careful."

He hung up. Spooked, she did the same. Noah raised a brow. "How is Antonio?"

She flushed. "Better, I think."

"Some of us are trying to sleep," Jamie said loudly.

"We should sleep too," Noah said to Jenn. He handed her a pillow. She lay down facing away from him, hyper-aware as he lay down too. His breath was warm against the back of her head.

Jenn began to doze, imagining the sun shining on Antonio's face. They would save her father, and Heather would be human again . . . so many dreams . . .

Holgar yipped. Jamie was snoring.

Behind Jenn, Noah moaned in his sleep. "Chayna," he muttered. He turned his head, and she saw the large silver Star of David pendant around his neck.

Suddenly the van stopped, throwing Jenn against Noah, who grabbed her. Pushing her hair out of her eyes, Jenn sat up. Noah thrust a submachine gun into her arms.

"What the bloody hell?" Jamie shouted.

Shouts and gunfire erupted, and the panel door slid open.

A dozen soldiers in flak jackets and helmets held sub-machine guns on them. Jenn kept her weapon up. Noah did the same, and by the sounds of clacking, the rest of Salamanca had as well. Jenn's heart was thundering.

"Who are you?" she shouted.

The soldiers parted, and Greg stood before her. Black suit, no sunglasses.

"It's all right, Jenn. Lower your weapons."

"Bloody hell," Jamie said. "That's the voice, Jenn. The man with Dantalion. White cammies."

"What?" Holgar and Skye said in unison.

Jenn stared at Greg, who looked puzzled. "Excuse me?" he asked.

"It *is*," Jamie insisted. "Shoot him!"

As if on cue, Greg's soldiers took a step forward. Noah grunted. Jenn sighted down her weapon directly at Greg's face.

"Woof," Holgar said.

"I can assure you, I have not been to Russia, and I have never met Dantalion," Greg said.

"Liar!" Jamie bellowed.

"Jamie, easy, please," Skye said. "We don't want to start anything."

"Uh, *yeah*, we do," Jamie shot back.

"Jenn, listen. We got wind of your operation, and we're shutting you down. We need the tape," Greg said. "The one you want to play at the conference."

"Tape? What century are you living in?" Jamie said, snorting. "We're digital. We got backups from here to County Cork. We got people all over the place. That convo's going to be played at that press conference, you feckin' traitor."

"Jamie-*kun*, please stay calm," Eriko murmured. "Please."

"Recording, then. That was a misstatement by an old man," Greg said. "You're going to waste it, Jenn." Greg was speaking directly to her. "No one's going to believe you. It'll cause a minor stir, and then Solomon and the president will smooth it over. They'll say it was a fake. And you'll have died for nothing."

"We ain't planning on dying, thank you very much," Jamie said.

"He's right," Noah interjected. "This man." He gestured at Greg with his chin.

"But isn't this what you want?" Jenn asked Greg. "For us to distract everyone while you do whatever it is you're doing?"

"Jenn, think," Greg said. "We took Dr. Sherman. He was working on the virus. Dantalion sent Solomon his data on supervampires."

"How do you know that?" Jamie demanded.

Greg just smiled at him sadly. "Son," he said, "we're on the same side."

"Go on," Jenn said.

"We're in the process of stealing the files from Solomon," Greg said. "But we don't need any flags on our play."

"I *heard* you," Jamie cut in. "He *was* in that lab, Jenn. We can't trust him."

"It doesn't matter if we trust him or not," Noah countered. "They have more guns than we do."

Greg ticked a glance at Noah. Appraised him. Nodded.

"This one's a keeper," he said to Jenn. Despite everything she blushed.

She couldn't decide if she should tell him that the Voice of the Resistance was going to help them. What if Jamie was right? What if Greg was one of the bad guys? For all she knew, Greg might use them as bait for Kent.

What should I do?

Just then, Gramma Esther approached the van. Her face was grim, and she was unarmed. Her gray hair was tousled around her shoulders. Greg saw her. She raised a hand and moved past Greg to Jenn. Jenn lowered her weapon. Noah did not.

Gramma Esther gave Jenn's shoulder a pat.

"Greg and I talked," Gramma Esther said, "I've discussed the situation with the other Defenders. We're going to do it his way."

"But you didn't discuss it with me," Jenn argued.

"With *us*," Jamie corrected her.

Noah cleared his throat. He shrugged his shoulders and made a face as if to indicate that Jenn should listen to her grandmother.

Gramma Esther turned to Greg. "Did you tell her?"

Greg shook his head. Esther exhaled and gave Jenn's shoulder another squeeze.

"Honey, Greg's people have gotten word about your academy. While you've been here, the Catholic Church ordered Father Juan to disband it. He's refused. He and a bunch of students are occupying the buildings, but something's going to happen one way or the other. I don't know when, but I think you're needed."

454

"No," Jenn said. "I just talked to him a little while ago. Just now."

"Then he was keeping it from you," Gramma Esther said.

"There's been a lot of movement around the university," Greg cut in. "We're thinking they might try to forcibly evict them."

"Oh, God, no," Jenn breathed. *What will happen to Antonio, then? And Heather?*

"This is all a lie," Jamie said. "They're setting us up to abandon the mission."

There was a long silence. Another. Then Jenn said, "That's because this isn't our mission. We're going home."

SALAMANCA
FATHER JUAN AND ANTONIO

"Find peace, my son," Father Juan told Antonio, who was praying inside his fortified cell. He had given Antonio a rosary and a missal. The arcana of the Church.

In the cell over, Heather had pulled her blanket over herself again.

"Gracias, Padre," Antonio replied.

Buoyed, Father Juan climbed the stairs to the ground floor of the building. Antonio seemed much better. Jenn had called him back, given him some grief for having hidden the dire situation at the university, and told him that the mission to Washington had been canceled. Jenn and the team—plus the two men from the Middle East—were already on a flight home.

Thank you, God, for all these blessings.

Juan walked outside, the night air cool on his face. Antonio *was* better. Had he and Skye done something permanent to him with their magicks? *Something we can do to other vampires?* When Skye returned, they could attempt the same rituals and magicks on Heather. He was certain the Circuit would prove to be a big help.

Statues of saints gazed down on him as he pulled a set of stones covered with ancient runes from his pocket and showed them to the moon. It was three-quarters full, large, and yellow. When he had aided Skye in Drawing Down the Moon, he had been filled with the love of the Goddess.

As a gesture to the Lady in addition to the Lord, he went into the chapel and took the lilies meant for the Holy Virgin and spread them on the chapel steps, beneath the moonlight. Who was She but the Goddess, in another form? Then he lit a white candle and set it among the lilies.

"Are you with me?" he asked the Lady.

A wind blew up, and the flame of the white candle flared.

"Blessed be," he said.

He prayed over the runes in Latin and tossed them. His heart seized as he read the signs. Everything pointed to something dark on the horizon—*this* horizon, Salamanca. More than that he couldn't discern. He couldn't even tell from which direction danger was coming, or whom it was targeting. Perhaps it was the trouble they were already in— the closing of the school, the war.

"Jenn," he murmured aloud, as if calling to her. "Be careful, my child."

He gathered the stones and put them in his pocket.

En Route to Salamanca
Team Salamanca Minus Antonio

As was their habit while flying, Jenn's team scattered through the cabin of the plane. Skye cast glamours on each of them to make them less interesting, but when it came to Noah, the glamour was not working for Jenn. He was sitting beside her, reading a book in Hebrew, and she kept staring at his hands without meaning to. What Antonio had said had cut her to the quick. Rededicating himself to the priesthood?

Breaking up with me, she translated. As if they had ever really been together. That was just some crazy dream she'd been having all by herself. *But he said he loves me.*

But he's a vampire.

She became aware that Noah was looking at her, and ticked her glance up at him.

"Reading over my shoulder?" he asked her, chuckling.

457

"Yeah, sorry." She started to pull away. He made a show of moving the book closer.

"This is one of the good parts," he said.

"I know. I've read it before." Of course she was kidding.

He chuckled again.

"Where did you even get a book in Hebrew?" she asked him.

"Your grandmother, oddly enough. She said she found it 'during her travels.' It's a bestseller, too."

"My grandmother gets around."

"She does," he agreed. Then he cocked his head. "Are you okay?"

"Define your terms."

He nodded. "Crazy world. I'm looking forward to seeing your home."

"It's not —," she began, then realized that of course it was. She grimaced. "My room's a mess."

"I'm sure I'll like it." His smile made that place at her lower back grow warm and tingly. Noah went back to reading. "One more hour till we land," he added. "Don't get eyestrain looking over my shoulder."

"I'll just wait until you're done, then read it myself."

"It's a long book," he warned her.

"I'm a patient person."

"So am I, Jenn," he replied, grinning as he resumed his reading.

SALAMANCA
FATHER JUAN AND THE STUDENTS

Father Juan passed from the chapel to the building that
had become the dormitory. In his absence they had completed the move so that everyone on the campus grounds
was housed in the same area. It had built an even stronger
bond of respect and camaraderie among the students and
the teachers. It also made it difficult to have private conversations. And it made for close living quarters. Tempers
were flaring. Students were complaining. Some of them had
cause: Apparently, there was a young student named Sade,
from Africa, who bathed in garlic salve to protect herself
from the Cursed Ones. Literally coated herself with it. Once
it dawned on the rest of the students that if they applied the
salve as well, no one would be able to smell the garlic anymore, they slathered it on as liberally as sunscreen.

When the troops garrisoned at the university had been
ordered to leave, a few who were loyal to the cause had set
up an academy-wide security system complete with motion
sensors. Father Giovanni, who had once studied to be an
electrical engineer, was in heaven. Father Juan told himself
that the alarms would give them fair warning, but he still
had the sense that he would be blindsided at any moment.

The runes had been tossed. Father Juan had put the lilies back on the chapel altar and set his votive candle in front
of the statue of St. John of the Cross. Now his hand was on

the door to the dorm building when the hair on the back of his neck rose. Something was wrong. Before he could open the door, it was flung wide by Father Giovanni. The young priest's face was ghostly pale.

"What is it?" Father Juan asked.

"Father, the alarms are going crazy. We've got dozens of signals from the sensors."

"Dozens?" Juan asked. That couldn't be his hunters, then. They should still be in the air.

Juan pushed past Giovanni and entered the hallway. He began pounding on the doors on the left-hand side. "Get up! Intruders!"

Giovanni raced along the right side of the hall doing the same thing. By the time the two priests reached the end of the corridor, the students there were already up and preparing for battle. The hallway was filled. Everyone stood in front of their door, more or less dressed, strapping on stakes and vials of holy water and wielding crosses. So young. So fierce.

Giovanni's pale face turned ash gray.

"You saw this in your vision?" Juan asked softly.

Giovanni nodded.

"Someone's coming," Juan said, raising his voice enough to be heard by all. "We don't know who or what is out there, but it's a good bet they're not friendly." He made the sign of the cross over each row, then over Giovanni, then over himself.

"Bless you, my children," he said. Then he turned to Giovanni. "I have to go downstairs to check on Antonio and Heather."

"Father, *prego*, don't go anywhere," Giovanni begged him.

Juan hesitated. Then he nodded. There was no time.

Juan ran back down the hall, his student hunters and instructors falling in behind him. They burst out into the night, and the air felt electric. Giovanni kept pace.

"Is it a good idea to leave the building?" he asked.

"We're not set up to handle a siege in there," Juan replied.

"We should have been better prepared," Giovanni said.

A roar boomed through the night like the tide coming in and crashing against the shore. It buffeted Father Juan's eardrums and rattled his spine.

Father God. Blessed Mother, he thought, crossing himself.

"I don't think we could have prepared for this," Father Juan replied.

"What do you—?"

A wave of Cursed Ones came over the wall, dropping down inside the university walls. There were a dozen vampires dressed like soldiers in black clothing, their eyes molten rubies, fangs extended like stilettos. A dozen more appeared at the top of the wall. And they kept coming. There weren't dozens of invaders, Juan realized. There were hundreds.

Just on the other side of the gate, Father Juan heard the howling of werewolves. Up and down the line students gasped.

"Holgar?" he said aloud. *Are the werewolves coming to help us?*

Next to him Sade, the tall, willowy Ethiopian girl with the ebony skin, slathered more garlic-infused salve on her face, then popped half a tin of garlic mints in her mouth. The stench was overwhelming even to his human nose. Smart girl, that one.

"Use your garlic!" he shouted up the line.

And then, then the vampires rushed over them like a flood.

In her cage, Heather hissed and shrieked. Eyes scarlet, fangs glistening, she hurtled herself at the bars in an uncontrolled frenzy. Screams from above pierced Antonio's eardrums, and explosions rocked the foundations of the ancient building. Smoke and the smell of blood poured into the tight space. His fangs extended. He hissed.

Vampires, attacking. *It must be Aurora,* he thought. *Here for me.*

Antonio gripped the bars and shook hard, fighting to get free. Aurora didn't have to do this. He'd go with her, if she'd spare the others.

But he couldn't get out. He and Father Juan had been careful to make sure he couldn't escape his confinement.

"They're coming!" Heather screamed, panicking. So Heather was afraid of the invading Cursed Ones. She didn't see them as liberators. That was good . . . if he could get her to be quiet. Her shouts would alert the vampires to her

462

location—and his. If he'd been alone, he would have called out to the vampires himself. He would have demanded that they take him to Aurora. But Heather was Jenn's sister, and he would die to protect her.

"Look at me, look," Antonio said. He had to calm her down. "Heather. When I say for you to do a thing, you must do it."

The room shook hard, and bricks and plaster rained down on him. For a few moments he lay dazed on the wooden floor of his cell while Heather screamed and screamed. Along the floor, smoke rolled like a dark gray carpet. A fire had broken out in the catacombs. He felt the heat against his cheek.

"Get me out of here!" Heather yelled.

Werewolves howled, creating a crescendo of wild sound. He thought of Jamie, whose family had been murdered by werewolves. Thought of Father Juan and the others aboveground. Worried about Heather.

"Heather," he said soothingly, calmly, as he got to his hands and knees. He pushed up from the rubble; just as he did, more fragments cascaded from the ceiling. "I can help you, *mi luz*. I'll save you. Listen to me, and I'll tell you exactly what to do."

"No!" she shrieked, but as she turned to look at him, he caught her eye. Pushed. She thrashed and looked away.

Then looked back.

Another wolf howl erupted somewhere close by. The *rat-a-tat* of gunfire.

"Heather." He lowered his voice to a whisper. She was a vampire; she would be able to hear him. He pushed warmth into his voice. Enticement. Seduction. "I'm here, and I will keep you safe."

He heard the shouts of humans dying. The cruel laughter of vampires on the hunt. More howls. The smoke grew thicker. Plaster dusted his shoulders. They were locked in.

Vampires could burn to death.

"Escúchame," he said distractedly, then switched to English. "Listen to me, Heather."

Focusing, he finally got her to lie in the corner and pull her blanket over herself. He wished he had the power to mesmerize from afar. Then he could summon someone to come let them out.

The building rocked again. *Dios,* would it fall down around them? That was one way to get out of here.

The wood beneath his shoes began to smoke.

Above him there were fewer shouts.

No gunfire.

A single wolf howl.

And a vampire was coming down the stairs.

Ay, here it is, then, he thought. *I won't let them take me alive again. I won't go back to what I was.*

There was no movement in Heather's cage. He had to get her out.

He reached into his pocket for the rosary given to him by Father Juan upon their return. Then smoke billowed around a tall, dark figure, and Antonio left the cross in his pocket. Orange flames danced behind the figure. Two red glowing eyes lasered directly at Antonio.

Then the figure took a step forward, and Antonio jerked in surprise. It wasn't Aurora.

It was Sergio, his sire.

Sergio Almodóvar, whom he had humiliated before all vampiredom. Sergio, whose unnamed sire wanted the renegade Antonio de la Cruz brought before him.

Sergio, whom Antonio feared more than Aurora, despite everything she had done to him.

Antonio felt a horrible tug, as if on his very soul. A call from the darkness, where it was cool and where there was no fire raging around his cell. From the shadows, where Antonio could be invincible, immortal.

Ay, no, he thought fearfully. *No, I won't go back.*

The darkness tugged. *He is my sire. I owe him my existence.*

No! I won't be damned.

Sergio looked hard at Antonio, and then he smiled as Antonio fell to his knees and bowed his head.

"Antonio," Sergio said. He smelled the fear rolling off his erstwhile protégé. Which did Antonio fear, himself or the flames? This basement was a death trap. He'd thought simply to collect Antonio, not to rescue him. "Long time."

"My lord," Antonio whispered. "Orcus has brought me to you at last."

"You don't fool me," Sergio replied, testing him. He watched the smoke rising from the floor in Antonio's cell. There was another cage beside his, apparently empty. "You're a traitor."

"I was. And for that I accept any punishment you offer. But I was . . . I recently found myself again. I don't know what happened to me, Sergio. But whatever it was, it's gone."

Antonio de la Cruz raised his head. Brilliant red eyes, such cheekbones. Perfect fangs. Sergio felt an ache. The young vampire was so handsome. He'd been such an excellent killer. Had Aurora really brought him back into the fold?

Smoke was rising from the floor beneath his own boots. He would have to make this quick.

"Why are you locked in here?" Sergio asked him.

Antonio smiled bitterly. "Why do you think?"

Sergio covered his head as fiery debris plummeted from the ceiling. By Orcus, there was a lot of it! Wooden beams, a desk, books crisping in a flash fire. Ironically, Sergio's young quarry was safer inside the cage—at least for the time being.

"Why did these people not kill you?" Sergio asked, dodging a shower of embers.

Antonio smiled lazily. "They want to make me good again."

"Can that happen?"

Flames licked the floor and began to devour it. Sergio

466

stepped closer to the cage, and the section he'd been standing on broke apart. Embers flew up. He looked around, assessing the danger. His sire wanted Antonio alive.

"I don't know if it can happen. But if you will take me back, perhaps we can prevent it from happening to others," Antonio said.

Cagey.

"Let me out. Let me join you in the fight," Antonio said. "I know I need to prove myself to you. But I *am* back, Sergio."

The wall behind Antonio's cage burst into flame. Antonio darted to the front, put his hands on the bars, and hissed. He let go, and Sergio saw burn marks on his palms.

"Sergio," Antonio said. His eyes matched the flames licking at his back. His fangs gleamed in the ruby light. "Sergio, please."

"Why did you leave? What happened to you?" Sergio asked.

Antonio inched as close as he could to the front of the cage without holding on to the bars again. He hissed and hopped from one foot to the other.

"Tell me," Sergio demanded.

"I don't know," Antonio said. "It was like . . . waking from a dream. I was suddenly revolted by what I'd done." He shook his head. "I can't explain it." He brushed the bar with his hand, and it sizzled against his skin again.

"Sergio, *please*," he said.

"Repudiate your god," Sergio said, "and I might begin to believe you." He smiled, recalling his sire's story of rescuing Aurora from the hands of the Spanish Inquisition. Those men of God had barbarically tortured her entire family and burned all of them alive, leaving her for last. Antonio had killed their descendants. Now Antonio was threatened with the bonfire unless he renounced his heresy.

"He is not *my* god. I spit on Him," Antonio said fiercely. And when he did spit, Sergio heard a sizzle.

The room was getting very hot. Antonio might only have seconds before the flames grabbed him. Sergio had made his point.

"*Bueno.* Good," Sergio said.

Then the wall behind Sergio burst into flame. Surprised, he leaped out of the way of a fiery flare. Moving backward, he stumbled against the hot metal of Antonio's cage. If Sergio didn't act fast, he and Antonio would soon be sandwiched between two walls of flame.

"Antonio!" cried a voice. It was a girl's, coming from the empty cell—not so empty after all. A vampire had been hiding there.

"Antonio!"

"Who's that?" Sergio asked.

"A new convert," Antonio replied. "I'm not sure how much you know about what's been happening."

Sergio ducked as a large chunk of burning plaster plummeted from the ceiling. Antonio didn't flinch.

"Try me," Sergio said.

"Her name is Heather," Antonio replied in English, so that Heather would know what was happening. "Aurora converted her to use as bait for the Salamanca hunters, so she could get to me. Her sister is Jenn Leitner, their leader."

"You bastard! Shut up!" the girl—Heather—shouted.

"It worked," Sergio said, also in English. "Aurora *did* get to you."

"Aurora has a Dark Witch with her. I think he helped her bring me back."

"Antonio, you are *evil*!" Heather started shrieking. "Get me out of here! Help me!"

A Dark Witch? Sergio was fascinated. What *had* Aurora been up to? He had to know.

So . . . I won't kill her. And I'd better tell Philippe the deal's off before he does it for me.

"Very well. I warn you, Antonio," Sergio said in Spanish, bending down and grabbing a sharp piece of charred wood. "One false move and I will kill you."

"I deserve death for what I've done," Antonio replied, then showed his fangs. "But I'd rather live another ninety years at least."

"There must be a key to this thing," Sergio said, examining the cell's lock.

"No. It can be easily unlocked from the outside. Just not the inside," Antonio said. He mimed twisting first one latch, and then the other. "This cell was strengthened so that

I . . ." He trailed off as a round of howls echoed off the burning buildings above them. "Sergio, do you have werewolves in your attack force?"

"Come and see," Sergio said, as he set to work freeing Antonio. He looked at Heather. "We'll leave her here."

Antonio hesitated, then shrugged. "As you wish, Sergio."

"Unless she's special to you."

"I like her, but it would be extra baggage, to have the sister of a hunter around."

Perfect answer, Sergio thought. But Antonio was no one's fool.

"Is she 'good,' as you were?"

Antonio waggled his hand. "On the cusp, maybe."

"Then perhaps we should take her with us."

"Whatever you decide."

Sergio suddenly wasn't so certain of Antonio. The vampire was being awfully passive, not the rash, fierce bloodsucker who had terrorized Madrid. Was it an act?

"I'm burning!" Heather screamed.

Very slowly, Sergio opened the door to Antonio's cage. He took a few steps back to give Antonio room to escape, but kept the charred stick pressed against Antonio's chest, directly where his unbeating heart lay. One false move, and he would thrust it into Antonio's chest and turn him to dust. Antonio was his height. They could have been brothers—*were* brothers of the fang. He searched him for weapons and found nothing.

"Okay, now let the girl out," Sergio ordered him.

As Antonio turned around, Sergio pressed the piece of wood into Antonio's back. It was long enough to hit his heart if Sergio pushed it through.

Above them the screaming and dying continued. The old buildings were going up like tinderboxes. The were-wolves cut loose with another round of howls.

"Get me out, get me out!" Heather shouted.

Antonio slid back the latch and poked in his head.

"Stay calm," he said in English.

She flew at him. Antonio made a fist and slammed it in her face as hard as he could. Her head snapped backward. He did it again, and she tumbled to the floor.

Antonio took one step into the cage. Then another chunk of burning ceiling dislodged, slamming against the top of the cage. Antonio stumbled and reached down with one hand to steady himself.

He whirled around, shoving Sergio away as he held the cross end of a rosary in his fist. He showed it to Sergio, who was forced to look away.

"I *knew* it," Sergio said, crestfallen, enraged.

"No. You didn't," Antonio replied.

Lightning fast, Antonio rammed a fist into Sergio's face, then into his stomach. Sergio doubled over, then head-butted Antonio. Antonio's back pressed against the super-heated bars, and he roared with pain.

Clenching his jaw, Antonio grabbed on to the bars. His skin crackled and popped. His hair caught on fire. He brought his knees to his chest, extended them, and kicked Sergio hard, toward the flames. Sergio staggered backward.

"¡*Traidor!*" Sergio bellowed.

Sergio lunged for Antonio. Antonio kicked him again, driving him closer to the flames.

"I loved you!" Sergio shouted.

Then the floor gave way beneath Sergio, and he fell.

"Antonio!" It was a cry of disbelief, a wounded plea, and a pledge of white-hot hatred.

Down, into the fire. Flames engulfed him. His skin broiled, charred. It flaked away. His bones ignited. Burning, blazing; he felt it, felt every assault as the fire claimed his flesh.

Above him Antonio made the sign of the cross over him. *Abomination! Monster! Betrayer!*

Father, Son, Holy Spirit, as the priests had done in the Spanish Inquisition, as the monks had done when they burned the Jews; as all Christian tormentors had done to insult their victims—

"Rest in peace, Sergio," Antonio called.

My sire, Sergio called out in his agony. *My sire!* He no longer worshipped Orcus. He worshipped the true god, his sire, whose name was—

Sergio was gone. Antonio had killed his sire. He spared a moment for victory and remorse.

Then Antonio dashed into Heather's cage and scooped

her up. He flew through the basement as it crumbled like a house of cards.

"Please, Blessed Virgin," he prayed, taking the stairs two, three at a time as the staircase burned. "Please let me get her out of here. Please let me save her."

But once he reached the exterior of the building, he saw that he should have prayed for a lot more than that.

CHAPTER NINETEEN

I HAVE LEFT THE SEMINARY. TONIGHT MY CONTACT WILL
FIND ME AT THE TAVERN CALLED EL COCODRILO, AND I
WILL JOIN THE FREE FRENCH FORCES. I WILL BECOME A
MAQUIS, AND I WILL PROBABLY DIE.

I'M READY.

—FROM THE DIARY OF ANTONIO DE LA CRUZ,
FOUND ROTTING IN THE CATACOMBS

SALAMANCA
TEAM SALAMANCA

Holgar glanced over at Jenn as she clicked off her cell
phone. They were standing just off the N-630, about a kilo-
meter from the university. The air was redolent with oily
smoke. Holgar wondered where the fire had been, and if
anyone had been hurt.

"Still no answer," Jenn said, as their two taxis sped off. Given the precarious status of the school, they had decided it wasn't safe to ask the drivers to take them all the way to the gates. Wearily, they hoisted their luggage and started walking.

"Maybe they're tidying up the place to welcome us home," Skye said.

Despite Jenn's inability to get Father Juan to answer the phone, Holgar couldn't help but feel a sense of relief. It was good to be back in Spain. He, for one, was looking forward to a hot shower and some raw meat.

"Do you smell that smoke?" Holgar asked the others. "There's been a fire."

"Yes, I smell it," Noah said.

"You don't have to be a feckin' werewolf to smell *that*," Jamie said. "When we get home, I'm talking to Father Juan about that black-cross bastard, Greg."

"Jamie, please, leave off," Skye said wearily. "You've been talking about that nonstop."

"Hai," Eriko murmured. "I think you need to calm down." She looked terrible. Holgar was very worried about her. Everyone had been focusing on Antonio, but at least as a vampire he was guaranteed good health.

Taamir walked by himself, looking a bit lonely. Holgar slowed down until they were walking side by side, giving him a pleasant smile.

"Ready to see your sister?" Noah asked Jenn. He took her hand. "And Antonio?"

Holgar looked at their clasped hands, and the troubled expression on Jenn's face.

Life at home would be interesting, that was for sure.

They rounded the bend in the road. Holgar glanced in the direction of the university, expecting to see the gates and, behind them, the beautiful gingerbread buildings.

He stopped dead in his tracks.

The university wasn't there.

"What the hell?" Jamie shouted.

"Am I hallucinating?" Jenn cried.

"No," Skye said slowly, her voice thick with pain. "It's . . . gone."

They all ran. The buildings were piles of rubble and ash, as though they had been toppled over and their contents burned. A few walls remained amidst the destruction, but not many.

Bodies littered the ground everywhere they looked.

"What happened here?" Eriko asked, voice shaking.

"Oh, my Goddess, dear Goddess," Skye whispered, swaying as if overcome.

"Do something," Jenn shouted at her as she slid to her knees before a heap of smoking brick and wood. "Heather! Antonio! Father Juan!"

A howl escaped Holgar as he grabbed burning bricks and tossed them over his shoulders.

"Vampires," Noah said, as he joined Jenn. He pointed to several nearby piles of ash. They began to dig together, through the rubble, searching for survivors.

476

"And werewolves," Holgar added, a deep sense of anger and shame filling him. He could smell the wolves, their musk lingering in the air just under the stench of death.

Jamie swore so long that Holgar began to think he wouldn't stop. Skye's gasps blanketed the terrible destruction. Stakes, crosses, and intact vials of holy water littered the ground.

"I don't see them," Jenn said, plowing through burned timbers and shattered bricks. Her hands were bleeding. "Heather!" she shrieked. "Antonio!"

"Father!" Jamie bellowed.

"The students, the teachers—are they all dead?" Skye asked, her voice a high-pitched wail. "Father Juan?"

"Only one way to find out," Jenn said, her voice breaking. "We need to be systematic. Cover the grounds slowly. Move forward in a wave. Don't run off."

She moved woodenly over to the nearest body. A girl lay on her stomach. Jenn turned her over. Blank eyes stared upward, bloody bite marks providing the only color to her pale throat.

"Feckin' hell," Jamie said, crossing himself. Slowly they spread out and began checking the bodies for signs of life, or for the faces of friends or mentors.

Holgar knelt next to one body and felt deep regret as he saw that it was Master Molina. The martial arts instructor had taught him so much about fighting in human form and hadn't been afraid to spar with him. Another involuntary howl escaped Holgar.

Sensing movement off to his left, he inhaled the stench of garlic so strong it nearly gagged him. The smell was coming from a body lying underneath a stone pillar. Its legs were starting to move.

Holgar picked up the pillar and threw it off the darkskinned girl who was trapped beneath it. He couldn't remember her name, but he recognized her. She groaned and moved her arm up to her head, then slowly opened her eyes.

"Over here!" Holgar shouted. "Survivor!"

Moments later the others gathered around. "I think she's one of the new students," Jenn murmured.

Holgar helped the girl sit up while Skye began working some of her healing magick.

As the girl slumped forward, she looked around at them, recognition lighting up her face. Then her eyes focused on the destruction all around them, and tears cut a path down her cheeks through the dirt and the ash.

"What's your name?" Jenn asked.

"Sade," the girl said hoarsely, pronouncing it "Sha-day."

"What happened here?" Jenn gently wiped the ash from Sade's forehead.

"We were attacked. Vampires, werewolves. Some of the werewolves looked like wolves and some like people. They overran us." Sade's voice was hollow. "There were so many."

"It wasn't a full moon. How were the werewolves in wolf form?" Jenn demanded, turning to look at Holgar.

He cleared his throat. There was so much about his kind that he had never bothered sharing, had never thought he would have to.

Before Holgar could answer, Eriko asked, "Are there any other survivors? Do you think so, Sade-*chan*?"

Sade held her head as if she were in great pain. "I don't know. A lot of people died before the vampire hit me with the pillar," she said. "But I didn't see . . . *all this*."

They stared at her for a silent moment.

"'And I only am escaped alone to tell thee,'" Jamie whispered at last, muscles working in his cheeks, the vein in his neck throbbing.

Something is still wrong here, Holgar thought. He sniffed the air and could smell —

"Let's finish checking the others," Jenn said, her voice quavering as she looked around.

"I'm afraid that won't be necessary," a voice called mockingly.

Holgar's heart plummeted. Then he growled deep and low in his heart.

"Oh, Goddess," Skye murmured beside him. "Protect us."

Clad in a black catsuit, body armor covering her chest, heavy boots protecting her legs and feet, Aurora stood at the place that had once been the entrance gates.

Estefan stood beside her, dressed for battle. Behind them, a dozen vampires, spread out.

And . . . werewolves.

There were at least ten, most in wolf form, a few of the younger ones in human form. Holgar recognized Acton and Balduin, his former schoolmates. Falentin, who got him drunk when he was only twelve. It was his pack, from Denmark.

And they were led by their alpha: a huge wolf, golden fur rippling in the wind. Two gold eyes, teeth bared, lips flared. Ears back. Haunches taut, in preparation for taking down prey.

Holgar's father.

Betraying no humanity, no recognition, no pity.

Holgar fought his impulse to submit, to cower. Or let his heart break.

He trembled, but stood firm.

The wolf growled.

The Salamancans spread out in a line, protecting Sade. Like clockwork they raised the stakes and holy water they'd gathered from the ground.

"We make our stand here, now," Jenn said. "Stay strong."

"Salamanca," they all chorused.

Aurora grinned as she and her gang advanced. In the darkness behind them Holgar spotted more shapes milling and shifting.

"Did you come back to gloat, you bitch?" Jamie shouted.

"Where's Antonio? Where's my sister?" Jenn screamed at her.

Ignoring them, the vampire approached, stepping through the rubble. "Oh, Sergio. This is so like him."

"Sergio is Antonio's sire," Skye said, somewhere behind Holgar.

"Yes, I know," Noah replied.

"His humiliated, mortified sire," Aurora confirmed. "I was going to do this so much more . . . tastefully." She bared her fangs. "But Sergio is so macho. He gets messy when he's angry." She gestured to the rubble. "And he likes explosions, no?"

"Antonio!" Jenn called desperately. "Heather!"

Aurora tsk-tsked. "This was such a beautiful university. It was founded three centuries before I was born. I had relatives who studied here. I would never have burned it down."

"Tell us where they are," Noah said, "or we'll open fire."

"Really." Aurora's red eyes focused on him. "And you would be?"

"A fellow Jew," Noah said.

She laughed. "Good try. You're macho too. Maybe tonight you'll live . . . the longest."

"No one here is dying tonight," Taamir said.

Aurora chuckled. "Oh, dear. This is so very, very sad. Sergio must be hitting his head against a wall in frustration. You weren't here, were you? He showed up and he didn't get to kill any of you." She hesitated. "Did he get Antonio?"

"*We* fought Sergio," Eriko said. "We *killed* him." Then she coughed.

"Ay." Aurora burst out laughing. Estefan, the vampires, and Holgar's former friends joined in.

"He does appear to be long gone. But he left his wolves behind, to clean up, so to speak. Amazingly, they're easy to seduce too." She smiled at Acton, who smiled back, ignoring Holgar.

"His pets," Aurora drawled, amused as Falentin wandered over to her and lowered his head, a wolf gesture of submission.

Pets. Holgar stared at his father, hoping the word had penetrated his wolf brain. But his father appeared to be lost to bloodlust, as he had been the night he had killed the man in the forest back in Denmark.

"Vale," Aurora said with an exaggerated eye roll. "It's all right. Sergio can make his grand gestures. I know who our sire loves best."

Holgar's father eyed Holgar. Holgar's mother had died when Holgar was a pup. His father had raised him, had taught him everything. His father had been hard on Holgar when he'd needed it. He'd killed a man to save Holgar. Now his father's wolf eyes were burning right through, looking at him and through him with disdain. His muzzle was coated with the blood of the students. Holgar pulled his lips back from his teeth and felt a rumbling start deep in his chest.

His father licked at the blood.

Unchanged in body but wolfed in mind, Holgar leaped

forward, closing the gap in bounds, eager to rip his father's throat out. But Holgar was a man, and he couldn't accomplish that. He'd have to be happy with breaking his neck.

A roar went up as the others on the field joined the battle. Eriko sprinted past Holgar and made a beeline for Aurora.

The vampires and werewolves surged forward. Holgar staked one vampire . . . and then he faced his father.

"Where is my sister?" Jenn shrieked, as she leaped forward and threw holy water into the face of an approaching vampire. The creature fell, clawing at his eyes. Beside her Taamir grabbed a piece of wood and staked the abomination.

"Noah!" Taamir shouted.

Jenn turned. A wolf had pinned Noah and was ripping into him with its muzzle.

Silver through the heart killed a werewolf, but Jenn had nothing silver. She threw herself forward and leaped on the creature's back, striking it time and again with the same piece of wood. Taamir kicked wildly at its face. The creature finally turned on them, and Noah reached up and yanked his large silver Star of David pendant from his neck. He slashed at the creature, and the silver evidently burned, because it roared and turned its attention back to Noah, who jammed a point of the star into the beast's eye.

The werewolf arced backward in pain. Jenn leaped out of the way, but Taamir was slower. It landed hard on top of him. Taamir flailed, trying to get out from underneath it.

"Taamir!" Jenn cried, throwing her arms around the wolf's massive head. Noah tried to drive the Star of David farther into its eye. Instead it came free in his hand.

"Jenn, Noah, go," Taamir said, gasping.

With a howl the wolf brought up a mighty paw and laid open Taamir's stomach with one swipe.

"Taamir!" Jenn cried.

Taamir reached out for the Star of David, and Noah thrust it into his hand. And then Noah handed him the same knife Taamir had given him in Russia, when he had been left alone with Svika. Jenn hadn't known he'd had it all this time.

Taamir angled the knife upward underneath the creature's rib cage, slicing it open. As the creature roared and bled, Taamir pushed his hand through the wound.

"Go for the heart!" Holgar shouted.

Slowly, with his waning strength, Taamir pushed his hand more deeply inside. The wolf howled and thrashed. The pack howled.

"Have it."

The wolf chomped at Taamir with its massive jaws. It panted and struggled.

"Allah . . . ," Taamir murmured. Blood coated his arm.

With a final howl the wolf collapsed on top of him.

"Ah," Taamir breathed. Then he went slack, and his eyes became glassy, and vacant.

"Taamir," Noah said, his voice strangled. "Taamir, no!"

"Jenn!" shouted a voice.

It was Antonio.

Skye choked on her own terror as Estefan approached her. She kept trying to engage vampires, but they shied away from her, as if they knew that she was marked as his. Dark hair, eyes blacker than black, he smiled a smile that was easy and mean.

"I don't want to fight you," she told him, raising her hands to ward off his magicks.

He sighed. "You might not want to, *borachín*, but you're going to."

He lobbed a fireball at her, and she extinguished it in midair.

"Very good," he said with a smile. "But is that all?"

He raised his hands toward her, and fireballs rolled off his fingertips with the speed of bullets from a machine gun.

Skye cried out and threw up a shield. The first ten dissolved against it, but her shield shimmered in the air, weakening, and the next three fireballs burrowed into it, lodging for a moment before dissolving. She desperately tried to repair her protective shield, but the next fireball came right through, buzzing her head and setting one of her Rasta braids on fire.

As she slapped it out, Estefan approached. "You know, Skye, if you won't fight me, I can only conclude that you still love me. You want me."

"That's a bloody lie."

She didn't love him anymore. She hated him. But her vows to harm none prevented her from hurting even him. And all her magick was defensive. *But he's attacking me. I should be able to defend myself*, she thought.

She glanced over at Holgar, hoping that he would see her distress and come to her aid. Maybe he would kill Estefan, and she would be free. But Holgar was battling a werewolf, his bare hands against the creature's fangs and claws. And even though he was in human form, Holgar was biting back, snapping his jaws so hard she could hear the sound carrying through the air.

"*Ay*, Skye," Estefan said.

He was grinning from ear to ear; suddenly he moved super fast, and he was standing next to her.

"Miss me?" he whispered in her ear as he clamped a wet rag over her mouth. Panic surged through her as she realized he was drugging her. His face melted like wax. Then, a moment later, the world went black.

"Jenn," Antonio said, fighting his way toward her. The moon ranged over his features and hair, slapping him with shadow, flooding him with light. Then he became a blur as he moved faster than her eyes could track him. When she saw him again, a vampire was disintegrating into a shower of dust in front of him. "Heather is safe."

"Antonio," she said, tears and sweat flying. "God, God, what's happening?"

Antonio blurred again; she tried to fight her way toward Aurora, but Cursed Ones blocked her at every turn. Safety in numbers; they were cocky, but she just kept moving, spinning, twisting, stakes flying off the ends of her fingers.

The combatants were all moving closer together as the survivors kept pushing forward to find the next adversary. Jenn tried to keep Aurora and Eriko in her sights, but like Antonio the pair was moving at staggering speed, no more than a blur of motion.

Still Jenn kept moving, working her way toward them. She would see Aurora dead if it was the last thing she did.

Antonio had brought Heather to Father Juan, who was saying last rites on the chapel steps for a dying student. She had been unconscious, and Antonio had told him that she should remain that way. Father Juan had put a blanket over her and left her there, taking up stakes and holy water to join the battle. Next thing Father Juan knew, he saw her fleeing the scene of destruction at the university, heading in the opposite direction, into the rocky hills outside the school.

"Heather!" he shouted. He gave chase, but she had too much of a head start. Then she waved her hands over her head, and the darkness devoured her.

"Father," Holgar cried, despairing, as he threw his father's body off himself.

Then someone rammed into his back and bit him with

human teeth, ripping out a chunk of flesh. He yelped and spun, seeing only a flash of long blond hair as he drove a stake into the chest of the person who had attacked him.

It wasn't a vampire; it was a werewolf in human form. And as she fell to the ground, blood gushing from her chest, Holgar recognized Kirstinne. His heart stuttered as he saw her face contorted in pain and surprise. He dropped to his knees beside her.

"Why?" he whispered. "Why did you do this?"

She stared up at him. "You're my enemy," she said, blood bubbling on her lips.

"I'm your pack mate. We were promised to each other."

"Not anymore."

Her head fell to the side, and the light left her eyes. He heard a roar of rage and grief behind him, and in his heart he knew it came from Kirstinne's mate.

The man slammed into him from behind, flipping him head over heels, tearing at him with teeth and nails as he tumbled. Holgar came down on all fours and turned, snarling and snapping his jaws together.

Kirstinne's scent was all over the other as they circled one another, looking for an opening. Holgar wished he could shift; everything in him wanted to tear the other man's throat out.

And then he realized he didn't have to be a wolf to do that.

He lunged forward, diving downward as if he were

going to try and break the other's arm. The man swiped at him with a hand, nails drawing blood against Holgar's cheek. And then Holgar contorted his body, pushing off from the ground, and locked his teeth into the other man's throat—his teeth, which were sharper than a human's, slicing through skin until they punctured the jugular vein.

Blood spilled over both of them. The other jerked backward, tearing his throat more in the process. He whimpered once, twice, and then collapsed on top of Kirstinne. Joined in death as in life.

Holgar spat into the dirt and wiped his mouth on what was left of his shirt. He stood slowly, limbs shaking, wondering who had seen what he had done. The others were engaged in their own life-and-death struggles and weren't paying attention to him.

He threw back his head and howled. He had killed his father. And he had killed the wolf he had loved.

Holgar staggered, punch-drunk with grief. He would have given in to it, would have lost himself in remorse, until his heart began to pound even harder than it had when he'd killed Kirstinne.

Where was his hunting partner?

Where was Skye?

Jamie staked another Curser. His eyes flashed to Eriko. Six vamps stood between Jamie and her. Eriko was still fighting Aurora, and Jamie, Antonio, and Jenn were pounding through the suckers to close in on them. Jamie registered briefly that Antonio appeared to be fighting on the proper side again.

Eriko thrust a stake at Aurora's heavy chestpiece, but the vampire blocked it with ease and knocked it to the ground.

Quick as thought, Eriko pulled out another stake and brandished it before her, feinting left and right. Aurora rushed forward, knocking her off her feet, and Jamie screamed as he saw Aurora sink her fangs into Eriko's neck.

He ran forward, kicking someone's leg out of his way. Then that someone's hand grabbed Jamie's ankle, which sent him sprawling on the ground. It was a Curser. He gave the feckin' bastard a pounding until the fanger let go, then staked him good. Wiping vampire dust out of his eyes, Jamie picked himself up and saw Eriko and Aurora grappling together, rolling back and forth as each strove for the upper hand.

Eriko threw Aurora off and jumped to her feet. Her quiver was empty, and with a warning shout Jamie prepared to toss her a stake. But she was moving so fast that Jamie couldn't see her. Calculating her trajectory, he flung the stake into the air; Eriko reappeared as she plucked it out of the air and leaped after Aurora, who lay sprawled flat on her back.

As though in slow motion he watched Aurora's hand wrap around one of the fallen stakes on the ground and bring it up, just as Eriko closed on her.

"No!" he yelled. "God, Eri, no!"

Too late.

Time dragged to a near standstill. His shout echoed in his mind.

Aurora sank her stake into Eriko's chest. Eriko grunted, dropped her stake, and collapsed.

Time stopped.

It stopped.

It bleedin' stopped.

"Eri," he whispered, hurtling through the air.

Aurora pushed Eriko off like a feather and raced for the high wall surrounding what had once been the university. In a flash she stood on top of the wall, laughing hysterically.

Jamie slammed against the ground. He crawled to Eriko. The blood was pumping out around the stake embedded in Eriko's chest. Her chest rose. She was *alive.*

"Skye! We need you *now*!" Jamie shouted.

"Skye?" Jenn echoed, falling to her knees beside Jamie. "Skye?"

Jenn grabbed Eriko's hand. To the fallen Hunter she said, "Eriko, listen to me; you can deal with this. Just concentrate and let your body heal."

"Bloody hell, Eri, damn you, don't you leave me," Jamie bellowed.

Eriko smiled—actually smiled. She never did that. She looked up at both of them and gazed with something that could have been love, had there been more time, at Jamie.

"*Hai.*"

And then she was gone.

"Sergio?" Aurora called. "*¿Mi amor?* Time to go, don't you think?"

"He's dead!" Antonio yelled at her, shoving and staking his way through vampires and leaping over freshly killed werewolves. Holgar was howling. Jenn and Jamie were crouched over someone on the ground. Skye, where was she? And Heather?

"He's dead!" Antonio shouted again, gaining on Aurora. Kicking, punching, staking. Vampire after vampire fell in his wake. He had never fought so hard nor so savagely. Antonio's mind raced backward in time to Madrid, when he and Sergio had brutalized the humans, their death-dealing an evil whirling dervish of destruction. He moved that way again, everything inside him focused on one goal—to kill Aurora.

Aurora stopped laughing. She gaped at him. "*¡Mentira!*" she finally shouted. Lie.

"I killed him myself," Antonio said. "And I'm going to kill you!"

The expression on her face spurred him on. She was genuinely frightened. "Estefan!" she shouted. Then she looked past him to the grounds, to her left and right. "Louis!"

Something hit Antonio on the back of his head. He was

undeterred, whipping his arm around and flinging a stake into the chest of a vampire, then crawling toward Aurora, bloodlust washing over him in waves. He would rip her apart. He would drink her filthy blood and grind her to dust.

"No!" she shrieked. "Keep him away! My sire! My sire! Help me!"

His hands dug into the dirt as he dragged himself forward. He brought up his legs, preparing to spring—

"Lucifer!" she screamed.

A wall of flames shot between the two of them. It was the basement all over again, except this time the fire separated him from his target. He felt the heat licking at him; his skin prickled, then ached; the pain intensified to a nearly unbearable level as he kept moving forward, kept going. Through the flames he could see her bewilderment.

"Kill. You," he managed, and then the fire took him over. He was ablaze. He thought of Jenn; he was failing her. God, he was burning.

"Antonio, Antonio, stop," Jenn said. Fire raged around him. Burned him. He cried out for it to stop.

Then he became aware that Father Juan was speaking in Latin over him. He was calling on the angels. On the archangels. His voice penetrated Antonio's panic.

I am safe, Antonio thought.

He lay still.

"Oh, my God, Antonio," Jenn cried. She threw her arms

around him, but Father Juan dragged her backward.

"Stay away from him," Father Juan said in a high, fearful voice. "I'm exorcising him. Aurora called on the Devil, and next thing we know, he's out of his mind."

"Oh, God, oh, God, Antonio," Jenn said.

Antonio bolted upright, then got to his feet. He whirled around, then stared down at his hands.

Then at Jenn.

He was bewildered.

"I was burning," he said. "I was set on fire."

She shook her head. "No."

"She called the name of Lucifer," Father Juan said, crossing himself. After a beat Antonio did too.

Then the truth dawned on Antonio:

"She was calling on her sire. She called him Lucifer."

"Can that be the name of a vampire?" Father Juan asked.

"We—they—worship the gods of death," Antonio explained.

"Lucifer is a fallen angel. A creature of light," Father Juan said.

"Many of the dark gods promise light to their followers," Antonio replied. "It is said that through them vampires will walk in the light." His lips parted. "She called upon him, and I felt the flames."

"She mesmerized you," Jenn ventured.

He reached out to touch her. Father Juan held her

tightly. Whatever ground Antonio had gained with them, with *her*, he seemed to have lost. *What else did I do, while I was hallucinating?* he wondered, worried and ashamed.

"I don't think so. Maybe her sire can mesmerize from afar. Or . . . I was bewitched."

Antonio heard a wild, ragged howl, and his eyes sought out the source. Holgar was standing, holding a piece of black cloth, his head thrown back. A few feet from them one of the first-year students Antonio had seen during the fighting was sitting cross-legged on the ground.

Twenty feet away, Noah knelt over the body of Taamir, whispering prayers to Adonai and Allah for his friend.

Antonio became aware of quiet sobbing, and then next to him Father Juan swore. Antonio followed the priest's gaze. There, a ways apart from the others, Jamie was draped over Eriko, crying and praying and swearing.

"No," Antonio whispered, even as his senses told him what he didn't want to know.

"She's dead," Father Juan said quietly.

Antonio started forward, but Father Juan put a restraining hand on his shoulder. "Don't. He will kill you."

"Where is Skye?" Antonio asked.

Jenn's face contorted. She was trembling.

"They took her," Jenn said. "Aurora and Estefan."

So Aurora had escaped. Emotions crashed through him: sorrow, rage, fear, and, most horribly, relief. Aurora still had a hold on him.

The Devil *had* had a hand in this.

Antonio turned away so that no one would see his struggle even as his fangs pricked his lower lip and he thought about killing the others in her name.

"Antonio," Jenn said, pulling herself away from Father Juan.

Antonio struggled to control himself as her arms came around him. He tried to remain very still, and after a moment he turned to face her. Sobbing, she covered his chin and lower lip with kisses. He didn't return her kisses, and she didn't seem to notice.

"I thought you had died. I thought I'd lost you," she said, weeping. "My sister, Antonio. Heather!"

"Yes, we have to look for Heather," Father Juan said urgently. "It will be light soon."

Antonio nodded slowly. "But all the other students, the teachers, dead?"

"I'm afraid so," Father Juan confirmed. He gestured with his hand. "Father Giovanni fell. He had a vision that he would die defending the academy, and it came true. We are all that is left of Salamanca."

Antonio expected Jenn to cry again, but she surprised him by wiping her eyes and raising her chin.

Her voice was too calm. She had to be in shock.

He wished he could comfort her, but he couldn't touch her again. He was intoxicated by the smell of her blood. He wasn't in full control. He folded his arms across his chest and maintained his distance. He had to, for both their sakes.

What should I do? he thought.

Estefan and Aurora were smart. Jenn had no idea what spells Estefan had used, what herbs, but he had managed to cloak their trail — even from a werewolf. They couldn't track them and Skye. There was absolutely no sign of Heather. Jenn could barely function. She had lost her again.

She turned to Antonio, but he was distant. Maybe he was blaming himself. Maybe . . . something else was bothering him.

"We need to rest and regroup, and then we'll take action," Father Juan said. "And we must honor those who have fallen."

They piled more stones on the resting places of the students and teachers, and dug graves for Eriko, Taamir, and Father Giovanni. They couldn't chance remaining at the ruins long enough to bury all their dead properly.

Holgar took off his wooden cross decorated with wolf heads and laid it in the pile of rubble on top of Kirstinne and her mate.

Father Juan spoke over the three graves, then over the burial ground in general, and then they all retreated up into one of the caves that dotted the countryside, to rest, and to hide Antonio from the rising sun. They stood or sat in a loose circle, all of them bone weary and hungry, but unable to sleep and having no food among them. The kitchen and pantry had burned to the ground.

Jamie prowled around the edges of the group, his pain radiating from him, as they discussed what to do next. He was making them all even more uptight.

"Jamie, sit down," Jenn said at last.

"No!" He whirled on her. "This is your fault!"

"Stop it, Jamie," Father Juan said.

"Why should I? Eri's dead, Taamir's dead, Skye's gone, and she's too wishy-washy to stake the vampire who stands in front of her." He pointed a shaking hand at Antonio. Then Jamie faced her square on. "This is bollocks, and I'm not going to take it anymore, you stupid, inept bitch."

But at that moment Jenn Leitner had had enough. She stood slowly and turned, every muscle coiled, and she stared at Jamie. She stepped closer to him. Her breath came out in ghostly puffs in the frigid air.

"Okay, Jamie, you want to go, let's go," she said softly.

His eyes dilated slightly, and she could see the hesitation in them as he glanced quickly at the others.

"Jenn," Antonio said, in a cautioning tone.

"Just you and me," she said. "This has been coming for a long time, and it ends now. Agreed?"

He spat in the dirt and then met her eyes. "Agreed."

She nodded and then hit him first. Jamie's nose made a satisfying crunch under her knuckles. Jamie staggered back. She followed up with a kick to his knee, hoping to take him down fast, but he twisted out of the way. Jenn was off balance, and as she struggled to recover, he cracked his fist on her jaw. Her head snapped back painfully, and pain seared through her.

He dislocated my jaw, Jenn realized. But she knew she had broken his nose. The question was, how far was too far? Or how far would be enough?

Jamie answered that for her when he leaped forward, knocking her onto her butt. He dropped on her, straddling her and pinning her to the ground. He raised his hand to hit her again, aiming for her jaw.

She spit in his eyes and then rammed her fist into his groin. While he was incapacitated, she flung him off of her and leaped to her feet, kicking him in the ribs until she could actually hear them breaking.

Sade screamed, and Holgar leaped forward and grabbed Jenn, dragging her back. She bit his hand, and when he yelped in surprise, she turned and punched him in the eye. The werewolf staggered back, eyes wide in shock.

"Let her go," Jamie panted, struggling to his feet.

Holgar hesitated, and Jenn lifted her chin, glaring at him. She bared her teeth and did her best to imitate one of his growls. Holgar whined low in his throat, ducked his head, and backed up a couple of steps, acknowledging her as alpha.

Jenn spun around just in time to duck as Jamie threw a punch at her. She dropped to the ground, grabbed a handful of dirt, and flung it into his eyes. He grunted and half tripped.

She slammed her hands against his ears before punching him in the eye too.

He roared in fury and swung blindly at her.

And that was when she knew she had him.

She pressed forward, kicking him in the solar plexus, and finished with an uppercut to the jaw that felled him like a tree. He lay on the ground for a minute, unmoving. She bent over, trying to catch her breath, daring to hope that it was over.

Which, of course, it wasn't. Jamie exploded up from the ground with a roar and kicked her in the chest before she could get out of the way. She staggered and went down, but caught herself on one hand before springing back up. She punched him twice in the stomach before dancing out of his reach. She moved in again to clip him on the jaw and took a left to the side of her head. Her ears rang, but her jaw didn't break.

She feinted to his left, and when he moved to block, she swept his feet from underneath him. She followed, landing on top of him, raining blows down on his face. She took careful aim at his throat and jabbed, and he coughed and grabbed at his throat. She had hit him hard enough to dislodge his Adam's apple. He could choke to death.

She punched him again in the side, doing more damage to his broken ribs. Blood began to trickle out of the corner of his mouth, and she leaned down close to him until their faces were an inch apart.

"Do you yield?" she said, biting off every word as she continued to stare at him.

He hesitated, then nodded.

"Will you acknowledge my leadership and stop your sniping, your whining, and your bitching?" she demanded.

He wanted to say no, she could see it in his eyes, but his throat was beginning to swell, and he had little time before he lost the ability to breathe. He finally lowered his eyes and nodded.

She stood up. "Father Juan," she said, "he's going to need prayer and magick if he's going to survive."

The priest hurried forward to work on him while she faced Holgar, Sade, Noah, and Antonio. They stood facing her, their expressions mixed. "Will you follow me?" she questioned Antonio.

He nodded, staring at her almost as if he didn't know who she was.

She turned to Sade. The girl reeked of garlic and fear, but she was still standing, still there, still willing to do her part. They needed someone to replace Eriko as Jamie's fighting partner, and she was the only candidate. "Will you follow me?" Jenn asked.

"Yes." She nodded like a bobblehead, terrified and wide-eyed.

Jenn turned to study Noah. He had proven himself time and again, and even now, after the loss of Taamir, he stood stoic, strong. He was a good man. He was a good hunter. "Will you follow me?" she demanded.

"To the ends of the earth," he said, eyes clear and intense.

She cleared her throat. "You'll be my partner." She avoided Antonio's gaze. "For now."

"Good, Jenn," Antonio murmured.

Finally she turned to Holgar. The werewolf had killed his father and his intended, and his partner had been kidnapped. His wounds were deep. So was his guilt. And the look of vengeance was in his eyes.

"Will *you* follow me?" she whispered.

"You didn't need to ask," he said.

He was right. She didn't. Of them all he had never once questioned her, had always supported her. She would trust him to be Antonio's partner until they could rescue his. Of all of them he would know when, if, Antonio needed to be . . .

No. She couldn't even think it.

Father Juan was working feverishly over Jamie. It would be easier if the Irishman died. Easier, but not better.

"What do we do now?" Sade asked softly.

Jenn put her hands on her hips. "We hunt down Aurora. We make Estefan sorry he ever laid eyes on Skye. We take back this world."

"We don't have many people," Antonio said.

"We don't need many. We just need a few courageous souls to stand up, to say they aren't going to take it anymore. And they're not going to have the courage to do that unless we show them the way."

"To fight the Devil?" Father Juan asked.

"If it comes to that, yes," Jenn replied.

"What about Heather?" Holgar asked.

Jenn shook her head. "If we find her, we find her. But that's not our immediate mission." She ignored the looks of surprise on her teammates' faces. It was true. It broke her heart, but they didn't know if her sister was alive or dead, holed up somewhere or running with the other Cursed Ones. They had a world to save. With any luck, when they did, her sister would still be in it.

"We need to find somewhere we can plan," she said.

Father Juan paused in his ministrations to Jamie long enough to look up at her. "I may have a place. I've been preparing for something like this for a while now."

"Good. As soon as Jamie can move, we'll go."

"You need help too," Noah said quietly.

Jenn had been struggling to ignore the pain that was raging through her. Talking was a special agony. She shrugged. Jamie was worse off. Father Juan could deal with her second.

Noah stepped forward. "I have some field medical training. May I?"

She nodded and tried not to cry while he pushed her jaw back in place. The relief was almost instant, producing a sort of euphoria throughout her body that allowed her to, at least temporarily, ignore the other damage.

She turned and looked down the hill at the pile of stone that used to be their university. The damage was fearsome. A few walls of the dormitory still stood, precarious, though the roof was gone. She thought of her diary, the new Hunter's Manual, which she hadn't risked taking with her.

"Do you think anything is salvageable?" she asked no one in particular.

"I'll go in," Antonio offered.

"You'll go *first*," Father Juan corrected him.

That night they rested. The next day and night they made forays onto the grounds. They took turns entering the ruins, finding treasures—some apples, a dozen protein bars, Sade's salve. Father Juan's statue of St. Teresa of Avila, who swooned in religious ecstasy while a little cupid speared her. Jenn was relieved that her diary—the Hunter's Manual— was safe under the charred remains of her bed. Holgar, by far the most practical at the moment, returned with changes of clothes for all of them.

Jamie asked Noah to retrieve a box from under his bed and then clutched it like a drowning man. Jenn suspected it was the gun he was building, the one that used silver bullets. She grimaced, but they could have used those bullets against the werewolves.

Father Juan used his cell phone to make some calls. A priest in Toledo offered them sanctuary, even though Rome had forbidden anyone to aid and abet any hunters.

They got into two university vans that still ran, and drove the four hours to Toledo. It was a beautiful, ancient city, though that beauty was marred by the presence of armed

Spanish troops everywhere. Nervous Spaniards skirted around them. Vampires swaggered like arrogant noblemen.

"Toledo has a violent past," Father Juan said. "The Grand Inquisitor, Torquemada, burned heretics and Jews in the central square. He targeted our patron saint, Saint John of the Cross." Father Juan patted the statue of Teresa of Avila on his lap. "And Saint Teresa as well."

"Nice," Holgar said. "A violent past, and a violent present."

The priest, Father Sebastian, offered them sanctuary in the gothic monastery. With the help of Father Sebastian's housekeeper, the group arranged bedding. Jenn and Sade would stay together in another room. The poor girl was shell-shocked. She didn't want to wash off her garlic, but Jenn pointed out that they were in a church, and vampires couldn't enter.

"Except for him," Sade said, pointing at Antonio, as the priest's housekeeper led Sade away to take a good hot shower.

Except for Antonio. That gave Jenn hope that he really was coming back to them.

The Salamancans met in the *sala* for a meal of simple omelets and tea. Everyone was quiet, dejected. Then Jenn spoke up.

"Holgar," she said, "I thought werewolves only changed during the full moon."

Cutlery clanked against plates as everyone waited to hear his answer.

Holgar shook his head slowly. "We are forced to change then, but more mature wolves learn how to do it at will."

"How mature?" Jenn pressed.

Holgar shrugged. "It varies from wolf to wolf. Sometimes when you reach your thirties, but it can happen much older than that."

Jenn was disappointed. She'd hoped Holgar would be able to do it sooner. It would be a huge help to them in battle.

"How about younger?" Jamie asked, his voice hoarse.

Holgar shrugged. "It has been known to happen, though it is uncommon. Like I said, it varies, different for each wolf."

"Like puberty?" Father Juan asked.

"Something like that." Holgar sounded uncomfortable, as if it were too personal a topic to discuss.

"And you don't have the ability to change at will?" Jenn asked.

"Not yet," he said.

"That's too bad," she said grimly. "That could have been useful."

"I know," he replied softly.

"And the silver thing. That's only when you're wolfed," Jamie said. "Otherwise, when you look like us, you can be killed like us."

This would be the place where Eriko would tell Jamie to be quiet, Jenn thought sorrowfully. *Or Skye would yell at him to leave off.* She could almost hear them.

"Yes. When I am in human form, I can be killed like a

human," Holgar replied, as if he needed to punish himself by saying it aloud.

"Thought so," Jamie said.

"I'd like to say Mass," Father Juan told them. "I know you're very tired, and not all of you are Catholics, but we need to mourn and acknowledge our losses." Father Juan looked at Antonio. "Will you assist me?"

"With pleasure," Antonio said, inclining his head.

Jenn swallowed. Antonio had told her that he was rededicating himself to God. Maybe that would help him stay true to his path. But she felt a terrible, wrenching loss as she, Holgar, Jamie, Noah, and Sade sat in a pew, while Antonio put on a stole and knelt with Father Juan before the altar.

Noah conducted himself with quiet dignity, and when Father Juan invited them all to pray, he knelt on the prayer bench beside Jenn and lowered his head. She felt tears welling. Noah placed his hand over hers, warm and strong.

Antonio moved through the ritual easily, bowing, crossing himself, holding a large missal for Father Juan. Jamie took communion. So did Father Juan. And after a long hesitation Antonio put the communion wafer in his mouth and crossed himself.

"Go in peace. The Mass is ended," Father Juan said.

Noah lifted his head. "That was beautiful," he told Jenn. She nodded, wondering if Antonio had seen Noah's hand on hers.

"I suggest we all get some sleep," Father Juan said.

"Agreed," Jenn said.

"May I talk to you, Father?" Sade asked. "I'm so scared."

"Of course," Father Juan replied, although he looked exhausted. "Let's sit here awhile, shall we?"

Both Noah and Antonio gazed at Jenn as she rose swiftly from the chapel and entered the room she would be sharing with Sade.

She was overwhelmed with sorrow. Eriko was dead, and Skye and her own little sister might be joining her soon. If she had known there was a chance of never seeing them again, she would have told Heather how much she loved her, and she would have thanked her teammates, told them how much she valued their friendship.

She had never thought of them as friends, but that was what they were. You couldn't live and fight and risk your life for years with someone without forming a bond. Her heart ached for them, and for Heather.

So much pain.

She curled up on the narrow bed and opened the Hunter's Manual.

She picked up a pen.

They had to keep the Cursed Ones from killing any others.

She took a deep breath and began to write.

I know who I am now. I am Jenn Leitner. I am the leader of Team Salamanca. We are this world's crusaders, and this is our quest. We stand where others fall. We fight where others run. We triumph where others cower in defeat. And I lead the way. Together we will save the world, because we have to. Even in the darkest night, there is hope. I will save the world, because I am Jenn.

And I wouldn't want to be anybody else.

Clouds undulated against the moon, then drifted away. Silvery beams hit the pages of her diary, transforming her tears to silver filigree. Outside, a wolf howled in deep mourning. A hardened Israeli solder patrolled.

And ruby eyes beyond her window burned with longing.

Don't miss the dramatic conclusion to
Jenn and Antonio's saga as they battle
against the Cursed Ones in

Vanquished

Coming Soon

ABOUT THE AUTHORS

NANCY HOLDER has published more than seventy-eight books and more than two hundred short stories. She has received four Bram Stoker awards for her supernatural fiction and is the coauthor of the *New York Times* bestselling Wicked series. She lives in San Diego with her daughter, Belle, their two cats, and their two Corgis. Visit her at nancyholder.com.

DEBBIE VIGUIÉ is the coauthor of the *New York Times* bestselling Wicked series and several additional Simon Pulse books, including the Once upon a Time novels *Violet Eyes* and *Midnight Pearls*. She lives in Florida with her husband, Scott, and their cat Schrödinger. Visit her at debbieviguie.com.

Read how Jenn and Antonio's
story began in

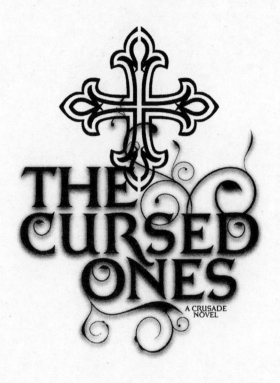

THE
CURSED
ONES

A CRUSADE
NOVEL

CHAPTER ONE

*For thousands of years the Cursed Ones hid in the
shadows, fooling mankind into thinking they didn't
exist. Then one day they just . . . stopped. Skeptics
turned into believers one fateful dawn. And no one
was ever safe again.*

*No one knows why they made themselves known.
Why they chose a Valentine's Day in the early
twenty-first century to reveal their presence. Some
say it had something to do with the end of the world.
Others that they simply grew tired of hiding.*

*I was twelve when Solomon, the leader of the
vampires, first appeared on TV and lied through
his fangs to all of us. Thirteen when the war broke
out. Fifteen when the United States declared a
truce . . . when, in reality, we surrendered, and the
nightmare really began.*

Even after that, many of us couldn't bring ourselves to actually say the word "vampire." It was as if once we admitted it, then we'd have to believe in extraterrestrials or government conspiracies, too. Or in witches and werewolves . . . in anything and everything that could destroy us. Because we could be destroyed. We lost something so precious—our faith that eventually everything would be all right. Because it wasn't all right . . . and few believed it ever would be again.

So among those of us who swore not to abandon all hope, vampires came to be called the Cursed Ones. We learned that it was the name given to them long ago by those few groups who knew of their existence yet never shared the knowledge. But the vampires weren't the cursed ones—we were. They had seduced us with their hypnotic smiles and talk of peaceful coexistence and immortality even as they had mounted a war against us. Then they sought to turn us into their slaves, and drink from rivers of our blood.

I'm nearly eighteen now, and I have learned something about myself I might never have known, if I'd been able to live an ordinary life.

But there is nothing ordinary about my life.
Nothing.
Including me.

—from the diary of Jenn Leitner,
discovered in the ashes

The village of Cuevas, Spain
Team Salamanca: Jenn and Antonio,
Skye and Holgar, and Eriko and Jamie

Barely sunset, and death exploded all around Jenn Leitner.

It was a trap, she thought.

The sky crackled with flames; oily smoke choked the air and burned her lungs. Jenn struggled not to cough, fearing that the sound would expose her. On her elbows and knees, her dark auburn hair loose and falling into her eyes, she crawled from beneath the red-tiled roof of the medieval church as it collapsed in a crash of orange sparks. Fragments of tile, stone, and burning wood ricocheted toward the blood-colored moon, plummeting back down to the earth like bombs. She dug in her elbows and pushed forward with the toes of her boots, grunting as a large, fiery chunk of wood landed on her back with a sizzle. She fought to stay silent as the pain seared through her. Biting her lip hard, she tasted coppery blood as she rolled to extinguish the flames.

Next to her, Antonio de la Cruz hissed a warning. The scent of her blood would fill the night air, attracting the vampires they'd been sent to hunt—but who were hunting them instead. When Jenn was little, her grandmother had told her that sharks could smell a drop of blood in the water half a mile away. She hadn't gone in the ocean since. Cursed Ones could smell blood more than a mile away. With sharks you could choose to stay out of the water. With Cursed Ones it was different. You couldn't leave the planet. You were trapped.

Like we are now.

Antonio studied her with his deep-set Spanish eyes. Jenn gave her head a shake to let him know she was all right; she could keep going. She had no time to search through her jacket for the garlic-infused salve that would block the odor of her blood. She prayed that the stench of the burning buildings—and burning bodies—would cloak the scent long enough to allow them to escape.

Past the church grounds the oak trees were on fire, acorns popping, leaves igniting like tattered tissue paper. Smoke filled the inky night sky, smothering the faint glow of the moon, but the hellish light from the fires illuminated Jenn's and Antonio's every move. Combine that with her bleeding lip, and they were two very easy targets for the savage monsters bent on massacring the village.

Antonio stopped suddenly and held up a warning hand. She watched him closely. Wisps of his wild dark hair escaped from his knitted cap; his full eyebrows were raised slightly, and his jaw was clenched. Like her he was dressed all in black—black sweater, black cargo pants, black knee protectors, and black leather boots—and now coated with ash. She could see the glint of the small ruby-studded cross that he wore in his left ear. A gift, he had said, when she'd asked about it. His face had darkened when he'd answered her, and she knew there was more to that story. So much of Antonio was a mystery to her, as intriguing as the sharp planes and hollows of his face.

He was focused, listening. All Jenn could hear were the flames and the terrorized, outraged cries of the villagers from the surrounding houses and office buildings. Her world became Antonio's face and Antonio's hand, blotched with soot, and she tensed her muscles so she'd be ready to move again when his hand dropped. She wished she could stop shaking. Wished she would stop bleeding and hurting. Wished someone else could do the rescuing, instead of them.

But somewhere in the darkness the Cursed Ones were watching. She imagined them staring at her, and could almost hear their cruel laughter dancing in the acrid air.

Three vampires and six hunters stalked one another through the steamy inferno. *If the other hunters are still alive. If they escaped the burning church.*

Don't think about that now. Don't think at all. Wait. Watch.

Cuevas, a small Spanish town a couple of hours from their home, had been terrorized by a group of vampires for weeks, and their mayor had begged for help. Jenn was one of a group of trained vampire hunters called the Salamancans, graduates of the Academia Sagrado Corazón Contra los Malditos—Sacred Heart Academy Against the Cursed Ones—at the centuries-old University of Salamanca. Father Juan, their master, had sent them to Cuevas to rid it of the Cursed Ones.

Instead the vampires were hunting the hunters, as if they had known they were coming, as if they had lured them there. Jenn wondered how they'd known. Father Juan always sent the team out covertly. Was there a spy at the university? Had someone in Cuevas betrayed them?

Or is the Hunter's Manual right about all *vampires?*

Don't think.

Late that afternoon Jenn, Antonio, and the other hunters had parked in the woods and silently made their way to the church, where they waited, meditating or praying, and preparing for the battle ahead. The vampires appeared with the flat shadows of dusk, and in the literal blink of an eye — they moved faster than most people could see — they set fire to the stone ruins of the *castillo*, the brick-and-mortar shops of the nearby plaza, and the glass and steel of a handful of modern office buildings. Flower boxes lining the plaza, which had brimmed with pink and white geraniums, crackled like sparklers; windows shattered; car horns blared like Klaxons; and everywhere, everywhere, fires roared.

In their short two months' hunting together as a team, the Salamancans had fought greater numbers — once there had been as many as eleven — but those Cursed Ones had been newly converted. The younger the bloodsucker, the easier to defeat, as they would not have fully adapted to their new abilities . . . or their weaknesses.

Against older vampires, like the three lurking in the darkness, you could only hope they hadn't yet run up against a hunter. That they would have grown so used to slaughtering the helpless that they would underestimate those who knew how to fight back.

But the Cuevas C.O.'s had struck first, which meant they knew what the six hunters were capable of. By the time Jenn and the other Salamancans had smelled smoke, there had only been time to rouse Antonio from his meditations in the chapel behind the altar and crawl outside.

Now they were exposed and vulnerable. And—

Jenn blinked. Antonio was no longer beside her. Panic wrapped around her heart, and she froze, unsure of what to do. Directly in front of her an oak tree shuddered inside its thick coat of fire, and a huge limb snapped off, cascading into the dirt with a *fwom*.

He left me here, she thought. *Oh, God.*

Breathe, she reminded herself, but as she inhaled, smoke filled her lungs, and she pressed her hand over her mouth. Her balance gave way, and she collapsed onto the dirt. Jenn grunted back a hacking cough. The welt on her back burned like a bull's-eye; she was a prime target. And alone.

Where are you, Antonio? she silently demanded. *How could you leave me?*

Tears welled. Jenn gave her head a hard shake. She had to hustle. If she didn't move, she would die a horrible death. She had seen vampires kill people. But he wouldn't let that happen to her. Would he?

Don't think. Just move.

Jenn's fingernails dug into the dirt as she lifted herself up. Commando-style she worked her way forward, scrambling to the left when another large oak branch cracked and fell toward her like a flaming spear. She had to get away from the collapsing buildings and the falling trees before she could think about going on the offensive.

There was a whisper of sound, a *shushshushshush*, and Jenn rolled farther to her left just as a vampire landed on his back beside her. His pale blue eyes were opened wide in a death mask, and his breath reeked of rotting blood. She thought he groaned a word, maybe a name.

Then all at once the vampire collapsed into dust and was scattered by the hot winds. *One down,* she thought, covering her mouth and nose to avoid inhaling any of the vampire's remains. The first time Jenn had seen that happen, she'd been unable to speak for over an hour. Now she couldn't help the triumphant smile that spread across her face.

Jenn struggled to her feet; Antonio stood a breath away, his eyes blazing, the stake that had killed the vampire still clenched in his hand. He towered over her, six feet to her five-five. As she reached out to touch his arm, a blood-curdling scream ripped through the night air, and she took off in its direction, expecting Antonio to do the same.

Instead his body hurtled past her, landing in a pile of burning branches and leaves.

"Antonio!" she screamed, then wheeled around in a fighter's stance, facing off against the vampire who had tossed him through the air like one might toss loose change onto a counter. The Cursed One was tall and bulky, grinning so that his fangs gleamed in the firelight. His face was covered in blood. Her stomach lurched, and she tried not to think about how many of the villagers were already dead.

Jenn swiftly grabbed a stake from the quiver on her belt, gripping it in her right hand, and ripped open a Velcro pocket with her left to retrieve a cross. She desperately wanted to look back at Antonio. She dared not.

The vampire sneered at her and snarled in a thick Leonese-Spanish accent, "*Pobrecita*, I can hear the frightened beating of your heart. Just like the rabbit in the trap."

He slashed her across the cheek with his talonlike nails before leaping back in a dizzying blur. Jenn felt the blood running hot and sticky down her cheek before she felt the sting.

Jenn circled him warily. *I'm a hunter,* she reminded herself, but the hand around her stake was shaking badly. Surely he could see it. If he attacked, there was a good chance she wouldn't be quick enough. The specialized training she had received at the academy had taught her how to anticipate a vampire's moves even when she couldn't see them. They moved so fast, the Cursed Ones. Father Juan said that they moved faster than man could sin. He said they could kill you and you would never know it had happened, but if you had been a brave and just person, the angels would tell you all about it, in song.

I'm not brave.

She took a deep breath and turned her head slightly to the side. Her best bet at tracking him was not to look directly at him. Movement was most effectively caught out of the corner of one's eyes. She had learned that at the academy, and it had saved her before. Maybe it would again.

But maybe not.

The vampire stayed visible, stalling, but more likely toying with her before he made his kill. Some vampires were matadors, drawing out the death dance like a ritual. For others the hunt was a means to an end—fresh human blood, pumped by a still-beating heart.

Movement in the shadows caught her eyes. Jenn fought not to react as one of the other hunters—*the* Hunter, Eriko Sakamoto—crept toward the vampire, her tiny frame belying her superior strength. Dressed in night hues like Jenn and Antonio, she wore a turtleneck, leather pants, and thick-soled boots that Velcroed halfway up her calves. Her short, gelled hair made her look like a tribal warrior. Fresh streaks of soot were smeared on her high, golden cheekbones.

The sound of the fires masked any noise from her approach. Eriko caught Jenn's eye, and Jenn began to edge to the right, placing the vampire between them.

"Hunters . . . *jóvenes* . . . you're nothing special after all," the Cursed One snarled.

"We're special enough to turn you to dust," Jenn growled, trying to hold the vampire's attention. She focused on his fangs instead of his eyes, so as not to be mesmerized by him. That was one of the first rules of survival—to resist the Cursed Ones' hypnotic gaze, designed to put their prey in thrall. "You'd better say your prayers. You're about to die."

The vampire scoffed, weaving closer, seemingly unaware that a hunter advanced behind him with her stake poised. The smell of Jenn's blood cloaked the subtler scent of unharmed human flesh.

"Prayer is for mortals," he said, "who must beg some deity to save them. And as we know, those prayers always go unanswered."

"Always?" Jenn asked, feeling the blood oozing down her cheek. The vampire stared at it as if he hadn't drunk in centuries.

"Always," he replied.

Eriko kept her distance, and Jenn had a terrible thought: *She's using me as bait.* Jenn began to back away, and the vampire made a show of taking a step toward her. Her hands were slick with sweat—from the heat, from her fear—and her grip on the stake began to slip. She worked her fingers around it. The vampire snickered.

Jenn took another step backward, her boot crunching

down on something. Her stomach lurched as sparks flew upward. What if it was Antonio?

She couldn't stop herself from glancing down. It was only a branch. The vampire launched himself at her with a hiss.

"No!" Jenn shrieked, falling backward.

The vampire landed on top of her, his eyes filled with bloodlust. His fangs were long and curved; she flailed, forgetting all her training, every maneuver that could save her. His breath stank of fresh blood, and she heard herself whimper.

Antonio.

Then, suddenly, the Cursed One was gone. Jenn pulled herself into a crouch, aware that she'd lost her cross. Eriko had yanked the vampire to his feet and was on his back, legs wrapped around his waist. He batted at her as she laced her fingers underneath his chin, forcing back his head. He hissed and grabbed her ankles, trying to peel her off him.

"Jenn, stake him," Eriko shouted. "Now!"

Jenn blinked. She took two steps forward, and then she stopped for a fraction of an instant. Just stopped.

She could no longer see Eriko or the vampire. They were moving too fast for her to track. She lunged forward, stabbing at the air. There was no contact. She caught flashes, blurs, but not enough to give her a target. Through her exhaustion Jenn kept swinging, as her mind raced. If Eriko died, it would be on Jenn's head.

Then she saw them. The vampire had been forced to his knees, and Eriko stood behind him, her hands still laced beneath his chin. Jenn ran to stake him as Eriko flashed her a fierce smile and twisted off his head. His headless body held its shape; Eriko threw the head into the advancing flames. It was something Jenn could never have done; she didn't have Eriko's superhuman strength.

"At least someone's prayers were answered," Eriko said, panting, as the body disintegrated. She trotted toward a crumbling stone wall to their left, which marked the north end of the church's cemetery. "Let's keep moving."

Jenn looked back to where she had last seen Antonio, but he wasn't there. Another surge of panic washed over her as she raced toward the spot. He was simply *gone*. He wouldn't have just abandoned them, though; he couldn't have *left*.

"Antonio!" Jenn screamed. "Wait, Eriko. Antonio!"

"*Sí*," he called. "*Sí*, Jenn."

Antonio pushed through the burning brush a few yards away, wisps of smoke curling from his charred clothes as he batted at them. His hands were blackened and peeling.

She ran to him and then stood hesitantly in front of him, frightened and ashamed of her doubts. "Are you okay?" she asked.

He nodded grimly. "I will be."

She began to shake. "I was worried. I thought . . ." She trailed off. It didn't matter what she had thought. All that mattered was that he was alive and there.

"You didn't think I would leave you?" Antonio questioned, his gaze intense as he reached out to cup her cheek with his hand. "I was coming to help you and Eriko." Then his soft expression flickered, and she saw his despair. He hid it well . . . though not well enough, at least for someone so focused on him as she was. The shadow in his eyes spoke of something he had refused to share with her—his deepest wound.

His darkest secret.

Tears stung her eyes. Jenn loved Antonio, and she wanted to trust him. But trust was something she'd left behind two years ago when she'd crossed the threshold of the university. She'd had to learn not to trust her eyes, her mind, or even her heart. Every time she forgot that, she nearly got herself killed.

"*Ay, no,*" Antonio whispered, gazing at her. "I would never leave you."

Antonio stroked her cheek with his thumb, and she closed her eyes, leaning into the touch. Calloused, velvet. When his lips brushed hers, she returned the kiss with a sob. She threw her arms around his neck and clung to him. His lips were soft and yielding against hers, and the taste of him mixed with the faint metallic flavor of the blood in her mouth.

Leaning against Antonio, she whimpered, wanting more. Then, suddenly, he *was* gone.

Jenn opened her eyes and saw Antonio hunched over

a few feet away, eyes glowing and fangs protruding. Eriko strode up beside Jenn, a thick stake clasped in her hand. One throw and she could kill him.

"Estoy bien," Antonio growled deep in his throat. He wiped something dark off of his lips and onto his black cargo pants.

Her blood.

"Eriko, I'm all right," he said in English.

His deep voice always made Jenn shiver, but with fear or desire she was never quite sure. Sometimes when they were kissing she would forget, just for a moment, all that kept them apart.

Antonio was a vampire.

She forced herself to take a good look: the gleaming teeth, the hungry, feral look that had crept into his eyes, the way the muscles in his face contorted as he tried to overcome his bloodlust. He didn't like her to see it, but she needed to. She needed to remember so that she could protect herself—and him.

Some vampires claimed to be able to control their cravings, but Antonio de la Cruz was the only one she had ever met who could actually manage it. Years of meditation, study, and prayer had given him the strength he needed. Or so he claimed.

But deep inside Jenn knew that every moment they spent together was eroding that strength. One day he wouldn't pull away, and then she would have to kill him. If she could. Or one of the other hunters would. Like Eriko. Or Jamie—

"Good," Eriko said. "One down." But she didn't lower the stake. Muscular and petite, Eriko was a couple of years younger and a couple of inches shorter than Jenn. When they had graduated from the academy two months before, Eriko had been chosen from their class to receive the sacred elixir that bequeathed astounding speed and strength. The elixir was so difficult to make, there was only enough for one Hunter, capital *H*. Their leader.

"Antonio killed one too," Jenn said.

Eriko raised a brow and glanced at Antonio, who nodded. His face was returning to normal. "There were only three, right? We're nearly done."

"Three's what we were told," Jenn said, relaxing only slightly. She pulled out her garlic salve and quickly applied it to her cheek and lip.

Eriko sighed and pressed the fingertips of her free hand against the spiky stubble of her hair. "The villagers might have miscounted. It wouldn't be the first time that happened."

Jenn swallowed hard. "I'm sorry, Eriko," she said. "I didn't back you up."

Eriko shrugged. "You don't have the power I do, Jenn. You did fine."

But Jenn knew she hadn't. She had panicked. She'd been more worried about Antonio than anyone else, including herself.

Eriko looked past her to Antonio. "Antonio, on the other hand . . ."

"He was burned," Jenn said, angry and defensive at the implication. "Look at his hands."

"Bloody hell, that was all arseways," a familiar voice fumed. Jenn turned as two figures approached. One was tall, with a nearly shaved head and heavy tattoos on his arms and neck, which made him look like a demon in the firelight. The turtleneck he had been wearing was gone, and only an undershirt remained. That was Jamie O'Leary.

For once the girl at his side didn't disagree. From her black battle clothes—padded jacket, leggings, thigh-high boots—to her white-blond rasta braids, to the silver crescent-moon ring on her thumb, Skye York was covered with soot except where tears had cut paths down her pale cheeks.

Skye made circles in the air with her hand while muttering an incantation with the Latin refrain "*desino.*" Cease. One by one the fires in her vicinity were extinguished.

"Cursers all dead?" Jamie asked, gazing around. He looked at Antonio. "The ones we're *allowed* to kill?" he added pointedly.

"There's one more," Eriko said. "I got one, Antonio got one, and that leaves—"

"None," Jamie interrupted. "I got one on my way out of the church." He showed them his singed palms. "Staked him through the back with a piece of burning timber. It was good and long and caught him in the heart."

"That's great; we're done, then," Eriko said, grinning at her fighting partner. Jamie grinned back, clearly relishing that both of them had managed kills. They hadn't been near each other when the church went up in flame, but they had still caused the most damage. Energy practically sizzled between the two. They did seem to belong together, somehow.

After fasting, praying, and working magicks, Father Juan had matched them into fighting pairs, insisting that each fulfilled some complicated balance of yin and yang, light and dark.

Strength and weakness.

Jenn was paired with Antonio, much to her relief. Eriko and Jamie were matched, and they pushed each other hard and themselves harder. Skye and Holgar were the third pair, and they had a quiet closeness with each other that was enviable.

Like Jenn, Jamie had no special gifts or powers. But his ferocity and the fighting skills drilled into him by his family during his childhood in Belfast more than made up for it.

Eriko seemed unaware of the way Jamie looked at her. . . . It went beyond a Hunter-hunter relationship. It must have been obvious to Skye, too, as she turned away to concentrate on her incantations. Their gothy witch carried a torch for Jamie, and Jamie had no clue. Jenn wasn't sure if the other team members knew, or if she was the only one who had figured it out. She felt both sorry for Skye and, frankly, bewildered, because Jamie was a jerk. He made no secret of his desire to be elsewhere; he didn't even believe that there should be a team of hunters. Jamie was only there because Father Juan had asked him to stay in Salamanca and serve the cause. If it hadn't been for his deeply ingrained loyalty to his church, Jenn was sure that even Jamie's attraction to Eriko wouldn't be enough to keep him from going home.

Finished with her incantation for the fires, Skye gently touched Jamie's palms, and his skin began to heal. Her delicate face nearly glowed as she infused him with her nurturing energy. Jamie sighed with pleasure but said nothing.

Skye turned next to Antonio. Moving into position while the sun was still up had weakened his system. He held out his hands, palms up, and Skye moved her hands over them and whispered in ancient Latin. Jenn felt herself relax slightly. She hated it when Antonio came close to fire. Fire was one of the few things that could kill a vampire. Vampires could also be killed by sunlight, a wooden stake through the heart, and decapitation.

"How many dead, *brujita*?" Antonio asked softly, calling Skye "little witch," as he flexed his fingers. "Villagers?"

Skye shook her head, her rasta braids swaying down her back. "At least fifty. When the fires started, the vampires killed the first few people who tried to escape the burning buildings. The rest were so afraid . . ." Her voice broke.

"Some of them stayed inside their homes and burned to death," Jenn bitterly finished for her, sick knots twisting her stomach. "Then we failed."

Eriko shook her head. "No one would be alive if we hadn't come."

"And about that," Jamie said, spitting into the dirt. "How the bloody hell did they know—"

"Where's Holgar?" Skye asked, glancing around for her fighting partner.

"Fried, extra crispy if we're lucky," Jamie muttered.

"Sorry to say it, Irish, but my ears weren't burned off," Holgar quipped, limping toward the group. His clothes hung in tatters from his body. Gaping wounds on his chest and legs had already begun to scab over. Holgar's hands were bloodied, though whether it was his or someone else's, Jenn couldn't tell.

Jamie swore under his breath, but Jenn only could make out ". . . bloody werewolf."